THE BELL HOUSE

www.**booksattransworld**.co.uk

THE BELL HOUSE

Ruth Hamilton

BANTAM PRESS

LONDON · TORONTO · SYDNEY · AUCKLAND · JOHANNESBURG

TRANSWORLD PUBLISHERS
61–63 Uxbridge Road, London W5 5SA
a division of The Random House Group Ltd

RANDOM HOUSE AUSTRALIA (PTY) LTD
20 Alfred Street, Milsons Point, Sydney,
New South Wales 2061, Australia

RANDOM HOUSE NEW ZEALAND LTD
18 Poland Road, Glenfield, Auckland 10, New Zealand

RANDOM HOUSE SOUTH AFRICA (PTY) LTD
Endulini, 5a Jubilee Road, Parktown 2193, South Africa

Published 2005 by Bantam Press
a division of Transworld Publishers

A catalogue record for this book is available
from the British Library.
ISBN 0593 053125

Typeset in Baskerville

Printed and bound in Great Britain by
Clays Ltd, Bungay, Suffolk

1 3 5 7 9 10 8 6 4 2

Papers used by Transworld Publishers are natural, recyclable
products made from wood grown in sustainable forests. The
manufacturing processes conform to the environmental regulations
of the country of origin.

For Larry Finlay.
Mazel tov, sweetheart.

Much gratitude is owed to:

My family for encouragement and love.
Linda Evans, my editor, who suffered every up and down with me.
Gill, Lyn and John, who kept the home fires burning.
Simon Topliss of Bolton, for research into the Mesolithic era.
Dorothy Ramsden of Bolton, for chasing up place names and dates.
Christina Abram of Bolton, for choosing the Feigenbaums' new name.
Caroline Sheldon, my agent, who supported me every inch of this too-long road.
Angela Kelly of the *Bolton Evening News*.
My wonderful dogs, Samson and Fudge, for being themselves.

Peter Kay and Dave Spikey for being as mad as hatters.

As ever, I thank my readership for letters, information and unswerving support.

Disclaimer, explanations and some special people.

Rivington is a real place.

Because I wished not to offend the people of Rivington, I turned it into a hybrid of itself and Bromley Cross – another favourite of mine. Thus was born the fictitious village of Rivington Cross with its two churches, two schools, Post Office/General Stores, stocks and, of course, an ancient cross for which this non-existent location is named.

On a beautiful summer day, I visited Rivington with Barbara and Bert Kerks, two wonderful people without whom I might have been lost. Churchwarden Gerald Hesford – lovely man – took us inside the church and it was a show-stopper – so beautiful and well-kept. I thank him for his kindness and generosity.

Then I went to the bell house and shut myself inside and, in complete darkness, felt my way around a place that once held human bones. There I discovered a tranquillity that defies description even for a supposed wordsmith. Into that bell house I have placed the six children at the centre of my story. It is important that I write this disclaimer myself for the people of Rivington. No one here is real, but I pray that you find the characters believable.

Lastly, I need to express my love for Bolton and all its villages. Rivington is amazing. To its residents I want to say how much I envy you.

Ruthie.

PROLOGUE

The end, 1961

The view from the rear window was beautiful, had always been stunning. Undulating moors stretched away to a horizon made dark by pendulous clouds whose contents threatened to spill at any moment. Even in shadow, the Pennine foothills remained splendid. A grey day. There had been many such days of late, because even sunshine could not lighten the burden carried by one of the prettiest villages this side of the mountains.

John Horrocks turned and considered his handiwork. 'Not a bad job,' he muttered under his breath. He stood back and surveyed the satin-lined casket, larger than usual and of the best quality; no expense spared for this dead man. There had been a few quid salted away, enough for decent handles of solid brass, a pillow, a shroud of the finest material.

What the shroud hid was not the business of

John Horrocks, Undertaker, Rivington Cross, Lancashire. What the shroud hid was the evidence of murder and marks left by pathologists in their search for truth. Would anyone ever know the full truth about the current occupant of this chapel of rest? Would anyone want to know? The undertaker shivered involuntarily. How many victims? How many lives had this piece of evil shattered? 'Unclean,' said John clearly. 'Unclean and a nasty piece of work – may God forgive me.' But not him. God should never forgive the article in this wooden box.

The coffin contained one of the ugliest clients it had ever been John's misfortune to handle. The meeting between deceased and undertaker was invariably a subdued affair, but today the air hung heavily in the silent room, as if a malevolence had invaded the area, a dark shadow which penetrated brick, mortar, roof tiles. Wickedness. The man in the box was as ugly as sin and his sins had been particularly hideous.

'John?' Yvonne Horrocks stood in the doorway. 'You've done your duty. Don't be stopping in here – you'll only get depressed.'

'I'd sooner have left him to someone else.' John prided himself on his professionalism, on his manner with the bereaved, on the respect with which he had always handled the dead. This was the final service to be performed by a man for other men and John was one of the best in the business. But he hadn't wanted this one; he would rather the Co-op or some other parlour had taken the job.

'There was nobody else,' his wife replied.

The undertaker nodded. No family had come forward to claim the corpse, no friend, no colleague. 'The village kept him all those years, and now we're stuck with him for ever. I hope they dig the hole deep.'

'He won't climb out, John. Even he had to come to an end some time. There'll be no need for garlic flowers and crucifixes, love. Come on – let's make a cuppa and have an Eccles cake with best butter, eh?'

He awarded her a tight smile. 'You go. I just want to make sure everything's tidy. You know what I'm like – it all has to be just so.' But he would not light the candles. At each corner of the bier, a thick, creamy candle rested in a huge sconce, wicks white and virginal. No, John Horrocks would waste no beeswax on this occasion. 'I'm all right,' he told his wife. 'It's the living we've to worry about next.'

She knew it was pointless to argue. Anyway, it was just a corpse now, just a shell that would soon decay in the graveyard. But it didn't deserve a Christian burial, she told herself as she closed the door in her wake. No – that man should have been laid in unconsecrated ground alongside murderers and other unclean people. He had done great damage, yet he would be interred in a Christian cemetery among decent, goodly folk . . . why? Why hadn't he lived to face the courts, the fury of his neighbours?

Yvonne raised her eyes and listened as her daughter paced about in the room above. Madeleine was about to take one more step, a stride too far. Eccles cakes? Who wanted to drink tea and eat pastries at a time like this? Everything had gone wrong. But Madeleine was unstoppable, had always been a determined little madam. 'She'll not start listening now,' Yvonne whispered to herself, 'not at twenty-one. God knows who her drummer is, because she's a one-off with a pace all her own.'

The salon was closed. Yvonne sorted out a jumble of perm curlers, combed the hair from a brush, emptied an ashtray, placed shampoos and conditioners in tidy rows on shelves between mirrors. In this small room, she had beautified the women of Rivington Cross for over twenty years. She remembered the old days, when perms had been achieved by the scorching of hair, when waves and curls had been the order of the day, rigid, hair-netted, waves down to the ears, neat rows of curls below. 'It's getting more like topiary now,' she muttered as she rinsed out a basin. People wanted their hair sculpted, shaped, lacquered, perfect, unreal ... 'I don't know about scissors – I could do with garden shears and a bucket of weedkiller.'

She sat down wearily, throwing aside cleaning cloth and scouring powder. It didn't matter. Making the place clean, burying the dead, cooking, washing, ironing – what difference would any of it make? It was a circle, a never-ending shape in which people were trapped, a merry-go-round that was no longer merry. People were born and they grew up. They had their hair done, then they died and had their hair done one last time. And Maddy was out of order.

14

Maddy, the perfect child, the leader, the philosopher . . . No, Yvonne would not cry. Sometimes, Maddy made the sort of sense that dissolved all Yvonne had learned from parents, teachers and priests. Yes, she would go far, would Maddy. Too far – out of reach.

A tap dripped. It had always dripped. No matter how many new washers had been applied over the years, that damned tap had never managed to hold its water. It dripped five times while the minute hand on her watch completed its course. Sixty minutes in one hour, twenty-four hours in a day – how many gallons were disappearing in a week, a month, a year? How would Madeleine manage in London? A teacher was on less than ten pounds a week – was that enough? Drip, drip, drip.

Maddy had broken all the rules. A dispensation, reluctantly awarded by the Bishop of Salford, had allowed Madeleine Horrocks to attend Didsbury Training College, a non-Catholic institution where teachers were shaped. Not content with that one small step, Maddy had opted for RE as her main subject, had plodded through Islam, Buddhism, Hinduism and several Christianities. 'All because of the bell house,' mumbled the troubled mother. In ten short years, the group known by all and sundry as the Famous Five-Plus had eradicated saints, prophets, the Bible, the Qur'an and any other religious tomes available in libraries.

And the plodding continued overhead. Drawers opened and closed, a wardrobe door clicked into position. Maddy was leaving home, was leaving everything, was leaving childhood. Emotion bubbled its unwelcome way towards Yvonne's throat and spilled into sobs. She didn't know what to think, how to feel, how to cope – and she must not weep! She had but one child and that child was precious beyond diamonds, but the precious child was a woman now, a wayward and determined young person whose convictions were leading her away to the big, bad city in the south. Maddy wanted a fresh start, anonymity, a chance to become herself. 'Jesus,' sobbed the mother. But Jesus was no longer trusted by Maddy. He had done some good, but He had divided man from man and was, therefore, to be questioned.

'Where did we go wrong?' Yvonne asked a mirror. But the answer was already a part of her. Maddy was bright. She was bright enough for university, for medicine, for law, for politics. But no, the girl had decided to help frame the future of her country, had been awarded a distinction in the principles and practice of education, was a star in the field she had chosen for herself. And life would be lonely without her.

Yvonne had borne two stillborn boys and had suffered countless early miscarriages. Yet her term with Maddy had been as smooth as silk – no sickness, very little pain at the end, just a few hard pushes and a perfect result, so pretty, so wanted. Right from the start, Maddy had focused on life, had delivered comments in unformed language, had made her wishes clear. She had read early, had sailed through school in an effortless sweep, had devoured book after book in a seemingly endless search for truth. Truth? There was none. There was just this dripping tap and some tiny hands moving across the face of time on Yvonne's wrist.

John came in. 'Don't cry. She'll be back.' His words carried little conviction. He strengthened his tone. 'Our Maddy's a northerner to the bone – she'll not stop long down yon, all that smog and noise. She's used to the Pike and the open fields, Yvonne.'

'And the bell house.'

He sighed heavily. 'Aye, and that, too. Famous Five-Plus, eh?'

'They called themselves the Cave Dwellers or the Cavemen. Remember? I wish she'd never found all that meso-whatsit stuff.'

'Mesolithic.'

Yvonne nodded, then drew a hand across wet eyes. 'All that about flints and caves and ancient burial grounds.'

'And standing stones,' added John. 'But some of it made a kind of sense.' He raised a hand against the startled expression on his wife's face. 'Nay, don't look at me like that, because I'm not saying I agree with her. What I mean is that it's a point of view. Even the Unitarians had to practise in secret for years – once folk start changing things and coming up with new ideas, there's always trouble. And at least she stopped being a Buddhist. That lasted about three weeks if my memory serves me right.'

'Which was that one?'

He pondered. 'I think it was sitting still and doing nowt – nirvana and some eightfold path.

17

What she's got now isn't a religion as much as a philosophy. And she has every right to it. It's a bit like votes for women – somebody has to kick off. Just leave her be and she'll come round in the end.'

'The women didn't,' replied Yvonne. 'They threw themselves under horses and chained each other to railings until they got their own road.'

'And were they wrong?'

'No, course they weren't wrong. But Maddy might be – oh, I don't know. What she's doing is different. I wanted a white wedding with bells and bridesmaids. I wanted a nice reception and a little house somewhere near, a couple of grandchildren, a normal daughter.'

'She is normal.'

'John, it's a register office job. She's marrying out and it's not right. Sometimes, I wonder whether it's deliberate just to hurt us.' She bit her lip. No. Maddy's generosity of spirit would never have allowed for so mean an action. 'I don't know what to do,' she whimpered. 'I can't argue sensibly with her because she's cleverer than I am. What am I supposed to do?'

John knew what to do. With or without his wife, he would be at the Bolton Register Office in a few days' time. He would witness with pride the marriage of his only child, would support her through thick and thin, would travel to see her even if she moved to the North Pole. 'Religion's done all this,' he said as he patted her shoulder.

'You sound like your daughter now.'

18

'Happen I do. Have you never thought that she might be just a little bit right? I mean, look at what I've got laid out in my chapel now – that's proof of a kind, isn't it? All this argufying all over the world, all these rules and regulations from God – how do we know? Because somebody said so? Because a pope said so?'

'Stop it,' she begged. 'I'm confused enough.'

'I'm confused, too, Yvonne. I can't pretend to keep up with our girl and neither can you, yet what she believes is so simple – it has a kind of purity – it's clean, you see. There's no Bible and no commandments and no sin as such.'

'Because somebody said so? Because our Maddy said so? How do we know? Is she from God and was Jesus not from God?'

He didn't know. He didn't know anything any more. A Catholic to the core, John Horrocks had been so shaken by recent events that his very soul seemed to ache. And it wasn't just recent events, because since childhood, Maddy had questioned the 'rightness' of this and that, of state law, of religious edicts, of governments and kings. 'Leave it, Yvonne,' he begged wearily. 'I've yon fellow to shift tomorrow and it could well be just me and a couple of old folk.'

'I won't be there,' she told him.

'I know.'

'Nor will Maddy, nor will poor Amy. He goes out with a whimper, eh? I bet there won't be a single flower.'

'And very few mourners.' John left her to cry out her grief. In the small hallway that separated beauty salon from funeral parlour, he leaned against the wall and listened to the sounds of his daughter's imminent exit. What she was doing broke every rule in just about every book, yet he found himself smiling. Maddy's destiny had been mapped out years ago, because she had arrived in this world to change it. The changes she was making would not echo down the centuries, would not leave fossilized foot-prints in soil and rock, would break down no huge barriers, yet they would stand as Maddy's own memorial.

'You're doing the right thing, girl,' he told the ceiling above his head. 'Follow the dream and be true to your heart.' Then he turned left and entered the chapel of rest. There was a lid to be screwed down, there were flowers to be refreshed. Come what may, the business would carry on in its usual way. Yet he felt nothing but hatred for the man in the coffin and that made him uneasy. The dead should always command respect, no matter what . . .

Sometimes, the 'what' was too much. Sometimes, there was no forgiveness.

It was a beautiful suit, well tailored and in a shade of ivory that was more flattering than white. White was a cold colour, empty, devoid of feeling. Maddy hooked the hanger onto her picture rail, then sat on the narrow bed. This had been her domain for ever. She could not imagine life without this small space of her own, without the pictures on the walls, without the scarred furniture.

Her dolls sat in a row on a shelf, each one

worn and slightly tattered by loving attention. Photographs of herself with her parents, with Amy and with various other friends were dotted about the room, as were awards for swimming and life-saving. The view from her window was spectacular, leading the eye out of Rivington Cross and towards Rivington itself with its beautiful, lush hill topped off by the famous pike. It was heaven.

But there was more than one heaven. London, a different kind of paradise, bustling with life and commerce, was beckoning. She would be living with her soon-to-be husband in the top half of a tall, narrow house with a walled rear garden terminated by a railway embankment. She would be teaching at a school near Spitalfields and would need to become inured to crushes on buses and tube trains. There would be street markets, buskers in the Underground, museums, theatres, the Palace of Westminster just a few miles along the road. The Tate, the Natural History Museum, the Victoria and Albert, dinner cruises on the Thames, wonderful shops. Well – eventually. For a few years, there would be little money for excitement.

Maddy's eyes rested on a picture of Monty. The tears welled and she blinked them away angrily. Yes, he had been a wonderful dog and yes, there had been some wonderful times, but life had to move on into the next phase and she must stop looking back, must stop gazing at the pike and the cross and the post office. The cross was so old that metal railings had been built round it to protect it from dogs like Monty, from children like herself and her precious companions. And Monty had died a hero's death, had lived a hero's life. If there was an afterwards, a place where the dead gathered, Monty would be there, because there could be no sense without animals.

In London, she would keep a cat. London was not the place for dogs. Behind closed eyelids, she saw the ridiculous Monty streaking his way up the hill towards Rivington Pike, black-and-white spotted legs moving like pistons, feathered tail curled, black ears flattened against a narrow head. The runt of a litter, Monty had never seemed to grow to full size, but his courage had been enormous. Everyone died, she told herself firmly. The one inescapable fact of life was that every man, woman and child would finish up in the hands of her father or of someone like him. It was the same for animals and she had to look ahead, should wear blinkers.

Yes, it was a wonderful outfit. The man she loved, the person in whom she had placed all her faith, would soon stand next to her in a dark suit and a crisp new shirt. They would make promises, exchange rings, then take a coach to Victoria Station. Perhaps few people would come to the ceremony, but that didn't matter. If Madeleine Horrocks wanted to count her blessings, the love of her life would come right at the top of her list. Nothing and nobody would divert them from their course. She would teach English, history and RE; he would teach mathematics and the sciences. Their furniture would be shabby and second-hand, but their love would stay as fresh and as young as if it were newly discovered with the birth of each dawn.

'I will be all right. Everything will be all right,' she told herself as she rocked back and forth, a pillow clutched to her chest. There came times in life for reflection, when it seemed natural to do a census, a taking of stock, and this was one of those times. The horror, the nastiness, the fear – these were all part and parcel of her life and of the lives of those around her, but she would not concentrate on those aspects just now.

She curled into a position that was almost foetal, the pillow still held tightly in her arms. Turning to face a wall of buttercup yellow, she allowed her mind to skip back through the lanes and hedgerows of childhood, up hills, down dales and right to the edge of the reservoir. In her mind, she entered the bell house with its makeshift seating formed by orange boxes and beer crates, with the waxy, smoky smell created by the burning of stolen church candles; could almost taste the sticky toffee and jam tarts pooled by the members of her gang.

They had been not the Famous Five, but the Famous Six plus dog, and their adventures would not have made stories pretty enough for the fans of Enid Blyton. She grinned to herself. 'We were more like William Brown and his motley crew, seldom clean, always naughty.' And a small part of her wished that those days would come back just for a little while, that she might re-enter the innocence of childhood and relive the joy of discovery of such valued companions. Amy had always been there, but the others had arrived in stages, each one of them special, each one of them valuable. One of them was now her fiancé. The engagement had raised eyebrows and tempers, but they had stuck steadfastly to their plan and nothing on earth would divert them now.

Her eyelids grew heavy and she entered sleep gratefully. Now, she could relive all of it, but it would not be real. Tomorrow was the only reality.

1951

Across the road from Hair By Yvonne and Horrocks Funerals, a woman gazed out of a front window of St Faith's Vicarage. Her twins, Sarah and Simon, were outside somewhere, were probably engaged in a conversation that excluded all others. Since birth, they had performed as a single unit, complete in themselves, settled – almost adult. They did not need her.

Derek needed her. He valued her, made her laugh, made her a young woman again.

In the church, her husband would be supervising some ongoings – flowers, orders of service, plans for the choir. He sermonized. He bored people. He was a good man and he did not need her. He was safe, predictable, gentle, generous and stodgy. No, he did not need her – he had Jesus.

Derek needed her. There was a hint of danger, an excitement, a promise of new territory, a fresh beginning. Caroline Butlin saw beyond the slight lisp and the moustache; she saw a man who needed love and passion. She saw her future, picked up her cases and followed her instincts.

From today, her life would begin.

ONE

Madeleine Horrocks was renowned for two things.

Her parents ran a pair of businesses judged by locals a 'queer combination' and Madeleine herself was far too pretty and outspoken for a good Catholic girl with a grammar school scholarship under her belt. She took little notice of people's opinions, was usually sunny, especially when arguing with an adult, and she made no bones about her ambitions. She was going to be a famous actress, or a famous writer, or a famous something-or-other. The something-or-other changed with the wind and she wasn't particular as long as the word 'famous' could be woven into her personal tapestry.

Amy Bradshaw, as dark as Madeleine was fair, was a total contrast to her special friend. Quiet by nature, made quieter by parents who had had no business producing a child so late in life, Amy was a dependable sort. She, too, had won a scholarship to the Catholic grammar school and she would be accompanying Madeleine on two buses, one into Bolton, the other up Deane Road to the convent of St Anne's, where, under the rather less than gentle guidance of Cross and Passion nuns, she would be educated towards teaching, law or some other respectable profession.

It was the last day of school. The two friends stood side by side outside the gates of the Holy Martyrs' Infant and Junior School, each of them blinking back a few tears.

'It's a bit like dying,' said Amy, 'as if that part of us has passed on. In July 1951, we stopped being the people we were.'

Madeleine, too, was upset, though she hid it well, as was her wont. 'Well, I'm not ready for my dad yet, are you?'

'No,' replied Amy, 'but what I mean is, we die in bits. Chunks. We can never go back in there, because Amy Bradshaw and Madeleine Horrocks are not on the register any more.' She glanced sideways at her companion. 'On our notes at the doctor's, there is a space at the top called "date of death".'

'Start worrying when they fill it in,' said Maddy. 'We're only eleven.' Not for the first time, she added, 'Amy, you read too much of what your mother tells you to read.'

'Jinny Anderson died when she was twelve,' replied Amy. 'Mam was there when they filled that space in. She said it was like looking into hell, because nothing can be worse than a child dying of cancer. Even the doctor cried.'

Maddy shook her head, causing blond curls

28

to tumble into her eyes. She swept them back with a careless movement. 'Your mother and my dad have very sad jobs. She sees people sick and my dad sees them dead – and we have to make the best of things. That's what my mother says, anyway.'

Maddy's mother, the local hairdresser, saw and heard a great deal. In fact, between the four of them, the Bradshaw and Horrocks parents knew just about everything connected to their village. John Horrocks was the undertaker, his wife was the local stylist, while Amy's mother and father worked for the doctor and the post office respectively.

The two girls turned their back on infancy and walked away from the school gates. They passed St Faith's, the local Church of England, and noticed the boy. He was there every day at this time. Perched on top of the ancient stone wall, he sat for hours on end, his heels beating a rhythm against the sandstone blocks. Even darker than Amy, he wore an air of mystery, because his family had come from abroad and the circumstances which had brought his parents and grandmother to England were unusual, to put it mildly.

'What about his shoes?' Amy asked. 'My mother would kill me if I did that. He must spoil them.'

Maddy shrugged. 'Well, he's lucky to be alive. They escaped from somewhere just before the war started. I suppose they're not bothered about shoes. Anyway, my mother says they have loads of money.'

Amy slowed down and placed her hand on Maddy's arm. 'Stop a minute. They're not Germans, are they?'

'Polish. Warsaw, I think,' replied Maddy. 'And Jewish.'

Amy sighed. 'They killed Jesus, didn't they?'

Madeleine, an avid reader herself, had formed her own views on that subject. 'The Romans had a lot to do with it. And Rome is where the pope is, so even Catholics aren't all that clean. Anyway, Jesus had to die. My dad said it was written into His contract.' She frowned. In religious education, she and her classmates had been taught about free will, that special God-given treasure visited upon mankind and only upon mankind. If Pontius Pilate and Herod had decided not to kill Jesus, then what might have happened? And if Jesus had really been sent by the Father to die, wouldn't that have involved the influence of God to a point where free will became meaningless?

'Maddy?'

'What?'

'The Jews are condemned to wander the face of the earth,' whispered Amy. 'It's in the Bible.' Amy's parents were devout Catholics. With their own hearts hardened against the Jews, they had instilled in their daughter the belief that Catholicism was the only route to heaven. 'They can never be forgiven.'

'Don't be silly.' Maddy marched on. She owned her thoughts, yet the language in which she might express herself often evaded her. Sometimes, though, she lost patience with Amy.

Amy listened too much, took notice of everything she was told, had been forced by her family into a straitjacket within a religion that was already rigid. He was just a boy; a boy who talked posh, but just another young male person. Before she reached his place on the wall, Maddy crossed the road and Amy caught up with her. 'Sorry,' breathed Amy, 'but it's just that they say at home—'

'Oh, stop it.' Maddy placed her heavy school satchel on the ground. 'The Jews have got their own homeland. And that boy's family escaped from the Nazis just before the war started. Hitler killed millions of Jews – and other people as well. So, was Hitler right?'

Amy shook her head.

'Then there's your answer. The lad over there lost uncles and aunties – my mother said so. She said his mam and dad feel guilty because they never got gassed. They are alive, Amy, but only by the skin of their teeth. According to Mrs Shuttleworth, another ten days and they would have been goners. But they got to London and the dad worked translating stuff for the War Office. Now they're here and you can please yourself, but I am going to make friends with him during the holidays.' Even for Madeleine Horrocks, this had been a long speech. She picked up her bag. She should walk across there now, right this minute, but Mother was expecting her home.

Amy tagged along silently. She didn't share Maddy's certainty, but she believed in her friend with most of her heart. Maddy made life interesting; she didn't moan and groan when she couldn't have something, never complained when she had to sweep up hair in the shop, when she was asked to sort out flowers for the hospital after a funeral. Useful, was the word for Maddy. But beyond that, she was imaginative and unafraid.

They reached the long frontage across Horrocks Funerals and Hair By Yvonne. Some folk went to town for hairdressing, because it was common knowledge that Yvonne Horrocks did the hair of dead people. Maddy had the answer to that one, too. When questioned, she would answer quite haughtily, 'There is no better hairdresser than my mother and yes, she tidies up dead people. She says it is a privilege, because it's the last thing that can be done for a person in this world and it pleases the relatives.'

The two girls entered the salon. As it was Friday, the interior was crammed with women who were 'doing themselves up' for the weekend.

Yvonne almost cheered when she saw her daughter and Amy. 'One of you get the sweeping brush and the other can put the kettle on – my stomach thinks my throat's cut, and thirsty? I've a tongue like the bottom of a birdcage.'

Cheerfully, Maddy got the dustpan and broom while Amy made tea. Maddy enjoyed every moment in her mother's shop. She learned more in here than from any teacher, because, as Mother said, the hairdresser was a bit like the confessional. Something happened to a woman when her crowning glory was wet. It was as if dignity went down the drain with shampoo and conditioning oils, because confidences poured as freely as tap water in Hair By Yvonne.

Mildred Cookson was speaking. 'It wouldn't be so bad for somebody normal, but with her being a vicar's wife . . .' She raised thin shoulders. 'Can you do me a couple of kiss curls near my ears, Yvonne? Put some setting lotion on. Anyway, she upped and left without so much as a by-your-leave.'

To make herself less noticeable, Maddy got down on her knees to retrieve some long strands of dark brown hair from beneath one of the dressing tables.

'She had her hair done in town.' Yvonne's words had to struggle past a few hairgrips clasped between her teeth. 'Round here was never good enough for her. It's the kiddies I feel for. I mean, he's a grown man and he can fend for himself, but the young ones have done nothing to deserve it.'

This was interesting, thought Maddy. A woman of what some might term loose morals had been married to the vicar of St Faith's. Vicars' wives were meant to be all nice cardigans and sensible shoes, good at flower arranging and visiting the sick, but it sounded as if Mrs Butlin had been another type of person altogether, one who was certainly unsuited to marriage with a man of the cloth.

Mrs Cookson, kiss curls plastered to her cheeks with setting lotion and steel slides, carried on with her tale. 'Seems he came back from a meeting with the organist and there she was – gone. They say she never even left a note. Even took the dog with her. And them kiddies loved that dog. It's a shame and no mistake. You'd best put me another colour rinse on next week, Yvonne – I think we need to tone me down a bit.'

Hilda Barnes awarded Mildred Cookson a withering glance. Mildred Cookson had bleached hair and wasn't worth much in Hilda Barnes's book. Hilda sniffed, then chipped in with her tenpennyworth. 'He's boring,' she pronounced. Nobody ever disagreed with Hilda Barnes. She was old and her husband was on the Town Council, so what she said went. 'You wouldn't need sleeping pills.' She patted the net that contained her newly corrugated hair. 'Just sit through one of his sermons and you could sleep from Boxing Day till Pancake Tuesday. Sermon on the Mount? He'd be better off on the mount, because the sheep might listen to him up yon.'

Maddy wondered why Mrs Barnes bothered going to church, but she held her tongue. Crossing swords with that lady was beyond most adults, let alone a child only just out of primary school. She prayed that Amy would hang on for a while, but she came in with the tea tray and began the business of distributing cups to the congregation.

As the ladies drank, Maddy picked up a few more snippets before dragging her friend through to the living quarters. 'Mrs Butlin's gone,' she whispered.

Amy swallowed. 'Is she in there?' She jerked a

thumb towards the chapel of rest. 'How did she die?'

Maddy looked to heaven for guidance, then, with her hands on her hips, she put her friend in the picture. 'Not that sort of gone – gone, disappeared, wandered off. And I think she left her children and took their dog. It must be terrible when your mother leaves you and takes the dog instead.'

Amy blinked and swallowed a lump of guilt. A part of Amy Bradshaw envied the Butlin children and she hated herself for it. Mam and Dad were strict, but they stayed, at least. She didn't wish they would go away – not really. 'Where's she gone?' she managed finally.

Maddy shrugged. 'No idea – but the salon's full of it. They say he's boring. That's one thing you could never call old Fire-and-Brimstone Sheahan, eh?' Father Sheahan, parish priest of Holy Martyrs – which church was known to infidels as Holy Tomatoes – was a man of unpredictable temperament. His mood swings were directly connected to the collection platters – if there was enough for a couple of bottles of Irish whiskey, he was calmer; but when the support of his habit was poorly upheld, every non-contributor was silently allocated eternal hell and several decades of the rosary. 'I can't stand him,' was Maddy's final pronouncement.

Amy did not quite shake in her shoes. Inured at last to her friend's tendency to undermine the priest, she simply made no reply. As Mam and Dad had explained many times, a priest was just a man and he had his own sins to tell. 'Judge not lest ye be judged', was one of Celia Bradshaw's oft-spoken rules. Which was strange, because Celia had plenty to say about other folk and was judgemental on all issues from the price of cod to the king's being a Protestant.

They drank milk and ate biscuits through Children's Hour on the wireless. This was Amy's second home, as her mother would be working at the doctor's and her dad, who had to rise at an ungodly hour each morning, needed his nap in the afternoons. She loved being in Maddy's house, though she needed to work hard not to worry about those dead bodies just a few feet away. In Maddy's house, there were proper conversations; there were jokes, there was laughter, there was fun. According to Celia Bradshaw, Maddy Horrocks had an old head on her shoulders because she heard too much. Amy, on the other hand, heard very little in her own house.

'I wonder what will happen to them?' pondered Maddy.

'Who?'

'The vicar's children. Who'll make their dinners?' She immediately added the vicar's son and daughter to her list for the holidays. Now, she had to break two lots of new ground – the Church of England and Judaism. 'I know we're not allowed to go inside the church without permission, but we can play with them, can't we?'

Amy attempted no answer. Her mam had enough to say about Maddy – what would her response be if she discovered that her daughter was associating with Protestants? Oh, she didn't dare think about that.

Maddy Horrocks motored on regardless. 'It's all daft,' she announced crossly. 'What are they frightened of? Do they think Protestantism is a disease we can catch? If we went to evensong or something, would we come out with spots and a temperature? Or do they think we might hear some sense?' She was repeating stuff she had overheard in the salon, which was the biggest source of information for her over-active mind. 'We should be allowed to choose,' she concluded.

'But we're chosen,' said Amy.

'The Jews were chosen, too,' insisted Maddy. 'That's in the Bible as well – the chosen ones. They were led out of Egypt and . . .' she struggled to remember, 'then Moses parted the waters and there were loads of frogs and locusts. A bush set on fire all by itself and he found the tablets. They were given to the Jews and our God is the same God as their God.'

As far as Amy was concerned, Maddy Horrocks was already fit for university. At the age of eleven years and some months, this friend of Amy's was extraordinarily well informed. It was because of her dad, really. During quiet periods, John Horrocks was a keen reader and he imparted a great deal of information to his only child. As for local knowledge – that was all freely available within the confines of Hair By Yvonne.

'Jesus was a Jew,' finished Maddy.

Well, there was no arguing with that. Amy chewed thoughtfully on a gingernut biscuit. But she could never communicate these things to her own parents, because Celia and Arthur Bradshaw were frozen in a time all their own. Bernadette, their older daughter, had been forced to leave home because she had been far too broad-minded for her parents to appreciate. 'I wish I knew what you know, Maddy. I wish I could be as . . . as clever.'

Maddy laughed. 'But you are – don't you see? You've just got to allow yourself to think. Stop doing as you're told without thinking about it. I mean, you can still obey people, but you can know inside what's right for you.'

Amy stayed silent. Her mother could see right inside Amy's skull. She knew what everyone was going to say and she knew when a person was harbouring bad thoughts. Whilst there was not much said in the house, Celia Bradshaw watched her daughter like a hawk; one daughter gone 'bad' was enough for Celia. So every expression on the younger child's face was noted, scrutinized, and probably recorded in a notebook somewhere.

'Amy?'

'What?'

'Can you keep a secret?'

Could she keep a secret? She was an expert at secrets. The biggest of all Amy's secrets was shared with no-one – not even with Maddy. 'Of course I can keep a secret.' Would going to the grammar school make things difficult? The big secret was hard enough now, let alone when there was homework to be done.

'The bell house.' Maddy's voice registered just

above the whisper mark. 'That's where they go, the vicar's children. I even know the grave where they hide the key – it's called Evelyn Partington. She died in 1802 and was a beloved mother and wife. Nobody visits her, so the key is in a gap under the urn.' She thought about the urn. 'She can't have been all that bad.'

'Who?'

'Mrs Butlin. She always put flowers in that pot. Mind, that might have been because it's near the church and it made things look a bit more cheerful. Anyway, that's where they keep the key.'

'Oh.'

'And I've been in.' Maddy's tone was trimmed with pride. 'And I'm going in again. And I'll be talking to them.'

Amy could see that Maddy's journey through the summer holidays was going to be adventurous. Where Maddy led, Amy followed; had she not done so, her own life thus far would have been conspicuously lonely. 'Then I shall come, too. But if my mother finds out . . .' Amy raised thin shoulders.

'You could meet Nettie there. It's bound to be a lot safer than the woods.'

Amy's jaw dropped.

'Yes, I know you meet her on the sly. If you both went to the bell house the back way – from the woods – you would have a better chance of getting away with it. As it is, anybody chasing a rabbit might see you with Bernadette and tell your mother. Where would you be then? Locked in a bedroom with the Sacred Heart and the

Book of Saints? Safer behind the closed door of the bell house, that's what I say.'

'How long have you known?'

It was Maddy's turn to raise her shoulders. 'I can't remember. But I've distracted people who were not far behind you – I can tell you that for nothing. This village knows everything about everybody. If you carry on meeting your sister, your mam and dad will find out as sure as eggs. We need a plan.'

The relief was so overwhelming that Amy broke down. Tears poured through long, slender fingers as she hid her face. Maddy had been looking after her; Maddy had made sure that no-one found out about the secret meetings. And it was so wonderful to know that Maddy knew.

'Don't cry.'

Amy uncovered her face. 'You're like my mother, but nice,' she managed finally. 'She guesses things, but not nice things. And this would not be a nice thing for her.'

'I know.'

Amy mopped her face with an ink-stained handkerchief. 'I don't even know why she threw Nettie out, but I sometimes wish I could go and live with her. She's twenty-six now and she could look after me. And she does normal things like going to the pictures and having ice cream.'

'I know,' repeated Maddy.

Amy breathed a long, shuddering sigh. 'I just want normal. To talk at the table, to play games with my mam and dad. Dad's all right, but he's always tired or at work. Mam's . . . well . . . she's

. . . what does your dad call people like her?'

'Fanatics. She's fixed in her mind, and she can't help it – it's just how some Catholics are. I mean, look at Father Sheahan. If he thought anybody ate meat on a Friday, he would probably set the village stocks up again and we'd be throwing tomatoes and rotten apples at each other. I don't want to feel like that. I don't want to be a Catholic just because I'm frightened.'

'I know.'

'So.' Maddy tossed the yellow curls away from her face. 'So, I ate a slice of ham one Friday and nothing happened. I confessed it in town – just in case the Catholics are right – and I never got struck down dead. Because it's all a load of rubbish.'

There was a pause before Amy answered. 'If it's a load of rubbish, why did you confess?'

Maddy laughed. 'Because I *am* frightened. Because they frighten all of us. And God shouldn't be about being frightened. God should be like a good friend, somebody you can talk to when things get hard. He shouldn't be a threat, Amy. I'm fed up. I wanted to go to Bolton School, because they do more science there, but even my mam and dad wouldn't allow that. It's as if Rome would choke them.'

Amy nodded and returned the handkerchief to her gymslip pocket. Maddy was right. Children had been caned for not learning catechism, for missing Mass, for getting the words to a hymn wrong. Father Sheahan kept well in with the richer people among his congregation, often neglecting those who were in real need of help and advice. There was something radically wrong with Catholicism, but two eleven-year-old girls weren't going to get to the bottom of it.

'Is your Nettie still a Catholic?'

'Is she heck,' answered Amy. 'She was a Methodist for a bit, then she started going to one of those spiritualist places where they talk to the dead. I couldn't do that.'

'My dad does.' Maddy had often heard John Horrocks talking as he laid out friends and neighbours. Sometimes, there was a break in his words and Maddy had heard him weeping on more than one occasion. He would tell them they had been too young, that they should have drunk less beer, that he had enjoyed their company. Then Maddy's mother would go in to do hair, nails and make-up just to make the bodies look nice for that one last time.

'Have you ever seen one of the dead people?' Amy asked.

Maddy nodded. 'I'm not supposed to go in and I suppose that's why I did. It was a lady and she looked beautiful. It was as if she was asleep. It's not frightening at all. Dad says a body is the house a person lived in, no more.'

'So what about ghosts?' Amy bit down on a nail.

'Stop chewing your fingers,' ordered Maddy, 'and there are no ghosts. Not here, anyway . . .'

'I hope not.' Amy shuddered.

A mischievous moment visited Maddy. 'I don't know about the bell house, though. It's creepy.'

Amy swallowed audibly. She had heard tales

about the little building and she didn't want to hear any more. 'I'd better go,' she said after a short pause. 'Mam likes the kettle on when she gets back from the surgery. And Dad might be awake now.'

Maddy could not share her friend's fear. Even if there were ghosts, what could they do? With no arms and legs, with no substance whatsoever – how could they hurt a living being? Death was a matter-of-fact business in the Horrocks household – Dad had even been heard to say that death was his livelihood – so perhaps that was the reason for Maddy's simple acceptance of the fact that life ended, that the spirit left its shell and . . . And what? What did she believe?

'Maddy?'

She looked into the thin, worried face and decided to keep her thoughts to herself. Because Maddy wanted the end to be the end; she required neither heaven nor hell, did not want eternity, not in flame, not in everlasting light, either. It should be quicker than that, simpler than that – and she did not understand herself. What she was thinking and hoping was probably a sacrilege, a sin so mortal that it could never be cleansed . . .

But. If there was no God, there was no sacrilege and—

'Maddy? I'm going.'

'All right.'

Maddy sat and stared into an empty grate. To whom should a child pray when the prayer was, 'Let there be no God'? To whom could a child speak about doubts and fears such as these? She was alone. She was one apart, a creature who belonged nowhere and with no congregation. 'I think it's called an atheist,' she told the fireplace. 'But there's another word – ag-something-or-other. It's for people who aren't sure.' Then she went to find a dictionary, because she needed to be sure of her words, even if she could not manage to be certain about eternal life.

They always died in the middle of the night. Why couldn't they pass on during daylight hours? Father Michael Sheahan was no longer a young man and he needed his rest. The whiskey helped him sleep, but even half a tumbler of Irish would not have seen him through repeated door-banging such as this.

He dragged himself out of bed, wished he could have kept a resident housekeeper, someone who might judge the severity of a situation and, on occasion, leave the master of the house undisturbed. But his help went home every evening and, with no curate, the whole parish looked to him when the reaper called.

Staggering from bed to chair, he dragged on some trousers and a shirt, throwing a cassock over his untidiness before descending the stairs. It was all but four in the morning, an ungodly hour for such disturbance.

When he opened the door, he stopped breathing for a second, then tried to push the door closed again. But she was quick; she had always been quick in both mind and body and he was no longer a match for her. Also, she was holding something in one hand, was digging it into his ribs – a piece of weaponry, no doubt.

'Sit,' she snapped.

He sat, eyes narrowing against the light when she switched on the central chandelier. 'What do you want?' he whispered.

'You,' she replied. She noticed how old he was, that his breathing was laboured. 'Just you. I have come to see you on your way and to cheer you along.' She leaned against the closed door. 'Satan is waiting for you. For such a loyal servant, he will have kept a special place. I bet you will have a cell all to yourself – with plenty of heating, of course.'

She could not be in her right mind. The presbytery was over fifty yards away from the next house, but surely the shot would be heard? She was levelling a gun at his chest. 'No use going for your heart, as you have none.' Her tone was conversational – she might have been discussing the weather or prices down at the local Co-op stores. 'Years I've waited for the courage to do this. Years and years and more years. How many little girls have you meddled with, eh?'

He gulped again. 'None,' he managed. 'I prayed – I got help from God and from the saints.'

Her laughter was chilling. 'So I was the only one?'

The priest nodded. 'I swear it.'

'But can you prove it?'

'No, but who could?'

She walked towards him. 'Don't move, bastard priest. Don't even breathe. There can be no punishment fierce enough for you and your kind. And even if it was just me – if I have been the chosen one – isn't that evil enough? Did you confess?'

He nodded.

'Who heard you?'

'Father Flanagan at St Patrick's.'

She nodded as if considering his reply. 'But you didn't go to prison, because Flanagan protected you. He is bound by the laws of your faith not to tell anyone how filthy you are. In a prison – where you should have been for the last fifteen years – other men would have dealt with you. But there's no-one here, Father. There's just you and me. And my special friend.' She brandished the firearm.

'You can't do this,' he blustered. 'You'll be caught and—'

'And what? Sent to jail? Don't you know anything? I have been in prison since the first time you laid hands on me. I have been in hell since the first time you raped me. Remember? How God had picked me out for you? How we always prayed afterwards? How I had nowhere to run because you were the parish priest and no-one would have believed me?'

His heart was thudding in his chest like a wild beast trying to escape confinement.

She backed away again. Her eyes shone, the absolute hatred she felt blazing from their depths. This was the worst kind of man, one who had opted for supposed celibacy because of his inability to cope with women, one who indulged himself with little girls who could be silenced because of his position in the village. 'I'm still near enough to blow your head off,' she said.

Urine soaked the chair, while terror threatened to open his bowels right where he sat. She was a woman now, an angry woman. Michael Sheahan would have preferred to face a furious man any day. Women went past reason; women came from emotion, from great depths, from wisdom that was born in all the daughters of Eve.

The uninvited guest was smiling now. He was like a great, ugly fish that could not escape the hook. But he did not wriggle as a salmon might have done, did not move at all. 'Have you ever been so afraid?' she asked quietly.

'No.'

'I have. I had an ugly man thrust into me, a great, hideous piece of so-called humanity that needed a bath. Did any of them ever tell you that you stink of sweat and booze? Huh? And I know why they have to be little girls, because you don't last five seconds, do you? A couple of huffs and puffs and you're gone, because it's all too exciting for you.'

He shivered as the urine reached his legs.

'And then you would collapse on top of me and start crying and whimpering, telling me I was doing God's work and that I would go straight to heaven for helping you. It was up with the trousers and out with the rosary beads, me kneeling beside you with your filth pouring into my knickers.'

He bit his lower lip until he tasted blood. Why

wouldn't she get this business over and done with? Ah, he had the answer to that: she was here for her pound of flesh and she was talking of flesh now.

'You were always heavy. You're even fatter now, but you were never the Adonis. A dead weight, you were, especially for a ten-year-old child. It's a wonder I didn't suffocate underneath you. It's hard to breathe with a fat man squashing you into the floor.' She glanced at the clock. 'I have to be at my job early in the morning. I need to have this business over and done with so that I can get a bit of sleep.' She cocked the gun. 'Amazing what you can find when you need it,' she remarked casually. 'I hope it works.' She raised the gun, her left hand supporting the barrel.

He had expected that he would pray at the end, but no prayers entered his mind. All he knew was that he would soon be dead and there was nothing he could do to protect himself. The clock ticked away the final seconds of his life. With eyes closed tightly against the sight of her, he waited for pain and darkness.

'Open your eyes,' she commanded.

He obeyed and saw that she had returned to the door.

'I'm not in the mood for killing just now,' she said.

His bowels opened then, but the emission was liquid and it burnt his skin. What the hell was she doing? Had all this been for nothing, had it been a game? The questions died; he was alive and for that he must be grateful.

'Phone the police if you like,' she advised him. 'And I shall fight like a tiger. I shall get a lawyer to knock on every door in this village and on doors of houses well away from here, places where your victims live now. Because I know I am not the only one. And anyway, I have not been out tonight. I am asleep in my bed, Father Sheahan, and I own no gun.'

He dared not move in case she changed her mind. The piece was still held aloft and he had heard no click, so it was still in the firing position.

'I shall come again,' she told him. 'I don't know when, but I shall be back. Wherever you are, look for me. I could be at the other side of the confessional grille for all you know. From tonight, you will never sleep easy in your bed again.' She left the house, slamming the door in her wake.

For at least five minutes, Father Michael Sheahan remained riveted to the chair. He could summon no help, because if the woman were to be arrested, his whole life could well be spread across the *News of the World* within days. Was she still out there? Was she using the blessing of darkness to stand unseen while he sat here in a pool of glaring, artificial light? And a pool of something else. The fumes hit his nose and he gagged.

The chair would be ruined – he would burn it in the garden. Would he be safe in the garden? The woods spilled right across the back of church and presbytery, stretching beyond St Faith's, too, and off towards the moors. She could be anywhere at any time – and there was nothing to be done.

Easing himself into a standing position, he felt his own waste draining away down his legs and onto the floor. He heard her all over again. 'With your filth pouring into my knickers . . .' Speaking softly to a statue of the Immaculate Conception, he said, 'Every man has a weakness and mine has been . . .' He could not say it, could not frame the words. Even now, well into middle age, the urge to place his hands on young, female flesh was strong.

He was no longer safe. Twice, he had applied for a move; twice he had been refused. It seemed that he would be here at this church until the day he died. And when would that be? Tomorrow, next month, next year? She no longer lived in Rivington Cross – she was somewhere in the town—

When the clock sang the half-hour, he jumped almost out of his skin. Half past four. The episode had lasted just minutes, yet he felt as if he had been fastened for ever to that chair. He had to clean himself, had to hide clothes, the chair, his guilt, his dreadful sins.

As he made his way to the upper storey, he found himself weeping. He wept not for the children he had abused, but for himself, because he had been born cursed and. God had abandoned him. The Boss up in heaven had never appreciated His servant, a man who had fought to be decent. 'With your help, I could have avoided this,' he muttered as he scrubbed garments in the washbasin. He lit the

Ascot, a gas boiler that provided constant hot water, filled the bath and lowered his soiled lower half into water that almost scalded him. It wasn't fair. It had never been fair.

Outside, the young woman placed her gun in the saddle bag of her bicycle and wheeled the vehicle out of the village. Soon, milkmen, postmen and paper boys would begin their day, so she needed to get out as quickly and as silently as possible. She must not be noticed, or her plan would be spoilt.

Once safe, she placed her bicycle in a roadside ditch and lowered herself onto the verge. She had finally got him. He would never fetch the police, would never run for help, because she had the ability to finish him – and yes, she might well find the others. There had never been anywhere for her to run, so she had waited for adulthood and had moved towards the source of her pain. Sometimes, the devil had to be faced.

The devil was a vestmented man whose colours changed with the dictates of the church, though his soul remained blacker than coal. He wore greens and purples, and white, sometimes with gold and silver running through. He blessed bread and wine, was there when the Lord entered these gifts; day in and day out, he celebrated the Last Supper, the Holy Mass, heard confessions, distributed Communion, blessed the dying.

The devil did the work of God and that was not right.

There had never been anywhere to turn. In the end, she had waited and, rather than running away from the evil, she had girded herself and had moved towards it. Sometimes, one had to face Satan, had to grab him by the horns and shake him until he fell apart. God, from where had she got the strength, the craziness? The enormity of what she had done made her shake, and she spread herself out on the grass, willing herself to feel the chill wetness of the morning dew as it soaked into her clothes. She was alive. Some victims died. Some were found mangled, drowned, suffocated, but he had allowed his to live. And yes, she would find some others, would seek out girls who had fallen victim to the man's lust.

The cold made her shiver and the shivering enlivened her. Even as scalding tears coursed down her cheeks, she rejoiced, because she had achieved more on this day than ever before in her life. No, he must not be allowed to remove everything from her. She wanted to be a wife, a mother, a proper person. She could not permit him to stop any of that.

When her weeping was finished, she dried her face and began the long ride down into the town of Bolton. She had work to do, a life to begin. And she had a priest to destroy.

TWO

Betty Thornton, whose aim in life had been to remain unnoticed, lived the ordinary life in an ordinary street between Deane Road and Derby Street in Bolton. She was clean, upright, a Methodist and a widow with a nine-year-old son from whom she pretended to take no nonsense. It wasn't easy, but no-one had ever promised that it would be. In fact, her existence was a sore trial, the embodiment of which stood silently in front of her at this very moment. She could not bring herself to slap him; no matter what was said to her by minister and congregation, no matter what the opinion of any other being, Betty Thornton was unable to lay a hand on her son.

James, the supposedly well-reared child, was quiet, polite and self-effacing when in the presence of his mother. Once allowed loose, however, James let rip with all the energy available to a child of his age, and was always in a great deal of trouble at Sunning Hill, the county primary school through whose portals he had wandered some four years earlier, face scrubbed, clothes fresh, the expression of an angel on his handsome face.

He had seldom been clean since. Betty, planted in the doorway between kitchen and scullery, surveyed her son and heir. 'Dragged home again?' she asked, though the question was not necessary. His teacher had just deposited the dishevelled boy on the doorstep of number 14, Claughton Street, and had left Betty in no doubt about her son's behaviour. 'You've been fighting,' she sighed resignedly. 'Miss Eccleston said so.'

'It weren't my fault,' he began.

But she cut him off. 'It's never your fault, James. Two and three times a week, it's not your fault. For somebody who's not at fault, you get into more than your fair share of trouble. You should just walk away. How many times must I tell you to just walk away?'

He kept his face expressionless. There was no point in explaining that folk at school mocked him. They laughed at him because of his girlish looks and his name, which was not to be shortened to Jim or Jimmy; he was James. His mam had told the school that he was James and that no other form of address would be accepted – and no-one messed with Betty Thornton. 'Why?' she asked now. She had raised him to be plain and God-fearing, yet he was turning into one of the very tearaways she feared and despised. 'Your father would be disappointed,' she said. Her husband, who had not been sent abroad until 1942, had never seen his son, was not here now to keep him under control. For a woman on her own, James was a handful.

James was disappointed, too. He owned a grey mother who went to a grey church in the company of many other grey people. They praised the Lord quietly, as anything ostentatious might have seemed Roman or Church of England; no-one ever took a drink, no-one laughed and the pianist could not find a right note to save her life.

'You will have to be taken in hand,' she told her son sadly. He was so good in the house, so perfectly behaved that she had taken time off from her job in the weaving sheds, had walked up Derby Street, had stood out in freezing weather to watch him fighting and carrying on like a wild young animal in the school play-ground. All that the teachers had said was true – James was a pest and no mistake.

'Why?' she asked wearily for the hundredth time. 'Why do you make a show of me? You carry on like a lunatic as soon as you're away from here – and you won't even tell the truth.'

James stared down at his clogs. His dad was dead. His mother's family wanted nothing to do with her because they were Liverpool-Irish Catholic and she had turned Methodist. He had a daft name. He had yellow curls and the face of an angel. He was clever and he couldn't help it. He had always been able to read and could not remember learning. His mother talked differently, because she had a Liverpool accent. And he was fed up.

'Well?'

If only Mam would stop being so nice. Nice got him down. Everybody at chapel was nice – they had all signed the pledge and were sworn to live cleanly and charitably for the rest of their lives. What was wrong with him?

'James?'

He lifted his head; it was time to own up, to give an account of himself. 'I . . . er . . . I don't like my name – anybody else would be Jim or Jimmy and I want my hair cut as short as it can be so that the curls will be smaller. I was getting beaten up because I was top of the class, so I feel like not trying any more. And everybody else has a dad. Well – nearly everybody.'

'That's not my fault,' she replied. 'God took him.'

'Hitler took him, you mean.' Mam accepted things. She never questioned what happened around her, never railed against life and all its cruelties. It was as if she had been born to be a victim, a leaf blown in the wind, no resistance, no fight in her.

'Whatever you like,' she answered, her tone almost cross. 'I can't give up work. I can't stay at home to look after you during the summer holidays and I can't afford to pay anyone to look after you. I would be ashamed to ask anybody to have you. So you'll have to stop in here all by yourself where you can do no mischief. At week-ends, we'll go for rides on the buses, but you are not to go anywhere Monday to Friday. Have you got that?'

He nodded.

'And there's nothing wrong with your name and nothing wrong with being clever as long as you stay humble. As for your hair – we'll get it cut off as soon as we can. All right?'

He nodded again.

She dismissed him and listened with a heavy heart as his footfalls resounded on the stairs. With Jim gone, the rearing of this child was all down to her and she didn't feel fit for it. The mill was hard, hot and wearisome, the work repetitive, the hours long. Sometimes, at the end of the week, she had insufficient energy even for chapel – and there were still chores to be done. No rest for the wicked?

She must have been extremely bad in her time, because she toiled morning, noon and night just to keep her house straight, her son dressed and fed and her own bodily require-ments fulfilled. From the fireside rocking chair, she looked up at the picture of Jim in his uniform. She would not remarry; marriage had not suited her the first time, so she had no intention of giving it a second try. But James showed no signs of improvement and, as he grew, he might well deteriorate even further.

Would not remarry? She smiled and shook her head. Who would want her? She had no choice in the matter, as men of her age were few on the ground and she was no raving beauty. There was no need to look in the mirror; mirrors were there for the straightening of hair and hat, no more. But even had she wanted to look at herself, the sight would not have been cheering. She was ordinary – ordinary was the best way to be.

The piece of paper was curled in a pocket of her apron. If she responded to it, her life would no longer be ordinary. There was no-one to ask; she might have spoken to the minister at chapel, but he wouldn't have understood, because the situation was unusual. Betty was a Methodist through and through, had been glad to escape into the faith after leaving Catholicism and all its stupid pomp. But there was countryside up at the village referred to as The Cross – there was Rivington Hill with its famous pike, the place where heathens rolled their painted eggs every Easter. There were woods and fields and moors; there were places where James might run off his energy.

'Church of England,' she informed the rug. 'Church of England – and why did his wife run off? And do I want to be stuck in a house with a vicar and his kids?' She didn't know and there was no-one to ask. But there would be no harm in keeping the appointment, surely? Going up and talking to the vicar would not commit her. Yes, James would have to attend the C of E school, but it had a good reputation. 'You don't need to take it. Anyway, it might have been snapped up.'

In the second after these whispered words left her lips, Betty knew that she wanted first refusal. The idea of another person's having been taken on panicked her slightly, because she wanted it. It had been a backward way to go about things, but she had her answer. She wanted a chance at the job, wanted the promise of a better life for James, somewhere away from the slums and from the school in which he caused so much trouble. Sunning Hill was overcrowded, but St Faith's would be smaller.

Mam and Dad had moved inland, too, were living in Bolton. She couldn't even ask them to look after James, because they would have him kneeling in front of the Immaculate Conception counting beads. Yes, she needed to get away from them, too, needed to save her son from Catholicism. There was nothing on God's earth worse than Catholicism. Church of England was a close second, but the chance needed to be taken.

Betty walked to the bottom of the stairs. 'James?'

'What, Mam?'

'Get washed and changed. We're going for a ride on the bus.'

'Where to?' he called.

'You'll see when we get there.' The iron was hot and it was time to strike.

Sarah and Simon Butlin shared a birthday and a great deal more, including mutual respect, love and support. They were not alike in temperament, but neither could imagine life without the other. She, a strawberry blonde with even features and a temperament to match, was an easy-going child with plenty of confidence and a sense of adventure that often startled her father. Simon, on the other hand, was quiet and imaginative, a painter of pictures, a reader of books, a boy who practised the piano without being prompted, who sang in the choir and was polite to all who met him. They were a pair of gloves and one could not fulfil its function without the other.

They had one particular hobby in common and that was the bell house. It was their sanctuary, their escape from a pompous and sometimes overbearing father, from a mother whose restlessness had finally caused her to abandon her family. The bell house was their secret retreat, a place into which they could take their troubles and share them. 'She won't come back, will she?' Simon sighed deeply into the dank air of the bell house's lower chamber.

Sarah struck a match and lit the wick on a large church candle in a tall wooden holder. 'No, she won't come back. I think she ran off with that man who used to visit sometimes – the one who couldn't talk properly.'

'The lisper with the moustache?'

'Yes. He sells clothes on Bolton and Bury markets and he makes her laugh. Dad never made her laugh and she needs some fun. The man made me laugh, but not in a nice way – I never heard such a silly voice and never saw a droopier moustache.' She was exaggerating the more obvious failings of Derek Ramsden, but she didn't care.

The twins sat and stared at each other through gloom illuminated by one frail source of light. This was their safe place, their refuge. The key to the bell house, supposedly lost, had been in their possession for a couple of years and they had allowed Evelyn Partington, beloved wife and mother 1802, to take care of it for them. So far, Mrs Partington had never failed them; her urn continued to conceal the precious device which opened the door to their own little kingdom. Escaping from Father was a necessity rather than a luxury, as he might have driven a saint to distraction with his humourless lifestyle.

'What are we going to do?' asked Simon now.

'He's advertised for a housekeeper.' Sarah's reply was delivered in a tone that fell a long way short of enthusiastic. 'If he approves of her, I am sure I shan't. It will be some miserable old woman who asks questions about our bowel movements so that she can dose us with syrup of figs. She will be as boring as he is. If she is in the slightest way interesting, she won't last a week.'

Simon clicked his tongue in agreement. 'Thank God we have this place. Let's hope she never finds us.'

The bell house was a strange little building. From one side, it seemed single-storey, but the other side held a door much lower than the one at the front, so they sat in a type of cellar, with no windows, and no light save from candles and, sometimes, a torch or a paraffin lamp. Designed to contain a bell purchased from a Wigan church in 1541, it had been built too small, so a man had been forced to run in with a hammer to hit the bell when services were about to start. The eventual removal of the bell to the tower of St Faith's had left room for the storage of charnel, though bones had not rested in this cellar for many years. The thick stone walls contained noise very well, and no light showed from the little subterranean chamber.

'Why didn't she take us?' asked Simon. 'Why did she leave us here?'

Sarah raised her shoulders. 'Who can say? Perhaps she won't have much money, or perhaps her new man friend doesn't want us.'

'But she took Stella. Seems to me she loves the dog more than she loves her own children. A cocker spaniel is more valuable than we are.'

The girl smiled. 'A cocker spaniel does her bidding. I didn't. You did. So she should have taken you, but twins should never be split. Children should not be separated. At least we have each other and the bell house.' In spite of sadness about the departure of their mother, Sarah felt a small bubble of excitement in her chest. That girl had been hanging about the graveyard again. Daughter of the undertaker and the hairdresser, Maddy Horrocks looked promising, as if she might turn out to be good fun.

Simon opened a book and leaned in towards the candle in search of better light. The best way he knew of forgetting things was reading, so he entered the world of Tom Sawyer and left his sister to her musings.

Sarah had spoken to Maddy on several occasions. Mr Horrocks did funerals for everyone from several parishes in the area, so he was well known – he was well liked, too. Mrs Horrocks styled everyone's hair, though Sarah's mother had preferred to go to a salon in the town, probably in order to meet her new companion from the market, but everyone else, including Sarah, had their hair cut at Yvonne's.

Simon closed his book. 'We need some more paraffin for the lamp,' he pronounced, 'I can't read with just one candle.'

They rose to their feet and Sarah blew out the flame. It was time to go home for tea, time to sit and watch while their father burned food. 'We shall need a housekeeper,' she informed her twin, 'or we may starve to death. In fact, you and I could probably fry eggs and bacon – let's go and help ourselves, shall we?'

They returned to a joyless house and to a father whose situation might have commanded pity had he been easier to approach.

Brian Butlin was still suffering from shock. Caroline, his wife of some fifteen years, had driven away in a Morris Minor van with most of her clothing and a cocker spaniel bitch – no note, no reason given, no apology. She had telephoned just once to enquire about the twins, had spoken briefly to him and for a slightly longer period of time to Sarah, then to Simon. She was heartless. For all those years, he had lived with a viper in his bosom, had protected, nourished and clothed a woman with no feelings, no thought for anyone save herself.

He had never cooked in his life, had no idea about washing, ironing and organizing uniform for two children who were about to begin their secondary education at Bolton School, an establishment famed as a feeder for Oxford and Cambridge, a school where scholarships were now available, a school known as one of the best academic institutions in the north-west of England. Brian needed his God now more than ever before. How on earth could he run a parish and raise two children single-handedly?

He stared gloomily through French windows and surveyed his rear garden. Where did one buy uniform? Would it be from Henry Barrie's on Churchgate, from Whitehead's, from Manchester? Where were the letters from the school, one from the girls' division, one from the boys'? He turned on his heel and began to rattle through the upper section of an antique bureau. Dinner money – was that paid weekly, monthly, termly? They would need sports equipment, tennis shoes, racquets, shorts, swimwear. Sarah might well want a lacrosse stick, Simon a rugby kit.

'How could she do this to us?' he asked the empty room. He was a vicar, a man whose family should provide an example for those he served. Looking people in the face was becoming difficult, while sermonizing on the subject of adultery promised to be uncomfortable for the foreseeable future. And there was the house to tend, too. A woman from the village had been doing the basics, but he needed a housekeeper, someone who would assume responsibility for his children, for meals, for laundry, for the smooth running of life at home. How could he minister to the sick and needy while a pair of eleven-year-olds needed him? They were sensible enough children, but they required a female guardian, a mother figure, someone who would help them through their early years at the big school.

Papers spilled to the floor and he stood back in confusion as they spread themselves across parquet and onto rugs. It was hopeless. There was but one option available to him and that was not palatable. He would need to find his errant wife, must take himself to Bolton, to the market on a Tuesday, a Thursday or a Saturday. There, he must seek out the man who had brought cut-price clothes to the vicarage, slight seconds available at a fraction of their normal cost. He bit his lower lip. The man had brought more than clothes for Caroline. Crude thoughts entered Brian Butlin's mind, bringing with them pictures that were not suitable matter for a man of the cloth, and he banished them with a shiver. The day was warm, but he felt cold right through to his bones.

The kitchen door opened. He heard his children chattering as they entered the house and he pulled himself up. A man should not show his feelings, should not allow himself the luxury of sadness or shock. Everything had to continue as smoothly as possible so that Simon and Sarah would survive this hiatus in their lives.

Sarah came in. 'We shall cook, Pa,' she told him. There were papers all over the floor. 'You get on with whatever you are doing, while Simon and I do some bacon and eggs.'

Brian kept his face as expressionless as possible. They were trying so hard to convince themselves and him that everything was normal, that there had been no unusual events to ripple the surface of life at the vicarage. His Adam's apple seemed to move of its own accord, as if emotion tried to escape from the trap in which he hid it so determinedly. The twins were looking after him and it ought to have been the other way round.

Sarah watched him. 'It's all right to be sad,' she said.

He nodded. 'I'm not sad, just hungry,' was the white lie he returned to his daughter. 'And rather confused about uniforms and so forth.'

She crossed the room and raised the lid of a small Victorian writing slope on the sideboard. 'The letters are here in Ma's box,' she said, placing them on the dining table. 'Simon and I have had our measurements taken at Henry Barrie's, and there is a full list of everything we need.'

Brian allowed a sigh of relief to escape his lips.

'You should have asked me in the first place,' chided the daughter, though her tone was gentle. 'I know where most things are.' She left the room, her brother a couple of steps behind her.

The man lowered himself into a dining chair, his eyes still fixed on the spillage on the floor. The mess seemed to illustrate excellently the state of his mind, of his marriage. Like the letters and bills, his thoughts were becoming fragmented and scattered, while his dreams, usually forgotten, left him with a feeling of unease when he woke each morning. She was in the dreams – of that he felt sure. Caroline, the woman he had loved and trusted, was now a source of great torment and his heart was close to breaking.

But a man with two children to care for and a parish to run could ill afford the luxury of a breakdown. He had to pull himself together, needed to act as vicar, as mentor to his flock and as father to the twins. Self-pity was a sin. He forced himself to pick up every last piece of the mess he had made, then to organize the top half of the bureau, sorting bills and letters into proper sections and neat rows.

The doorbell cut into his thoughts and he rose swiftly from his task. 'I'll get that,' he called to the children before making his way into the hall-way. The next few moments contained a blur of activity, blue smoke, some screams and a woman who pushed past him, a young boy moving at a slower pace in her wake. Brian blinked, closed the front door, then followed the new arrival into the kitchen.

The fire was out in a few seconds. Betty Thornton, who was good in a crisis, had already proved her worth before a word had passed between herself and her prospective employer. With a dampened tea towel, she starved the chip pan of oxygen and killed the flames. 'Is anyone burnt?' she asked. 'Who screamed?'

'I did,' replied Sarah. 'But we aren't hurt. It was just so frightening. And thank you so much.' Her tone was shaky,

Betty tutted. 'Well, you had too much fat in there, you see. When you put the chips in, it overflowed and caught fire. You'll have to be more careful if you're going to fry chips – you could have had the house and everything in it burnt to a crisp.'

'Sorry,' wept Sarah.

Betty was filled with remorse. She hadn't meant to shout at the child, hadn't meant to upset anyone. 'It's an easy mistake to make,' she said, 'so don't go getting yourself in a state. If we all got in a state every time we made a mistake, the whole world would be in a right mess every minute of every day. You ask my James – he's an expert at mistakes.' She turned to look at her son. 'Aren't you?'

James nodded. 'I could start a fight between angels – Mam said so.'

Sarah Butlin dried her eyes and allowed her gaze to rest on the self-confessed maker of mistakes. He was beautiful, just like one of the angels he had mentioned, with a cherubic face whose features included rosy cheeks and clear blue eyes. The whole pleasing ensemble was topped off by a shock of yellow curls which were surely the envy of every female he met. 'I'm Sarah,' she said. 'And this is my brother Simon and my father, the Reverend Brian Butlin.'

James shook her proffered hand. 'I'm James Thornton and this is my mam Betty. She's come about the job.'

Betty nodded at the vicar. He looked a bit green around the gills, as if he had suffered one shock too many. 'Tell you what,' she said, 'why don't you all go in the other room while I make you something to eat? Don't worry, I can find my way around a kitchen – I'll not be needing any help.'

Thus Brian Butlin acquired a housekeeper and the first decent meal he had eaten in over a week. Furthermore, he collected a nine-year-old boy who, though a self-confessed sinner, looked like a saint. He also promised to drive the two of them to the Methodist chapel in Horwich whenever possible, to move them from Bolton to Rivington Cross the very next day and to talk to the owner of Betty Thornton's mill with a view to having her released immediately from the man's employ.

Betty refused to allow the vicar to drive her home. 'No,' she said firmly, 'you stop here where you're needed. We'll be all right on the bus and thanks for giving me the job. James needs a fresh start away from the town.'

'And a haircut,' said the lad.

'Hair By Yvonne,' offered Sarah. 'She does boys' and men's hair, you know.'

'I want rid of these curls,' James insisted.

'At least you don't have pink hair.' Sarah patted her own offending locks.

'Strawberry blond,' amended Betty. 'There's many a woman who tries to get that colour out of a bottle.' She sniffed. 'Not that a person should worry about looks. It's what's on the inside that matters.'

Brian agreed with her, though he said nothing. For many years, he had enjoyed the company of a whited sepulchre, decent on the outside and decayed within. Caroline Butlin, wife and mother, had proved Betty Thornton's statement to be true. Betty Thornton was plain and decent, as was her religion. Methodists, in the Reverend Brian Butlin's books, were no-nonsense people who served God as best they

69

could. And he did not want a decorative woman about the place, as such a female might have caused tongues to wag. He would have preferred her childless, but this poor widow and her son needed him and he had been put into this world to help people.

Alone while their father prepared a sermon, Simon and Sarah discussed the events of the past hour. 'She's dull,' pronounced Sarah, 'but we get James with her. He seems interesting.'

'She'll be strict,' replied the boy. 'Not like Ma.' Ma had allowed them a free hand whenever Pa had been away from the house. Or had she simply failed to care about their activities? 'But she's a good cook and I bet she'll keep the house nice.'

'She will.' Sarah rubbed at a spot of egg on her dress. There was a great deal of washing to be done. 'Do we let him in?' she asked.

Simon knew what she meant. 'I don't know.' Sarah made all the decisions, anyway, and she was considering letting quite a few people into the bell house. Two of those people were Catholics and Pa would not have approved, because he disliked the parish priest intensely. To be fair to Pa, he was not prejudiced as such, yet he had been heard to aver that he hoped the parishioners of Holy Martyrs would not listen too carefully to the preachings of a fool.

'There can't be many,' mused Sarah aloud. 'It's too small. And we can't risk using the front, even though the key fits both doors. There's a window in the downstairs-upstairs.' Downstairs-upstairs had always been the term they had

70

used for the upper level of the bell house. Downstairs-upstairs had a wooden floor, but downstairs-downstairs was a windowless cellar, a perfect place for secrets. 'It won't hold more than six,' she added, 'and even that would be a squeeze. But I think we have to let James in.'

'What if he tells? Pa would be angry if he knew we had the key. The bell house would be useful for storage – he still talks about getting a lock-smith to break in so that the gravediggers can use it – their shed is falling to bits.'

Sarah shivered involuntarily. 'God forbid,' she begged. She would hate to lose the bell house. It was their den and she wanted a gang like the Famous Five or the Secret Seven, a place where plans could be made, where ideas could be discussed beyond the reach of adult human hearing. 'All we can do is hang on to the place for as long as possible. Don't think about it, Simon. We've escaped Pa's seriousness and Ma's silliness for a long time – let's just hope our luck doesn't run out.'

Simon, betraying a wisdom worthy of adult-hood, shrugged. 'Luck always runs out in the end,' he said. 'Ask Mr Horrocks.'

'I don't need to. Just step outside and look at the graves – they are enough proof. So we just have to hang on to the bell house for as long as we can. And we'll grow out of it. Even if we don't grow out of it in our heads, our bodies will get too big for it. The gravediggers would be forever banging their heads if they kept their tools there. Yes, James comes in. He's only nine, but he's not a babyish nine, is he?'

'No. He's all right,' agreed Simon. So James Thornton was co-opted onto the committee in his absence, and the twins went up to their beds.

Yuspeh Feigenbaum enjoyed a mixed relationship with her adopted country.

She loved England, because England had received her and she had enjoyed her freedom since 1939, when she, her son and his wife had escaped from Warsaw while storm clouds thickened over Germany and threatened to float across to Poland. She was lucky and she knew it. Most of her family had perished at Treblinka, but she, Jakob and Anna had been safe in the bosom of England for most of the time.

London had been unsafe, though, night after night of bombing, Jakob away translating for the War Office, Anna terrified while they hid in the Underground with the baby. The baby had been named George in honour of a great king who should never have been king; his second name, Josef, had been chosen in memory of his dead grandfather. A girl child would have been Elizabeth in deference to the Duchess of York, that wonderful woman who had been installed at Buckingham Palace after the abdication of the cowardly and stupid Edward VIII. That poor girl hadn't wanted to be a duchess, let alone a queen, yet what an icon she had become, God should preserve and guide her, what a blessing she was.

But food? The one kosher butcher in Bolton knew little or nothing, it seemed. He was an English Jew and English Jews were not quite up to scratch when it came to food. She poked at the flaccid breast of an uncooked bird. 'They don't know from chicken,' she declared for the umpteenth time. 'This could be a crow with a weight problem, because I never saw a chest so flat.'

Anna grinned. Jakob's mother was a sore trial, yet she loved her dearly. 'It will be fine, Mamme. We have vegetables enough—'

'Thank God for that, or we would starve before night. And my poor boy, he works so hard in the business, he will be hungry. He should have stayed in London to work with his head, but no, he says the tailoring is in his soul and he doesn't care to work with words. My son, he can translate from three languages, so he makes suits and makes no sense. Two spoons of honey in my tea, Anna, I have a cold beginning.'

Anna smiled and shook her head as she set the kettle to boil. The move from Bolton to Rivington Cross had been for Yuspeh's sake, yet the old woman chose not to take advantage of the fresher air. She stayed indoors for most of the time, her hawk's eyes fixed on her little family, her heart given totally to Jakob, to Anna and to George. 'You should take a walk, Mamme.'

'To where should I walk?'

'To nowhere – just walk.'

'And the point of that would be?'

The younger woman turned and looked at her mother-in-law. Clad in black – as ever – Yuspeh looked as if she had stepped out of some old picture book, a relic, an example of times gone by. 'The point would be exercise to make your legs stronger, also to meet people.'

'I should meet people? For why should I meet people? I have people here, you, my son – God save him – and George Josef, my grandson, the light of my life. I need no more; I am satisfied with my lot in this world. For why do you want me out? Must I move to another house that you might become English and leave the old ones to rot, as they do?'

Anna sighed, smiled and shook her head. 'You are troublesome and your grandson is the same. Hour after hour, he sits on that wall, heels kicking, talking to no-one. But at least he is out in the air. And you know well enough that we would not part with you for a king's ransom. Just walk. Keep your legs moving while they can and breathe in the air.'

'There is air in here. Without air in here, none of us would be breathing. So for why should I be blown about? What happens if the wind should tip me over and break the legs you wish me to exercise? Worse still, should I break an arm, there would be no darning and sewing done in this house, for you are not a woman for the needle, Anna.' Yuspeh sniffed. She owned a whole dictionary of sniffs, and this was the *I am right* version.

Anna swallowed a laugh and brewed the tea. When she brought the pot to the table, she looked through the window and saw George in his usual place, alone on the wall. A great sadness stabbed Anna in her chest. George had just left a junior school in Bolton, a place to

74

which his father had driven him each day. The two schools in Rivington Cross were unsuitable, as one was Church of England, the other Catholic, and George's education had, of necessity, been non-denominational. But he had made no friends up here and Anna felt his loneliness acutely.

'Don't worry.' Yuspeh was suddenly at Anna's shoulder. 'There are other Jewish boys at Bolton School – didn't the headmaster tell you so?'

'Yes, Mamme, but they might not live round here. He needs other children near his home.'

'He needed a brother or a sister, but that was not to be.' Yuspeh placed a hand on her daughter-in-law's arm. 'For all the tea in China, we would not lose you, dear girl, and a second could have killed you. Yes, I would have wished for more children myself, but Josef – he died young, may he rest. And for you, I wished more. But we were not to be blessed and this we must accept. George will find friends with the Jewish boys at his new school. They will come to the bar mitzvah and all will be well.'

All would be well? Anna poured tea and scooped honey into Yuspeh's. As it dripped from the spoon, the words *life is sweet* popped into Anna's mind and she agreed in a sense, because she was among the most fortunate of all those she had known and loved as a child. From the Warsaw ghetto, her family, like Jakob's, had disappeared into the gaping maw of Hitler's camps and she was here, free, happy.

But her boy was not happy. Sometimes, being a Jew was hard. The local schools were good, yet

George had been forced to attend a non-denominational school in Bolton, one in which there had been no danger of indoctrination. But what did it really matter? Yet she dared say nothing to her mother-in-law, nothing to her husband, as they were slightly more orthodox than she was. George was English, yet he was not, because Judaism was more than a faith – it was a way of life – and because his parents were Polish. Would he ever fit in? Would he meet a nice Jewish girl in time, would his life become whole?

'Drink your tea,' snapped Yuspeh, 'and the world should do the worrying.'

The dog came round the corner at about twenty miles an hour. In its wake ran the pretty girl, the blonde one whose parents were undertaker and hairdresser to the villagers of Rivington Cross. She stopped next to George and doubled over. 'I have a stitch,' she gasped. 'Here, take this.' She thrust a lead at him. 'Monty's owner died and we have to save him. Mrs Appleyard, he belonged to, but she died – he'll probably go back to her house. Run! Hurry up!'

Compelled by the sheer force of her voice to obey, George set off after the dog. He saw it turn into the gateway of a cottage and he slowed his steps. The poor thing had probably gone home, but there would be no-one to greet him. Gingerly, George tiptoed up the path and watched the sad creature as it shivered not from cold, but from fear. He lowered himself onto the step next to the animal, placing a hand on its neck and taking hold of the leather collar. 'You will be fine, just fine,' he said, his voice low. 'Someone will take you, feed you and walk you. I know you think you have lost everything, but you haven't.'

Monty continued to tremble. This was his territory, yet it was not, because his howling had brought the others and the others had taken away his beloved owner. Like most animals, he knew about the absence of spirit, had felt the passing of his mistress and had done his mourning loudly and clearly. After licking that cold hand for over an hour, he had realized that the essence had gone and that he was alone.

Maddy, at the other side of the hedge, listened to the boy's gentle words. This Jewish boy had a heart and his heart made her eyes wet.

'The girl who chased you,' George went on, 'she is from the family who will look after your mamme. The lady will do her hair and the man will prepare her body. They will be kind to her and someone will be kind to you. It isn't over. You are young and someone will love you.'

Maddy joined him and sat at the other side of the dog. 'I'm keeping him,' she said. 'My dad felt so sorry for the dog that he persuaded my mother, so I am taking Monty home. But we could share him if you like.'

George fixed his eyes on her. 'How?'

She shrugged. 'We can walk him together, you and Amy and I.'

'Amy is the dark girl?'

'Yes. Her dad's the postman and her mother works for the doctor.'

77

'I know. I have often seen the two of you together. I sit on the wall and watch the world go by.'

'Yes,' she replied, 'we noticed you, too. Now, put his lead on and we shall take him back to my house. You can meet my parents and have a glass of lemonade. Would you like that?'

He nodded. This was not the time to worry about plates, cups and glasses, not the time to wonder whether milk and meat had met in washing-up water. He had a friend and a part-share in a dog, so life was promising to improve.

The dog took some shifting. Although he knew that his best friend had died, he could not yet imagine another life in another place with another owner. Thinner than most border collies, he still displayed an enormous strength when the children tried to shift him from the step. In the end, they carried him, Maddy's arms under the chest, George's supporting the hind quarters. 'Thank God he's the runt,' breathed Maddy, 'otherwise we would have needed more help.'

'How old is he?' George asked.

'Only about a year.' Maddy blew some hair from her eyes. 'Nobody wanted him – Mrs Appleyard had to take him. Those cottages have huge back gardens, so he was quite happy and very well behaved.'

George laughed. 'Was,' he repeated. Then he added, rather hastily, 'He will be good again when the fear stops.'

They arrived at the back door of Maddy's home, put the dog on the kitchen floor, then stood back when he streaked out of the room and into the hallway. He began to whimper softly, then John's voice was heard. 'Come on, then. Come in and say ta-ra to your mam. Our Maddy'll look after you, don't be fretting.'

George stared at Maddy. 'Has he taken the dog to the body?'

She nodded. 'Yes. He's done it before, for somebody's guide dog. Dogs have to be shown. They get mixed up unless they are sure about what's going on. We've had them at funerals before now, in the church and in the graveyard. Very intelligent, you see.'

'I never thought about it.'

'Most people never think, but dogs need explanations the same as we do. They can't understand what we say, but they know a tone of voice and they take notice. Once he gets it into his head that Mrs Appleyard is properly dead, he'll come round. I have to feed him. I read about it somewhere. When I give him his dinner, he'll know he's mine.'

George took the proffered glass of lemonade. 'I'm George Forrester,' he told her. 'We were Feigenbaum, but my father changed it to Forrester – easier to spell. My grandmother is still Feigenbaum. It means fig tree, so we changed to Forrester, as it still begins with F and it implies a connection to trees.'

'And you are Jewish?'

'Yes, but I was born in London.'

'Your dad makes clothes.'

George nodded. 'He does, bespoke and some ready-mades – he opened a small factory on

Halliwell Road for the ready-to-wear clothes. He employs quite a few machinists. Mamme was supposed to help, but Papa says she could not sew on a button properly. Soon, my mother will help at the factory in the office. My grandmother sews, but she is too old for work.'

He was nervous and Maddie sensed his discomfort. 'Well, I'm Madeleine.' She was determined to put him at ease. 'I hate it, so I get Maddy. You know what my parents do as jobs. I was born here and I have never been to London. I like ice cream and dogs.'

'But not on the same plate.'

'No,' she agreed. 'And I never managed to eat a whole dog, but I reckon I could shift a bucket of Manfredi's vanilla.' He had a twinkle in his eye. She liked the twinkle and was glad that he could keep up with her. 'You going to Bolton School?' she asked.

'Yes.'

'Convent for me.' Her tone was mournful. 'Amy and I will be with the nuns up Deane Road. I am trying not to think about it, but Amy thinks about nothing else – she's more nervous than I am. Her parents are very old and quiet and Amy doesn't get a lot of fun at home. Do you?'

George thought about that. 'Yes, I suppose I do. My grandmother is funny and my parents play chess and Monopoly with me. But I have no friends here.'

Maddy laughed. 'Come back later. You have me and Monty.'

'Yes. Yes, I suppose I do.'

There was no *suppose* about it, thought Maddy

after George Forrester had left. She had always sensed that the boy would be interesting and he had not disappointed her.

But she had a dog to settle and a salon to sweep. George Forrester was filed in the pending tray of Madeleine Horrocks's brain while the child got on with her duties.

George's step was light as he made his way along the road towards his own house. There was a bubble inside his chest, a warmth that threatened to burst and engulf his whole body. For weeks, he had tried to pluck up the courage to talk to those two girls, but he had never managed it. The dog had made it happen. If George thought about it, the old lady had played her part, too. Her death had caused Monty to run loose and Monty had needed catching. Grandmother Yuspeh was always saying that there was a reason for everything and she was probably right.

Yuspeh pounced as soon as George entered the house. 'You left the wall.'

'Yes,' he replied. 'I had to help a girl catch a dog.'

The old woman tutted. 'Anna?' she called through the doorway. 'Your son, he is chasing dogs and girls.'

George laughed and went upstairs to change. He was chasing no-one. But the warm glow stayed with him all through dinner . . .

THREE

Mr Weston was not pleased.

Betty had decided that it would have been unfair to leave without telling anyone. The vicar was clearing the way with her employer at the mill, so it was only right that she should tell the minister, as the chapel was the sole place she visited when not at work. He was worried about her. She was gravitating towards a religion that was flamboyant, too colourful and noisy. The Church of England would take money from her, as it needed a great deal to keep up to scratch with its pomp and circumstance. She would be contaminated, diseased, disempowered. She would need fancy clothes and good shoes, because it was all about dressing up and being seen.

For once in her life, Betty stood her ground. 'I'm doing my best, Mr Weston. The vicar's giving me and my son room and board and I will be getting a wage as well. There is a Methodist chapel not too far away, and Mr Butlin will drive me and James there whenever possible.'

Charles Weston's lip curled slightly. 'You'll find that won't be very often. Next news, he'll be asking you to do the flowers and fill up the communion wine decanter.'

'The church has its own cleaners,' she said.

'Aye, till one of them gets sick, then you'll be polishing pews and I don't know what. And I've heard all about him. Did you know his wife walked out and left him with two children? She ran off with some market trader, so what sort of a family is that? Not decent, I can tell you.' The man glared. 'You don't know what you're letting yourself in for.'

'He told me his wife had left, yes.' But he hadn't told her the details and she understood why. No man wanted to explain about a wayward wife; no man wanted to admit that the mother of his children was a loose woman who could be tempted by a few cheap clothes. 'All I know is this, Mr Weston,' Betty continued, 'my husband is dead and I need some help with my son. He is running wild at school, good as gold at home. If fresh air and fields will help him to use up his energy, that will be a good thing. And I don't care what Mrs Butlin did – her husband seems a decent man and he needs help, too. He has twins who want a woman to look after them. They nearly had their house on fire. It wouldn't be Christian for me to leave them in that state.'

'Mrs Thornton, I only—'

'I only wanted us to part on good terms, Mr Weston. Now, I am leaving today. My neighbour will sell my bits and pieces of furniture – not that they're worth much – and I ask for the congregation here to pray for me and James. So, that's that. I wish you all the best.' She turned on her heel and left the manse, closing the door sharply as she stepped out.

In the street, she felt stronger in her heart, though her legs were rather wobbly from the shock. She had stood up for herself, had argued with a minister, so she was experiencing mixed feelings that were not completely unpleasant. She was a person in her own right, a house-keeper, a woman with a proper position and a nice big house to care for. And although she did not approve of Mr Butlin's faith, she no longer resented it, because his job had created hers. She would work hard. The biggest sin was her wish, her hope, that Mrs Butlin would never return to her children.

She crossed Deane Road and shivered. That was a terrible thing to want, she told herself firmly. Even if the woman did come back, a housekeeper might still be a good idea, because that vicarage hadn't enjoyed a good bottoming in years. It needed some concentration, some organization and plenty of elbow grease. Well, Betty Thornton was not afraid of hard work and she would make herself indispensable.

All the way up Emblem Street to its junction with Claughton Street, she made her plans. Closing the door of number 14 in her wake, she leaned on its solidness for a few seconds. In two hours, the vicar would be here. 'James?' she called. 'Find all your toys and put them in that trunk of your dad's.' She would pack the clothes. By this afternoon she would have a new address, a new job and a different life. And if Mr Weston didn't like it, he could lump it. Her heart fluttered. Was she making the biggest mistake of her life? Was she a sinner?

Someone knocked on the door and her heart missed a beat. Had Charlie Weston followed her? Was he going to try to force her to stay? She opened the door to find a lad with a bicycle and, for a few beats of time, she was transported back to the days when young boys had brought messages of death from the battlefront via the War Office. No. All that was over. The lad handed her a letter. 'He said no reply, missus.' Then he rode off without waiting for a tip.

She ripped open the envelope and almost wept when she absorbed the contents. Described as thoroughly dependable and industrious, Betty Thornton sat on her stairs and read the reference. It was with regret that the mill dispensed with her services to allow her to help out a cleric whose household required the very qualities so valued by the mill. This was to be taken as a reference and character of the highest calibre and, should she ever require work as a weaver in the future, she would be given first refusal at any of three mills owned by the company. She was useful; she was valued.

Betty found herself smiling through unshed tears. So she had been noticed. Never one for gossip or a sly cigarette in the toilets, she had completed each shift to the best of her ability and her absences from work, which added up to one

85

week in five years, had been caused by an influenza so severe that she had been unable to lift her head from the pillow without serious discomfort. In fact, the mill nurse had been to the house with a basket of fruit and some flowers from management. 'I was noticed,' she whispered. Then she thanked God for all His infinite goodness and went on to pack her few paltry possessions. It was time to begin a new and better life.

Phil Bennett practised from an end-terraced house that was really two stone cottages knocked into one. A bachelor, he was currently courting a nurse from Bolton Royal Infirmary and they were planning to marry next year. But the ceremony would be held in Wales, his fiancée's native country, because Enid's family wished for that; also, the patient who currently sat opposite Phil was a man he disliked intensely and he would not have wanted him involved in the wedding. Professional to the core, Dr Bennett parked his voice in neutral. 'The tests are positive,' he said. 'You have diabetes, Father Sheahan.'

The priest shifted his bulk in the straight-backed chair. 'And what will that involve?' he asked.

Phil thought about that. 'You will have to stop drinking. The readings are high enough to warrant insulin and, if you drink, you may well have difficulty in stabilizing your blood sugar levels. The mechanics are not fully understood, but alcohol interferes and can cause hypoglycaemia. You will also need to eat a great deal less and you must avoid refined sugars. I shall give you a diet sheet.'

Michael Sheahan blinked rapidly. 'Will I need to inject myself?'

'Yes. I can show you how. It's intramuscular, so there is no particular need for precision. Cakes and chocolate will become an occasional treat, I'm afraid.'

The priest considered that. 'So, if I drink, I might lose blood sugar?'

'Yes.'

'And I would have to eat more?'

'Yes, but that isn't the way to manage diabetes. The best way is to stick to the diet and stay away from drink altogether.'

The patient had been drinking for most of his adult life. Food was important, too – what pleasures were available to a man of the cloth if he could not enjoy a drink or a good meal? 'And if I carry on as normal?'

Phil took a deep breath. 'You will die.'

'We all die.'

Some did not die quickly enough for Phil Bennett's liking. There was something about this man, an oiliness that rendered him markedly unattractive. He would rant and rave from the pulpit in a church Phil had ceased to attend and, on more than one occasion, Phil had suspected . . . No. Surely not? Children became disruptive and naughty for all kinds of reasons . . . Yet not one of those anxious youngsters had been pupils at St Faith's – every last one of them had attended school and church at Holy Martyrs.

'I never see you at Mass these days,' said Father Sheahan.

'No.'

'May I ask why?'

The doctor was leafing through papers in search of a low-sugar diet. 'I go to St Patrick's,' he replied offhandedly, 'with Enid. That is unless I am tending the sick and I am sure that God will forgive me on those occasions.' He found his target. 'All points are listed. You may have twelve points each day and, for now, just one dose of insulin per day. I shall come along to the presbytery later to do a demonstration.'

'You should support your local parish.'

Phil, the red-haired descendant of three Irish grandparents, felt his temper slipping out of neutral and close to second gear. 'The commandments of the church dictate that I should contribute to the support of my pastors, Father. It does not specify an address. I give at St Patrick's.' He also confessed at the church in Bolton, because he could not have trusted this man with the slightest thing; also, he had no intention of helping the cleric buy five or six bottles of whiskey each week. 'I do my duty,' he concluded.

'Bless you for that.' Tiny eyes disappeared further into rolls of adipose tissue. Below those bulging pockets, thready veins gave the countenance a falsely healthy appearance, because these rosy cheeks were the result not of fresh air but of over-indulgence.

'Diabetics have strokes and heart attacks,' Phil continued, all emotion deliberately stripped from his tone. 'If you follow the diet and take your insulin, you may live another twenty years. If you do not . . .' He raised his shoulders.

'I shall have less.'

'Yes.'

'Then I must make an effort.'

'Yes.' In that moment, Phil Bennett knew. As he looked into those narrowed eyes, he began to realize that he was in the presence of true malevolence. A Catholic priest was revered by his flock. A Catholic priest was in a position that was almost unassailable, because all his parishioners – plus some non-Catholics – would choose to believe the best and ignore the worst of a shepherd of Christians unless they had been actual eyewitnesses to sin.

Sensing a slight change of atmosphere, the patient rose to his feet, weight making the shift in position a little unsteady. 'I shall see you later, Dr Bennett,' he said.

'Yes, Father.' He pressed his buzzer and waited for Celia Bradshaw to replace Father Michael Sheahan.

Celia passed the priest, nodded a greeting, closed the door, then walked to her employer's desk. 'Yes, doctor?'

'After surgery, leave out on my desk the notes for Philomena Shaw and Claire Greenhalgh.'

'Yes, doctor. Anything else?'

'No, thank you. Send in the next patient.'

Outside, Michael Sheahan stood next to the famous Rivington Cross, a time-worn article with railings protecting what remained of the ancient relic. He had lingered near the surgery door, had heard the doctor's words, the names of the girls whose notes he had requested. The priest's eyes darted from side to side as he looked for the one who had entered his house, the woman with the gun, the one who was threatening his life.

Behind him, in the doctor's house, now a man was plotting, too. Did no-one realize how hard life was for a priest? Oh, let them try rattling round in a presbytery with just a part-time cook and cleaner, with no family, no company, no release. A man needed his release, needed his whiskey, his food and . . . and the other thing, too. He was the victim. God had called him, he had answered and life was difficult.

Inside, Phil Bennett, spatula in one hand and torch in the other, was peering into the throat of a young patient. He saw the pustules of tonsilitis and raised his eyes until, over the child's shoulder, he was looking through the window to where a dark, robed figure lingered near the village cross. That was a guilty man and, not for the first time, a doctor resented the oath of Hippocrates. The priest was interfering with little girls and there was not a damned thing the doctor could do.

He removed the spatula from the boy's throat and spoke to the mother. 'Penicillin again, I'm afraid. When this bout is over, I think we must get tonsils and adenoids removed.' If only it were as easy as that to excise the root of many other problems in this village. But neither surgery nor medicine would remove the priest. Mind, an overdose of insulin might well do the trick . . . As he wrote a prescription, Dr Bennett shook his head slightly. A doctor should not entertain thoughts of that nature; for a Catholic doctor, such ideas were probably a mortal sin.

Amy Bradshaw was afraid of dogs and the fear made her ashamed. She was afraid of several things and some of them were very silly. There was the tree-and-building problem for a start. She could not climb a tree, because she feared she might slip – or was she afraid that she might jump? Similarly, she had been unable to join her friend Maddy on the flat roof of the kitchen below Maddy's bedroom window. Scared of *wanting* to jump? Whoever had heard of anything so silly? Even when Maddy's dad had put railings round the roof, Amy had remained tremulous.

She had recovered from the puddle thing. As a small child, she had been unable to 'plodge' in larger puddles, because she had been afraid of falling 'up' into the reflected sky. So, while other children had plodged, Amy had deliberately forgotten to wear her wellington boots and no-one paddled in shoes.

But now there was the dog thing. And, because a boy was involved, the business with the dog was even more embarrassing than it might have been. George Forrester, a Jewish boy, was probably not the sort of company of which Amy's mother would approve, so that was another factor in her nervousness. Maddy's parents, who were definitely more *laissez-faire* in their attitude to child-rearing, did not appear to mind when Maddy entertained the lad in her bedroom, but

Amy was petrified. Celia Bradshaw blamed Jews for the cold-blooded murder of Jesus Christ. Celia Bradshaw had been heard to opine that Jews would wander the face of the earth for ever, as they had been guilty of the worst crime ever committed by mankind.

And now, there was Monty.

'He doesn't bite,' pleaded Maddy for the umpteenth time.

George, who was hanging on to the dog's collar, agreed. 'He has never bitten me and I am all kosher,' he quipped.

'All what?' Amy's voice was a whisper.

Maddy laughed. 'He means his meat is killed the Jewish way.' She turned to George. 'The dog may not be Jewish, but he hasn't bitten me either and we get our meat from an ordinary butcher. So he probably isn't religious and just doesn't bite anyone.' Her head swivelled. 'Amy, for goodness' sake come in.'

'I can't. I daren't.'

Maddy tutted. 'Put his lead on, George, and fasten him to my bed railings. Poor little thing – he's been through enough.'

Amy backed off. 'I'll go home,' she volunteered. There were two reasons – the boy and the dog – and she couldn't explain either of them.

Maddy read her best friend's mind in an instant. 'It's all right, I've told him your mother can't stand Jews. But we can help you with the dog and you don't need to say anything about George. What your mother doesn't know won't worry her. We'll find a way round your mother –

it's her loss, anyway, because George is good fun. But the dog – we have to get rid of your fear. Amy, you cannot go through life terrified of dogs.'

'Dogs are our friends,' said George. 'Even Bobbee likes them. She says they were put here for our amusement and protection.'

'Bobbee is Grandma,' Maddy explained. 'It's Yiddish.'

George grinned broadly. 'Bobbee says she is fluent in four languages – Polish, Yiddish, English and Rubbish. Really, she talks rubbish all the time, but we love her. And actually, Bobbee is a name I made up as a baby. She's really Bubbah.'

Amy wanted to smile, but her fear of the over-active dog held her back. He was straining on the leash, was almost managing to pull the bed across the room. But she had to do this. Her love for Maddy and her need for Maddy made her put one foot in front of the other until she was established just inside the door.

Maddy closed it. 'Right,' she breathed, 'so far, so good. Are you still alive, Amy?'

Amy nodded, though her heart threatened to escape from behind her ribs into the room. She perched on the edge of a chair, eyes fixed to the frantic animal. It looked like a wild thing and it was staring straight at her.

Maddy decided to go for shock tactics. There was no point in pussyfooting around; Amy was not a baby and a short, sharp shock might be just what the doctor should order. She flattened herself against the door in case Amy tried to escape.

'Let him go,' she mouthed silently at George.

George hesitated, then decided to obey. Although he had enjoyed but brief acquaintance with the girl, she seemed sensible enough – and she knew Amy well, had been through school with her, had kept company with her for many years. He unclipped lead from collar, his own heart becoming unsteady when the young dog leapt forward.

Amy screamed as the animal landed on her lap, front paws digging into her thighs, tail waving madly, tongue reaching for her face. She hid behind her hands, waited for death and received a thorough wash. Slowly, she opened eyes and separated fingers. The dog was laughing at her; he knew about her fear and was doing his best to cheer her. The teeth were big for such a small dog, especially the four pointed ones whose shape was exaggerated for the sole purpose of tearing flesh from bone. But she had to do it, had to face this now or she might lose Maddy for ever.

'Sit,' Maddy ordered.

The licking stopped and the dog leapt away and sank to his haunches.

Slowly, Amy lowered her hands.

'And stay,' Maddy said.

He stayed. Amy raised a trembling hand and placed it on a head so silky and soft that she had to comment. 'He feels like my satin First Communion frock,' she said. The ears were magic, one folded over, the other at a crazy angle, part down, part up, part sticking out sideways. He was a mess, a wonderful misfit, an unbeautiful beast who needed love and comfort. 'He's nice,' she concluded. 'I'll get used to him, I promise.'

'And he has to get used to you,' George told her. 'His owner died and he is confused. But Maddy's father showed him the body and he seems to have accepted things now.'

Amy's rate of breathing slowed to normal. 'Let's take him for a walk,' she suggested. 'Then he can get used to all of us. If we go the back way, my mother won't see us.' She glanced at George. 'I'm sorry,' she said lamely.

'I'm Jewish,' he grinned, 'so I'm used to it.'

'Mrs Bradshaw doesn't like anyone who isn't Catholic,' announced Maddy cheerfully. 'She doesn't like Church of Englanders, Methodists, Unitarians, Jews, Conservatives and the man who comes round with the coal. Amy, stop backing away from Monty – you've had him all over you like measles. Here – hold the lead, and if he pulls just tell him, "Heel". Come on, we'll take him to the woods.'

Amy Bradshaw took the dog downstairs and the others followed. It was only one little dog, but it was a huge stride for a small, frightened girl and she experienced a new emotion as she walked towards the woods. She was proud of herself.

Betty felt slightly uneasy. Her long-term employer at the mill knew the truth about her reasons for leaving Bolton, as did the minister, but the one person with whom she had not been completely frank was standing at her door, a big smile lighting up his homely, ordinary face. She hadn't told him about James.

The chip pan fire had been a distraction, as had the providing of a meal for the Butlin family, but those were not adequate excuses. She glanced down at James. 'Just run upstairs and see if we've forgotten anything. Make sure all my ornaments and photos are in this cardboard box.' She waited till the child had left, then led her visitor into a poorly furnished parlour. 'I should have told you yesterday – he's naughty at school.' She could get her job back at the mill, she reminded herself. She hadn't lost anything. Yet she had, because she wanted to move to Rivington Cross, wanted to look after that beautiful house and those motherless children.

'He will not be naughty in my school, Mrs Thornton. The pastoral side of education is very much emphasized – but don't worry about indoctrination. He will hear Bible stories and learn general Christian principles, no more. Please do not make yourself uncomfortable. Twenty-four hours ago, you and I had not even met – this has been a quick change for all of us. As I said when teaching my twins to swim – jump in at the shallow end and test the water. We shall do the same. And your employer had nothing but good to say about you. James will improve.'

'Thank you. If you can help him, if the teachers can help him, I shall be very grateful. I just needed to be honest about my reasons for wanting the job.'

Brian Butlin remained confident that he had made a lucky find in Betty. The only applicant, she was eminently suitable – cool in a crisis, industrious, plain in appearance and as honest a woman as he had ever known. Betty would not entertain spivs from the market, would not neglect the children, would tend the house carefully. A man of even temper, Brian could not help feeling angry when he thought about the magnitude of his wife's crime: Caroline had abandoned her children for the sake of baubles, had left a decent life in order to pursue shallow pleasures. She would have plenty of clothes now, but those clothes would be slight seconds, which term might be aptly applied to their wearer.

'He's not a bad lad,' Betty was saying, 'but he runs wild in the playground and hits other children.'

'Not at St Faith's.' The minister's tone, though quiet, was firm. 'Such a child would be dealt with immediately, Mrs Thornton.' Brian prided himself on the behaviour of the young among his flock. Sometimes, he even awarded himself permission to feel triumphant when he thought about Holy Martyrs' RC Infant and Junior School, because the Catholic children of the village were certainly noisier and more rebellious than were their C of E counterparts.

James re-entered the arena. 'Nothing left,' he told his mother.

'Then that's that,' said Betty. Now she and her son could leave these grimy streets for a better life, for fresh air, good food and decent company. Feeling a cut above her neighbours and knowing that this sense of superiority was a sin, she climbed into Mr Butlin's car while he packed her belongings into the boot. Moving onward and upward, she left Claughton Street without a backward glance – she was destined for better things.

Phil Bennett did not particularly approve of alcohol. There was a new school of thought which voiced the suspicion that a tablespoonful of Scotch before bedtime was good for the circulation, but Phil was not convinced; he had closed the eyes of too many dead alcoholics in his four years as a general practitioner and, as a result, he adhered firmly to the belief that any substance which caused an alteration in perception, in behaviour and in the proper conduct of major physical organs was a bad thing.

Yet he found himself in the Eagle and Child on a weekday lunchtime, a small Scotch in his hand. This was Dutch courage? It tasted more like poison and he hoped that this small measure would be enough. It would have to be enough, as he might find himself driving to sick calls out at one or two of the farms at some stage in the day. Like one of his own patients, he closed his eyes and took his medicine. Occasionally, a doctor needed a crutch. To tackle a priest, a Catholic needed the moral equivalent of a wheelchair, he told his conscience.

He was glad when he found himself outside and in fresher air. The stench of stale beer was not pleasant and he wondered, not for the first time, how on earth people managed to spend so much time in such an atmosphere. The Eagle was the centre of village life, particularly for the menfolk. Some managed an odd hour in church; many spent several hours each night at the bar. Even the women gravitated occasionally to the pub lounge, cares set aside for a time while they gossiped about whichever female was not one of their number.

He crossed to the presbytery and knocked at the door. Deliberately composed, he waited as heavy footfalls approached, then drew himself up in preparation for the imminent encounter. This promised to be nasty. For any doctor, the task would be difficult; for a Catholic doctor, it was Everest.

The door opened. Michael Sheahan's eyes narrowed when he identified the caller. Shoving a needle into his own flesh on a daily basis was not his idea of a good life. He widened the gap and allowed the doctor to pass into the house. He had to learn how to administer his own insulin, and he did not relish the concept.

But Phil did not even open his bag before addressing his patient. 'I shall show you the hypodermic shortly and you may practise on an orange. First, there is something I need to get off my chest.'

'A confession?'

'No.' Phil placed his bag on a table. 'I am not the one who needs to confess, am I?'

The clock ticked loudly. 'What?' said the priest.

'I wouldn't confess to you even if the saving of my soul depended on it,' said the doctor. 'I make my own arrangements regarding worship,

99

as well you know. During my years here, I have seen some terribly disturbed young girls. Several burst into tears at the mention of your name. Fortunately for you, the parents did not notice. But I did. Why are they so afraid of you?'

The priest dropped into a chair. 'I am the one who teaches them about sin and fear of the Lord.'

'You *are* the sin.' Phil's voice was dangerously quiet.

It was as if the girl had returned, the one with the shotgun and the nasty tongue. Michael Sheahan's own tongue was suddenly as dry as sandpaper and this was not merely the diabetic thirst; he was afraid, scared that his bowels might open again, too terrified to move a muscle. 'What are you talking about?'

'Sexual deviation.'

The clock whirred and gave out the hour. It was one o'clock in the afternoon. 'How dare you?'

'Because those children are my patients. It took me a while to realize what was happening, but one of them will speak up sooner or later. When that happens, when the police become involved, you will regret the day of your birth.' If Phil Bennett had doubted himself, the expression on his companion's face was enough to convince him. 'In a case such as this, my oath as a doctor becomes burdensome. If I refuse to treat you, the whole of Rivington Cross will wonder why. This will become a divided village if I take you off my list. You will say that I am a poor doctor and I will say that you are a deviant.

If you cease to be my patient, I can do that, I can go to the police. The result? Chaos. I wish to remain here when Enid and I are married; I have every intention of rearing my family in this area. With any luck, you will be dead before my children are of school age. Perhaps I should put in an order for sons, as you appear not to upset little boys.'

The cleric was beaten and he knew it. Here stood a man several years his junior and several notches his superior in the intellectual sphere. He would apply for early retirement, would tell his bishop that his health was poor, that diabetes made him too weak for the work. What then? A home for retired priests, his time lived out in the company of the senile? 'I am not a bad man,' he said.

'You are a sick one,' replied Phil. 'You should be locked away for your own good and for the benefit of society. Touch one more child – one more – and I shall take you off my list. If I were to question some of those little girls, if I were to concentrate my efforts on breaking down the barriers created by you, the walls built of their fear and your cowardice, I could make a massive case against you. I would have to leave the village as a result, but it would be worth the sacrifice. One more. Just one more. Do you hear me, Father?'

'Yes, I hear your nonsense.'

'Then we understand each other. Now. I shall go through the injection process with you.' He would also dispense tranquillizers, would sedate this man until he posed no threat. As a doctor, he could say nothing; as a doctor, he could dispense his own kind of justice. He wrote a prescription for barbiturates and thrust it at the clergyman. One way or another, he would slow this man down for the sake of humanity.

'Mamme, it would cost too much. There would have to be a shed, nesting boxes, runs – then the feed.'

Yuspeh stood her ground. 'I have found a *shoychet* in Horwich. He has been in kosher since he was a boy in Vienna, God should let him live to one hundred. I can rear the chickens and the *shoychet* will prepare them. In return, as favour for the good man, I do some small sewing. You tell me go out, I go out. I find some good birds and I feed them well, then you try to keep me in. How am I to understand?'

Anna shook her head.

'You are dearer to me, Anna, than life itself. When you married my son, you became as precious as any *tochter*. You *are* my daughter – we can forget the in-law business. You want me exercise, I exercise. The *shoychet* has found me some young birds, no disease, and we get clean eggs and good meat. These English Jews have not proper kosher butchers. How we sure these birds we eat are killed well? For all we know, God forbid, these could be birds of prey we eat. I see my birds, I feed them right, I know they are good.'

Anna knew it was time to give up. There would be chicken runs in the back garden and there would be chickens in and out of the house.

Yuspeh would get fond of them, as would George, and the trouble would start when the *shoychet* arrived to do the slaughtering. But there would be eggs and Yuspeh would have an occupation, something to interest her and take her outside. 'As you wish, Mamme,' sighed Anna. There was no point in arguing; Yuspeh was already dressed in her outer wear, black coat, black headscarf, black stockings and shoes. Looking positively funereal, she was about to set out on her search for chicken wire and timber so that Jakob could build the coop and the runs.

'I was out earlier, too,' pronounced the old woman. 'When you shopped, I walked, much good it did me on such uneven pavements. I saw George. He was with a dog and a *shikse*. Well, more than one *shikse*.'

Anna laughed. 'What other kind of girl is there here in Rivington Cross, Mamme? Do you want him to sit alone on that wall for ever? He is eleven, no more than a child, and he should have friends.'

'Did I say different from this? A comment I made is all. I walk, I look for chickens, I try to do as my *tochter* asks and now this? But I pray my great-grandchildren should not drown in holy water, may God forbid.'

Anna continued to laugh. Yuspeh in full flood was like the tide coming in – no-one could stop her until the moon phase changed. 'He is not getting married, Mamme. He has not even had bar mitzvah – why should the walking of a dog with two Gentile girls mean that his children will be baptized?'

'God forbid,' repeated Yuspeh. 'My blood would turn to soup and my hair would fall out, also all my teeth, but one would remain for toothache.'

Anna sank into the nearest chair, tears of glee pouring down her face. Life without Yuspeh would have been darker and colder. She made mountains from molehills and carried on as if the slightest thing meant doom to her whole family. She dictated, teased, interfered and was the most splendid nuisance. The Seder meal was always wrong, eggs too hard, too soft, not good. Shabbat blessings were mumbled by her son, he should speak up when he blessed her only grandchild, God forgive him. 'Mamme, you will be the death of me.'

'My own death will come first. I go now find about the chicken runs and see where is George. And yes, you laugh at me, Anna, laugh if this makes you happy. It makes me happy that you are happy and that Jakob and George are happy. Me, I worry. It is my burden.' On this final note of high drama, Yuspeh swept out of the room, grabbing a long black umbrella on the way.

'The sun is shining,' Anna called after her mother-in-law.

Yuspeh's head made a brief appearance at the door. 'The sun shone on Poland and Gestapo still came.'

'An umbrella will not save you.'

'With an umbrella, I feel safe. It is good that I feel safe, may you enjoy my chickens when they arrive.'

Anna listened while Yuspeh left the house.

Poor Jakob. To him would fall the task of building sheds and runs. And if the chickens followed the example of their owner, life promised to be noisy and disrupted. Whatever, Anna kept reminding herself, chickens were an interest . . .

Brian Butlin pulled into his driveway, alarmed when the little Jewish woman waved her umbrella at him. Dressed, as ever, in black, she had emerged from the trees as fast as a woman half her age. He jumped from his car. 'I am so sorry. Did I frighten you?'

Yuspeh awarded him a stern look. 'The Germans frightened me. You did not. But you should look better through the window of a car. If you wish to go around in that big thing, you need good eyes and some sense.'

Betty let herself out of the rear of the car, James hot on her heels.

Yuspeh studied the new arrival. Better-looking people had been buried, she told herself, but looks were not everything. The boy was pretty, all yellow curls and blue eyes, but the woman looked as miserable as sin soaked in bitter herbs. 'Good afternoon.'

'Good afternoon,' replied Betty. 'Would you like a glass of water?'

'No, I want for some chicken wire and some wood for my son to make use of himself in the yard.'

Brian could help there. 'Go up to Ernest Grimshaw's house,' he advised, 'the blue door and a white gate. He is a handyman.'

'Thank you.' Yuspeh stalked off, head in the air.

Betty stared after the old woman. 'She must be hot in all that black,' she said.

'As am I,' replied the vicar. 'Mrs Feigenbaum seems to wear black all the time.'

'That's a funny name,' commented James.

'Don't be rude,' snapped his mother.

'Jewish family. They escaped from Poland before the war started. I understand that all their kinsfolk were exterminated.' Brian lifted Betty's cases from the boot. 'Come inside and the children will show you to your rooms. James – yours is rather small, but I hope it will be adequate.'

James, round-eyed with wonder, stood at the vicarage gate. For mile upon mile, moors rose towards the horizon. The air was sweet and the houses, built of stone, looked safe and solid. He hadn't looked the first time, though the views from the bus had been interesting. But now that he was going to live here, he drank in every last drop. He could run here. He could find horses and cows, sheep, wildlife.

'Come on,' ordered his mother.

Brian smiled. 'You like it here, James?'

'I think I do. It's big, isn't it?'

'There is plenty of space, yes. And there are woods full of rabbits and squirrels. Come inside. Sarah and Simon will help you settle in.'

James found himself in a tiny room under the eaves. It was a funny shape, its window perched on the roof. He could stand at the window, but the wall on each side was very shallow, with shelves to the left and lidded boxes to the right, the slope of the roof making standing an impossibility.

'Storage,' said Sarah. 'You can keep your toys in the boxes and your books on the shelves, but careful when you stand up, or you might bang your head.'

James didn't care. His head had taken more than a few blows during playground fights. He turned to look at the rest of his room. Against the normal walls stood a single bed, two small chests of drawers and a wardrobe. 'It's grand,' was his pronouncement. 'It's like a secret.'

'Our rooms are the same, but a bit bigger,' Simon informed him. 'We like being under the eaves, too. Your mother and my dad have the two bigger bedrooms on the next floor down.' He hesitated for a second. 'Our mother left us,' he added as an afterthought.

'So did my dad,' answered James, 'but it wasn't on purpose – the Germans killed him. They killed all that old woman's family too, the one in black with the umbrella.'

'Mrs Feigenbaum,' Sarah said. 'She has a son and he makes suits in Bolton. The son is married and he has a boy called George after the king. They changed their name to Forrester, but Mrs Feigenbaum kept the old name. George is in the woods with Maddy Horrocks and Amy Bradshaw.'

'And a dog.' Simon opened the wardrobe. 'Will this be big enough? If not, you can keep some stuff in mine.'

James bounced on his bed. It was a satisfactory

bed, firm and comfortable. 'What do you do all day?' he asked them.

The twins glanced at each other. He was only nine and the two-year gap was a canyon. Nine-year-olds didn't keep secrets. Sarah raised her shoulders. 'This and that,' she said. 'When there's no school, we do as we like, mostly.' It was not yet time to mention the bell house.

'Does your dad read the Bible out loud a lot?'

'No.' Simon grinned. 'Does your mother?'

James perched on the edge of the bed. 'She did, but she won't here. I might get a few verses at bedtime, but we won't have it at the table like we used to. She's a Methodist. Methodists don't drink, don't smoke, don't swear and don't fight. I stop being a Methodist when I'm at school. I'm a good fighter. When you look like me, you have to be a good fighter.'

'You fight?' There was shock in the girl's tone.

'I used to. But Mam says I can have my hair cut. I am sick of looking like a girl. And I have to behave myself, or she will lose her job. The other thing I hate is being called James. She won't allow Jim or Jimmy. When I grow up, I'll be Jim.'

Simon closed the wardrobe door. 'What would your mother say if we called you Jay?'

James shook his head. 'No idea.'

'Well, that's decided,' Simon announced. 'Unless she stops us, you will be called Jay from now on. Jay Thornton. It sounds good, doesn't it? It could be your signature. Come and look at our rooms.'

Thus James Thornton acquired the name that

would accompany him through the rest of his life. He followed the twins from room to room, catching glimpses of a splendour he had never expected to encounter. Had he known anything about fine furnishings, he would have realized that this was a shabby house, a neglected place. But, coming from the poverty of 14, Claughton Street, James could only wonder at a house that owned proper couches, a piano, a sideboard, bookcases, and pretty rugs.

He would be as good as he could manage, because he had found his true place in the world.

FOUR

The dog leapt about as if he had just been released from prison. He attacked trees, loose branches, clumps of grass, and managed to find any bits of mud that lingered from earlier falls of rain. This had been a dry summer, but the collie was determined to seek out any mess available to him, and he collected it about his person, particularly on the white bits.

Amy, still rather timid, watched the animal's lunatic behaviour. She was no longer experiencing terror, but she hung somewhere between caution and fear, her heart skipping the occasional beat whenever Monty doubled back in her direction. Maddy and George seemed close, as if they had known each other for a very long time, but Amy, determined not to be jealous, made an effort to join in their conversations. It was important to be friendly, she told herself firmly; any sign of resentment and Maddy would not be pleased.

'Amy?' called Maddy. 'Come on, don't hang back – he won't hurt you.'

George seconded that opinion. 'He is a good dog.' His tone was meant to be encouraging, but he noticed an expression in Amy's eyes, a fleeting look of not-quite-resentment, as if she felt like an intruder. He was the intruder and he did not want to come between these two long-term friends, so he fell back and joined the smaller girl. 'You did well,' he told her. 'Some people are naturally timid in the company of animals and you have come a long way. See how silly he is.' He pointed to the crazy dog. 'That is half a tree he is pulling. How can a dog so thin drag along a bough of that size?'

'I don't know.'

'It's called determination,' he told her. 'Have you ever watched an ant? The ant carries food far heavier than itself. That is in order to feed its fellows.'

Amy laughed. 'But Monty isn't going to eat that, is he?'

'No, but he may have plans for it – a bridge, a tree house . . .'

'A raft?' asked Amy, her eyebrows raised. 'The reservoir is just beyond that last lot of trees.'

They caught up with Maddy and made their way to the water's edge. As they stared at the vast stretch that served many thousands of people, Monty's attitude changed perceptibly. He dropped the large piece of timber with which he had encumbered himself, then squatted on his haunches, a ridge of hair stiffening along the whole length of his spine.

111

'Hackles up,' murmured George thoughtfully. 'Which means he is either distressed or angry. What on earth is the matter with him? Calm down, Monty.'

Amy shivered slightly. The day was warm, yet she trembled, because she feared that the dog might just turn on her. 'What's that?' She pointed to something in the water. 'Are people tipping rubbish in here again?'

Monty remained completely motionless, though some teeth showed while he allowed a low growl to escape his throat. With his eyes fixed on the distant object indicated by Amy, he continued to grumble.

'Looks like an old carpet,' said Maddy.

'Or a bundle of clothes.' George's attention was still on the dog. Something was wrong. 'What is it, Monty?' he asked.

At last, the collie turned and gave his attention to George. His mouth opened and a strange sound emerged, a cross between a growl and a moan.

'Fetch,' ordered George.

'What if he can't swim?' Amy, fear forgotten, stepped forward and stood between boy and dog. 'He could drown.'

'All dogs swim,' offered Maddy.

'It's a long way out,' Amy continued, 'and he isn't a big dog. What will he do with it when he gets to it?'

'The water will help,' insisted George. 'It will float. Let him bring it. At least we shall know what it is. Go, boy.' He pointed towards the half-submerged object.

Monty launched himself into the reservoir and began doggy-paddling towards the bundle. He did not glance once at the children, choosing instead to give himself up to the task in hand. The water, which was extremely deep, seemed to try to pull him under as he progressed towards his target. But he refused to panic. Every instinct bequeathed by his ancestors dictated that he should finish his task. It was important. Heavy, wet fur slowed him as he neared the bundle. It was weighty. As he turned to drag it back to the bank, he sank beneath a surface of glass, cold and deadly smooth except for the path he had made on his way out.

Monty was not a dog to be denied. Designed to control large flocks of beasts, he was not prepared to be defeated by one object. His blood surged madly with adrenalin as he surfaced and drew oxygen into starved lungs. Here was his prize; his friends awaited the bundle and he would take it to them. It reminded him of . . . of days gone by, a fireside, a light no longer burning, cold hands, the trembling he had done until the others had come. This was the same; this was an important package of remains, of memories.

When he reached the children, he was exhausted beyond pain. George dragged him from the water and rubbed his belly until some feeling returned to his innards. There was screaming, but it seemed far away and Monty felt that he might just float off to a different existence, but then his senses returned, ears assaulted by the sound of raised voices, eyes focusing on a pair of distressed girls.

113

Maddy stopped crying, then slapped Amy, who was hysterical. 'Monty is fine,' she said.

Amy's eyes were fixed not on the dog, but on the bundle he had brought to the bank. A hand, mottled and blue in parts, protruded from wet gabardine. There was chipped pink polish on the nails; this was a dead girl. Maddy had been weeping for the struggling dog, but her friend had seen something far, far worse. 'Don't look,' Amy managed between chattering teeth. 'Don't look, Maddy.'

Maddy looked.

While the dog lay panting, the three children stood and stared at the horror at the water's edge. It bobbed about gently, as light as a flower, its bulk supported by millions of gallons.

Amy swallowed audibly. 'It's a drowned person,' she muttered. It was a drowned person who wore sugar pink nail varnish. It cost one shilling and elevenpence at Woolworth's and . . . Amy knew someone who liked it. 'Sugar pink,' she mumbled to herself. The head was covered by the ends of some sort of scarf and the rest of the body was enveloped in a navy blue raincoat.

George took a step nearer to the parcel. 'It may be a murder,' he whispered. Then he looked around, as if expecting to see the perpetrator close at hand. 'We need police.'

'A girl.' Amy's voice was shaky. 'Or a young woman. Old women don't use that colour on their fingernails. Murdered?'

George nodded. 'She has been wrapped up and dropped in the reservoir. See that circle of rope? I bet that was fastened to a stone so that she would sink to the bottom, but the stone has gone and she has floated.'

Maddy's legs didn't seem to work any more and she dropped to the ground, an arm round the wet collie.

George grabbed the rope and placed it in Amy's hands. 'Hold on to that. Whatever happens, don't let go.'

Amy nodded mutely.

'I shall fetch some grown-ups and they will know what to do. If you don't hold the rope, she will float back again.' As he hurried away, George felt weakness in his own limbs. He had heard of horrors – Bobbee was full of tales about concentration camps, massacres, dead relatives, but this was England and people did not get murdered in small, northern villages with nice little shops and pleasant people. Here was too ordinary for murder, wasn't it?

The two nearest houses were the vicarage and the presbytery. Instinct guided George away from the latter, as the priest seemed an unapproachable type. He leapt over a wall and into the graveyard, passing a yellow-haired boy as he neared the vicarage. 'Hello?' He threw open the back door.

Betty Thornton was starching shirts. 'Who are you?'

George attempted to regulate his breathing. 'I need the vicar. I need the police.' He needed a chair, but there was no chair in the kitchen, so he slid down the wall and sat abruptly on the hard floor. 'Please,' he begged.

115

Betty tutted as she dried her hands. 'Do you want a glass of water?'

He shook his head. 'There's a dead person out there.' He waved a hand in the direction of woods and reservoir.

There were a lot of dead people out there, thought Betty as she studied the seated boy. There was a graveyard full of dead people . . . But no. She didn't like the look of this young lad at all; he seemed shocked, as if all the blood had drained away from his head and into his boots. 'Stop there,' she ordered. 'I'll go and fetch Mr Butlin and you can tell him.'

James, who had been listening outside the doorway, stepped into the kitchen as soon as his mother had removed herself. 'Is there a dead body?'

George nodded.

'I've never seen a dead body.' The younger boy joined George on the floor. 'I'm new. My mam is looking after the vicar's family. We came because she wanted to get me away from town.' He was babbling away, just talking, using words to fill the gap between himself and the stranger. 'I'm nine. How old are you?'

'Eleven.' George's teeth were chattering.

James remembered something. On a rare visit to his Liverpudlian grandmother, he had heard her talking about the woman next door. The woman next door had witnessed an accident and had been shaking with shock. 'Sugar for shock,' Nan had pronounced. This was shock. The dark-haired boy was shaking because he had found a dead body. James jumped up and took

116

two lumps from the sugar bowl. 'Here,' he said, 'eat it. It'll stop you shaking.'

George placed the sugar in his mouth and found himself thinking about Bobbee. Bobbee liked honey in her tea, but if there was no honey she would drink the scalding, dark liquid through a sugar lump clenched between her teeth. He wanted his father, Bobbee, Mamme – wanted his family. Instead, he got James's mother and the vicar.

Betty shooed her son outside, then set the kettle to boil. Lancashire instinct told her that copious amounts of hot water would be needed for the brewing of drinks – a crisis always meant tea. She had come to Rivington Cross for a peaceful life, but, after just a few hours, she seemed to have landed in the middle of a nightmare. Yet the child might be mistaken, she told herself as she bustled about the kitchen.

Brian Butlin helped George to his feet. 'Show me,' he said gently. 'Take me to whatever frightened you.'

'A hand,' gasped the boy. 'Rope round her middle. Raincoat. There's pink polish on her nails. Amy's frightened. She was afraid of the dog and now she's afraid of what the dog found.' George closed his mouth determinedly. He wasn't making sense and he needed to make sense. As Bobbee might have pronounced – *If you can't say it good, don't say it at all.*

Betty Thornton looked through the window, her gaze following the progress of man and boy. Behind them crept James, his head held low, his mind clearly fixed on adventure. In a trice, Betty

117

had collared her son and he was in the kitchen once more. 'Mind your own business,' she ordered crossly.

James sighed. Come fire, flood or famine, he would be told to mind his own business. If Mam thought about it for long enough, she would find a piece about minding his own business in the Bible. 'I've never seen a dead body,' he complained sadly.

'Then think yourself lucky,' replied Betty smartly. 'Carry on like this and you'll be seeing mine. Now shut up.'

James shut up.

Yuspeh had found a solution. The cares of the world, which had rested on her shoulders for over half a century, had rendered her walking rather unsteady, so she needed a prop. The prop arrived from the shed in the form of a pram, the very vehicle in which George Josef had travelled during his early years. Its handle kept her supported and the wheels, once oiled, moved with reasonable ease over the ups and downs of village pavements.

Determinedly independent, Yuspeh used this form of assistance to get herself out more. Anna had told her to go out and she was out. The pram was good for carrying wood, rolls of wire and boxes of nails through Rivington Cross. Why pay a delivery charge when she had her own mode of transport? Soon, she would have her own chickens in her own pen and England could boil all its birds, because they were fit for no other method of cooking.

'Mrs Forrester?'

Yuspeh stopped in her tracks, turned, glared at the policeman. 'I am Feigenbaum,' she answered drily. 'My son, he can be this or that or whatever he chooses, but I remain Feigenbaum. My husband was a Feigenbaum and so it goes on. It means fig tree in case you wish to know.'

Sergeant Alan Shawcross didn't wish to know. 'Have you seen anyone suspicious?' he asked. The old woman put her head to one side. She did a fair imitation of an angry crow, all in black, head perched atop a scraggy neck, face set in deep furrows of disapproval. He watched the lines in her forehead fighting for position while she processed the question.

'Suspicious of which?' she asked. 'Of what is these people suspicious?'

'Eh?' The man scratched his chin. It was far too warm a day for the breaking down of language barriers.

'From where comes all the cars?' demanded Yuspeh. She pointed towards a row of black vehicles.

'Bolton police. What I meant was, have you seen anyone acting suspiciously?'

'Yes.'

His face displayed interest. 'Really?'

She nodded. 'Indeed. The man from which I buy these woods and wires. He should be arrested and spoken to, for his prices come too high. He takes money from a poor old woman who tries only to get good chickens for to keep her family in meat and eggs.'

Alan sighed. This was a waste of time – he

would have been better off talking to a dry-stone wall. 'There's a body,' he told her. 'That lad of yours found it. All I wanted to ask you was—'

'My George Josef has found a body? Why is nobody tell me this before? He is young for the finding of bodies. This could mark his mind for the rest of time, may God preserve him. Where is he?'

'In the police station.' Alan Shawcross waved a hand at a corner house where a blue lamp advertised the business it contained. CID officers had taken over the scene of crime, while the two village bobbies, whose experience of serious crime was negligible, had been left to deal with the nuts and bolts of the matter.

Yuspeh bridled. 'You have arrested my grandson?'

'No.'

'Then you will mind this while I go for my poor George Josef.' She turned the pram until the handle was next to the policeman's hand, then she applied the brake. 'The nails I have counted,' she announced.

Alan shook his head. So he was to be left with nails as well as with nuts and bolts. 'I can't stand here, Mrs—'

'And I, also, cannot stand here while my boy is in there. This police house is no place for a good boy who still waits for bar mitzvah.'

'Mrs Fie . . . Fie . . .'

'Feigenbaum. I shall be but a few moments. My son will not be pleased when he hears that our boy has found a body in England. In

120

England, we did not expect bodies. In Poland, many bodies, but here . . .'

'Folk die here, Mrs . . . er . . .'

'If George Josef is upset, this will at your feet be laid.' She stalked off, head held high.

Sergeant Alan Shawcross gazed down upon the rolled wire and lengths of wood in the pram. He wanted to leave the damned thing and get about his business, but what was his business? Whoever had dumped that poor girl in the reservoir would be long gone. And there was something terribly ferocious about Mrs Feigenbaum, something that put him in mind of his schooldays. Aye, she should have been a headmistress, ruler of a small domain, cane in one hand and Bible in the other. Did Jews have the Bible?

There was a great deal of fuss down by the lake. The body had been identified unofficially by Alan Shawcross, though formal confirmation by a family member would be needed. It was all a bloody mess. It probably wasn't suicide, was unlikely to be an accident and he was standing here with a pram, three rolls of wire, some lengths of two by four and several boxes of nails. He felt useless and upset. She was only in her mid-twenties, the poor dead girl.

There were already too many people at the water's edge: detectives, a couple of doctors, some folk from the infirmary mortuary getting ready to take that drowned body for post-mortem. There was nothing for him to do. Poor kid, though. She hadn't deserved to die like that – no-one did. As for those who had found her –

Amy Bradshaw, Maddy Horrocks and George Forrester – what a shock this had been for such tender young souls.

Suddenly feeling his age, Alan Shawcross sat down on a wall and removed his helmet. It was time to start thinking about retiring. He could polish his bowls and practise on the crown green, would have time to go fishing. But he wouldn't be going near that reservoir – never again.

Yuspeh muttered a few curses under her breath and wished she had brought her pram. It made walking easier on these English pavements with bits that weren't level because the land which supported them was uneven. But she would walk, oh yes, she would, because her beautiful grandson was in need of her. Suddenly, there he was, God be praised, his hair standing on end, clothes filthy, eyes widening when he noticed her.

'Bobbee!' he cried. She was walking without her usual support.

'Where is this dead body?' she asked when she reached him. 'And what were you doing that you should be the one to find it?'

He explained as best he could, words tumbling from lips that trembled too fiercely for syllables to be properly formed. He rambled on about a grieving sheepdog, an Amy, a Maddy, a housekeeper, a vicar and a bundle in the reservoir. A boy with yellow hair and sugar for shock entered the equation, then Yuspeh grabbed her grandson by his shoulders. 'Listen good,' she ordered. 'You go home now to Mamme. You tell her what you have told to me, then you stay inside the house. Me, I go to ask some question.' She watched George until he had disappeared into the house, then she leaned for a few seconds against a garden wall.

'Mrs Forrester?'

Yuspeh turned. She was tired and weighted down with sadness, but she still managed one word. 'Feigenbaum,' she stated wearily. After a long intake of breath, she continued. 'Ah, you are Mrs Bradshaw and you work for Dr Bennett.'

Celia Bradshaw bit her lip. 'I thought you were going to fall,' she said, her voice frail and shaky.

There was an expression in the woman's eyes that Yuspeh recognized only too well. It was terror. This was a woman whose fear-filled thoughts were on show and this was unusual, because Mrs Bradshaw was one who hid her emotions for the most part. But the furrowed brow and wet eyes gave away her state of mind. 'My dear lady,' began Yuspeh, 'I am just think—'

'It can't be,' babbled Celia. 'I have to go to the infirmary and say whether or not . . . And Arthur's not here – he's doing a day on parcel deliveries somewhere round Farnworth, somebody's on holiday, and . . . and . . .'

'And you are afraid.' This was not a question.

'Then there's Amy. Who'll mind my Amy?'

'I will. Mrs Bradshaw.' Yuspeh placed a hand on the trembling woman's shoulder. 'I may be just a foolish old Jewish woman, but I know how for to mind a child – even a Christian child. See, see, look at me.'

Celia obeyed.

'We are both mothers. We have suffered the pain and the disappointment from children, from husbands – may my dead Josef forgive me – and from being women. I shall take your child to my house and you will go to do what must be done. Police will telephoning to the post office people to bring back your husband so that you will not do this alone.' She paused for breath. 'Who is this poor body?'

Celia Bradshaw shivered. 'They're saying it's my girl, Mrs F.' She could not have struggled with the complete word. 'Bernadette. She was wild, you see, too wild for me and her dad. She got herself led astray, Mrs F, and she wouldn't listen. Out every night on the town, going to stupid churches when she should have been a Catholic, living with some other girls who were no better than floozies. We're a Catholic family, Mrs F. We're Catholics,' she repeated.

'This I know. And I tell you just one thing, Mrs Bradshaw. We are the same. You may not see this, but I am seeing it all of the time. The strictness, the difficulty, the rules of our church and of our synagogue, which say this and that and those and these.' She shrugged. 'Is guilt, that's what it is. We are born in guilt and we live in guilt. May God make you strong, my poor lady.'

Celia heard little of the old woman's message. It couldn't be Bernadette. Bernadette lived in the town, worked in the town, never visited Rivington Cross. The Cross was dead as far as

Bernadette was concerned – no picture house, no theatre, no dance halls, no cafés. 'Can I ask you something?'

'Of course.'

Celia swallowed noisily. 'Go and get my child out of there. I am supposed to be fetching her, but I don't want her to see me like this. And I am to travel in a police car to the infirmary.'

'You want I should come with you in the car in case your husband does not arrive?'

The younger woman shook her head. 'No. Thank you, but no. Put Amy first.' Amy. Poor Amy had found the body of her own sister. If it was Bernadette. A policewoman was walking towards the place where Yuspeh and Celia stood. The latter swallowed audibly; the former placed a clawlike hand on Celia's arm. 'I will pray,' she promised. 'Go now. Go with the police and see what has to be seen.'

When the younger woman had left, Yuspeh sagged against the wall. It was all so wrong. She closed misted eyes and her eyelids became a screen on which ran the newsreels she had seen in 1945: Belsen, Auschwitz, Treblinka. Skeletons walked. They stumbled past heaps of bones across which skin was stretched like translucent parchment. The walking looked no healthier than the dead, but many had survived to bear testimony to the inhumanity of mankind. The unnatural death of even one person was not acceptable; it was as bad now for Celia Bradshaw as it had been for all who had survived the Holocaust. Perhaps it would not be Bernadette; perhaps this might prove to be the daughter of some other woman whose heart would be torn apart by the pain of unbearable loss.

'Such grief,' whispered Yuspeh before walking on to retrieve the other daughter of the Bradshaw family. It was a hard world and a hard life and murderers were everywhere. Through narrowed eyes she surveyed the beautiful village that had become her home. One of these pretty stone cottages might well contain a killer. She would get Amy and take her home.

Yvonne Horrocks pushed her way through to the front. Few people visited this small police station under normal conditions, but now it was a sardine tin. 'Where's my Maddy?' she yelled.

A plain clothes officer pulled her past a line of people and placed her against the wall. 'The little boy has gone and the two girls will be out in a moment with their dog. Somebody dried the poor dog off and your daughter's been given a nice cup of sweet tea.'

Yvonne shivered. 'I hear it's Nettie Bradshaw they've found.'

'We're not sure. It could be.'

'So Amy might have found her own sister?'

'Yes.'

Yvonne sniffed back a tear. 'The number of times I've told our Maddy to stop away from that water. It's deep. It's water for thousands and thousands of homes all over the place. But will she listen?'

'Do they ever?' asked the man. 'Just hang on a minute and I'll try to find out what's going on. I know what you mean – it wouldn't have been so bad if an adult had found the body.' He left Yvonne sandwiched between a wall and half a dozen plain clothes officers. She heard snatches of their conversation, gathered that Celia Bradshaw was to be taken to identify the body, listened to a few curses as these men berated the person who had committed so heinous a crime.

Suddenly, everything stopped. A fierce voice lifted itself above all others. 'I am come for the child of Celia Bradshaw.' In different circumstances, Yvonne might have smiled. It was the voice of Yuspeh Feigenbaum and she meant business. Celia Bradshaw was a fanatical Catholic. She didn't approve of Jews, though she had been heard to express some disgust about the prison camps and gas chambers. But Jews had killed Jesus and would, therefore, be condemned to wander the face of the earth for all time. Which opinion, in Yvonne's book, was stupid because Israel was there and anyone could choose where he or she lived.

'Without her, I will not leave and I have things outside in the pram which are precious and paid for. Is for chickens. And mine grandson is white in the face from what has happened here today. So the other child is now to come with me, for her mother is taken to the infirmary.'

Yvonne shifted herself forward and pushed her way towards the voice. The woman could have been a town crier, because her words cut through flesh, bone and masonry. 'Mrs Feigenbaum?'

'Yes?' Yuspeh surveyed the hairdresser.

'Amy can come with me.'

But Yuspeh was closed to negotiation. 'I am asked by the mother to look after the child. This is responsibility of mine. Amy will come with me, just as I promised the mamme.'

'She's used to us,' Yvonne insisted.

'Then she will get used to me. What is problem here? Is it bad that she goes into my house because I am Jew?'

The ensuing silence was deafening. Then Yvonne spoke as clearly as she could manage. 'Bigotry travels in both directions, Mrs Feigenbaum. I have no prejudice against you or against anyone, but this is a bad time and Amy needs the people she knows. Amy and Maddy have been inseparable since nursery class. So she will stay with her friend – my daughter – and they will both come with me. That is an end to it. Everyone is upset and there's no point in making matters worse, is there?'

Yuspeh Feigenbaum had met her Waterloo. She quite liked this Waterloo, though. The woman had sense and dignity and she stuck to her guns. But Yuspeh, too, was fastened to weaponry. 'Then we all go together. You will have me in your house, yes?'

'Of course I will.'

'And pram can sit in shop?'

'Yes.'

Thus it came about that two shocked Catholic girls with one Catholic mother came together with a wise old woman in living rooms behind the hairdresser's shop and the undertaker's parlour. Yuspeh's pram was parked outside in the back garden and she drank tea from a cup whose correctness did not concern her at this point. Even if the crockery had been washed alongside meat plates on which had rested non-kosher food, this was not the time to worry. George Josef would be well, because he had his mother. Yuspeh had made a promise and she intended to fulfil it to the very last letter.

'I didn't reckon on murders.' Betty Thornton wandered to the front gate of the vicarage, James hot on her heels. He'd come out with some nonsense about changing his name to Jay, but a haircut was as far as Betty was willing to concede. 'Go on, then. Get across and ask her if she can fit you in. If she can't, you'll have to wait till tomorrow.'

She stood for a while and watched as he crossed the street to Hair By Yvonne. There was a small pang in her chest, a discomfort caused by the idea of losing her little lad, because he wouldn't look like James any more once the curls were gone. She shook herself inwardly. 'You're not the sentimental sort,' she mumbled quietly. Was it the country air? she wondered. Because she was changing, was enjoying cleaning a long-neglected house, was happy in the company of the vicar's twins, felt useful and needed – even valued.

She watched police cars coming and going, saw an ambulance in which probably rested the sad remains of the murdered girl. In all her time in Liverpool and in Bolton, she had never known a killing to happen so close to where she had been living. A hand strayed to her throat. Had she done the right thing? Was this a sign that she should go back to the mill, back to those narrow streets, back to a situation in which James might not behave himself?

No. She was further away from Mam and Dad here. They had come inland to be near her, to interfere, to try to persuade her to return to Catholicism – they might have indoctrinated James in the end. She wasn't having that. With grim determination, Betty returned to the task of cleaning a greased-up oven. It would take more than murder to shift her back to Bolton. God was good. If she stuck to her prayers, He would see that she and James were safe. And she hoped her lad wouldn't look too old without his curls.

James knocked on the door. The legend *OPEN* was displayed through the glass, but the lock was on and the shop seemed empty. He knocked again. With a few shillings in his pocket, he had the means to get rid of these wretched curls once and for all before his mother changed her mind. She wasn't a great mind-changer, but James sensed that she didn't really want him to have his hair cut, so he needed to strike now, before the iron cooled.

Maddy opened the door after the third knock. She wore an air of distraction, and her own curls had tumbled free enough to cloud her vision. 'We're closed,' she informed him, one hand on the door handle and the other pushing strands from her face.

'It says open,' he answered. 'Look.' A stubby finger pointed to the sign.

'Today's different,' she said.

'I know. I know what's happened. But please, please let me in. She might decide I've got to keep them, you see.'

'Keep what?'

'Me stupid curls. This lot.' He tugged at the offending mass. 'I don't want to go back to school – even a new school – looking like a girl. I'm fed up. Lads keep giving me their sisters' ribbons to tie it up with.' He stood his ground, feet together like a guardsman. 'Ask your mam,' he begged. 'Ask her if she'll just cut this lot off.'

Maddy stared at him. 'You know what's gone on, don't you?'

He nodded. She sounded fierce and he didn't feel equipped for fierce. His knees sagged and he was no longer standing to attention. 'Yes, I know. But me keeping my hair long won't stop it from happening, will it? I mean, it's already happened. I've got to have it done.'

She opened the door. 'Come in and sit in that chair. Don't move. My mother's upset and we've got company, but I'll ask her.'

James sat. After some moments, Yvonne came into the salon. 'Hello, love,' she said. 'I didn't intend doing any more today, but our Maddy says you're desperate.'

'I am. I want short back and sides. That's what all the boys have, isn't it? Can you shave it up my neck so it'll be like everybody else's? Can you use clippers? Can you make it lie flat?'

In spite of her sorrow, Yvonne felt a smile tugging at the corners of her mouth. This was the most extraordinarily beautiful child, but his

131

hair, so thick and wavy, probably gave other lads cause to take the mickey out of him. 'There's women who'd kill for hair like yours,' she said. He looked like an angel, she thought as she dragged a comb through yellow tangles. That poor girl would be with the angels now . . .

'Can I have a parting on the left?' he asked.

Yvonne looked at him in the mirror. 'You can have anything you like, son. And because you've nearly made me smile, you can have it for free.'

James beamed. Life wasn't looking so bad after all. He had money in his pocket and he was going to look like a proper boy in about ten minutes. The future promised to be a great deal better than the past, he mused as the yellow locks began to tumble to the floor. 'Mrs Horrocks?'

'Yes, love?'

He gulped. 'Nothing. Just thanks. That's all.'

Yuspeh was in her element. She'd never had a daughter, though she thought of Anna as her own, and she had missed out on young female company. This was hardly a circumstance in which she would have chosen to meet the daughters of Celia Bradshaw and Yvonne Horrocks, yet she felt privileged to be in their company at such a time.

When Yvonne had left the room, Yuspeh cast an eye over the girls. One was so thin and old for her years, dark-haired, worried and wise. But the child of this household was a blessing for any mother – bright, determinedly supportive of

Amy and with a million unanswered questions shining from her eyes.

Deliberate distraction was Yuspeh's goal for the moment. 'In Poland, you see, we never got to be anything but Jewish. We were poor and separated out from Christians. But we make their clothes and some was kind to us.'

'So you have no Jesus?'

Yuspeh grinned broadly. 'Jesus, he was good Jewish boy and he looked after his friends and his mamme. Me, I have great respect for your Jesus – may all our boys be as good as he was.' She straightened her spine proudly. 'Judaism is mother to all religion on the earth. Out of us comes Christian and Islam. We are not so different from you.'

'Then why did you kill Jesus?' The question was out before Maddy could enclose it behind her teeth. Perhaps it was the shock of today or perhaps she really needed an answer, but oh, how she wished she might have bitten back the words.

'I don't know.' Yuspeh kept her calm. 'But we have suffered for the mistake – if it was a mistake. I cannot answer for those who lived before me almost two thousand years. What I can say is this – Herr Hitler took six million of us. Was this payment enough?'

'I didn't mean . . . It was just a question.'

'It is good you ask. He is your Messiah and you give honour to him. I can honour your honour without making him my Messiah. Do you understand?'

Maddy nodded. So many more questions, but

this was the wrong time. Nettie – if it was Nettie – was dead and poor Amy looked half dead herself, face pinched, eyes closing, mouth in a tight line.

Amy wasn't hearing any of it. All she could see was a wet parcel which had recently been a human being, that hand so lifeless in the water. Sugar pink nail polish, one shilling and elevenpence from Woolworth's. She remembered meeting Nettie in town outside the junior library. It had been raining and the two sisters had shared an umbrella all the way to Woolworth's where Nettie had bought matching lipstick and nail varnish. Sugar pink. It was a bright, happy colour and it had chased away those miserable, black clouds.

One cloud had remained, of course. Over Amy's life had hung a darkness caused by deceit. She had been meeting the sister who was no longer welcome in the Bradshaw household.

'Come here, Amy. Come to Bubbah. I know I am not your bubbah, but I can be a borrowed bubbah. It means the grandmother.'

Amy lifted her tear-stained face. 'It's my fault,' she whispered.

'No!' shouted Maddy. 'It is not your fault.'

But Amy persisted. 'She came here to see me, only to see me. There was nothing else here for her – only me. And she died because of that.'

'Come to me now,' insisted Yuspeh. 'My legs are too tired to come to you. Use your young legs and save my old ones.'

Amy obeyed and found herself seated in the bony lap of the old woman. She could feel

134

whalebone on the lower body, too, so the experience was not comfortable. An almost overwhelming scent of lavender rose from the black clothing, but the eyes were kind, gentle and full of empathy. 'In my life, I lose many peoples I have loved. But I am old and this thing happens when a person is old. My friends, my husband, my brothers and sisters are all gone. And I am come here, to England, for to find a future for my son and for his son and for Anna. It is hard for me to understand why things are happening when God is a good God and those who die is good, too. Hard life. I am sorry you find out while you are still so young.'

Amy leaned her head against a bony shoulder. She came from a family where physical contact was not the norm, but this knobbly old woman was offering her comfort, so she grabbed it. She heard the beginning of a song whose words she would never know, because they were in a foreign tongue. In spite of her misery, Amy Bradshaw drifted towards sleep, her Catholic soul lulled into tranquillity by a Yiddish lullaby.

Simon and Sarah were in the downstairs-downstairs part of the bell house. They lit their stolen candles and sat in silence for a while, each thinking of the dead girl, their heads bent as they considered what had happened today so close to their home.

After a while, Sarah stood up and took a small bottle from her pocket. She shook it and held it up to the flame, noting that the contents were slightly cloudy. Did a blessing do that?

'What is it?' asked her brother.

Sarah bit her lip. 'It's holy water.'

'Why? Where from?'

'Because if it is Nettie Bradshaw, she used to be a Catholic and her family are still Catholics. And I got it from one of the fonts in Holy Martyrs.'

'But . . . but we don't use holy water. We don't believe in holy water.'

'Who said that?'

'The Church of England.' He shook his head. 'Dad wouldn't like it.'

'I'm not asking him to have a bath in it,' came the terse reply. She placed the bottle on an orange box. 'I found a new word,' she announced. 'It's not an easy one.'

'Oh, yes? Daft, is it?'

She pretended to glare at her brother. 'No. It's ecumenicalism, I think. Or it might be ecumenism.'

'Right.' He shook his head. 'Is it like the last word you found?'

'No. It's not like transubstantiation. It's about people being allowed to believe in transubstantiation.'

'They are allowed. They think the bread and wine change to the body and blood of Jesus and nobody's stopping them if they want to carry on like cannibals. It's a free country.'

'It's about accepting,' she said, patience etched deliberately into the clearly separated words. 'It's about divisions and beliefs and charity. Pa always says the greatest virtue is charity, doesn't he? Well, isn't it time he

136

practised what he preaches?'

'He doesn't do any harm.'

'Sometimes, just doing no harm isn't enough,' she replied. 'Sometimes, somebody has to make things happen instead of just sitting there doing no actual wrong.'

Simon sighed deeply. His sister was all for changing the world for the better. Again. She had spent the previous Christmastide following the Salvation Army all over Bolton, had even been allowed to rattle a tambourine for a while. What now? Holy water? And if so, what next?

'You can't change anything by yourself,' he said.

Sarah laughed. 'There always has to be one person at the beginning of something. Jesus was on His own till He met His apostles. All we need now is common sense. We all believe in Jesus, so why can't we all be together?'

'We can,' he snapped. 'At football matches, the pictures, the theatre, in shops. We just go to different places to say our prayers, that's all.'

Sarah decided to ignore him. Boys were beyond redemption when it came to new ideas. If the world had been left to the male of the species, humanity would probably still be living in caves and wearing animal skins. She walked across the small area and opened a wooden box which had once contained some of her baby toys. Into its hollow interior she placed the first piece of her collection. From her dad's church, she would remove a tattered copy of the Book of Common Prayer and she would try to find something belonging to a Methodist. The new housekeeper should be able to provide an item.

'Why are you doing this?' Simon asked.

Sarah faced him. 'I have no idea,' she answered. And that was the absolute truth.

Caroline Butlin was not content. She had been bored with life at the vicarage, but it hadn't improved enormously since her move, so she had returned to assess the lie of the land. So far, the lie of the land seemed to consist of comings, goings, police cars, an ambulance and a strange woman standing in the gateway of St Faith's vicarage. A boy, too, had been in the same place, but he had disappeared into the hairdresser's only to return half an hour later with a very short haircut and a very large smile.

The advertisement in the *Bolton Evening News* seemed to have borne fruit, then. Brian must have grabbed at the first or second applicant, because the newsprint had scarcely dried, yet here was the usurper, face like a promise of storms to come, clothes saggy and brownish-grey, hair scraped back as tightly as piano wires.

Caroline drummed her fingers on the steering wheel of Derek's Morris van. He had lent it to her for a limited period and she would have to return soon to the bosom of her lover. God, what had she done? Could she come back? Would Brian have her back? Or must she return to the top of Wigan Road and to a man who adored her to the point of nausea? He never left her alone. The neglect she had suffered in the company of Brian now seemed like a blessing she had failed to recognize. And she missed her children to the point of physical pain.

Why was it that life in Rivington Cross, once so hated, should now seem like a remembered heaven? The natives would have been gossiping, no doubt. She would be a scarlet woman, a harlot, an unnatural mother who cared nothing for her twins. 'I don't want to be in either place,' she told Stella, the cocker spaniel who was her constant companion. 'I don't know where I should be, but it isn't here and it isn't there.'

Stella snuggled down on her cushion in the back of the van. She had recognized familiar places and scents, but her mistress was showing no sign of allowing her back to her former haunts, so she resigned herself to snoozing through what promised to be a boring time.

Caroline remained undecided. There was no sign of the twins, so she could not use them as a ticket to get back into the house. Would they want her, anyway? 'Time to go home – wherever that is,' she told herself. She was trained for nothing real, had no chance of making her own way in the world and was guilty of a huge mistake. 'Frying pan and fire,' she muttered as she drove off. There was only herself to blame and she could find no comfort in that sad fact.

'What do you mean, Phil?' Enid Jones leaned across the desk and touched her fiancé's cheek. He had been muttering and mumbling for at least five minutes while checking through files of expected patients.

'I don't know,' he answered. 'I'm just not sure enough. And I suppose he wouldn't have had the strength.'

Enid frowned. 'You want to make a complete fool of yourself, Phil? Who will listen when you start shouting about a priest and murder? And there was a boulder tied to her?'

'Probably. The rope had been fastened to some kind of weight.'

'Could he have managed that?' she asked.

He paused for thought before replying. 'It depends where she was killed. If she was killed near the water, he could have tied her to one of the surrounding rocks and pushed her in. It would have taken effort, but desperation is a good motivator. If it's the last thing I do in this village, I shall prescribe some sort of sedative for him. I'll explain it away in his notes as medication to prevent him becoming agitated when he stops drinking.' Not that Michael Sheahan would stop drinking. Phil rose and walked to the window. 'I shall miss this place,' he said.

'So will I.' Enid joined him and took his hand in hers. 'And if you really want to stay, I can go alone to look after my mother.'

He squeezed her fingers. 'No, it's all decided. Your mother will need you once your sister goes back to London. From the sound of things, that stroke was quite a bad one. And I want to be with you. There are plenty of openings in Wales for a GP, so let's go and make the best of it.'

Enid Jones kissed him on the cheek, walked across the room and picked up her bag. 'You can't mend the world,' she said.

'I want to see him in prison.' Phil Bennett swivelled on his heel and faced the woman he

140

loved. 'But it won't happen. He'll just disappear on health grounds and he'll get away with it. I know he interferes with girls. No-one has said anything and I have to think about my oath. But how I regret Hippocrates. I want to prove what the priest is, advertise it and see him get his punishment.'

'He won't.'

'I know. But . . .'

'But what?'

'I may have a word with the new doctor when she arrives.' The flat of his hand crashed onto the desk. 'He killed that girl, Enid. I don't know why and I don't know how. But he did.'

'Do what you feel you must. I have to go now – some dressings to do. See you later.' She let herself out of the surgery.

Phil Bennett sighed heavily. He loved Enid with every fibre of his being, but what a time to have to leave Rivington! 'Barbiturates it is, then,' he told himself softly. 'And if, by some chance, he takes a drop too much of the hard stuff, he'll be incapable of wrecking any more lives.' The pills might even kill him, thought the doctor as he wrote the dose into Sheahan's notes.

There was no receptionist this evening, because Celia Bradshaw had gone into Bolton to identify the body of her daughter. Phil strode to the door and flung it open. He looked at the patients who awaited treatment, noted sadness and bewilderment in their faces. 'I'll do my best,' he told them. 'Let yourselves in one at a time and I'll try to have your notes to hand. I'll ring my bell when I am ready.'

141

Mildred Cookson spoke up for all of them. 'Was it Nettie Bradshaw, Dr Bennett?'

He shook his head. 'I have no idea,' he lied. 'I only saw the body for a minute. Celia will know the answer by now.'

Back at his desk, Phil took a deep breath. It was Nettie. Not that he had ever met the girl, but even after lying in water for however many hours, the similarity to Amy had been clear. Had she been a victim of the priest? Had she been silenced by a man of God?

He crashed his hand onto the bell. Time to get on with his job. Come war, pestilence, fire or flood, a doctor's work continued.

FIVE

Caroline Butlin was reading the *Bolton Evening News*, while she had time and peace during which she might do exactly as she pleased. It contained an account of the murder of Bernadette, daughter of Celia and Arthur Bradshaw. The body had been discovered by children in the reservoir behind St Faith's vicarage. Caroline knew that the finders had not been her own children, as she had spoken to them several times on the telephone following the grim event, but she was scared. What if this were the work of a serial killer? After some weeks, no suspect had been arrested, no-one had been charged and the body had been released for burial. So whoever had perpetrated the crime was still on the loose and was probably living somewhere in the Rivington area. But what could she do about it? Nothing. Her life now was not one into which she would choose to bring her children.

She threw down the newspaper and gazed at

her new home. It was a decent enough house, she supposed. It stood in a block of similar houses built into the rise of a hill, all gardens and paths to front doors being terraced into deep steps. It owned a sitting room, a living room, a kitchen, three bedrooms and a bathroom and it seemed to own her, too. Well, its master owned her. He would be home shortly and the business would begin all over again, the groping, the squeezing, the prickly kissing, the pre-prandial conjoining on the floor, on the stairs, against a wall – wherever. She felt sick. This was all her own fault, but she had seen no sign of the monster in Derek Ramsden. Until now. Now, she knew what he was and was forced to live with it, because she had nowhere else to turn.

Caroline had never considered that she might bring her children here. They were settled in Rivington Cross and Brian, who had bored his wife senseless, was the better parent. But she had brought Stella, the cocker spaniel. Stella did not like Derek, so Stella lived in a shed in the back yard whenever Derek was about. Dogs were good judges of character, it seemed. As Derek would soon be home, the dog was outside where she would not become upset.

'Then supper,' she sighed. After supper, the wireless for an hour, then a repeat performance, so urgent, so rapid and painful. She hated the smell of his breath, the feel of his skin, the sight of his face. Bed. At least that didn't hurt so badly, as a mattress was an ingredient in the mix, but he would wake her from time to time and he was always savage. He didn't slap her, didn't leave her marked, but he was eradicating her soul, was wiping out her character. Fortunately, all encounters were brief; unhappily, he never took time to prepare her, to court her, to love her. Even if he were to change, she could never feel anything for him, not after the agonies she had suffered.

'I am a total fool,' she told her echo in the mirror over the fireplace. Derek Ramsden, a childless widower, had brought what she had once seen as light and colour into her drab life in Rivington Cross. A seller of affordable clothing, he did the rounds of regular customers in his van, then hired a stall on Bolton Market three times a week – Tuesdays, Thursdays and Saturdays. What had she done? How on earth had she managed to convince herself that Derek was going to be the love of her life? What a mess. And to whom might she turn for comfort and advice when she was so ashamed of her own rashness?

Brian and Derek were chalk and cheese. Brian had indulged his bodily needs infrequently and apologetically, was not an exciting man, had seldom managed to make her laugh. The result was that she now cohabited with a jealous fool who kept her on a very short rein, who satisfied his sexual needs whenever the mood took him and who lasted just seconds once he had achieved his goal. He adored her. He adored her so avidly that he had expressed his intention to keep her for ever for himself. It was not love, no – it was obsession, greed, a bid for total owner-ship. She could never look at another man and she was forced to account for every moment she spent out of his sight. Caroline was afraid. Never before in her life had she known such confusion and terror. She was also a prisoner.

'This is just a different cage,' she mumbled as she peeled half a dozen potatoes. And there were no young in this cage. When an unbearable thought entered her mind, she sliced into her left index finger and watched the scarlet result as it flowed into a pan of water. What if she became pregnant by him? His wife had borne no children, but that was no testament to his infertility – the problem might have been hers, not Derek's. The thought of bearing a child by him was truly unpalatable. 'You hate him,' she told herself as she bound the wound. Angrily, she tightened the bandage, pretended that she was fastening it round that thin neck with its prominent and mobile Adam's apple. 'I am unused to feeling hatred,' she told herself aloud. 'I never hated Brian, never hated anyone before in my whole life.'

The real pain was not in her finger. The digit throbbed when contained in its dressing, but the pale rhythm simply kept time with the heavier beat inside her body where he had ripped into a place whose almost permanent dryness was a demonstration of her loathing. He was raping her. He was raping her three or four times in every twenty-four-hour period and was ill-tempered when she menstruated. During those few precious and blessed days, he could not invade, yet he forced her to use other methods to achieve his relief. She had not expected to be

146

subjected to such degradation, was angry with herself for being too afraid to speak up, to defend herself against her attacker.

'I am his prostitute.' She rinsed the pan and started peeling all over again. She had to escape, but where might she go? Her parents, neither in good health and both disgusted with her behaviour, would not help her. Her husband, a good, steady, rather pompous man, would not want her back. As for the parish of St Faith and the villagers of Rivington Cross – they were probably damning her out of hand on a daily basis.

She was not a good woman. Good women did not desert husband and children in order to follow an ill-conceived adventure. Good women washed, ironed, shopped, cooked and cleaned. They underpinned and cared for their husbands, encouraged their children and certainly did not drive off towards an orange sunset in a Morris van with a silly man and his almost-good clothes. She should have been running coffee mornings, fêtes, bazaars, charity race-days with the schoolchildren.

She had done those things, of course, but had always allowed parishioners to play the leading roles. Brian had praised her often, had approved of her placing faith in other people. But that had not been the reason for Caroline's repeated delegatings. The real cause had been boredom, plain and simple. Oh, what would she not give to be bored at this very moment? An almost paralysing stiffness arrived in her spine, its source lying in tension and apprehension.

Derek would soon be home. He would say little or nothing until after the first session of sexual exertion, might talk during the meal about his day, his sales, his success. He never enquired about her, never asked about her day, her well-being.

While the wireless was playing, he would suck his teeth and poke about with a matchstick for bits of food wedged in the uneven spaces between them. Sometimes, there was debris in his moustache; always, always, there was the inability to roll his Rs and to form a proper S. Every evening, Caroline took her time with the washing of dishes, but she had been attacked once while standing at the kitchen sink, so that was no real escape.

Had she been normal, she would have remained at the vicarage until the children no longer needed her. Countless women stayed in situations that were not completely satisfactory. How many parents used children as cement, hanging on and trying to make life good for the young? Why had she been unable to act as other women did? Children should come first. She missed them more acutely than she had expected, needed to reach out to touch Sarah's strawberry blond hair, wanted to see more of Simon's drawings and writings, longed to hear his clear treble as he stood in the front row of the choir and sang his little heart into the body of a spellbound congregation.

'I want to go home,' she told the vegetables. Derek, like the vegetables, had no answers to offer. There was no-one here in whom she might confide. Brian had listened sometimes, when his flock's needs had not been acute. But Derek, bound up in cardigans and dresses, cared more for his business than for her. In fact, he cared nothing at all for his partner – she was a mere vessel into which he poured bodily fluid that might otherwise have been spilled into bed sheet or handkerchief. She was nothing. She was less than nothing and she was beginning to dislike herself.

Yesterday's newspaper now contained vegetable peelings and she folded up the top three sheets in order to transfer the contents to the bin. Then she saw the advertisement. St Anne's Roman Catholic School for Girls wanted a bursar. A bursar? What did that involve? she wondered as she threw away the debris.

Carefully, she tore out the piece and placed it in the cutlery drawer. Didn't a bursar keep books and accounts? She could do that; she had done it for years, had never even thought about it. Brian's bent was for sermon-making and pastoral matters, while Caroline, always the practical partner, kept records in order, balanced the books, acted as treasurer for the parish. But for a Catholic school? For the sisters? Would they want to nurture in their midst the wife of a vicar, a woman who had walked out on her responsibilities?

Hawthorne Road was nearby. All she needed to do was leave this house by the front door, walk to the corner, turn right, ascend the steep hill and the school was at the top. Furthermore, the approach commanded a view to the other side of

Bolton, so that she would be able to see Bolton School from the place where she would be working. She would not be able to see Sarah or Simon, but she might take some comfort from the ability to look at the buildings in which they were being educated. She would be working. Well, could be working . . . might be . . . Derek. What were the chances of Derek's allowing her to take a job?

As she set the table, she arranged her mind into a shape he might just accept. With nuns, she should be safe. Even he could believe that a convent was unlikely to be a seat of iniquity and debauchery, surely? She needed the money, wanted to save so that she might start a new life nearer to her children and away from the man whose key she could hear turning in the lock. Caroline swallowed. When he entered the room, she looked straight through him and spoke in a voice which betrayed no emotion. 'I am ill,' she informed him, the lie sliding easily from her tongue. 'So please, no nonsense tonight.'

He threw down a briefcase. There was nothing in the case, but it allowed him an air he imagined to be professional. 'I see. What's wrong with you?'

'Slight cold and a headache,' she replied. 'It's been coming and going all day, so I have taken aspirin.' In the kitchen and scarcely ten feet away from her lay the knife with which she had prepared the vegetables. The temptation to retrieve it, to sink it into a belly that was strangely soft for so thin a man, was almost over-powering. Within a matter of weeks, she had managed to learn to loathe this creature. There had been no sign of his obsessive tendency when he had visited the vicarage – a few kisses, a hug, a joke, a cup of tea. She had bought clothes and had been flattered by his attention, but in truth he was subhuman, evil, nasty. And she had no idea of how she might extricate herself from a situation into which she had walked voluntarily.

'I need my bit of comfort,' he moaned now.

'So do I,' was her rejoinder. 'So let me rest – please.'

Unsure of how to respond, he edged towards her. 'Don't you love me any more?' he asked, eyelids fluttering stupidly.

Caroline made no reply. She walked into the kitchen and banged a few dishes about. She would get a job. There was no chance of her crawling back to Brian and even less chance of her remaining here. But she would find a home in which Sarah and Simon might visit her, would gain independence from this—

Suddenly, he was behind her. She could feel his hot breath on her neck, could hear a quickening in its rhythm as his urge to mate overcame him. He lifted her skirt, tore away her underwear and penetrated a part of her body not designed for such assault.

Quick as lightning, she picked up an empty frying pan and swung it behind her own head, crashing it into his temple. He shouted, removed himself from her and fell to the floor. But he did not remain down for long. With blood dripping from an ear, he jumped up, swung her round and punched her in the chest. Winded, she staggered back and he finished what he had begun, this time raping her in the usual way. As his thrusts quickened, he lisped excitedly into her hair. 'Now you're playing well,' he said. 'Worth fighting for, isn't it?' Then he shivered and was quickly spent.

She watched as he made himself decent. Decent? There was no decency in the man, no dignity, no normality. 'How did your wife die?' she surprised herself by asking.

'What?'

'How did she die?'

'Beryl?' He ran a hand through thinning hair. 'She was unstable. She killed herself, took a lot of pills and whisky. The doctor put it down to a form of depression. She'd always been a miserable sort of woman, not the kind a man wants to come home to after a day at work.'

Caroline Butlin tidied herself, waited for her breathing to return to normal, lifted roast ham from the oven. She understood Beryl Ramsden perfectly. If this animal had treated his wife as badly as he now treated his mistress, then the wife's behaviour was thoroughly understandable. But Caroline would not kill herself. No. She would wait until he slept, would empty his pockets and his wallet and would leave this house tonight. With no particular destination in mind, she would walk away from here and towards . . . towards whatever. Because anything at all would be better than this.

Celia Bradshaw was no longer alive. She rose every morning, made a large pot of tea, cooked bacon and eggs, toasted bread under the electric grill, took food to the table. While her husband and daughter ate whatever they could manage, she drank tea and stared from her place in a fireside rocker into an empty grate. When Amy and Arthur had finished eating, she cleared up crockery, scraped leavings into the bin, washed dishes, returned to her chair. An automaton, she simply reacted without taking part in life. There was a temporary receptionist in her place at the surgery and Celia showed no signs of getting back to normal. Perhaps, once tomorrow was over, she would begin to feel alive again. Tomorrow. God, she did not want to think about it.

Arthur went to bed after breakfast. He had already made one delivery, and instead of returning to the post office he took advantage of the extended compassionate leave granted by his employers and went upstairs to lie down and stare at the ceiling. Amy, abandoned to her own devices, usually left her mother and went down to Maddy's house. Talking to Celia was no use. Celia did not weep, did not speak, scarcely moved. Dad was the same, but he took his silences upstairs.

On the day before her sister's funeral, Amy decided that it was time to grow up. After endless questions, after post-mortem and various resulting formalities, Nettie's body had finally been released for burial and Amy, whose parents were less communicative than ever, took it upon herself to ask a favour of Maddy.

Maddy was taken aback. 'Are you sure?'

Amy nodded. She was terrified, but she was certain. 'Somebody has to do it,' she said. 'It's an open coffin, isn't it?'

Maddy answered in the affirmative. 'I heard Dad saying he had done his best and that the . . . that the water hadn't done too much damage. Mum dressed her hair.' Mum had been crying, but Maddy held back that piece of information. And, of course, Nettie's body had been kept refrigerated in the morgue, so there had been no visible deterioration. 'Amy, what if you have nightmares afterwards?'

'I'll still be alive, won't I? Alive with night-mares is better than dead like Nettie is. I won't forgive myself ever if I don't say goodbye to my sister.'

'All right.' Dad was out and Mum was busy in the salon. 'Come on, Amy.'

'Maddy?'

'What? Have you changed your mind?'

Amy shook her head vehemently. 'There's a secret. The police know it. Mam and Dad know, but I'm not supposed to. Only I listened on the stairs.'

Maddy kept quiet. Sometimes, it was best to allow her friend to travel at her own pace.

'She had a baby.'

Maddy frowned. 'Who had a baby?'

'Nettie. It didn't go in the newspapers after Nettie died, because it wouldn't have made any difference. They haven't caught the murderer and talking about a baby wouldn't have helped. It looks like she had him adopted. He was Adam. I heard Mam telling the police. When the doctors looked at Nettie's body, they could tell she'd had a baby. Mam doesn't know exactly what Nettie did with him, but he was named Adam.'

'So you have a little nephew somewhere.'

'Yes – and no hope of ever finding him.'

Maddie folded her arms. 'A baby has a dad as well as a mam.'

'I know. Mam told the police it could have been anyone. She said Nettie was wild and had a lot of boyfriends. There's nothing in the register office about a baby, so he might not have been adopted properly – Nettie could have just given him to somebody who wanted a baby. And we'll never know now, will we?' Her voice began to break.

'Do you want to wait till later on?' Maddy asked. 'To see Nettie, I mean.'

'No. I have to do it now. Mam's no use, Dad's no use, so there's only me. I have to see her. She'd want to see me if this had happened the other way round. But . . . but I wish they'd find the person who killed her, Maddy.'

'So does everybody.' Maddy opened the door to the chapel of rest. Slowly, she drew back purple velvet hangings round the first cubicle and beckoned. 'Here she is. Don't be frightened.'

Amy felt strangely calm as she stood next to her sister's coffin. The container was lined with cream satin and Nettie's head rested on a pillow edged with lace. 'She looks asleep.'

'Yes.'

'And she's got a bit of lipstick on and nail varnish.'

Maddy blinked. Her mother had been all the way to town to buy Nettie's sugar pink cosmetics. 'She can't hurt any more now, Amy. That's what my dad always says. Your Nettie's gone to a better place.'

Amy gulped. 'Yes, but she went on the wrong bus, Maddy. She should have waited for a later one. Only somebody made her go on the early bus.' She lifted her face and looked at her friend. 'I want him found and hanged, you see. I won't ever rest until they've caught him. He's walking about out there somewhere . . .' She waved a hand at the opaque window. 'He's walking about and eating his dinners and having a life. And my sister's lying here ice-cold. It's all wrong. What makes people do these things?'

'I don't know.'

Amy touched her dead sister's hair, then pulled a small pair of blunt-ended scissors from her pocket. Carefully, she lifted Nettie's fringe and cut a lock of hair, spreading the remaining strands across the white forehead. Then she replaced the scissors, opened a silver locket at her throat and placed her prize inside. There was a little bit of Nettie that would never be buried and Amy would wear it close to her heart for the remainder of her days.

Celia Bradshaw opened her door. It was sitting there again, head on one side, one ear at half mast, a front paw raised as if in supplication, the whole animal a picture of misery and doom. 'You don't live here,' she said. 'Go on – shoo.'

Monty pushed past her and into the house. He

wasn't sure why he was here, yet he knew he had to be in this place. There was a smell about the house, an emptiness, a sadness. He wagged his tail very slowly.

Celia marched past him and sat where she had sat for days and days, in the rocker next to a grate that wanted no fire because the summer was hot. Oh, this was all she needed, a blinking dog with no fixed abode. It usually stayed at Maddy Horrocks's house, but it had been known to wander. Sometimes, it sat on the grave of Mrs Appleyard, the woman who had been its former owner; at other times it stayed in the vicarage or at the house of George Forrester, the little Jewish lad whose grandma still kept their old Polish name. Oh well, Amy could shift it when she got home.

Monty studied the woman. She wasn't right, wasn't sitting as she should. He walked up to her and spread himself out at her feet, nose between his two front paws, eyes staring up at her.

Celia tutted. She didn't want anything or anyone near her, couldn't be doing with words of condolence, with sympathy and small talk. Tomorrow, once the funeral was over, she would start trying to pull herself together again, would make an effort to carry on as if nothing had happened. At least dogs didn't say anything. This creature wasn't coming out with words of regret that cut to the very soul because ... because she had thrown Nettie out. Nettie hadn't been a good girl, hadn't been decent, hadn't kept herself to herself as a good Catholic girl should.

She'd tried a few funny religions, too, had Nettie – even spiritualism had entered the arena at some stage. The dog owned a very hard stare, yet there was gentleness in those brown, unblinking eyes.

'And the greatest of these is charity,' she heard herself saying. Who *should* cast the first stone? And hadn't Jesus loved Mary Magdalene in spite of all her sins? Celia remembered a parable about a lost sheep, about the shepherd who had abandoned his flock to go in search of that one small, wandering sinner. The dog sat up and licked her hand. Her stomach rumbled ominously – when had she last eaten? There was a strange comfort in having this daft dog here. It didn't say anything, didn't judge her, yet it . . . it loved her.

'I don't know how to feel,' she whispered.

Encouraged, he licked her again.

'It's as if I'm not a mother at all. Somebody killed her and I've even been blaming her for that. Am I bad? Am I?'

Monty whined softly, the sound coming from the very back of his throat.

'I've not even been to look at her, not since that day at the infirmary when I had to say who she was. She looked . . . she looked so young, just a bigger version of our Amy. And I had to stand and say, yes, it was my daughter. Tomorrow . . .'

Tomorrow would mark the very end of Nettie. In a few years, she would be no more than a name, a young woman who had been killed. If they caught the killer, Nettie would get a few more days of notoriety in the papers and on the wireless, but she wouldn't be real, wouldn't be the kiddy who had learned to read at Celia's knee, who had run in for a wash and a bandage after a fall, who had . . . Oh, God!

Monty sat up. It was going to happen and he would be here and the woman would feel better. It was noisy. She was so loud that his ears hurt, but he stayed exactly where he was, because he was needed.

Arthur stumbled down the last few stairs. 'Celia?'

'She's dead! My girl's dead!'

The man held her while she howled her anger and pain, while she screamed at the world and all who inhabited it, while she poured out her own self-loathing and agony. Arthur, too, was weeping openly. Monty lay down again. All he had to do now was to wait for the storm to pass. These two-legged creatures were very strange. Suddenly, there were three of them. Amy threw herself at her parents and they clutched at each other, a heap of human grief glued together by tears.

Monty, who knew he had been needed, had no idea why he had been an essential part of this human equation. But his job was done, so he scratched an ear and went to the door. Sooner or later, one of them would allow him outside and he would move on to the next task: a dinner – perhaps two dinners – and a nice, warm bed.

'What do you think you're playing at?'

Caroline swung round to face him. He was sleepy, angry and very tousled. She placed the white blouse on a chair and folded her arms. 'I'm getting ready for a job interview,' she told him. 'They're seeing people tomorrow and it's only round the corner, so I thought I might as well—'

'You don't need a job. You never had a job when you were with the other fellow, did you? Am I keeping you short of anything? Or are you trying to get some independence, eh?' He glowered, eyebrows settling in a single line above unforgiving eyes.

Caroline exhaled and thanked her lucky stars that she had changed her mind about leaving in the middle of the night. She would go in the day-time when he was safely out of the way, but she needed to find work and a place to live, some-where for Stella—

'Well?'

If push came to shove, Stella could go back to the vicarage. 'Well what?'

'Why do you want a job?'

He couldn't even talk properly. He lisped and limped his way through the shortest sentences and was not a man. No real man behaved as he did. She could have forgiven him his slight speech impediment if he had owned normal feelings, but he had driven one woman to her death, and if Caroline couldn't manage to get away she, too, might be forced towards desper-ate measures. 'It's at the convent,' she told him. 'St Anne's.'

'The school? What do you want to go there for? Haven't you had enough of bowing and scraping and hymn-singing?'

'It's nothing to do with religion,' she replied. 'It's the bursary. They want someone to look after the finances, that's all. I could save up for extras – holidays, a television set. And it would keep me occupied while you aren't here.'

He scowled. 'You've the cooking and cleaning to do.'

'I can still do those things as well. Anyway, I probably won't get the job – there'll be Catholics going for it. They'll choose a Catholic before me.'

'Then why bother?'

She gritted her teeth. Why bother? To get away from him, to find a place of her own, a place where she would not be assaulted by a creature who had not the first idea about love. 'I want to try,' she said lamely.

Suddenly wide awake, he leapt across the room and grabbed her by the throat. 'Get back to bed.' He forced her onto the mattress, his fingers continuing to squeeze her neck. 'Just remember who's boss round here,' he said. Then he went about his usual business, ripping into her and bouncing heavily three or four times before climaxing. Kneeling between her legs, he stared hard into her eyes. 'You'll never get away from me,' he growled.

He had absolutely no idea about his own abnormality, she mused as he lay down beside her. His first wife had killed herself in order to escape him – probably because she had realized that there was no other way out of the predicament. Caroline closed her eyes and allowed the tears to course down her cheeks. Would she get away? Could she?

161

He snored. Wide awake, Caroline made a decision. She would go back to Brian if she didn't get the job. Even if he didn't want her, she would stay there. The village could talk all it liked, because gossip was not as threatening as this snoring man. If she did get the job, she'd find a bed-sitting room somewhere and Stella could return to Rivington Cross. Forcing herself to breathe evenly, Caroline courted sleep. Tomorrow, she would need her wits about her.

Both sides of the main road through Rivington Cross were lined with people. Nettie's hearse had but a short distance to travel, so there were no other cars in the procession. So silent was the crowd that trees rustling in a gentle breeze could be heard, while birdsong seemed unusually noisy.

Arthur and Celia Bradshaw walked behind the single vehicle with their younger daughter. Celia, white-faced and stumbling, clung to her husband; Amy, who walked to the left of her parents, was supervised by two children who steered her gently towards the church. Maddy Horrocks and George Forrester walked behind Amy and were ready to set her to rights if she faltered.

As the chief mourners made their way towards Holy Martyrs, those on the pavement peeled themselves away and followed. Catholics and Protestants walked together, no division, no segregation on this sombre day. And at the front, just inches behind the family, a young Jewish boy wore his circular black cap as a mark of respect.

He smiled at his parents and his grandmother, was pleased to note that they, too, were joining the slow-moving queue in the middle of the road. It was right that they should join this community, right that they should offer support to bereaved Christian neighbours.

Phil Bennett kept his eyes on the priest who stood at the gateway of the church. Sheahan looked tired – as, indeed, he should, sedated as he was. Phil had done all in his power to contain the man and to warn his successor about him, although a part of him now doubted that Michael Sheahan had killed Nettie Bradshaw – he had not the physical strength for it. And yet . . . and yet . . . Phil was leaving tomorrow and Dr Linda Marshall would be in his place. There was no more he could do and he had to make himself live in hope.

Enid squeezed his arm. 'You did all you could,' she whispered. 'Are you coming in?'

The doctor shook his head. He had a call to make at an outlying farm whose owner was suffering from angina. 'I have to put the living first, sweetheart.' He turned away and walked into the surgery to collect his bag.

Yuspeh, Jakob and Anna remained at the back of the church, but George walked to the front with his new friends. For the time being, he was there for Amy and for Maddy – the dictates of his faith did not matter at the moment. He didn't like the priest, was glad that his own rabbi at Temple was a clearer speaker – even the bits spoken in English here were garbled. The clergyman stumbled and fumbled his way through the Requiem Mass, then six large men picked up the coffin and led everyone out to the graveyard.

In beautiful weather, Bernadette Marie Bradshaw was placed under the sod. George looked into a sea of faces, noted that Bobbee and Mamme were both weeping and that Jakob, too, seemed close to tears. So many Feigenbaums had been gassed, shot, worked to death; perhaps this Catholic funeral prompted George's family to remember all those who had been granted no proper blessing when their end had arrived. He clutched at Amy when it was her turn to throw soil into the grave – she stood so near to the edge that he feared she might fall in. 'Careful,' he whispered.

Celia managed a smile. 'Thank you,' she said. This little Jewish lad had taken care with his appearance – beautiful dark suit, shining clean face, dark cap perched on the back of his head. 'You are a good boy.'

George blinked away some wetness. Did it take death to bring people together? Was death the only true equalizer? If that were the case, the world was a very sad place indeed. 'I am sorry for your loss,' he replied. 'May God give you comfort.'

Celia patted his shoulder and glanced across at the lad's grandmother, another good soul who had tried hard to give assistance at a time when there could be no help. And in that moment, a fanatical Catholic woman allowed some of the prejudice to slide from her mind. What was right and what was wrong? Wrong was a girl in a

coffin long before her time, a second child grieving, parents heartbroken and a whole village in
mourning. Right was a dog that opened a
woman's eyes and heart, and an old Jewish lady
who wore strange clothes, pushed an old pram,
stuck to her old name and planned to keep
chickens. Right was here and now with all those
she knew standing together in defiance of faiths.
Most of all, right was Amy. From now on, Amy
must become the focus, the centre of Celia's
world.

Mother Olivia was a tiny woman who taught
Latin and Greek, took no nonsense and had the
ability to sum up a person's value in ten seconds
flat. The interviewee was a confused and
unhappy woman. She had been disarmingly
open about her circumstances and about her
own faults and seemed not in the slightest way
impressed or intimidated by the headmistress of
St Anne's RC Grammar School for Girls.

'So, I decided to apply,' Celia concluded.
'Because I am used to running things, you see.'

Mother Olivia saw. She saw fear, pain and
something almost akin to despair. 'You are living
with a man who is not your husband?'

'Yes.' Caroline did not lower her gaze. She
believed in meeting the truth head-on and was
not reluctant to admit to her own shortcomings.

Mother Olivia poured a second cup of tea for
the visitor. 'It is a warm day,' she remarked
nonchalantly.

'Yes. Yes, it is.'

'Then why the scarf round your throat?'

For the first time, Caroline was hesitant. A feeling of self-pity almost overwhelmed her and, in an effort to hide her uncertainty, she gulped down a mouthful of tea. She was hiding more than mere uncertainty – she was trying to conceal marks on her neck, bruises bequeathed by the monster with whom she currently shared living space. 'I am injured,' she said finally as she replaced the cup in its saucer.

'By him?'

'Yes, by him.'

The tiny nun rose from her seat and walked round the desk. Slowly and carefully, she undid the scarf and lifted it away from Caroline's neck. 'You poor child,' she said.

That was all it took for both of them. The headmistress made an instant decision, one she might well live to regret, but she meant to go through with it. The woman needed help. She seemed a sensible type – apart from the mistake she had made in leaving her husband – and was clearly bright enough to fill the position of bursar. 'Where will you live?' she asked.

Caroline dried her eyes. 'No idea, Mother.'

A corner of the nun's mouth twitched slightly before she spoke. 'I suppose you have never considered the possibility of living in a convent?'

'No.'

'We can give you a little flat – one we use for visitors. We seldom have visitors, but if a passing bishop does decide to honour us, you will have to sleep in a smaller room for a while.'

Caroline could not believe her ears. A home? A little flat of her own? She didn't know what to say.

166

'It will give you somewhere to stay while you think your way through the predicament,' continued Mother Olivia. 'There is a cooker – you need not eat with the sisterhood – and convent rules will not apply. Oh, except for one. You must bring in no men.' She smiled encouragingly. 'We have a tendency to avoid men. It comes with the job.'

Celia mopped her face with a small handkerchief. 'I have a dog,' she said. 'I probably should have left her with the children, but she obeys me and only me. Cocker spaniels can be wayward.'

'A sinner, then.' Pale blue eyes twinkled under the black veil. 'The sisters would love a dog, I am sure. And we can offer you safety, at least. What do you say? Would you like to go away and consider your options?' If the poor woman possessed any options. 'The position is yours, by the way – on a month's trial basis. The sister who had the job became senile, you see. So we sent her back to Ireland to be cared for. Yes, I think you should do very well.'

'You are kind.'

'We are all sinners, Mrs Butlin. Even in a place like this – which is dedicated to the Passion of Our Lord – there is jealousy and ill-feeling from time to time. We are human. This I feel I must stress. Go away now and think about what you must do.'

Caroline glanced at her watch. 'When may I move in?'

'At any time.'

'Today?'

167

'Yes.'

Caroline jumped up and grabbed her bag. If she hurried, she could be out of his house and back here with Stella in less than an hour. 'I don't know how to thank you, Mother.'

'Prayer will do. Oh, and a little cup of tea in your flat from time to time. There's a wireless. I like to listen to the wireless, you know. If you jiggle about with the knobs on the front, you can sometimes hear Dublin. Ah, you'll be grand. Away now and collect your belongings. My sisters will have your little home ready for you in a couple of shakes. God bless you.'

If anyone had ever told Caroline Butlin that she would kiss a nun, she would have laughed her socks off. But she kissed Mother Olivia's hand, then sat like a child while the nun rearranged the scarf. 'All hidden now, my dear. Go with God and come back with Him.'

Caroline floated on air all the way down Hawthorne Road. She packed her belongings into two suitcases, leaving behind all the clothes he had bought for her in recent days. Without pausing even to wash her hands, she collected her dog, picked up her suitcases and walked out of his life, stopping only to post the house keys through his letter box.

Outside on the road, the air smelled so fresh and clean that she wanted to drink it in, but there was no time. With the larger suitcase in one hand, a dog lead and a smaller case in the other, Caroline Butlin walked away from her biggest sin and towards the rest of her life. The world was a wonderful place and she would have the chance to regain some dignity through labour. There would be safety, too, because she would be surrounded by many women.

Above all, she was free. He would never hurt her again.

Betty Thornton knew that she was leaving herself out of things. The vicar had bought a beautiful white wreath for the dead girl, had signed *Rest in Peace, Bernadette. From Brian, Sarah and Simon Butlin, from all parishioners at St Faith's, also from staff and children at school*. But Betty hadn't done anything. She was out of step on this occasion, because her fear of Catholicism had kept her away from the service.

It was wrong, she told herself as she scrubbed a shelf in the under-sink cupboard. The village was in mourning and she hadn't even made an effort. Why? Why was she so stubborn?

She stood up, placed the kettle on the hob, found tea and milk. A crack across the head, the cane for missing Mass, a crazy priest chasing her halfway up Scotland Road because she hadn't learned her catechism and refused to take her punishment. Benediction, a clergyman scowling at her because she had dared to cough during the singing of *O Salutaris Hostia*, another crack of the cane when she had failed to learn the *Credo* in Latin plainchant.

Confession. That voice growling through the grille, five Our Fathers, five Hail Marys, five Glory Bes and the longer act of contrition because her sins had been so heinous. Saints' days, Sundays, no meat on Fridays, no food before Communion, children almost fainting on cold winter mornings, stomachs grumbling when digestive juices searched for something to work on. It had been cruelty.

Methodism had become her haven. It was strict, predictable and simple. She had turned her back on her family, had refused to listen to their endless moanings when she had chosen a faith of her own. But was she right? Did she need to be afraid?

The mother had looked so awful when the funeral procession had passed by. What if that had been James in the coffin? She shivered and took a mouthful of tea. 'I should have gone,' she informed herself. 'Out of respect for that family, I should have gone.' James had gone. Sarah and Simon, too, had attended the service – as had their father, a Church of England vicar. Even Jews had walked into a church dedicated to Jesus, who was not their Messiah. 'So why am I so important?' she mused.

She placed her cup in its saucer and walked into the back garden. From a bush under the kitchen window, she plucked a single rose, a perfect flower with curling, scarlet petals. 'I can do this,' she whispered. She could walk into a graveyard, could pay her respects to a girl she had never known, a poor thing whose body had been dragged from that huge reservoir. There was nothing to stop her, nothing to dictate that she must stay away.

Wearing her customary work clothes minus apron, Betty Thornton walked along between the two churches until she reached the gateway of Holy Martyrs. It was only a cemetery. The

Gothic-styled building was just that – a building, stone and mortar, a tower with a clock in it, an inanimate creation pulled together centuries ago by the hand of man.

Inhaling deeply, she took the first step, then the second. How many years had passed since she had last stepped on ground consecrated for Rome? But it was just earth and grass and gravestones. The new mound was covered in flowers, a cross-shaped wreath from the family, circular wreaths round the edges, sprays of flowers piled into the centre of the grave.

Into the middle of the white arrangement donated by her employer, Betty placed her blazing rose. 'That's from me and our James,' she told a girl who would never hear her, a girl whom she would never know. 'I am sorry,' she concluded before turning round.

She felt much better. That single flower had made all the difference and it was hard to understand why. It was probably something to do with common decency, she told herself as she neared the vicarage. A van stopped by the gate and a man leapt out. He had a moustache and a wild look in his eye. 'Is Mrs Butlin in?' he asked.

Betty didn't know what to say. The village surely knew that Mrs Butlin had left, so this man had to be a stranger. He had a lisp and a shifty expression; he was not a man Betty would have trusted. She decided to tread carefully. 'She's out at the moment,' she said. 'I'm Mrs Thornton, the housekeeper. Who shall I say was asking?'

He offered no reply. After looking up and down the road, he climbed back into his van and drove away. Then Betty remembered. She had overheard the twins talking about 'Daft Derek', the market trader with whom their mother had gone to live. 'Oh, well.' She dismissed him from her mind and went in to start baking.

It was none of her business and she had best keep out of it.

SIX

'Jakob, they cannot stay out in the night as well as all the day. Chickens will get cold when winter comes, just as we get cold. There is snow here in these parts. They will be froze. So a hut I will have.'

Jakob Forrester, a man endowed with patience enough to make a straight seam in the most difficult fabrics, to supervise two dozen workers and to deal with all their working and domestic problems, was not driven easily to the edge. But sometimes, his mother was a trial. 'Mamme, I have a factory to run and a living to make.'

'This I know and I am proud. I have a chicken business to start and with the hammer I am not good. Thank you for the runs you have made, but I am still wanting chicken house. This you will get for me because you are good son. You will not do as the English and put me away in a home.'

The 'good son' should have been elsewhere. His chief supervisor was staying in Blackpool for a well-earned rest and mice often played while the cat was away. 'I cannot do this now,' he said firmly. 'Firmly' attracted but one result every time. Invariably, she insisted and persisted. 'Is the farm over by Marsh Lane – you know where I mean. They will sell chicken hut for small price and you will borrow vehicle for to bring it. Unless you are wishing to give me your shed and to throw away all this rubbish you are collecting, then we make chicken boxes on walls inside. That we can do instead, I suppose.'

Jakob did not wish to lose his shed. He had a gift for whittling – as the locals termed wood-carving – and the little building at the bottom of the garden was a refuge, somewhere he could sit away from the noise and bustle of his factory. Noise and bustle? What peace would he achieve once the garden was full of chickens? There would probably be a cockerel and, although people hereabouts were inured to countryside sounds, the thought of a bird crowing under his window every morning did not appeal. 'Mamme, not today.'

'But you do not work in evening. Can you not go then? If we do not go, some other person may buy my hen house and the shed will be used.'

He sighed. 'Mamme, you are a torment.'

'Son, you have been torment all my life, but for what is woman born? For to be tormented by her son and to wait until he find the time to be a help to her. This I am doing for whole family, so that eggs will be had and chicken enough to eat. Anna tells me get an interest, so I am interesting in chickens.'

She was interesting altogether, he thought as he hid a smile. Her English was improving, but she still managed to lose articles definite and indefinite, throwing away a 'the' or an 'a' in every other sentence she uttered. He adored her. She knew that and would play on it until she got her own way. 'Mamme,' he said, 'I shall telephone and inform the farmer that he must keep his hen house for you. I hope it is not enormous. We have a big garden, but there are limits.'

'Limits?' she scoffed. 'A mother knows no limits. She will lay down her life for her children – look how many Jews of Europe stayed to die but put children on trains while there was time.' She frowned, plainly deep in thought for a few seconds. 'So many gone of my people. Jakob, we have had good fortune.'

'Yes, Mamme, we have.'

When he had gone, Yuspeh returned to the house and drank hot, black tea, this time with a cube of sugar clasped between her teeth. Sugar was a treat and she savoured it.

Her daughter-in-law was ironing. 'Did Jakob say he would buy the hen house for you, Mamme?'

'Is the rain wet? He does as I ask, because he knows what is good for family. I have to ask more than one time, but that is ever the case and this you must remember. The man, he must think he make decisions. But in truth, he does not. Is always the woman who does thinking and making happen. You let him believe he is captain of ship and we all will be happy sailors.'

'As long as we steer the ship away from the rocks?' Anna laughed.

'This is truth. If women was in charge, world would be safer and better place, so we learn slowly, put men in front and we do pushing.' She sighed and placed her cup in its saucer. 'Our George Josef, he is steered by nice little *shikses*. There is the Amy who lost her sister, may God be good to her. There is daughter of Hair By Yvonne and daughter of the vicar man. I am hearing they are to make a gang like the books of Enid Blyton named Famous Five. They will be Famous Six plus dog.'

'Monty.' Anna folded a shirt collar. Monty was a funny little dog, almost a gypsy. He went from house to house, and were he not such an active little chap he would be the size of an elephant, because everyone fed him. 'Well, George must play and he will be with boys, too. The vicar's daughter has a brother and the vicar's housekeeper has a son. So, three boys and three girls.'

'And no Jews.' Yuspeh placed a second cube of sugar between her teeth. Taken all round, England was not a bad place to live. Except for murderers. Of course. George Josef would be safer in a gang.

'There are Jews in the town, Mamme.'

'This I know. I am thinking more about that murder, Anna. Our boy will be protected good with five children at his side. Also, he was having loneliness sitting all the time on that wall. It is good to hear him laughing and shouting now as he runs about. But may God deliver to us this

176

killer, my *tochter*. Until he is caught, we is none of us safe.'

Yuspeh stood by the window and watched members of the new gang as they passed the window. Amy was forlorn, Maddy pretty and laughing, George kicking a stone. Ah, that boy went through shoes faster than a cat consumed sardines. They would all look after each other, she supposed. 'Where is their place?' she asked.

'Which place?'

'The gang. Do they not have place where they meet?'

'I have no idea, Mamme. Now, come and press this lace collar for me. I don't want to spoil my new blouse and you are good with the iron.'

Yuspeh grinned. Anna was learning to steer. And a woman who could steer a woman was a gem among blocks of granite.

Derek Ramsden came almost every day to Rivington Cross. He sat in his van and watched the vicarage, making sure that he varied the positioning of the van each time he parked. He saw the husband, the cleaning woman and Caroline's children, but he never once caught sight of her. The damned woman had upped and left without so much as a by-your-leave: no letter, no telephone call, no visit to explain herself.

Where the hell could she be? At the convent of St Anne? He doubted that. Why would nuns employ a woman who had turned her back on husband and children to live 'over the brush' with another man? She must be hiding in the vicarage, he thought. Perhaps he should speak to one of her kids, ask whether they had seen her. But, on his fourth visit, he found himself to be the focus of attention from an unwelcome source, a policeman who seemed to be writing in a little hard-backed notebook. Convinced that the constable had copied down his number plate, Derek did a neat reverse out of the pub car park and drove back towards the town.

Once he had rounded a bend, he stopped and steered his vehicle up a narrow, unmade path. There was no-one about, so he crossed the road, climbed a fence and made for the woods. That was where Caroline's children played; perhaps if he eavesdropped on their chatter, he might hear something to his advantage. Because she would not escape – oh, no. He would have his day with her as sure as eggs were eggs.

Keeping an eye on the steeple of St Faith's, he made his way through the trees until he came to the graveyard. There was no sign of either child. But a dog sat on a grave, so still that it seemed at first to be a statue highly unsuitable as decor in a Christian cemetery. The statue saw him, growled, then leapt in his direction. Hot on the heels of the dog, a boy hove into view, but Derek was not going to hang about to be caught by a child.

The boy called out, 'Monty!' and the dog seemed to give up the chase. Panting, Derek stood behind the trunk of a large oak. The boy was shouting. 'We haven't to go in the woods, Monty – not since the murder. Come on, now. Come to heel.'

Derek sat on the forest floor. The boy was not

known to him; he was certainly not the son of Caroline Butlin. Oh, well. There was nothing else for it – he had to give up and go home. Home? Empty house, no supper, no clean sheets on his bed. But he would find her eventually. If it was the last thing he ever did, he would bring her to book and no mistake.

Betty Thornton found herself humming 'Fight the Good Fight' as she cooked the evening meal for Mr Butlin, his children, herself and James. There was no segregation in this house. The housekeeper and her son sat down each evening and ate with the vicar, Sarah and Simon. Mr Butlin had declared that all were equal in the eyes of the Lord and that children behaved better when a goodly adult female was at table. So Betty, in her position as goodly adult female, became used to decent silver and good crockery, learned to deal with linen napkins, napkin rings, proper table settings, water glasses and cheese boards.

She was unbelievably happy. Never in all her life had she wakened so refreshed, so alive and ready to face her day. When she looked back at her time in Bolton, she had difficulty in coming to terms with the idea of that dark little house and the huge, hot and noisy mill in which she had toiled for so many years. Occasionally, she almost pinched herself just to make sure that this was not a dream, because she could scarcely believe her good fortune.

James burst into her reverie, Monty at his side. 'Mam, there was a man.'

She tossed salad in a glass bowl. 'Where?'

'In the woods. He were sneaking about.'

'Was,' she said patiently. 'He was sneaking about.'

'Did you see him, too?'

'No, I was trying to make you talk properly.' She stopped what she was doing. 'What did he look like?'

'Too far away and Monty went mad. I came straight back.'

'Good boy.' She peered through the kitchen window. 'Has he gone?'

James nodded. 'He ran off when he saw me and Monty. Do you think it might be him, Mam?'

'Who?'

'The man who killed Amy Bradshaw's sister. The one they've all been looking for.' It had been very exciting for a nine-year-old boy with too much energy and imagination. Police everywhere, some tramping about in the woods and prodding the ground with sticks, others questioning every person in the village, comings, goings, lots of happenings. It was quieter now. But if the murderer had come back, perhaps things would liven up again.

Brian came in, noticed that Betty was almost glued to the window. 'Is there something wrong?' he asked.

James produced the answer. 'Monty were sitting on Mrs Appleyard's grave – like he does – and he started barking. So I went to fetch him, because Mam says dogs shouldn't be barking in a graveyard. And there were a man at the edge of the woods. Monty wanted to chase him, but I stopped him. The man ran off. He'll be well gone by now – that were about five minutes ago.'

Brian placed a folder on the kitchen table. It was nearing September and he had been making notes about harvest for his special sermon. 'Betty?'

'I saw nothing,' she said. 'You were a good boy to come in and tell us, James. I think you should tell the police about it. After all, what happened here was very, very serious.'

Brian agreed. 'I shall take James up to the station after supper.' He smiled. 'I thank the Lord for the two of you every day. You have looked after us very well, James and Betty. Yes, very well indeed.' He picked up his folder and wandered off towards whichever task was next on his interminable list.

Betty stopped short of preening. The whole house shone like a diamond in sunlight. Every wood or glass surface had been cleaned to within an inch of its life, all upholstery had been scrubbed, rugs had been batted and shaken until almost threadbare and she was proud of herself. More than that, she was comfortable.

'Mam?'

'What?'

'I like Mr Butlin. He reminds me of a teacher, only a nice teacher, not one who gives you the cane or tells you off all the time.'

She offered no response.

'Do you like him?' he asked.

She stopped slicing chicken breasts for a moment. 'He's a very decent man, James, and he has given us a very decent life.' She was even managing to save, because he took scarcely a penny piece for board and Betty had got into the habit of buying a few supplies herself in order to ease her conscience. Yes, she liked him. He didn't preach, shout or threaten, didn't try to force her in any particular direction when it came to religion. And he had driven her three times to service at the Methodist chapel in Horwich.

'He'd be a good dad,' James pronounced.

'He is a good dad to Sarah and Simon.' She knew what the lad meant, but she had bread to cut. 'Go on, get from under my feet while I do the rest of this. And don't be coming to the table with dirty hands. Do you hear me?'

He heard. And he saw. With all the wisdom available to a bright boy of nine, he sensed that his mother had affection for her employer. He skipped outside to play with Monty until the meal was ready.

George lay flat on one of the deserted tables outside the Eagle and Child. He was looking for shapes in the clouds while Maddy, ever the organizer, scribbled notes in an exercise book. 'There's a sheep,' he said, 'and a ship. I wonder if the sheep is being transported by ship?'

Maddy looked up. 'The sheep's bigger than the ship.'

George agreed, turned and propped himself on an elbow. 'Are you still not finished?'

She glared at him. 'Unless you want some stupid Winnie-the-Pooh sort of gang, someone has to do the thinking. We need aims, secret

182

signs, reasons for forming a club. I don't know Sarah and Simon Butlin very well, but they agreed that we should have a purpose.'

'They would.' He chewed a pencil stub and asked about Amy.

'She'll be along,' replied Maddy. 'Amy's deep. She thinks too much.'

'And you don't?'

'She worries,' Maddy snapped. 'I try to be more . . . more positive.'

George sat up, climbed off the table and sat next to Maddy on the bench. 'I suppose we have to put our names to some sort of charter? In blood?'

'Don't be silly. Have you been reading Mark Twain again? We're not Injun Joe and Huckleberry Finn, George. We're English.'

'I'm not.'

'Yes, you are. You were born here and you live here. We're all mongrels, anyway – Vikings, Romans, Angles, Saxons, Celts—'

'Poles and Jews,' he said.

'Yes. Now shut up while I think.'

He shut up. There was no doubt in anyone's mind that Madeleine Horrocks, daughter of John and Yvonne Horrocks, would be leader. She possessed a quality that was difficult to pinpoint, though it was something to do with knowing a lot and being willing to research the rest. Her general knowledge seemed boundless. She covered most things from amoebae through ancient history to comparative religions and was given to eavesdropping in her mother's salon, a misdemeanour which

183

produced some hilarious and wildly inaccurate results.

'What did Mrs Barnes say last week about piles?' asked George with feigned innocence.

Maddy grinned. 'Don't sit on anything cold or wet, or you'll end up with a bunch of grapes to sit on. Everyone has to agree with her, because her husband's on Bolton Council. I think she should be on the stage – she's funnier than Tommy Handley.'

'Who?'

'He's on the wireless. Do you think James Thornton's old enough to be a member of the gang?'

George scratched his head. 'It doesn't matter, because we have to let him join anyway. If we locked him out, he would tell his mother and the Reverend about the bell house and we would all be evicted. Oh – I've found a paraffin stove for the winter. It's hidden at the bottom of our garden and we shall need to get it out before Bobbee starts keeping chickens.'

'Bobbee means grandmother?'

'Yes. It also means bossy nuisance who gets all her own way just because she's the oldest person in the house. We are to have chickens. They will be butchered kosher and will give us eggs.' It was grim. The back garden rang with colourful Yiddish curses whenever Papa hit his thumb instead of a nail. There was wire everywhere, the shed was filled with wood and a dismantled hen house leaned against the side of the house. 'We are doomed to live among squawking and feathers,' he said.

Maddy chuckled. 'I live among the dead and perm curlers – we all have our cross to bear.'

'Not Jews. We have no cross – just the Star of David.'

'We have Jesus and you don't.'

He nodded. 'Are you happy to be a Catholic, Maddy?'

'Not really,' she said. 'Some of it's OK and some of it's a bit mad. Our priest is slimy. He's not the sort of person you would want to open your heart to in confession.' Maddy looked at him. 'What about being a Jew?'

'A born Jew or a religious Jew?' he mused. 'I am Jewish by birth, so I follow the laws of Judaism. If I didn't, my family would never speak to me again.'

'Same here.'

They discussed their positions for several minutes, each reaching the conclusion that religion was a thing to be endured, because it could not be cured.

'Here comes Amy.' Maddy pointed to her slow-moving friend. 'We shall need to go easy on her, George. She's lost her sister and it isn't easy for her. A part of her blames her mother for throwing Nettie out of the house – it's all very horrible.'

'Blaming a mother is hard,' agreed George. 'Will she get over this?'

'Hope so. We start at St Anne's soon and she'll need a full set of chairs round her table if she's going to survive up there.' She saw his con-fusion. 'A full set of chairs means wits. She'll need her wits about her. Tough school, nuns, rules and prayers.'

'I go to Bolton School in September, as do Sarah and Simon.'

'Non-denominational,' said Maddy enviously. 'No nuns. And no prayers if you tell them you're Jewish.'

Amy joined them, looking strained. Her mother had started to cry the day before Nettie's funeral and her eyes had scarcely been dry since. She had not gone back to work, was upset about Dr Bennett's leaving the area, did not want to be employed by a female doctor, had hardly left the house since Nettie had been buried.

'I'll try to get there later,' Amy promised now. 'But it may not be easy.'

Maddy tutted. Tonight marked the first meeting of their motley gang. There would be the children of a vicar, the son of a Methodist, a Jewish boy, two Catholic girls and a dog. The dog was something of a movable feast, but he would probably show up at some stage, as he visited the grave of his owner at least once a day. 'Try to get there, Amy. It's our inaugural gathering.' She had found the word in a magazine in the salon. *Lancashire Life* had waxed on about an inaugural event involving quilt-makers in Preston.

'You must come,' urged George. 'We have biscuits and cakes and lemonade.'

Amy tried to smile, but the world hung heavily about her thin shoulders. Dad was back at work, had settled into his old routine. But Mam . . . Mam wasn't right. Even Monty could not cheer her. 'I suppose Mam won't notice if I go out,' she said. 'But I worry about her – someone has to keep an eye on her.'

Maddy, who owned strong opinions, kept to herself the near-knowledge that parents were supposed to look after children. Amy's mother had suffered a terrible shock and Maddy had not the right to intrude. 'Try,' she insisted. 'Sooner or later, you'll have to leave her for more than a few minutes at a time, Amy. What about when you're at school all day?'

'I know. But I can't help school. Choosing to leave her on her own is a different thing. I feel mean.'

They separated and went home for evening meals. As Maddy closed the door of the salon, she heard more monumental words from the mouth of Hilda Barnes, wife of a councillor, self-appointed eyes, ears and spokesperson of the village. 'A vicar shouldn't live with a woman. That Mrs Thornton should be sleeping in somebody else's house instead of bedding down with the vicar.'

Maddy sighed, shook her head slightly and went through to the living quarters. The world was mad and the most insane creatures inhabited the sphere of adulthood. Perhaps the answer was never to grow up.

Caroline Butlin had died and gone to heaven. Not because she was living within the walls of an order of nuns, but because she was enjoying herself. The good sisters, who, at first, had reminded her of a nest of fledgling crows with all their grounded flapping, were in a state of high excitement. They had a lay person in their midst. Any passing observer might have thought that a rare species had been captured, because the chatter and activity could have registered on the Richter scale. They fussed over her, made cakes for her, helped to rearrange furniture and were always hungry for gossip from the 'outside'.

She was to have a television set. This history-making event would occur not because she had asked for it, but because the brides of Christ all declared loudly that Caroline should have the comforts she might have expected at home and anyway, the bishop might like to watch the news if and when he came to stay. There was an air of anticipation while all awaited the arrival of the television and Caroline could imagine the whole convent crowding into her flat to watch *Andy Pandy* and *What's My Line*.

They were like children, she thought as she watched them tucking up their skirts to play tennis while the school was closed. Released from the prison that was academia, they ran, shouted, argued over points and were just as silly as anyone else on a break from work. The stories she had heard about their fierceness seemed to lose all credibility as she watched them enjoying a life as near to ordinary as might be achieved in those silly, burdensome clothes.

The flat was small, but lovely. She had a cream sitting room, a cream bathroom, a cream kitchen and a cream bedroom. She also had permission to change the drab decor and her little kitchen table was covered in wallpaper samples, swatches of curtain material and colour charts for paints. Sister Maria Therese favoured aquamarine distemper with white trim to doors and skirting boards, but Sister Vincentia thought Wedgwood blue would be a better option. Several other protagonists argued for and against moss green, ivory, buttercup yellow and a particularly nasty shade of mauve named Pale Whisper.

She watched them squabbling and was reminded of the playground at St Faith's – they might have been arguing over a game of conkers or a marbles tournament. Rosary beads rattled, black-swathed heads bobbed and nodded, spectacles and dignity slipped as agitation rose.

'You don't want miserable,' declared one with dark-rimmed glasses. 'She won't want to be living in miserable. That green is like something my daddy brought up when he'd been too long in the pub. Ah, no. That's a nasty shade altogether and she mustn't think of it.'

'No, 'tis a clean colour. The peach you like is horrible and not a real colour at all. As for the wallpaper with all the flowers on it, sure it looks like a Victorian garden gone to seed for lack of care. The room's too small to be taking a busy wallpaper – she wants plain or just a simple pattern.'

Stella, under the kitchen table waiting for scraps, was delighted with her new environment. She was ruined. Three or four times a day, someone took her for a walk in the grounds. They threw tennis balls and sticks for her and gave her biscuits as rewards. This house of women suited the cocker spaniel all the way

189

from her wet nose to the end of her feathery tail. She owned a warm basket, the freedom of the convent and even attended services from time to time, though she had been persuaded not to join in with the plainchant, as she was tone-deaf and, according to Reverend Mother Olivia, a sore distraction.

Mother Olivia entered the arena and silence fell very suddenly. 'I see you've the visitors as usual. They are like flies around a bowl of honey and I pray for your sake that they don't stick. I never heard such chatter in all my days, Mrs Butlin, and I apologize.'

'Caroline.'

'Very well, Caroline you shall be.' She looked sternly upon her gathered flock. 'Would you ever leave this poor woman alone? She's ground down by you all – you'll be having her worn out. She came here for peace, not to be locked in a cage of chattering monkeys. I see it's the usual suspects again. Maria Therese and Vincentia, have you nothing to be getting along with? Like timetables and class preparations?'

'We're all done, Mother,' replied one.

'Finished days ago,' said the other.

'Then should you not be praying instead of tormenting the life out of our guest? We've a world in total disorder and you would be better at your beads and contemplation.'

Caroline burst out laughing. 'I never had so much fun in my whole life, Mother Olivia. Oh, and I must thank you for allowing me to telephone my children and for arranging delivery of my shopping.' She inhaled deeply. Sooner or later, she would have to grab some courage and go to face the world. He was out there and he was not in possession of a forgiving nature.

When the twittering sisters had left, Mother Olivia parked herself in a fireside chair. 'Don't let them bully you,' she advised. 'They'll have you painted cardinal red with black doors if you aren't careful. It's all the excitement, you see. But worry not, they'll get over it. I'll help them over it with the toe of my shoe if necessary.'

Caroline laughed again. She hadn't expected it to be like this. Desperation had driven her here, but affection was holding her in the convent.

'We've surprised you?'

'Do you read minds, Mother?'

'Ah, I'm a student of people, so I am. People look upon us as strange, you see. But we're the same as the rest of you except for our bad habits.' She raised an arm and pulled at the sleeve. 'We are given to Christ, but also to the children of God. And I am not going to lecture you. Nor shall I make any attempt to convert you – I've enough trouble on my hands without getting you instructed and baptized. Now. The sadness underneath the veneer of laughter is those two children. Am I right?'

'Yes.' How had she managed to walk away like that, to take a dog and abandon her children? Perhaps a part of her had known that Derek Ramsden would not be a suitable companion for Sarah and Simon. 'I was foolish and selfish,' she told her companion.

'Yes, you were, but you are human. Most sins

191

are mendable. Get your children to come along whenever they please. We can even get a couple of camping cots and they may sleep here if they so wish.'

'You are very good.'

'I know.' The little woman grinned almost from ear to ear. 'But don't be telling my sisters that, or they might take advantage of my better nature. A woman in my position has to be firm.'

Caroline lowered her head. She should have been elsewhere, ought to have been with her children to offer support at this vital time in their young lives. They would be going to Bolton School soon, would be taking a giant leap into the big world. And where was their mother? In a convent choosing paint.

'We've a car,' said the nun.

'What?'

'Some of us have driving licences. If you like, we'll drive you up to Rivington Cross so that you may visit the children in relative safety. I realize that this would be a bad time to be taking the bus. The other fellow may be anywhere. Am I right?'

'Yes. Unfortunately, he is fixated on me to the point of obsession.'

'Which is why you must be careful. Remember what happened to his wife. I pray God will show her mercy for the sin she was forced to commit. Now.' She clapped her tiny hands together as if demanding the attention of a class. 'Away and put that kettle on, for I have a throat like the bottom of a parrot's cage. And a biscuit or two would be very welcome.'

This was the most normal life had ever been for Caroline Butlin. Her parents had been distant, had concentrated on their business rather than on their child. Brian? Brian was so predictable that she might have known the time without ever glancing at clock or watch. Coffee at eleven, lunch, tea and supper at the same time each day. He wrote sermons in the mornings, went about parish business each afternoon and was in bed by 11 p.m. each night.

Then along had come Derek with his levity, his risqué jokes from the market, cheap clothes, bunches of flowers, courtship. And she had believed in him, had left her children and her home behind and had placed herself in real danger. That part of her life had been the least normal of all. What had driven her to that? she wondered. Boredom? Was boredom a good enough reason for rampant stupidity?

But she was fine now, she told herself as she carried the tea tray into the living room. Soon she would see her children and that would ease her conscience in part, at least.

'You'll have heard about the murder of that poor young woman?'

Caroline set down the tray. 'Yes. She didn't live up there. I'm told she had a flat in Bolton and I believe she shared with another girl. What she was doing up on the moors I can't think – her mother threw her out of the family home years ago. She's . . . she's a fanatical Catholic. I think her older daughter didn't come up to scratch.'

Mother Olivia poured tea. 'I've no time for fanaticism, you know. It's a terrible thing no matter what its source. Look at Hitler. I know that business was all political, but it flew in the face of God, so it did. We have to make room for each other's mistakes and beliefs. Hitler made way for no-one.'

Caroline bit into a digestive biscuit. If anyone should embrace a faith without question, surely it should be a nun?

'I fight for my faith.' Once again, the Reverend Mother was mind-reading. 'It's not easy. If I didn't have to question the church, it would not have the same value for me. And no, it isn't a sin. Having a working brain is no offence against the Almighty. I pray hard for my faith and that is how I sustain myself.'

'I've never talked much about religion,' said Caroline.

'And you shan't now.' Mother Olivia rose, biscuit in one hand, cup in the other. 'Away to the kitchen with you. Those sisters of mine have very poor taste. Let's sort out your colour scheme while they're out of the way.'

The downstairs-downstairs of the bell house was reached by a back door. The upstairs-downstairs entrance faced the church, was exposed and was no use anyway, as that level boasted a couple of shuttered windows and offered no real privacy. At the back, in the lower chamber, there was no chance that light might leak and betray the children, so they planted themselves in a virtual cellar.

James – now Jay – was the first to speak. 'Is it true they used to keep bones here?' he said.

'Bits of dead people?' He shivered involuntarily.

'Are you going to be afraid of ghosts?' Maddy asked. 'Because we can't have scaredy-cats down here.' She surveyed the gang. Simon Butlin had lit the candles, and they sat on upturned orange boxes and a couple of beer crates acquired from the local hostelry. 'And this isn't going to be one of those Enid Blyton things.' She glanced at the Jewish boy who sat between herself and Amy. 'Anyway, Enid Blyton's George was a girl.'

Sarah snorted. 'I've read all those books – *The Famous Five* and *The Secret Seven*. Everywhere they went, there was burglary, kidnap and all kinds. It wasn't a bit like real life.'

Amy made a contribution. 'Real life round here hasn't been very good, has it?' She would rather be a part of Enid Blyton's nonsense than a resident of Rivington Cross, the place in which her sister had been strangled then thrown into the water like rubbish.

George patted Amy's shoulder. 'Not everything here is bad.'

Amy looked at the five other people in the room. George was kind and gentle, Jay was just a child, Maddy was strength, backbone and security. The two Butlins were, as yet, people with whom she had occasionally passed the time of day, though their inner qualities still remained a mystery.

Maddy, efficient as ever, unfolded a sheet of paper on which she had printed *WHAT ARE WE ABOUT*? 'That's the question,' she said quietly. 'We should all think about the answers, because we need a constitution. If this is not going to be

195

a silly club, it has to be about something. And I don't mean stamp-collecting or taking train numbers. Sensible ideas, please.'

George gave the opinion that the gang should be about friendship and loyalty. Jay was looking for adventure and fun, while Sarah declared that she simply wanted to know more about people. 'They're interesting,' she said lamely. 'Grown-ups, I mean.'

Simon agreed with her. 'I'd like to find the murderer,' he stated baldly. 'Sorry, Amy, but we are supposed to be saying what we want.'

Amy smiled wanly. 'Yes. And thank you. At the moment, I'm just glad to be out of the house.' She did not add that every minute was torture because she was worried about her mother. 'What about you, Maddy?'

Maddy's thoughts were, as usual, all over the place. 'I don't know yet,' she began carefully, 'but I'd like to change the way we think, the way we have been taught to think. We have to become ourselves and not what other people want us to be.'

George pondered that. 'Everything we learn is taught.'

'Yes.' Maddy stood her ground. 'But we want facts without them getting bent and twisted. Like . . .' She dug about for an illustration. 'Like Protestants killing Catholics, or Puritans behead-ing Cavaliers. They never tell us in a Catholic school that Catholics have done the same. The Spanish Inquisition was horrible. Then all those witch-trials – it was very brutal. But teachers and priests and vicars tell us what to believe.'

'And rabbis,' added George.

'And rabbis,' agreed Maddy happily. 'We need to unlearn stuff.'

'Not easy,' said George. 'We're all born into families and our families force things on us because the same things were forced on them. Schools give us books to read and we don't know where the authors got their ideas. Well, we do. They were probably taught. And if we change each other's way of thought, that's just learning from someone else – from us. But I know what you are trying to say.'

Maddy nodded. 'So it's about truth. And it's about knowing that one person's truth is another person's lie.'

Jay got down to brass tacks again. 'The police never found him. But I saw a man in the woods and Monty saw him too. So Mr Butlin took me to the police and I told them he was thin. He was too far away, but he was thin. Then one bobby told another bobby there's been a man hanging about for a week. He has a van and the bobby was going to write the number down, but his pencil broke and when he looked up the man had driven away.' He paused for breath. 'Well? It could be him, couldn't it?'

'Could be anybody.' Amy's voice was quiet. 'Could even be somebody we know. The police said it's often somebody the murdered person already knew.'

There followed an uncomfortable silence, then Sarah spoke. 'There aren't any strange people round here. Everyone's so . . . so ordinary.'

'But that's the point,' said George. 'Criminals look just like the rest of us. They don't have anything odd about them – well, there's nothing odd on show. They probably look just like other people. That's why it's so difficult to find them. If they all had two heads and four hands, it would be a lot easier.'

Amy stood up. 'I have to go back to Mam. I told her I wouldn't be gone long.'

Maddy rose. 'What are you afraid of, Amy?'

It was too late to ornament the truth. 'I'm scared she might put her head in the oven.' There, it was out. 'She made Nettie leave home because of all the boyfriends and staying out late. Mam blames herself, I'm sure she does. So there it is. I'm babysitting my mother.'

'So we do the constitution without you?'

Amy shrugged. 'It's done. We pledge to keep this place and the key a secret. We promise to look after each other for ever. Adults aren't our enemies, but they're not to be trusted just because they're older than we are.' She paused. 'And we try to find out who killed my sister before he goes and does the same thing to somebody else.'

Maddy took her best friend's hand. Her voice trembled as she spoke. 'Also, we find a way of living with what we know and a way of making the world a better place. Our world. Our lives.'

'Yes.' Amy opened the door, peeped out, saw that she was not overlooked, then left.

A heavy silence hung over the rest of the children. Jay broke it. 'It's not right that she should be so unhappy.' He jerked a finger towards the door through which Amy had just left. 'I know we can't bring her sister back. I know she's gone for good and all that. But we can try and find him. I mean, the police gave up, didn't they? They just said she'd been strangled. It's . . . it's as if she doesn't matter any more.'

'Or as if she never lived,' whispered Sarah.

Maddy shocked everyone by beginning to weep. Along with the tears, bits of Amy's story poured into the candlelit cellar. 'They're so . . . so Catholic. Lives of the saints, no meat on Fridays, always cover your head in church, don't go near St Faith's – that's not charity. It's nasty.'

'Don't cry,' begged Jay.

Maddy looked at him. He was only nine, but he definitely belonged. 'You're one of us all right,' she said, smiling through the downpour.

Jay felt so proud that he clasped small hands between clenched knees to stop himself applauding. He belonged. That was all he had ever wanted – to belong somewhere, with somebody, for some reason.

Simon decided to address the details. He discussed theft of candles and the acquisition of a heater from George Forrester's back garden. Then they might need blankets, some old cushions, an air-tight tin for supplies of biscuits and chocolates. 'And we'll need drinks,' he concluded. 'Bottles of pop. Failing that, water.'

'Paraffin for the heater,' said Sarah. 'And we've some old chairs in a shed at the back of the vicarage – I'm sure Dad wouldn't miss them. I think there's stuff in the attic, too.'

So the gang was formed. They went their

separate ways to think about rugs, small tables and cups. It was a new beginning, and their enthusiasm was boundless. But Maddy paused on her way home to look through the window of Amy's house. The girl's mother was sitting by the fire and Amy was bringing her a cup of tea.

Another day drew to a close.

SEVEN

Arthur Bradshaw was fast reaching the end of his tether. His wife had seemed to improve briefly once the grief had been allowed to escape, but now, a whole month after the burial of their daughter, she was locked in some world of her own and no-one could reach her. Amy had managed to get her to eat and drink, but, with the exception of basic bodily functions, Celia was not alive. He could not remember when she had last taken a bath, changed her clothes or cleaned her teeth. She simply existed.

In the kitchen, he spoke quietly to Amy. The child had dark semicircles under her eyes and was clearly fretting. 'This burden should not be carried by you,' he whispered. She was too young for it, was due to start at her new school in a couple of weeks, was suffering beyond measure. 'I have to get the doctor, love.'

'I know. But what can the doctor do?' Linda Marshall seemed a nice enough woman, but new doctors were always an unknown quantity. 'She's already given Mam tablets. What else can be done?'

Arthur, who had an idea about what needed doing, dared not answer. But nor could he allow the current situation to continue. He was back at work, making two deliveries each day, and needed his sleep. As the sole source of income in the house, he was forced to put food on the table and he could not ask his employers for any more time.

Amy was ahead of him. 'Will she need to go away, Dad?'

'I don't know.' That was the honest truth, but he could not tell the child that he was hoping for Celia's removal. As things stood, three people were in mortal agony. One needed to be removed so that the other two might get some breathing space, at least. 'If she does have to go away, it will be for the best. She needs help, Amy. She isn't even having a wash and she's stopped cooking. I'm not much use when it comes to making dinners – and why should you have to do it? You're only eleven and you've algebra to face. And French.'

'Latin, too.'

'That's nice, sweetheart.' He smiled at her. 'If you can go backwards in time, you'll be able to have a good old chinwag with Julius Caesar. Latin? What use is Latin except in church?'

Amy raised thin shoulders. 'Different kinds of Latin. Church Latin is spelt the same, but pronounced differently from classical. Doctors use Latin, chemists use it. And our teacher said it helps with English, because a lot of our roots are in the Romance languages. Romance means from Rome, not love stories.'

'Aye, right.' He dragged a hand through thinning hair. 'I've done a letter with everything in it. I made it like a diary of the past couple of weeks and I wrote down everything your mam did – and everything she didn't do. Anyway, I left it at the doctor's surgery. So we can expect a visit. It was easier, written down. I couldn't have said all that stuff – I'd probably have forgotten more than half of it.'

Amy's heart pounded like a trapped bird. She knew only too well that her dad was talking sense, but what about Mam? Would she be dragged off screaming? How long would she be forced to stay in a place she didn't know with people who were really crazy? 'Will they put her in a lunatic asylum?' she asked.

'I don't know, love. I've no idea what they're going to be doing with her. You see, we're not any use, are we? I'm sure you know I'd mend her myself if I could. But I've got to accept that I can't. You can't. We can't.'

Amy nodded. 'But I might know somebody who can. I thought of it a few days ago, then I decided it would be cheeky unless I asked you first. And the other person, of course.'

Arthur frowned. 'Who?'

'George's grandma.'

'What? That funny-looking little Jewish lady? Your mam isn't one for mixing with folk from other faiths.'

'I know.' Amy straightened her spine and firmed up her resolve. 'Mam never liked other

Christians, let alone Jews. But when they found
. . . when Mam had to go and look at Nettie's
body . . .' She gritted her teeth for a moment.
'She left me with Mrs Feigenbaum. We went to
Maddy's, but Mrs Feigenbaum stayed with us all
the while because she'd promised Mam.
Something happened. I think Mrs Feigenbaum
is good with Mam. I don't know why I think it,
but I do.'

Arthur was flummoxed and he said so. 'Well,
we'd best get knocking on Jakob Forrester's
door, then. Because if the doctor comes first, it'll
be taken out of our hands.'

'I can't. It's their Sabbath.'

'What? It's only Friday.'

'Jewish Sabbath starts some time in the
evening – I think – on a Friday and it goes
through all Saturday. They have to say prayers
and eat certain things in a certain order. George
says that rich Jewish people up Chorley New
Road in Bolton pay Christians to do jobs for
them on Sabbath days. They're supposed to do
nothing.'

'I see.' Arthur was scratching his head again.
'But if there's an emergency of some kind, can
they stop? I mean, they'd still send for an
ambulance if somebody got ill on a Sabbath,
wouldn't they?'

'I suppose so.'

'Then let's have an emergency. Do you want
me to go and ask?'

'George is my friend, so they know me better,'
said Amy. 'And it's worth a try.' Anything, anything at all to keep Mam out of the asylum was a

good idea in Amy's book. She remained worried because it was Friday evening, but she collected her courage and left the house by the back door.

As she walked along the street, the child realized how tired she really was. Her legs ached, as did her head, as did most points in between. She hadn't been sleeping, was always on the alert for the smell of gas, for the least noise out of her mother, who had not climbed the stairs in weeks. Celia slept and ate on the fireside chair and used the outside lavatory when she needed it.

Tentative at first, Amy tapped on the Forresters' door. When there was no reply, she used the lion's head door knocker.

Jakob answered. 'Good evening, child. Would you like to come in?'

Amy nodded and followed George's dad into the living room.

The table was set and she apologized. 'I am sorry to come at Sabbath time,' she said.

'No matter,' answered Jakob. 'We begin only when the sun has gone down and see . . .' he pointed to the window, 'we still have sun. Have you seen the Shabbat table before?'

Amy shook her head.

'Then be a guest and let me show you.'

Not wishing to be rude, Amy listened while everything was explained. There was a plaited candle on a side table. It had several wicks and all would be lit at the end of Sabbath. The wicks represented the many tribes and the plaiting brought those tribes together. 'This is a time for family, also for community,' he told her.

Where was everyone? Amy heard sounds floating down the stairs and realized that the other Forresters and Mrs Feigenbaum were probably getting ready for the Sabbath meal.

Jakob demonstrated the spice jar and the challah bread. 'In the desert we were fed by God on manna, but on Shabbat, He gave us double rations. Here, in this two-handled cup, we must wash our hands three times before we begin to eat. So.' He grinned from ear to ear. 'What brings you here this evening, Amy?'

She swallowed. 'The sun will go soon, Mr Forrester, so I don't like to ask for your help, but—'

'Ah, no.' He tutted. 'For our friends and neighbours, we are always here. We have a forgiving God and He will excuse us at a time of need. Your mother – does she stay in the house still?'

'Yes.'

'And this is why you are troubled?'

'Yes.'

'I think you are wanting my mother, then.'

Amy's relief almost resulted in tears, but she held them back. 'On the day when my mam had to go to hospital, she left me with Mrs Feigenbaum. Something happened. I think Mrs Feigenbaum talked to her. We just wondered – Dad and I – whether she would try again?'

'Will she try?' Jakob ruffled Amy's hair. 'Child, there would be more trouble making the effort to stop her. My mother is noisy and bossy, but she has a heart of solid gold.' He sighed. 'She lost many in the camps, you see. You know about these camps?'

'Oh, yes,' replied Amy, 'we all do. We did it at school, so we understand why you came to England.'

'We lucky few,' he mused. 'My family – those who are not here – they died. So, we who are fortunate are here now to help those who gave us home and work.' He went to the foot of the staircase. 'Mamme? You are needed in the house of Mr and Mrs Bradshaw. Amy is here for you.'

George rattled down the stairs first. 'Amy!' he cried. 'What's happened?'

'Nothing yet,' she answered, 'but Dad has written to the doctor and Mam may have to go away for a while. The only hope I thought of was your gran. I remember Mam saying that Mrs Feigenbaum – Mam calls her Mrs F – was a good woman. She is our last hope, George.'

The last hope came into the room. She smiled at Amy, then spoke to her son. 'Pray for this child's mother tonight, Jakob. She is troubled woman and prayers may bring comfort.'

Amy and Yuspeh walked the short distance to the Bradshaw home. When they were about halfway, Yuspeh stopped. 'If you wish, you may go back to Shabbat at the house of my son. This may be difficult for you now, what I am trying to do with your mother.'

'No, thank you. I want to be there.' Had she spoken the truth? Amy wondered as she opened the front door. Was she staying away out of concern for her mother or because attendance at a Jewish Sabbath might be a sin? After all, St Faith's was a sin . . .

They entered the house. Celia remained in her chair and did not look up even when the door slammed shut.

'Mr Bradshaw,' Yuspeh began. 'I am sorry for the trouble you endure, may God guide you in this time of need.'

Arthur smiled his thanks.

Yuspeh dragged a ladder-backed chair across the room, motioning with a shake of her head when Arthur offered to help her. She sat next to Celia and waited, but the woman's head did not move. 'Mrs Bradshaw? Celia? This is Mrs Feigenbaum who you are naming Mrs F. Feigenbaum is a mouthful, I know this, but I did not change to Forrester as did my son. He did that for the business, you see, so that people could say better the name.'

Celia did not even blink.

'So, I was wondering how you are getting along and I come now with Amy for to visit you. Amy is friend to my George Josef, who is my grandson. They are having a club and they meet for to put right the whole world – may God grant them such ability and the time to use it.' Yuspeh looked at Arthur, her thin shoulders raised in a gesture of near-defeat.

Arthur spoke. 'Sometimes, I reckon she can't hear us.'

'Sometimes,' replied Yuspeh, 'people is not wanting to hear.'

'Amy has to feed her. She cuts everything small and spoons it in. Mind, Celia takes herself off down the yard a few times a day to do the necessary, but she never as much as washes her hands.'

'Yes, she is dirty,' Yuspeh agreed. She turned to Amy. 'You have hot water enough for the bath?'

'I think so, Mrs Feigenbaum.'

'Then you will fill the bath and your father, you and I will get this mother of yours upstairs. She cannot sit here in this way for all time. The poor lady begins to smell and we cannot allow her to become any more unclean.'

Arthur stared at the old woman. She looked as if a stiff breeze might blow her over. 'It's not going to be easy,' he ventured.

Yuspeh awarded him one of her less powerful withering looks. 'Nothing is easy. We do not come in this world for it to be easy. You and Amy will push her up the stairs. If necessary, we shall get more help from my son and his wife, Anna. This will be done.'

Arthur knew better than to argue. The woman meant business and he would have stood a better chance of redirecting a boa constrictor chasing prey. He stood beside his seated wife. 'Come on, love. Get up – let's be having you.' This yielded no result, so he took her arms and pulled her to her feet. Almost carrying her, he dragged her out of the room and began the slow journey to the upper storey.

Yuspeh took Amy's arm. 'We will unclothe her. Put the beads of rosary round your neck, child. I am wearing holy amulet and, between us two, we shall reach Almighty help at some level.' Her eyes twinkled for a moment. 'You see, we cover all the possibilities – me the Jew and you the Christian. Get towels.' She walked upstairs.

Amy found herself almost smiling. The old lady had brought a sense of normality into the house, also a degree of wit that rendered her charming and amenable. 'I like her,' Amy told the crucified Christ before following the instructions of her Jewish mentor. Armed with rosary and towels, she entered the theatre of battle.

Celia was seated on the lid of the toilet. Arthur, breathing heavily, was being shooed from the room by his neighbour. 'If we need you, I call,' she said as she pushed him onto the landing.

Yuspeh rolled up her sleeves. 'Now, Celia, if you want a fight, we give you one, your *tochter* and I. *Tochter* is daughter, should you wish to know.' She turned. 'We attack firmly,' she told Amy. 'If she struggles, we struggle, and if she become too bad a job, we get your father and my Anna.'

It was like undressing a doll. Joints didn't want to bend, buttons stuck, socks didn't agree to leave the feet. 'Thank God she was not wear the stockings,' breathed Yuspeh. 'Suspenders can be a trial very sore even when a person is willing to move.'

At last, Celia was naked. Stained clothes were gathered up by Amy and placed on the landing. Before she re-entered the bathroom, an order was transmitted. 'Bring your father and he can put her now in this tub.'

Arthur came in from the bedroom, picked up his wife and placed her in the bath. When the shock of warm water registered, Celia blinked several times. Then, to the joy of the assembled company, she picked up sponge and soap and began to clean herself.

Yuspeh sat on the lavatory. 'Oy, oy, oy,' she cried. 'See how some things stay no matter how tired the mind? She is in bath, so she washes.'

Celia, who was swilling her face, looked quizzically at her audience. 'What are you doing here?' she asked. 'Can I not have a bath in privacy?'

Amy fell into her father's arms. 'Is she coming back, Dad?' she wept.

'She has been nowhere, child,' Yuspeh answered for him. 'Celia has been sleeping. Sometimes while awake, we sleep. Go now. I shall mind her.'

As Arthur and Amy made their way downstairs, they heard more words emerge from Celia's mouth. 'Will you wash my hair, Mrs F? I've not been myself lately, so I've no strength.'

'Thank God,' whispered Arthur.

But Amy, inside her head and in her heart, was thanking Mrs Feigenbaum. And in some strange way, it was all the one thing – God, Mrs Feigenbaum, Mam, the rosary. Yes, life on some levels was a lot simpler than some people wanted to believe.

Dr Linda Marshall snapped shut the lid of her bag. 'She's sleeping. Thank you for your letter, Mr Bradshaw. Sorry I could not get along sooner.'

211

Arthur inclined his head. He was glad that the doctor had arrived late, because Celia, shocked to life by something as simple as a bath, was showing signs of picking up. She had demanded toast with strawberry jam, had even complained about the weakness of tea brewed by her husband. 'I can't believe it was that easy,' he said.

Linda Marshall grinned. 'The human mind is an odd bag of tricks. She has probably been in deep shock, guilty because her relationship with— What was her name?'

'Bernadette.'

'Was your wife the one who sent her away?'

'Yes.'

'Then if they did not get on well together, your wife is feeling guilty. All that what-if stuff will have been running through her head continuously. It all overcame her and she closed the door. You see, the mind shuts down from time to time and it can be wakened by the cry of a baby or a knock at the door – it's a mystery.'

When the doctor had gone and Amy was in bed, Arthur closed his eyes and tried to remember happier days, but he could not quite manage to picture Nettie running on the shore at Blackpool or in the back garden at home. She had been gone so long before her death, and now . . . and now he would never see her again. He hadn't sent her away, yet he could not bring himself to blame Celia. She had done her best, had tried hard to work out a solution. And it had ended like this, with Nettie strangled and thrown away like a sack of old rubbish.

How could one plain, ordinary postman catch

a killer? Especially when a whole police force – together with forces from neighbouring areas – had failed. He was out there. Arthur's fist curled on the arm of his chair and he bashed it hard into the upholstery. It wasn't fair.

Linda Marshall closed the Bradshaws' door and glanced across the street. It was time to visit her least favourite patient and a brief shiver touched the base of her spine. She was not a Catholic, but her predecessor was – and Phil Bennett had made several near-allegations before handing over the reins to Linda.

'Watch the girls from the Catholic school,' he had said. 'They can be disruptive and noisy at home.' He had mentioned one family where a daughter had broken the arm of a sibling – 'She never had such a temper until she began going to school and church.' Oh, God. Sheahan was a creepy, smelly old bugger and she was forced under the terms of her contract to treat him.

The priest had telephoned earlier, had complained of stomach pain and vomiting. Such symptoms in an injecting diabetic had to be taken seriously, because the fine balance between insulin and food intake had to be maintained. A small part of the doctor hoped that he had slipped into a hypoglycaemic episode from which he might never recover. She chided herself. Life was life. It was in her oath and the oath prevented her – as it had prevented Phil Bennett – from doing harm by meting out justice to this horrible man.

Doctors found ways around the oath,

naturally. Phil Bennett, a decent, God-fearing man, had denounced the priest as a paedophile without actually using the word. Linda's medical radar had filled in the blanks and she found herself encumbered by the same albatross that had decorated the neck of Dr Bennett. Like Phil, she knew full well that an overdose of insulin would eliminate the creature; like Phil, she realized that such action would be criminal and that she should not contemplate it.

She rang his doorbell, heard him shuffling. He was on his feet, then. Besides the insulin, the prescription left by Phil was for sedatives and Linda had continued to prescribe the drug. It was, perhaps, unsuitable for a diabetic, as one of its side-effects was the inhibition of breathing – and diabetics were prone to chest infection. But there was no other way of containing him outside prison. There was no possibility of maintaining round-the-clock supervision, so the drug had become the babysitter. Priest-sitter, she reminded herself inwardly.

The door edged inward. 'Come in,' he said. 'It took you long enough.'

She followed him into a sitting room and she noted right away a tantalus on a small bureau. Good. He continued to drink. She could smell it on him; the stench seemed to be folded into his clothes, while his face, a road map of capillaries, advertised very clearly his fondness for spirits.

'So,' she began briskly, 'how are you now?'

'Dreadful.' He lowered his bulk into an easy chair. 'I can't keep anything down.'

'Have you taken a drink?'

214

His eyes narrowed. 'A little brandy to settle my stomach, that's all. I prefer whiskey, but brandy's supposed to be good for the digestion.'

She placed her bag on a low table. 'If there is no food in your system and if you have alcohol in your blood, you are courting coma and, quite possibly, death,' she pronounced, the words stripped of all emotion.

The priest blinked stupidly.

'The sugar content of your blood will be diminished if you have injected insulin and have not been able to ingest food. Alcohol will lower the levels again, so you are now hypoglycaemic.' She sniffed the air and caught a whiff of acetone wrapped into the scent of brandy. His blood sugar was dangerously low. 'You need to be stabilized in hospital,' she told him.

'No!' he shouted.

'Then how am I to help you?'

He glanced at her bag. 'He used to give me an injection.'

'Dr Bennett?'

'Yes.'

'Then I shall do the same. But these episodes will weaken your major organs, Father Sheahan. Your heart and kidneys will not cope with too many occurrences of this nature.' She drew liquid into the syringe, then dabbed his arm with antiseptic. His liver probably demonstrated the properties of a worn-out saddlebag, she mused as she drove home the needle none too gently.

'That hurt,' he complained.

'Did it?' She held his gaze.

His eyes narrowed again. In that split second

after the hypodermic had been applied, he saw her hatred for him. So, the other fellow had spilled his venom, had he? Michael Sheahan had lately come to realize that the female of the species was, indeed, far deadlier than the male.

She straightened, closed her bag, picked it up and walked to the door.

'Just a minute,' he snapped.

Ah, the glucose was doing its job, she thought as she turned to face him. 'Yes?'

'Will I be all right now?'

He would never be all right. 'You have a better chance. If you continue ill, we shall need to get an ambulance. I can do so much and no more under domestic conditions.'

He could not say it, dared not ask what she had been told by Bennett. His mouth stayed open, but no words emerged, because he caged them. She was staring at him as if he were an exhibit in a zoo. Was she a danger? he wondered. Would she go to the police and expound further on the previous doctor's theory? No, she was bound by an oath, so she could not do that. Could she? As his front door closed, he suddenly felt less safe.

The murderer of Bernadette Marie Bradshaw did not sleep well that night.

There were ten nuns crammed into Caroline Butlin's newly decorated sitting room. Not a sound came from anyone while the gathering stared hard at *Watch With Mother*. Caroline, who wanted to laugh at the silliness of the scene, backed away towards the door. The smell of

216

paint, combined with so many inhalers of oxygen, served to make her breathing difficult, so she stepped into the corridor and led Stella out to the grounds.

It was a beautiful day. But she had no right to feel as happy as she did, and the hole created by the loss of her children soon overshadowed her elemental joy. No, she had not lost her children; she had given them up. Tormented by this knowledge, she trudged around the tennis courts, down to the stables where horses were no longer kept, back to the small maze of cloisters, then homeward. Strange that she could call the place home. This was the first time she had felt at home in ages. Boring Brian and Desperate Derek had never allowed her to feel so settled.

Poor Brian. She threw a ball across the school yard and watched the silly spaniel leaping about in her efforts to catch it. So many years of plodding along, no cruelty, no quarrel, no excitement. But he was a good man. Perhaps she had never wanted a good man. Married to his parish and devoted to his calling, Brian had neglected his wife. Was that a sin? She doubted it very strongly.

Nor did she need a bad man. Memories of Derek's behaviour made her shiver in spite of the late August heat. Sometimes, she could smell him; often, she would wake in the middle of the night, her breath laboured as she felt his hands and inhaled the scent of him. He was sick. She wondered who his next victim might be, wondered, too, whether he had finished with her. Her groceries were being delivered to the convent, but, sooner or later, she would need to go out. She was not a prisoner and had no intention of allowing herself to be contained indefinitely. But the fear remained . . .

A small nun flapped round the corner. She waved. 'Caroline?'

'Yes?'

Mother Olivia arrived at her side. 'Where are they?'

She didn't want to inform this principal that the heads of geography, English, modern languages, art, history and mathematics were all glued to a television screen on which images of puppets bounced around, strings obvious, background voices very clipped and BBC. The strings needed clipping, she mused obscurely before answering, 'I saw some of the sisters earlier, and—'

'Ah. They're plugged in to the electricity, I take it? Watching programmes for babies, is it?'

'No idea, Mother.'

'You're a poor liar and that's a credit to you, so it is. They need firmer management, you know. They want talking about, every last one of them. What's the matter with them at all?'

'Perhaps I'm a bad influence?'

'Ah, away with your bother – you'd make a finer nun than any of them. They'll have to be fetched and I'm the man to do it.' She walked a few paces, stopped, turned. 'I very nearly forgot. Get your bonnet on, for we're away on an outing to see your children. That'll cheer you up no end.'

Caroline lifted her face to the sun. She

dreaded seeing Brian, longed to be with her children – and the longing overcame the dread within seconds. She arrived at her flat just in time to see a gaggle of nuns disappearing round the corner towards convent quarters. Inside the sitting room, Mother Olivia was staring at the TV. 'What's that?' she asked.

'The test card. It's there to prove the TV is working.'

'And it does nothing?'

'Nothing, Mother.'

The nun sniffed. 'Waste of money,' she pronounced before making for the door. 'We'll be back in a few minutes,' she threw over her shoulder before making off in the direction of her miscreant sisters.

Caroline prepared for her visit. She didn't want to see anyone from the village, didn't really want to see the man she now thought of as 'Poor Brian', but she desperately needed contact with her children. Would the visit disturb them? Arriving would be nice, but leaving would be terrible.

Sister Vincentia dashed in, red-faced after her telling-off from the Superior. 'Mother will be along in a minute. Do you drive? I've a licence myself, but I'm out of practice. And Mother Olivia is so short that she has to peer through the steering wheel and we need blocks on the pedals.'

'I'll drive,' said Caroline.

It was not an uneventful journey. The Reverend Mother, in the passenger seat, was terrified every time the car's speed approached thirty miles per hour. Vincentia, in the rear seat, ooh-ed and aah-ed over every pretty garden, every new shop.

'Would you ever keep quiet?' snapped Olivia after about ten minutes of enthusiasm from the woman in the back. 'Anyone would think you'd never caught sight of the world in your whole life. You're acting like a nun from a closed order, so you are.'

Vincentia leaned back and kept quiet by pressing anxious knuckles against an over-excited mouth.

'Mind the child,' ordered Olivia, her hand gripping fast the inner door handle. 'I know he's near the wall, but they do run and jump about so. And there's a bicycle up ahead – you never know when they'll slip sideways under your wheels.'

Caroline was beginning to wish she had taken a chance and a bus, because driving this pair was like sitting on the edge of a rumbling volcano. In fact, at the pace allowed by Olivia, walking might have been a quicker option. Then there was the idea of turning up at the vicarage with two Catholic nuns in tow. Why did life have to be so complicated?

They started the ride up Chorley New Road, the Reverend Mother in the front becoming more agitated when they were forced to pass a parked bus. 'Watch for passengers, now, they've a habit of crossing in a rush.'

Caroline swallowed a nervous something-or-other – she could not work out whether she wanted to cry or laugh. The whole situation was ludicrous. Here she was, wife of a vicar, mother of delightful twins, ex-mistress of a rapist, now in the company of a pair of Cross and Passion sisters who were enough to make anyone cross and passionate.

'There's a dog about to dash out, and—' Mother Olivia's words froze in her throat as Caroline ground to a halt. 'Is something the matter?' she asked.

Caroline inhaled. 'Now. We can do the rest of this journey in several ways. I can drive, Sister Vincentia can drive, or we can get the cushion and the blocks from the boot and you can drive, Mother. What is it to be?'

The little nun in the passenger seat leaned her head to one side. 'Is this you putting your foot down, Caroline Butlin?'

'It is,' came the swift reply. 'And as you see, Mother, my feet actually reach the controls of the car.'

A strangled cough emerged from the rear of the vehicle.

'Vincentia?'

'Yes, Reverend Mother?' The words were flattened by a brave attempt to hold back nervous laughter.

'You are the worst driver it has ever been my misfortune to meet. Caroline, drive on.'

'And you'll be quiet?'

'As the grave.'

They were passing through Horwich and the word 'grave' was sitting at the front of Caroline's mind. 'That murder was never solved,' she said quietly. 'If anything happened to Sarah or

Simon, I would blame myself.' The climb to Rivington began and she moved down a gear. 'God knows who or where the killer is. But I can't take the children away from Brian – I just can't.'

Olivia patted her arm. 'Things will work out, you'll see. Now, would you like us to sit in the car? People in villages are not used to seeing a couple of penguins flapping about on an August afternoon.'

Caroline made a decision. 'No. You'll come in. That's if anyone is at home, of course.' She swung the car into the driveway, then sat and listened while the two nuns exclaimed over the beauty of the vicarage. Caroline looked at it. Yes, it was a pretty house, built in 1881 and bought by the church just as the century turned.

'You could stick us in a field as scarecrows,' suggested Vincentia, who was rewarded with a hard look from her boss.

Mother Olivia apologized. 'Vincentia has scarcely been out of the convent since her poor mother sold her to us. Well, it was barter, really, because we paid with two pigs and a sheep. If she goes silly on us, she will be in a field, Caroline, because I shall drive her there myself and not in a car.' She turned to survey her companion. 'With a whip,' she concluded, a twinkle in her eyes, 'and back to the pigs and the sheep.'

There was a special quality to female friendship, mused Caroline as she continued to stare at the door of a house that had once been her home, a door now closed. She had closed it herself; she had erected that barrier between herself and the two people to whom she had given birth.

'Are you all right?' asked Olivia.

'Just thinking. Collecting my thoughts.'

'And your memories.' This was not a question.

'Yes.'

The nuns knew that this was a special moment in Caroline's life. She had made a monumental mistake, had suffered for it, was now forced to swallow her pride and . . . and what? She should come home, should return to Rivington Cross, thought the senior sister.

It was Caroline's turn to read a mind. 'I can't come back, you know. Not yet. Even though I am worried sick about the murderer. Derek may follow me and God forbid that anyone should hurt my twins. It won't take long for him to work out where I am. He may have moved on to some other poor woman, or he may still be . . . obsessed. Derek owned me – or thought he did. I cannot bring more danger to my children. There is enough danger already, with the murderer of Nettie Bradshaw unaccounted for.'

'I understand,' said Olivia.

Caroline turned to look at her. 'What if he comes to the convent?'

The black-veiled head shook. 'Would you face the wrath of Sister Saint Thomas when she has the mood on her?'

Caroline laughed. 'No.'

'Then we shall make sure she has the mood on her. Will we do this now? Do we go in?'

'Yes.'

They left the car and walked up the path, Caroline's heart beating like a sledgehammer, the two sisters praying that she would be accepted for a brief time into the bosom of her family.

James was up to something. He and the twins were forever disappearing, often in the company of that Jewish boy and those two Catholic girls. Betty Thornton had spoken to Mr Butlin about her concerns, but he had dismissed them. 'Children play,' he had said. 'They are mixing with other children, just as they should. I suggest you stop worrying about them.'

Betty scrubbed a shelf. She didn't want her son mixing with papists, the very people from whom she had escaped; nor did she want him back in Bolton, so she had to accept that with every good result came a little of the bad.

'This place hasn't had a good bottoming in years,' she told herself aloud as she cut new shelf paper. 'She wants talking about.' The front door opened. 'Mr Butlin? Sarah?' No answer arrived. 'Who's there?' she called.

She felt her jaw dropping when Caroline Butlin entered the kitchen. So. Here she was, then, the woman who had abandoned her children to go off with another man. 'There's nobody in,' said Betty.

'I have friends with me,' Caroline informed the interloper. 'I shall make some tea.' She could feel the housekeeper's eyes boring into her spine as she filled the kettle and set it to boil.

Betty knew one thing about a kitchen – there

should never be more than one woman in it at any given time. She excused herself and walked into the hall, only to be shocked yet again, this time by the sight of two nuns exclaiming over photographs of 'Caroline's' children. They were not Caroline's children at all. She had left them in order to enjoy the company of a common market trader. Those twins belonged to one parent only and that parent was the Reverend Brian Butlin. Where was he? Should she go to the church and look for him?

No. That was not a part of her job. Betty took herself upstairs, leaving her door slightly ajar so that she might monitor any further developments. Nuns. What was Mrs Butlin up to – bringing nuns into a decent Christian household? The woman was clearly out of her mind.

Caroline placed the tea tray on a table. 'Help yourselves, sisters. I must go outside to see if I can find those two. They aren't in the house – we would have heard them.' She left by the rear door and approached the graveyard. Yes. There they were, standing by the old plot where an urn hid the key to the bell house. She had known for some time about the bell house, but had kept her counsel. Children needed secrets, needed to live their magic before grim reality moved in on them.

Sarah saw her first. 'Ma!' she yelled before leaping across the graves.

Simon's response was slower. His emotions were mixed, because life had settled into a routine whose predictability was a comfort. And Mrs Thornton's cooking was a great improvement on Ma's. Anyway, he liked Jay and he even liked Mrs Thornton. She was strict, but straight – and she was always there.

Caroline noticed his coolness, kissed him on the cheek. Sarah would forgive quickly, she thought. But Simon would take a great deal longer. 'How have you two spent your holidays?'

They walked towards the house, Sarah rattling on about their new Jewish friend, about Maddy and Amy, about Nettie and the police, about Jay. Simon, feet dragging, did not know how to feel. He was guilty, he supposed, of not valuing his mother. A normal son would choose a mother over a housekeeper any day.

They reached the back door. 'I have brought some friends,' Caroline explained.

'Is he here?' asked Simon. If the lisping moustache should happen to be a part of the formula, Simon would have none of it.

'No.' Caroline placed a hand on her son's head. 'No, he is not here. I don't live with him any more. I am staying with other friends.'

The nuns were a further shock. After the brief introduction, Simon excused himself and went up the stairs. He didn't need this. The household didn't need it. He sat on the toilet seat and pondered. There was a bond between himself and Sarah, an invisible cord which would keep them joined for ever. Often, they communicated without needing words; within the exclusive bell house gang, Simon and Sarah had their own special arrangement, a relationship in which a glance could carry a whole chapter of information.

He opened the bathroom door, noticed that Mrs Thornton's door was ajar. He knocked and she opened it wide. 'Come in,' she said, seating herself in an easy chair while Simon hovered near the window. 'What's the matter?' she asked eventually.

He bit his lip. 'I don't want you to go. I want you and Jay to stay here with us.' He swivelled and looked hard at the housekeeper. 'Is it wrong for me not to want my mother back?'

Betty knew she must tread softly. 'Whatever's gone on, Simon, Mrs Butlin is still your mother and she always will be.'

'She ran away.'

'Folk make mistakes, son. Even the best people do things wrong sometimes.'

'If I had to choose, I'd pick you,' he whispered. Ma had hurt him too deeply and only now, when she had come to visit, did he realize how injured he must have been feeling. Caroline Butlin had not loved her children enough. 'She didn't even bring Stella,' he grumbled.

Betty offered no reply. She was flattered by what the boy had said, but this was, indeed, just a boy. He was a child confused by the actions of his own mother and now, settled as he was into a new way of life, he wanted no further disruptions.

'Am I a bad person?' he asked.

'No, Simon, you most definitely are not bad. Don't be thinking of yourself in that way. It's just been hard for you, that's all. And with the new school coming up and everything, you're facing more changes. Change is never easy, even for grown-ups.'

'I can't do anything about anything, can I? She's down there with two nuns, the sort of people who will soon be tormenting Maddy and Amy. Why is she with nuns?'

'I've no idea.'

He stared at his shoes for a few moments, then left the room. But he did not rejoin his sister, his mother and the strangely clad intruders. No. He opened the front door and ran as fast as his legs could manage, through the main street, past Maddy and Amy, past all the shops.

By the time he came to a halt with a stitch in his side, he was almost out of Rivington Cross and certainly out of breath. And, deep down inside himself, he knew that he was trying to run away from life itself. He also realized that he could never do that, so he simply retraced his steps and walked back home. There was nowhere else to go. For a child, there was no alternative.

EIGHT

The house was empty without her. Everything echoed – his footfalls, a cough, a dropped spoon. How had the presence of just one other person managed to make the house so much fuller and warmer? The daily grind was killing him, backwards and forwards to the homes of women who wanted bargain-priced clothes, then the market, wholesalers, factories where seconds were sold at a fraction of their cost. Work was all he had. He wasn't one for propping up the bar at his local, wasn't keen on cinema, did not relish the idea of hanging around in the Palais dance hall – he would never find the courage to ask anyone to dance, anyway.

There was nothing for him any more. Many women would not give him a second glance, because he was no oil painting and the lisp was sometimes a problem, so how could he go on? There was no-one to soak up the sound, to make a meal, to clatter about in that suddenly unproductive kitchen.

She had been different. She hadn't judged his appearance, his speech difficulties, his way of life. Caroline had seemed to slip into his life like an old glove onto a familiar hand, had accepted him, had walked away from a comfortable life with scarcely a backward glance. Her husband had bored her. 'She won't go back to him,' he informed the empty grate. 'So where the bloody hell is she?'

He had scoured the streets, had searched everywhere, had even driven past the walls of that convent just in case she had been given the job. But she was nowhere. 'Has to be somewhere. Everybody has to be bloody somewhere.' He picked a chip out of the paper and chewed absently. Since Caroline had abandoned him, his diet had consisted almost exclusively of ready-to-eat foods: fish and chips, pies, pasties. He took breakfast in a small café in town, lunch at a different location each day, and supper, which was now congealing in his hands, usually from the fish and chip shop.

Thinking back, he remembered making her laugh. His grandfather had once told him that women liked to laugh. 'If you can make her laugh, you're halfway there,' the old man had said. And it had worked. Up at the vicarage with cups of tea and scones, he had amused her for weeks on end. Vicars didn't tell jokes, it seemed. She had taken some persuading, of course, had worried about leaving her children, but gradually he had worn her down. The vicar was a good father, the children had each other for company and

Caroline had wanted to snatch back some life.

There was a nagging doubt at the back of his mind, a piece of discomfort which had driven him all the way to Manchester today. There he had found a bookshop with a second section in the back, a place where special titles were kept away from the general public. The password, given to him by another market trader, had opened up a whole new world for Derek Ramsden. He had paid a high price, but he was now the owner of two limited editions that concentrated on the etiquette of sexual behaviour. Some of the illustrations excited him, but when he had read certain texts he realized that he was easily aroused and soon spent, and that his behaviour was not designed to satisfy a woman. So. Now he knew.

There was something wrong with him. She should have said, should have told him, ought to have helped him. It wasn't his fault. He'd always been like this, even with Beryl . . . She had been highly strung and had killed herself. But it wasn't his fault, it wasn't, it wasn't!

Angry now, he jumped up, chips scattering all over the floor as he leapt to the overmantel mirror. The man who stared back at him was abnormal. It was in the books. A proper man kept going, knew how to prepare a woman, didn't go to pieces within a couple of minutes. Why had no-one ever taken the trouble to explain?

Then there was the other thing – the losing of his temper. Some part of him must have realized all along that there was something wrong. He always became frenzied and furious with his partner and ended up damaging her, hitting her, pretending to strangle her. 'You're not right,' he said to the looking glass. 'You never were right. Nobody ever cared enough to tell you, not even your own wife. All these years and you weren't doing it properly.' Would a doctor help?

Derek Ramsden could not envisage himself opening up to the crusty old tyrant who had been his general practitioner for at least two decades. And it would probably involve specialists examining private parts. He could imagine them all sniggering in the hospital canteen afterwards. No. He wasn't going to turn himself into a joke, no bloody way. A feeling of desperation and hopelessness overcame him. What could he do?

He picked up one of his purchases. It waxed on about men keeping going for twenty minutes, half an hour, controlling their thoughts and managing to hang on until the woman was satisfied. No way would he ever be able to perform satisfactorily unless he got some help. Help? Where could a bloke turn for the kind of education he needed?

A tiny seed took root in the back of his mind, its tendrils spreading forward while he made himself a cup of tea in his dirty, disordered kitchen. There were women who made their living on their backs. He stirred in an extra spoonful of sugar, because he needed energy to work his way through this one. He couldn't allow one of those women to come here – oh, no, he would never bring a prostitute home. But if he gave himself a different name and if she had her own place . . . or if he took a room in a bed and breakfast . . .

He sat down again by the fireplace. The only way of managing this was to ask a woman about it, find out what she needed. The books wanted reading from cover to cover, then hands-on experience would be the next step. He would show them all, by God he would.

Betty Thornton's feathers were ruffled, as were Simon Butlin's. James, who had been out looking for conkers during the unexpected visit, had not seen the mistress of the house and her two companions, but when he returned from his expedition he was aware of an atmosphere in the place. 'What's the matter?' he asked his mother's back. She was washing teacups and making quite a noise as she performed the task. 'You'll break something in a minute, Mam.'

Betty was muttering. 'You do your best,' she grumbled under her breath, 'try to make life easier for folk who have been left to starve . . .' She clattered a saucer onto the drainer. 'And what do you get? Two nuns and a loose woman swanning in as if they own the place. Me? Oh, I'm nowt a pound, me, just a servant. May God forgive me, but I don't like that wife of Mr Butlin's.'

James was hearing half a story and could not piece together the fragments, so he wandered off in search of more congenial company. With his mother in a mood like this, he might have expected better sense out of a brick wall.

Betty was still clattering when the vicar wandered in. She had finished with the tea things and had moved all the way up to cooking pots and pans. Deafened by her own noise, she did not hear him as he entered by the back door. 'Nuns?' She banged a large stockpot onto newly spread shelf paper. 'Nuns? They're the ones on sale at nowt a pound, not me.'

'Mrs Thornton?'

She froze for a split second before turning to face him. 'Yes?'

'Are you all right?'

Was she all right? Was she heck as like. 'I'm very well, thank you.'

He blinked. 'You seem to be unlike your normal self.'

It was time to come clean. She paused for another few moments to compose herself before speaking again. 'Will you listen to me for a while, Mr Butlin?'

'Of course. That's my job, is it not?' He sat at the kitchen table and motioned her to do the same.

She placed herself in the chair opposite his. 'I know we can all say we've had a hard life, but some of us get affected by it. My mam and dad – they live in Bolton now – he's an engineer and she's a full-time nuisance – are Catholics. Fanatical ones. I won't go into details now, but the main thing I remember about being a child is fear. Fear of mortal sin, fear of all the venial sins mounting up on my soul to make a mortal one, fear of hell, of purgatory, of confession. I was frightened to death by them.'

234

'By your parents?'

'Well – yes – but mostly by priests and nuns. An Irish Catholic life isn't easy. My parents were born in Liverpool – so was I – but all four grandparents were Irish immigrants – mad, they were. And drunk. But drunk was all right as long as you went to church. Hitting your kids was all right. Everything was all right as long as you went and put money in the plate so as the priest could get drunk, too.'

He nodded, noticing yet again how her accent slipped back to her Liverpool roots whenever she became agitated. But why was she upset today? Had her background suddenly caught up with her? Was she starting some kind of nervous episode?

'She's been here.'

'Your mother?'

Betty shook her head. 'She'll be looking for me, but she'll not find me here, Mr Butlin. No. Your wife was here.'

Brian Butlin frowned. 'You should have fetched me – I was in the vestry mending prayer books.'

'I never thought,' she answered. 'And the reason why I never thought was I went upstairs to my room and left her to it. Because she didn't come by herself. She's left her address on a piece of paper under the clock through there.' Betty waved a hand in the direction of the sitting room. 'And her address is St Anne's Convent, Hawthorne Road, Bolton. There's a phone number on it, too.' The woman had called up the stairs just before leaving, had informed Betty about the address 'for my husband'.

235

The vicar's eyes widened. 'Really? So she isn't with that . . . person any more?'

'Well, I can't see them letting a man and a woman live together in a convent, can you?'

'No, indeed.'

Betty inhaled deeply before launching into her next paragraph. 'She brought two of them here. Into your house, Mr Butlin. Two Cross and Passions, they were, them that teach up at the convent school. Hard as nails and bold as brass they sat there, both waiting for cups of tea and looking at photos and going on about what a lovely house this is.' She paused for breath. 'Mrs Butlin came in here to make a brew and I felt as if I was in the way, so I went upstairs for an hour. Then your Simon came up and begged me not to leave, said he's happier with me and James than he was with his mam. So she's got him all confused as well. It's a shame.'

Brian placed elbows on the table and cupped his chin in his palms. 'Oh, dear. Well, they are her children, Mrs Thornton, and she has every right to visit. But she should have informed me.'

'Shock of my life,' muttered Betty, 'seeing them sitting there in that parlour. It was as if I'd gone back to my childhood, back to Scotland Road and the cane for missing Mass. I mean, I know my James plays with those two Catholic girls and very nice they are, but I don't want him anywhere near nuns and priests. I don't like that religion.'

'So I gathered.' What Brian didn't like was the idea of Simon not loving his mother. She was the person who had birthed him and, whatever

236

her behaviour, she was an important figure in the boy's life. 'I shall have to visit the convent,' he said, almost to himself.

'Well, I'd rather you than me. Is it all right if I get on now, Mr Butlin? Only I've a couple more shelves to paper.'

He nodded, clearly distracted.

Betty continued with her work, but more quietly this time. She heard the scrape of his chair, knew when he left the room, listened to a small chime as he lifted the clock in order to retrieve his wife's note. 'I don't feel safe any more,' she whispered. 'Because if she comes back here, there's no way I can stay.'

She papered her shelves and rearranged their occupants according to size, pots at one end, pans at the other. The curtains needed washing, so she climbed onto the sink and dragged them down, all her anger going into rubbing, scrubbing and wringing out the material.

It wasn't right, she thought as she pegged out her washing on the line. The woman had made her choice and should be forced to stick to it. Comings and goings were bad for any child. Caroline Butlin was a bad woman and that was an end to it.

'You must come, Celia, for this is too much for a woman who has reached my age. Anna has gone to town to collect things needed for George's new school, he has gone with her, and everything is happening while I am alone.' She had arranged to be alone, but she didn't bother to mention that fact.

Celia, who was still a little timid about leaving the house, viewed the sight of Yuspeh Feigenbaum at her most excited. She looked like those two nuns who had visited the vicarage earlier, all black clothes and fussy movements. 'What are you talking about, Mrs F?' she asked. And why had nuns visited a Church of England vicar?

'They are come. I was sitting there doing my darning and a man came to the door and left them. In a big box. They cannot stay in big box for too long, because they need to get used to their new home. So you will help me, no?'

Ah. The chickens, mused Celia. The reputation of Mrs Feigenbaum's chickens had preceded them by a matter of weeks, as she had enthused on the subject to anyone who would listen. Should she have a cockerel? Would a cockerel disturb the neighbours? No, the hens needed no cockerel if they were not intended to breed and yes, they would lay eggs with or without a male bird in their midst. However, social groupings depended on a masculine presence, so the idea of a cockerel had not been completely ruled out thus far. 'How many?' she asked.

'I don't know. They sound like a lot, but they may be angry in a box. I am planning to start with eight, but there may be twelve. They are not tiny chickens no more, but they are not full-grown birds, I think. Well? Will you come?'

'Yes.' Celia picked up her cardigan and walked to the door.

As they made their way up to the Forrester/ Feigenbaum home, Celia noticed the housekeeper at the vicarage knocking the dust out of a door-mat. From the expression on the woman's face, she looked as if she really wanted to be kicking the life out of some human being or other.

Yuspeh followed. Thank God so far, because Celia was in want of a shove from time to time. She needed to get back into life and chickens were the ideal excuse for dragging her out of her home. And it was a very big box. 'Wait, wait,' she cried until Celia slowed down for her. 'Is the same in the Bolton markets – Anna is all the while rushing here and there while I am walking slower. I am old. Remember that.' There was a little colour in Celia's cheeks and Yuspeh was pleased to see it.

The box was in the back garden. Both women stood and listened to the noises from within, then Yuspeh undid the latch and opened the lid. She watched Celia's face, saw the smile tugging at her mouth's corners, noticed that the woman's hands were twitching and longing to pick up these sweet little birds. 'They pretty, no?' No female could ever fail to notice beauty in the young of any species.

'Very pretty. There are ten. I think there are ten, but they don't keep very still, do they?'

Yuspeh tapped the side of her nose. 'For this, we have answer. You pick up a bird and shout "one", I pick another and shout "two", then we shall know what we are having here.'

They were 'having' eleven. Eleven lunatics were released into their run. They scuttered up and down, entered the hen house, had a long conversation about the accommodation, then

239

re-emerged. They found water-feeders and chicken food and immediately set about the important task of growing bigger.

'We have tea,' pronounced Yuspeh. 'I got apple pie with the custard, and I know that English peoples like these things. I, too, am fond of Anna's apple pies. Come and tell me what you have been doing and how you have been keeping.'

They took tea at the kitchen table and Celia announced that she would be returning to work in a matter of days. 'The other lady will share with me at first. I am not good in the mornings, so she will cover those. As soon as I am able, I'll be back to full time.'

'Good.' Yuspeh scraped the last of her custard from the dish. 'This news is making me happier. You are not a woman for the idleness.'

Celia looked round the room. It had shelves, pots and pans, jelly moulds, a bread bin – it was just like anyone else's house. Why had she expected a Jewish home to be different? she asked herself. Had she been anticipating a crowd shouting, 'Death to all Christians'? 'What's it like being Jewish in a Christian country?' she asked.

'We are always in Christian country,' answered Yuspeh smartly. 'Christians killed six million of us not very long ago.'

Celia swallowed hard. She had never thought of it that way. Were Nazis Christians? If they were, she certainly knew no others who were so evil. 'Why did they pick on Jews?' she asked.

'Gypsies, too. Oh, why not? You think this is first time? No, no. In London the Mile End was

240

made to keep out the Jews and stop them handling the money. An Italian family was brought in and the Jews were forbidden to trade within that mile. Always, we are persecuted.'

Celia was uncomfortable. All that she had been told, all that had been drilled into her, seemed so vicious. They killed the Son of God and were therefore condemned to be unloved for ever? A whole race?

She happened to glance sideways out into the back garden and her train of thought was immediately broken. 'Oh, no!' she cried. 'There's a dog in with the chickens.' Monty had jumped onto the hen house and down among the chicks.

Yuspeh stood up and surveyed the scene. 'That is a sheepdog? Look at him. I think we have today invented a new breed – the hendog. He is happy, no?' The daft dog was lying there with chickens all over him. They pulled his hair, pecked at his ears, seemed to be grooming him.

'That is so funny.'

Yuspeh laughed. 'Is it? The dog lies with the chickens – why not? Why should not a dog live among chickens? Why should not a Christian break bread with a Jew? Is same thing.' She reached across the table and placed her hand on Celia's. 'We are all with the one same God. Remember that.'

'I will,' answered Celia.

Yuspeh raised her cup. 'Mazel tov,' she said.

Celia smiled. 'Mazel tov.' She had no idea what it meant, but she said it anyway.

* * *

'He'll have her back. It will be his Christian duty to have her back. Our dad's a vicar.' These words, spoken earlier in the evening by Sarah Butlin, echoed through Jay Thornton's mind. Being good hadn't been easy, but it was a heck of a sight easier up here than it had been down there. 'Down there' was Bolton, grey skies, narrow streets, too many people. 'Up here'? Oh, it was different, all right. He had seen rabbits, even a fox, was able to hear the hoot of an owl once night had fallen. There was space, oodles of it, vast expanses of grass and woodland, places in which a boy could run, climb and feel free.

'He'll have her back.' Jay swallowed. If Mrs Butlin came back, he and his mother would probably have to leave. Mam hadn't been able to keep still after that visit. She had washed everything that didn't move, had even washed Monty – who did move – after he had called round whilst covered in chicken droppings with feathers stuck into them. The dog had stood like a martyr in the old zinc tub on the path, had not complained at all when Betty had scraped away at him. Mam's behaviour meant that she, too, was worried about something – and the something was probably the idea of moving back to Bolton.

What could be done? Jay tossed and turned in the bed in his own little room under the eaves, this special place where he kept his collection of strangely shaped twigs, stones, even the skull of a rabbit – well, he thought it had once been a rabbit. A night bird trilled outside. It wasn't an owl, might have been a nightingale.

This could all be taken away if Mrs Butlin came back. Simon didn't seem to want his mother; he was happy with Jay and Mam, but Sarah was different. Sarah was a girl and girls always wanted their own mother. When would it happen? Tomorrow, the day after, next week? Back to Sunning Hill, to the streets of Daubhill, to the Methodists?

'I'm not going,' he advised his pillow. 'I am not, not, not going.' With every 'not', he bashed the same pillow with a clenched right fist. He would find somewhere, would become a free man, one who lived out under the sun, moon and stars. There were farm buildings all over the place, sheds, barns, even a few deserted houses. Food he would need to steal. As for clothes . . .

Running away was fast becoming a complicated business. He got out of bed, found torch, pencil and a scrap of paper. The list took several minutes to write. Food, drink, clothes, candles, matches, torch, bandages, notebook, pencils and sharpener, blanket, quilt for the winter, binoculars – where did Mr Butlin keep those? – as much money as he could find, soap, towels, compass.

It took three trips. By two o'clock in the morning, he had everything except the binoculars hidden in a large, hollow tree stump in the woods. The binoculars had been impossible to find, so he would need to depend on his eyesight. He sat on the sturdier edge of the trunk and wondered whether he was being daft. What he was doing was naughty and he could accept that, but was it silly? No. Silly would be sitting there until Mam said the dreaded word, 'Pack'. This way, he had a chance, at least.

Should he leave a note for Mam or for Sarah and Simon? Better not. He had stolen a couple of stamps and a few envelopes, so, once he was clear of Rivington Cross, he would go during darkness to another village and post a letter to Mam. That would let everybody know that he was all right and that they were not to worry and start a search. Jay knew what he was doing. He was nine now and nearly grown-up, so he could look after himself.

He gazed through the trees at the reservoir and realized how much he was going to miss Sarah and Simon. Living here, he had not felt like an only child, because Mr Butlin had treated him almost as he would treat a son, with firm kindness and respect. He would miss George, Maddy and Amy, too. He would miss the gang, the bell house and—

He knew where the key was. He could sneak back and leave messages there and they could do the same for him. His heart quickened. This promised to be a real adventure, adults versus children. But he would have to stay within reach of the vicarage, must not go further away than Horwich or Rivington itself, which was just a couple of miles along the road. So he had the rest of tonight in which to find a place for all his stuff and that would take another three trips. North, he told himself. He would follow the compass and find the nearest deserted farm building and that would become his base.

As he was deciding what to carry first, a

movement caught his eye. He turned, saw nothing, continued to sort his belongings. An unmistakable splash reached his ears. Putting his blanket back into the tree trunk, he stepped through the trees, noticing that some leaves had begun to crisp their way towards autumn. Cautiously, he approached the water. There was a killer about and he needed to be careful and very, very quiet.

Standing at the water's edge was an extremely fat man. He wore a long black cape and he seemed riveted to the spot, as if making sure that whatever he had thrown in had sunk. Jay did not need to get any closer – he knew this person, had seen him out and about in the village on many occasions. A Catholic priest? Why would a man of God be out in the dead of night throwing things into the reservoir?

It hadn't been a body, Jay decided. A body would have made a louder splash, especially if a weight had been tied to it. Nettie Bradshaw's body had been weighted and the rope had slipped from its anchor, allowing her to float to the top again. So had this been a smaller body, a child, perhaps? Was the Catholic priest a murderer? And if he was simply getting rid of household refuse, people had been in trouble for throwing rubbish into the reservoir, so why was the priest disobeying the rules?

A dry twig snapped under Jay's foot and he froze. The sound seemed to echo across the water, as if the trees served to bounce it back over and over again so that the whole world could hear it. He dropped to his knees. The priest was moving in his direction. Throwing caution to the winds, the boy decided to save himself no matter what. He stood up and launched himself in the direction of the graveyard. With his lungs heaving, he picked the key from beneath its urn, ran to the bell house and opened the door. Inside, his breathing bounced off the walls and he fought to contain it. He dared not move, was afraid to light a candle.

After what seemed like many minutes, Jay heard the heavy footfalls he had been expecting. The priest was not a quick mover and, with any luck, he would not have identified the child who had been spying on him earlier. The door handle rattled. Jay pressed a hand to his mouth and swallowed a scream. He had locked the door, yes, yes, he had.

This was a crypt, the others had told him, a holy place into which aged bones had been placed for storage so that newer graves might be dug. The bones had been allowed to pile up; then, once the pile had grown large enough, remnants of several Christians had been reverently returned to the earth in a shared grave. There were no ghosts, he told himself firmly. The people whose bones had rested here would not come back to haunt him now.

He heard the priest as he moved away from the door, and then, about half a minute later, the upper door of the bell house was rattled. That, too, was locked. Yet again, heavy footsteps walked past the back of the bell house and paused before walking away. As far as Jay could work out, the priest had returned to the woods.

What now? Would the priest be waiting? Had he found the cache of running-away things in that hollow tree? Too scared to shift even an inch in the blackness, Jay remained where he was for a period that seemed endless. For the first time, the idea of running away did not seem so wonderfully clever.

Michael Sheahan walked back to the water's edge. If that had been a poacher, it had been a very small one. Anyway, what had the person seen? Nothing. Just a man throwing a package into some water, that was all. Just a man? He looked down at his cloak, wishing he had not worn it. This particular mode of dress advertised his calling and, probably, his identity.

It was nothing to worry about, he told himself repeatedly. The shotgun would be under millions of gallons of water by now and would not resurface as she had done. He looked around, saw no movement, walked back to the presbytery. Inside, he poured himself a treble Irish and downed it in two swallows. Now he would have to eat, because the whiskey would affect his blood sugar. Not wanting to eat, knowing that food would take the edge off the alcohol, he made himself a cheese sandwich and forced it down.

What a mess. Insulin twice a day, cut down on the drink, eat sensibly, no quarter given. It was an unforgiving condition and it was ruining his already limited life. He sat down in an armchair and swallowed the last of the sandwich. Someone had been out there at well gone two o'clock in the morning, but such a person was probably a breaker of the law, a poacher or a burglar, so why should he worry? It had looked like a child, but could not have been a child, not at that time of night.

He drifted into a fitful sleep and was immediately plagued by nightmare.

She was at his door for a second time, the gun held before her. But she tripped over the mat and fell headlong into the house. 'Got you now,' he said as he retrieved the gun.

'Shoot me,' she shouted. 'Go on, shoot me.' But he chose not to shoot her. He hit her in the face with the butt of the gun, picked up her thin scarf and strangled her. It was so easy. She was a strong girl and he was a weak man, yet she went like a light, a thin, naked flame blown out in a draught. It was almost as if she had come here to die, as if she had volunteered.

He spoke her name, 'Bernadette?', and held to her nose and mouth a small looking glass taken from her handbag. Nothing. There followed a time of trembling while he came to terms with what he had done. But what choice had there been? It was self-defence, no more and no less. A couple of whiskeys helped the shaking to stop.

There was little else to do. He cleaned up the disorder, returned the mat to its rightful place, set straight a small table which had tipped over during the brief sequence. He found rope in the shed, sat with the body for some hours, waiting until he was sure the whole village would be asleep. Then, gathering every last ounce of strength, he tied her up in her raincoat and carried her to the reservoir. The most difficult part was the stone. He fastened the rope round it and round her waist, then tipped her and it into the water. She was gone; she could plague him no more.

But she did. As he half turned to set off homeward, she rose up and walked on the slick, still surface, water pouring from her mouth, from her nose, cascading from her hair. 'Murderer!' she screamed. 'Rapist!' Her eyes, wide and staring, seemed to burn straight through him – he could feel the pain in his head.

He began to run, but his legs had turned leaden. She came closer, so close that he could feel the icy breath of the dead on his neck. 'No!' he screamed. 'Get away from me. No, no no!'

The final 'no' woke him. His breathing was rapid and his heart was pumping like an ill-timed engine, but she was not here. She was in a grave – he had prayed over her, had watched as she had been lowered into the earth. Yes, she had come back, but not walking. And no-one suspected him. Who in their right mind would think a priest could commit murder?

That doctor, perhaps, and he had gone. The new doctor was not pleasant, but what could she do about Phil Bennett's suspicions? He was safe, was guarded by Hippocrates. Gradually, his breathing returned to normal and he made his way up to the bedroom. One thing was certain – he would never again eat cheese in the middle of the night.

*   *   *

As minutes dragged by, Jay began to discern the edges of items and he felt his way to a crate where he sat for what seemed like hours. Running away no longer seemed an attractive option. The family would tell the police and, in view of recent events, the bobbies would take his disappearance seriously. It was a bad idea.

So, what now? He could not very well go outside, not while there was a chance of the priest's being around. The man must have been up to no good, or he would not have followed Jay. There seemed no alternative but to sit here until morning came. He nodded, woke, nodded again.

When he came to, Jay was lying on the floor of the bell house. He was cold, almost frozen to the bone. What time was it? Cautiously, he felt his way to the door, turned the key and opened it. It was morning, but a mist lay over the graveyard and he knew that the dew was still falling. He had to be quick. Locking the door carefully behind him, he placed the key in its usual place and began the task of collecting his ill-gotten gains from their hiding place, all the time glancing around to make sure he was alone.

He managed to complete his task in two journeys, looked at the clock in the sitting room and saw that it was five minutes to six. Swiftly, he began the business of returning everything to its proper location, right down to the two stamps he had stolen from the bureau. As he closed the drawer, he made a decision. There was a person in this house whom Jay would have trusted with his life. He would find Mr Butlin later today and would tell him all that had happened. It was time to be a man and there was more than one way of achieving that. 'I'll talk to him,' he said as he slipped into his comfortable bed. 'Mr Butlin will look after us.'

Amy had been doing a great deal of thinking since Nettie's death. For the most part, she wondered about her nephew and where he might be, worried in case he should turn out to be unhappy or poor. She could not broach the subject with either of her parents. Even had her mother been in the best of health – and she certainly was not – Amy could not have discussed what she had heard while eavesdropping on the stairs. As for her father – well, he was a good man, but he didn't like complications, and Nettie's son would certainly have been a complication. An illegitimate grandchild was a source of shame, but it was not the child's fault. Wherever he was in this big, wide world, Amy wanted more than anything to find him.

Maddy was face down on her bed, elbows bent, hands propping her chin. She had taken to reading about different religions and was currently making her way through parts of a book named the Qur'an.

'Maddy?'

'What?'

'Where am I supposed to go if I want to find out about my nephew?'

Maddy rolled over and sat up. 'Well, there's the registry – that's where all births, marriages and deaths are recorded. I've heard Dad talking

251

about it when he has needed a death certificate from relatives before a funeral.'

Amy chewed a fingernail. 'I don't think they'd help a child, though. It would have to be a grown-up. And who can I ask? If people round here got to know about Nettie having a baby, my mother would die of shame. She's only just starting to think about going back to work properly. Anyway, I don't trust anybody.'

Maddy thought about it. 'The baby may not have been registered as Nettie's. When did she have him?'

'No idea.'

'Then with no date, all you have is Nettie's name. Somebody would have to go through all the details of births under Bradshaw, in case he was registered as hers. That could take ages. You don't know where she had him – at home or in a hospital. Oh, Amy, I wouldn't know where to start. You need to ask an adult you can trust.'

Amy shrugged. 'Well, there's Father Sheahan. He isn't supposed to tell secrets, is he?'

Maddy shook her head vigorously. 'Not on your Nellie, as my mother would say. He's creepy. I wouldn't trust him as far as I could lift him off the floor – and I'd need a crane to do that. No, not him.'

'Then who, Maddy? Who is there?'

'I don't know.' With a piece of gossip as juicy as this promised to be, Maddy could come up with no name. Even her own mother might let something slip in the middle of doing some complicated hairstyle. It wasn't that she didn't trust her family, Maddy told herself firmly. But people forgot themselves at times. It needed to be someone whose whole life was built on the confidence of others. 'We can't afford a lawyer,' she said.

'Or a private detective,' Amy added. 'Isn't it strange that we can trust our friends with just about anything? Yet when it comes to adults, we can come up with no names.'

'Mr Butlin.'

Amy stared at her best friend. 'What? Are you serious?'

'Yes, I am. You know how all the biddies in the salon keep saying he's boring? Well, that's because he doesn't gossip. You won't find him standing in the street pulling somebody to pieces. But I do know this – he goes and sits with sick or troubled people. When he comes back and Sarah asks where he's been, he just tells her he's been out and around on parish business. I reckon you could tell him just about anything. My dad trusts him.'

Amy's eyebrows shot upward. 'So the Protestant vicar is a better man than our Catholic priest?'

'Yes. One hundred per cent. Father Sheahan's horrible. You know it even if you won't say it. So, if you want me to come with you to see Sarah's dad, I will.'

'But—'

'Never mind the buts. Leave butting to the goats. You need to talk to someone and I've thought of the someone. He won't look down on you, Amy. He won't judge Nettie or anything she

253

did. And if he can find any answers for you, I bet he will.'

Amy felt uncomfortable. After years of indoctrination from school, from the church and from her parents, she could not but believe that Catholicism was the one true faith. Only Catholics would enter the kingdom of heaven and, even then, entrance would be restricted to Catholics with clean souls. Mortal sin meant damnation and hell happened to those who were allowed to look upon God before being forced to leave Him for all eternity.

With venial sin, there was some sort of bartering system in which a spirit had to serve time in purgatory until said spirit was as clean as a whistle. So, although heaven was timeless, hell and purgatory were clearly run by Greenwich or some similar base where experts handled the measurement of years, days, hours, minutes and seconds.

'You're thinking again.' Maddy's tone was accusatory.

'Yes.' The unbaptized went to limbo, but there was some kind of hope in that area, too, because an unbaptized man could enter heaven from his deathbed because he wished he had been baptized – that was Baptism of Desire. Then there was Baptism of Blood, where someone died for a just cause, and—

'Amy?'

'What?'

'Stop it. It's like going to see a doctor, that's all. Like your mother nearly had to – remember? How your dad was saying that she might have to go for a rest? Well, she would have seen head doctors and they are people who help mend your mind. They might not have been Catholics.' She waved her Qur'an. 'They could have been Muslims, Buddhists, Methodists – whatever.'

'I know, but—'

'But what?' Maddy was coming to the end of her tether. 'Who helped your mother get better at the finish? Who was it took her and threw her in at the deep end with chickens and chicken feed and Monty?'

Amy gulped. 'It was Mrs Feigenbaum.'

'Yes, it was. And what is Mrs Feigenbaum in the religious sense?'

'She's a Jew.'

Maddy hung on to her equilibrium by taking a series of deep breaths. 'So, Amy, a woman descended from the people who killed Jesus was the one who set your mam straight. Am I getting through?'

'I think so.'

'Well, it's not before time. Look at your mam and Mrs Feigenbaum – thick as thieves, they are. That old lady has done more for your family than any other person whatsoever – certainly more than Father Sheahan ever did. Your mother goes into a Jewish home and eats scones and drinks tea and gets advice from someone older than herself. I'd never have believed that could happen in a million years, with your mam being so . . . I think it's called prejudiced – I'll look it up. In your mother's case, it means Catholic to the bones. But that strange thing did happen. If your mother can do it, we can. So, we go to Mr Butlin. Right?'

'Right.'

'Say it as if you mean it, Amy Bradshaw.'

'Right. And I mean it.'

Maddy walked to her bookshelf. She would look up 'prejudiced' just to make sure she had used the correct word.

NINE

'Am I a good person?' Brian Butlin looked at the face in the mirror. This was no outstanding specimen of humanity, just a large man with ordinary blue eyes and ordinary mid-brown hair. Ordinary was the correct word. Normal. Nothing to write home about, not the sort of chap one might expect to see in a cinema film. But who was he inside, where it mattered?

His father had been a vicar, as had his grandfather, as was his one surviving uncle. It was as if the family passed the calling down along the line, rather like a chain of butcher shops or a circus background – here come the clowns. Brian was yet another Butlin pastor. He had a parish of a decent size and he did his duty wherever possible, was not the greatest maker of sermons on God's earth, did not possess any breadth of imagination. 'Which is why your wife left you.' He combed his hair and adjusted the dog collar. Had he not loved her enough? Had he ignored her to the point where she had become sufficiently desperate to run off with a man who sold tawdry clothes from a van and a market stall?

There came a point in almost every human's life when stock needed to be taken, an event or a series of events which caused a hiatus, a pause, a summing up of all that had gone before. For history was father of the future and mistakes formed the workbench on which all important plans must be reshaped. He needed to talk to himself and he needed to talk to Caroline. 'I must go to her,' he mumbled, 'but first, I need to know what to say. And to know what to say . . .' His words tailed away.

Finding the text meant finding himself first. Knowing how he had been formed was easy enough – good, decent parents, a minor public school where he had managed to avoid being buggered, a degree in religious studies, college, curacies, a parish. This parish. Here he had met and married Caroline, here they had produced their children, here they had lived together . . . together, yet separate.

'I have never been close to anyone,' he concluded, still staring at his image. He wanted everyone to be happy, needed the world around him to be inhabited by contented people whose lives were fulfilling and untroubled. And, as long as nothing glaringly horrible occurred, he tended to assume that all was well within the realm of domesticity and that no-one was in need of his attention.

Parishioners were different. As primary shepherd, he was honour bound to help the sick, the needy and the dying. These duties he performed as part and parcel of his vocation and, on a one-to-one basis, he invariably gained the trust and affection of his flock. But his family seemed to have no need of him. The twins had arrived as a ready-made pair; they confided in each other and, presumably, in their friends. Caroline? She had busied herself, had done the flowers, had attended functions and services, but had she been happy? It would seem that she had not; it was his fault.

What might he do to regain her affection and respect? He could not imagine himself stepping right out of character and into picture-book lover mode, all languishing looks and meaningful words, a serenade delivered to a balcony on which she was standing. 'No Romeo am I,' he said quietly. Nor had he ever been a bringer of gifts. When had he last presented her with chocolates, a scarf, a dozen roses? Was his neglect in that area the cause of her disappearance? 'Help me, God,' he prayed.

As he continued to stare at himself, an idea gave birth to itself. Perhaps Caroline hated this way of life. Could he give it up for her? Should he? There were possibilities, doors through which he might pass without too much difficulty into the world of education. He could teach – could even lecture – on the subject of Divinity. Or he and his wife might buy a business, a shop of some sort in which they could both invest time and effort.

But he was still skimming the surface, was continuing to think of things practical rather than of elemental factors. Brian Butlin needed to study himself, and not just in a mirror. The wife he loved was living in a Catholic convent for reasons he was yet to discover. Other people would mark the absurdity of the situation, yet he could not. Something had happened to her and he needed to find out the details of her story.

A wry smile appeared on the face in the glass. He had to understand just one single fact. He was a man who loved a woman and he would fight to get her back into his life. Through her and through the efforts he must now make, he would discover who he really was.

The salon was filled to capacity and buzzing with conversation. Yvonne rinsed shampoo from Mildred Cookson's bleached hair, noted some breakages, due, no doubt, to over-liberal applications of peroxide, rubbed in some conditioner. This particular head of hair needed glue to fix it, but Yvonne would just have to make the best of it again. Mildred, who was not particularly well off, thought she was saving money by colouring her crowning glory at home and allowing Yvonne just to set it. A pity. The blond hair aged Mildred, yet nothing could be said, because Mildred thought it suited her.

Hilda Barnes was holding court. As her husband was on Bolton Town Council, the lady had awarded herself a high position in Rivington Cross, and she occupied her invisible podium yet again. 'She's mad,' she declared. 'Wandering up and down with a pram full of wire and wood – and she talks to herself.'

Yvonne bit her tongue. Yuspeh Whatever-her-name-was had done Celia Bradshaw a great deal of good, had probably saved her from nervous breakdown, but what was the use? Going against the opinion of Mrs Barnes would have been like sacrilege, so it was best just to continue with hair.

'I don't want a parting,' said Mildred. 'I want it taken straight back off my face – like that one in the Beverley Sisters.'

Beverley Sisters? Mildred looked more like a prune in a yellow hat. 'It's thinning out a bit, love,' said Yvonne. 'You'll need to take it easy with the colouring.'

Mildred stared in the mirror, her eyes fixed on the hairdresser's reflection. 'Will I have to stop lightening it, then?'

Yvonne raised her shoulders. 'You might be better letting me handle it, Mildred.' The woman was going to end up bald if she didn't stop. What was she using? Lanry? Kitchen floor bleach?

'And what if she changes her mind and gets a cockerel or two?' Hilda Barnes's voice boomed across the room. 'Her back garden'll end up a disgrace. No thought for her neighbours, that one. The noise will be terrible if she decides to breed them.'

Doreen Hardacre took it upon herself to throw in a timid tenpenceworth. 'Hens should be on a farm or a smallholding. I know we all kept them in the war, but that was different. She wasn't here then.'

Yvonne took a small step over the line. 'No, she wasn't. Her son was translating for the War

Office and they were all dodging bombs every night. I believe young George was born in the middle of a terrible raid.'

'Oh, gracious, excuse me,' came the retort from Mrs Barnes. 'If I'm not allowed to speak my mind, I might as well shut up.'

Please do, thought Yvonne before continuing. 'As for the chickens, Jews have to eat stuff slaughtered in a certain way. She can't go wandering into a butcher's and get just any meat. It's got to be kosher.'

'Oh, well. Sorry, I'm sure.' Hilda Barnes patted her pin curls. 'I still think she's a very strange woman.'

Strange? Yvonne Horrocks struggled to get a comb through the tangle of porous wires which attempted to cover Mildred Cookson's head. Even with the conditioner, it was like trying to rake thistles. 'She's kind.'

'But not our kind.' After this supposed witticism, Hilda looked around the salon at the eight or so customers who had come for weekly beautification. With her eyes, she challenged each to disagree with her, was triumphant when not a single word was spoken.

Yvonne tightened her lips against a thousand words that threatened to tumble if she gave them space. If Hilda Barnes stopped coming into the shop, half of the customers might follow her into Horwich for their perms and sets.

'Then there's that vicar.'

Oh, the old vixen was well into her stride. 'Pass me that broad-toothed comb, Mildred,' was all Yvonne said.

'Nuns in his house yesterday. Not C of E, not the nuns from St Augustine's – oh, no. Roman Catholics.' She spat the final three syllables as if ridding her mouth of a nasty taste. 'And that strumpet wife of his. What's she doing with nuns? Is she going to take the veil? Never heard of a married woman doing that before. Wife of a clergyman, too. She wants talking about.'

Yvonne put down the comb. Every instinct of the businesswoman told her to keep her mouth shut, but she had taken enough. There were at least three Catholics in the room – not counting herself – and they had simply looked away when Hilda had emitted her latest barrage of mindless abuse.

The hairdresser swivelled on the spot and eyed the warp-tongued woman who had made herself queen of all she surveyed when her jumped-up bit of a husband had been admitted to the inner sanctum of the Town Hall. 'You *are* talking about her,' she said, her voice dangerously quiet. 'You do nothing else but talk about folk, decent folk. Some of them make mistakes and so do you. Your biggest mistake is that big, flapping gob of yours. It wants sewing up.'

Hilda Barnes's face underwent a sudden change of colour.

Yvonne continued. 'A few weeks back, you were saying you didn't blame Mrs Butlin for leaving. You said the vicar's sermons put you to sleep. What's changed?'

The red-faced woman seemed to be gasping for breath.

'I've heard enough from you to last me a

263

lifetime,' Yvonne said, her voice slightly stronger. 'You flounce in here, act as if you own the whole village, pull people apart.' She glanced around. 'There isn't one of you here who hasn't been stabbed in the back by this old witch.'

Mrs Barnes staggered forward. 'How dare you? I've been coming here to get my hair done for—'

'For long enough.' Yvonne stood tall. 'For too long, in fact. Now, take your nasty, mealy mouth out of my shop and don't ever, ever, set foot in here again. You are banned.' She looked at all the customers in turn. 'And if any of you feel like going with her, get on with it and don't come back. This place is beginning to smell of bigotry.'

Doreen Hardacre shifted in her seat, thought better of it and remained where she was. No-one else moved an inch or a muscle. Mrs Barnes tried to make eye contact with a couple of them, but they seemed engrossed either in the condition of their footwear or in some riveting article in an old *Woman's Weekly*.

'Put your scarf on,' snapped Yvonne. 'After all, it wouldn't do for the wife of a councillor to be seen outside in curlers, would it? You can take them out yourself at home, then shove them through the letter box while I'm shut. I don't want to see you in here again.'

Hilda Barnes regained a little equilibrium, though her cheeks remained bright with embarrassment. 'Are you coming, Doreen?' she asked.

For answer, Doreen Hardacre shook her head.

The angry customer snatched up her bag and coat. 'I've never been so insulted in all my born days,' she shouted.

'Haven't you?' Yvonne picked up her comb and returned to the task in hand. 'That was nothing – I was just warming up.'

'You've not heard the last of this.'

The hairdresser laughed. 'No? Will your hubby bring it up in a council meeting? What's that committee he's on – isn't it something to do with dustbins and street-cleaning? Tell him to stick it in with any other business at the end. Oh, and he can stick you on one of his bin carts, too. Now get out.'

The door closed behind Hilda Barnes. Yvonne was aware of two things – her legs were shaking and the whole room seemed to be holding its breath.

Mildred finally broke the silence. 'Hey, Yvonne?'

'What?'

'Lend us a headscarf, will you? I'll be back in a flash.' She grabbed the scarf and tied it over her wet hair. 'Five minutes. Just five minutes and I'll be here.' She reached the door, stopped, swung round. 'Get in the back,' she ordered Yvonne, 'and find some glasses – cups – jam jars – owt'll do. I'm going home for some of my Colin's parsnip wine. We should celebrate.'

As the door closed, a woman in the corner began to clap. The infection spread. Soon, the whole salon was a riot of 'hoorays' and 'well dones'. Yvonne stopped shaking and took a bow.

Doreen Hardacre stood up. 'A word, please.

Yvonne, can you come to our house tonight and have a talk to my old man? Because if you can get rid of him, I'll leave you all me jewellery.' She glanced down at her worn wedding ring. 'Such as it is, like.'

Yvonne grinned. 'All I want is to keep my customers. I thought I'd lose you, Doreen – and a few more.'

Doreen blew a raspberry. 'You must be joking. Now, where's that bloody woman with her wine? Time for a bit of a celebration.'

Jay knocked timidly on the door of Mr Butlin's little study. Mam had gone out shopping, so the coast would be clear for about half an hour. He knocked again.

'Come in.'

Jay entered the book-lined room in the middle of which sat Mr Butlin behind his desk. He looked very important, like some boss of an office, or, worse still, like a teacher. Jay noticed that he was writing in a large book – politeness was called for. 'Shall I come back later, Mr Butlin?'

'No, James, you step into my parlour, as the spider said to the fly. Sit yourself down and tell me what I can do for you.'

But the lad didn't want to sit. Advertising his agitation by hopping from foot to foot, he began his story, but it came out wrong, which fact served to confuse him even further. And he had planned what to say, but he couldn't remember the plan.

He liked Rivington Cross and didn't want to

leave it because it was green, interesting and had trees and he was a good climber. Methodists were miserable, as was Bolton, and he wasn't keen on the idea of returning to a place with mills and back-to-back houses with outside lavatories and no hot water. He hadn't even started at his new school, so he didn't know whether he would like it and it wasn't fair.

Brian took off his reading glasses and placed them on the blotter. 'I see.' He didn't see – with or without his spectacles – whatever it was the child was trying to communicate, but he was attempting to encourage the poor lad. 'Carry on,' he said.

'So I ran away. Well, I didn't, but I nearly did. I had all the stuff in the empty tree, then it happened and I came back.'

'Yes?'

'Yes. He threw something in the water, so I ran away and hid in—' Jay stopped suddenly. The bell house was a secret and he had better take care. 'I hid in the graveyard. He tried to find me, but he couldn't. I waited a long time, then I came back in and put all the stuff back where I'd pinched it from – even the stamps – you can count them. I didn't keep anything, honest.'

'Right. Now, James, you saw someone doing what?'

James sieved through the muddle. 'Oh, yes. I saw that priest throwing something in the water. Like Amy's sister got thrown in – remember?'

'I certainly do.'

'But this wasn't big. It made the wrong splash for big. But he were – I mean he was chucking something away and why would he do that?'

'When was this?'

'In the middle of the night, but I could see a bit because the moon was there even though it was a little moon. It might have been a new one or an old one, but it wasn't a full one. I snapped a twig with my foot and he heard me.'

Brian offered Jay a sweet from a jar. The boy took it, but placed it in his pocket for later – this was hard enough without trying to chew through a caramel at the same time. 'It was the priest. Fat and in a long, black cloak and he followed me. I ran and ran as fast as I could.'

Brian nodded. He knew for a fact that Father Sheahan had a habit of throwing spent whiskey bottles into the reservoir, but he would not impart that information. Father Michael Sheahan liked to think he could hide his habit from the cleaning lady. 'Why were you running away, James?'

'Because I don't like him.'

'No, I meant why were you planning to run away from Rivington Cross when you are so happy here?'

So Jay began all over again. Mrs Butlin had come with the nuns and Mam hadn't liked it, so her washing up had been loud and then she had started on shelves, curtains and the dog. Jay knew that Mam knew that there was a chance that Mrs Butlin would come back and then a housekeeper wouldn't be needed any more. 'I want to stay up here for ever,' Jay announced. 'So I thought I would run off and live in empty barns. Because I don't want to go back to town.'

Brian tapped the desk with the tips of his fingers. It occurred to him that he had a lot in common with this little boy when it came to expressing himself. In fact, James was probably making a better job than Brian would with Caroline.

'You will not return to Bolton, son. I know of other families round here who need help and we can certainly find lodgings for you. No matter what happens, I shall do all in my power to keep you in or near this village.' And there was no reason why Mrs Thornton and James should not remain at the vicarage. Caroline would settle to the idea – if she did come back and if he decided to continue as vicar.

Jay blinked to hide wet eyes. Mr Butlin was the best man in the world.

'A little trick for you,' said Brian, standing up and leading the boy to the door. 'The moon.'

'Yes?'

'If it looks like a C for coming, it is going. So C is an old moon and a C backwards is a new one.'

'Thank you, Mr Butlin.' Jay closed the door. He had been right in his judgement of the vicar. Not only had he given hope, he had given Jay the moon as well.

Yuspeh Feigenbaum was waxing as lyrically as she could manage to a captive audience of one. She could see that Maddy Horrocks was genuinely interested in life and, at the moment, in Judaism. This was a child who was hungry and thirsty for knowledge and enjoyed learning for learning's sake.

'So it's just one God, like ours?' asked the girl.

'Is same God. God of Israel is God of Islam and of Christianity. Your Jesus is said to be the son of our God. We wait still for our Messiah and he is taking his time.'

Maddy grinned. 'He could sort out Mrs Barnes.'

Yuspeh grinned. 'May her house be filled for seven days with her friends.'

The child's expression requested an explanation. Yuspeh giggled. 'Ah, you are not understanding. When we die, our families sit on low chairs for seven days of mourning. Friends visit and sit for a while. So what I was saying was not nice, because it was a Yiddish curse. We make fun a lot, you see. Sometimes the making of fun is cruel.'

Maddy understood. It was like when Mam said, 'Don't come running to me when your leg's broken.' 'So Abraham was the first – a bit like St Peter was our first pope. Then Abraham's twelve sons made the tribes and they all wandered about for a long time.'

Yuspeh sucked some black tea past her cube of sugar. 'You are nearly arrived, but not yet. It was Jacob, grandson of Abraham, who was having the twelve sons, then we got the twelve tribes of Israel.'

'We did Moses at school. He got everyone away from the Egyptians, didn't he?'

'Yes, he did that. So, you see, the stories you are given in your Catholic school shows you that your roots are same as ours.'

270

'The only difference being Jesus?'

'If you make everything simple, yes. But there is more to the Children of Israel than just that. Many things. Covenant, Shabbat, coming of age at bar mitzvah, taking responsibility for poor, giving charity. Most of all is look after the family. Family is core of Jewish faith. Family is important. My family now is small, but it is my life and this I offer to God, may He be in my house for always.'

'Amen,' said Maddy. 'So that table is ready now for the Sabbath?'

'It is and you must stay and sit with us. All are welcome. You do no harm to pray to your own God in my house. No matter what your rabbi – I mean your priest – is saying, we are all one. Prayers is different, Shabbat different, but we all go one way home. We live, you see, then we die. And the life we live says how we will be after death. So how are we different? There is more sameness than differences is what I want you knowing. You walk with God, I walk with God. You hold one of His hands, I hold another. Road is same, just some small paths goes off to side, but we come together on a bigger road at the end.'

Maddy felt privileged. She was sitting in a Jewish home just before the start of Sabbath and this dear old lady was educating her. Sometimes, a person could learn more out of school than she could in some bone-dry class with a trained teacher and books. 'So you can't work on the Sabbaths?'

'No.'

'Doctors do. And nurses – some of them must be Jews.'

'They will be given permission if the work is to save people. But anything they earn they should give away. My Jakob, he has a Christian associate who runs Jakob's factory from Friday evening until end of work on Saturday. Any money made goes half to Christian man and half to poor. Jakob cannot make money on Shabbat. And we are not strictest – some Jews much more careful than we are. But the rules – we obey most of them.'

Maddy was enraptured by what followed. Jakob, who wore a shawl and a little black cap, entered the room with his wife, who lit the candles. Because there was a visitor, he explained what the celebration was. 'First, Maddy, this is God's day – He rested, so we rest. It is the law. On this day we can neither create nor destroy. Second, we celebrate the escape from Egypt. When they were slaves, Jews could not have a Shabbat – they were forced to work. So now we have Shabbat not just because we must, but because we can.'

He prayed over the bread, broke it and passed it round. He also prayed over the wine and Maddy was reminded of Holy Communion at church – how similar this was to the Catholic service.

The meal was wonderful. Maddy had her first taste of kosher meat and enjoyed it.

Anna smiled at her. 'This kosher chicken we had from the shop in Bolton, Maddy. Although Mamme's chickens grow, she will find a reason every time why they should not be killed.'

Yuspeh tutted loudly. 'They not big enough for eating yet.' She turned to Maddy. 'You do the best for family and what you get? Laughing, joking, making fool of an old woman. For why I try? I ask myself.'

'Because you can,' said Maddy clearly. 'Because there's no slavery and you can, like Mr Forrester just said.'

The old woman laughed loudly. 'See? She has answers. But one word she say wrong. This is Shabbat, Maddy. On Shabbat, my son is Jakob Feigenbaum.' As ever, she had the last word on the subject.

It wasn't easy. He drove around Bradshawgate and the bottom of Deansgate, saw women who might have been prostitutes, wondered how to find out. They seemed to hang about on that corner and down into Churchgate towards the theatres, but they might have been just groups of friends on their way to a function – how was he meant to tell the difference?

After several nights with no satisfactory outcome, it was made easy for him. As he drove at walking pace down Bank Street, a female approached the van. He stopped and she bent to the open window on the passenger side. 'Looking for some company, love?'

He nodded, his throat too constricted to allow speech.

She opened the door and climbed in beside him. Derek breathed in cheap perfume and a whiff of ale.

'Go somewhere quiet,' she said. 'Is there room in the back of the van?'

Nervous now, he coughed to clear his airway. 'No, I've got stock in there. There might be something for you – a blouse or a skirt.'

'That's nice. So where can we go? It's not cold – what about the top of Tonge Moor? There's fields and woods over yon. It depends what you want. If you're just after – well – a hand . . .' she grinned lewdly, 'we could do that anywhere.'

Her accent was broad Lancashire, her teeth were not good and he could see dark roots where the bleached hair had begun to grow out. A picture of Caroline entered his mind and he tried hard to banish it. She had been classy, well spoken and decorative in a quiet way. If it hadn't been for his particular difficulty and his impatience with it, she might have stayed with him. 'I need help,' he managed to say.

'We all do,' replied his companion. 'I've two kids to feed and rent to pay.'

'I mean a different kind of help. I've a problem.'

'Oh. Right.' She waited.

'I'm too . . . too quick,' he said finally.

'And I'm Rose,' she replied with a smile that was meant to be winning. 'Look, love, I deal with all sorts of folk with all kinds of problems. It goes with the job.' Too quick was her idea of an easy customer. And she knew him from somewhere, but she couldn't seem to place him. 'You've not to worry about that type of thing. What's your name?'

'Derek.'

'All right, Derek. Now, it's a fiver for the full business and less if you just want a bit of relief. Do you get me?'

He nodded.

'So, what's it to be and where's it to be?'

'Erm . . . the full thing. I'll drive till we find somewhere quiet.'

She gabbled on about this and that while he drove northward towards the moors. He got a diatribe about the cost of food, nylons, gas, electricity and meat. She was fed up with coppers trying to stop a girl from earning a living, she considered her job to be a necessary service and she was clean, but she had a 'johnny' in her handbag if he wanted to 'use something'. This was hardly the language of love, but what had he expected? he asked himself as he pulled off the road onto an unmade path.

'We can go in them bushes,' she said. 'Then, if you don't mind, you can drive me home – I live in Laycock Avenue just off the ring road.'

He followed her, noticing how she teetered in her high-heeled shoes and how the muscles of her legs seemed over-defined – probably through walking the streets and standing on corners, he pondered. To think that he had come to this, that he had been driven to it through no fault of his own. He was shaking.

She peeled off her coat, spread it on the ground, removed her knickers and flung herself down. 'When you're ready,' she said.

He couldn't do it. He stood there looking down at her and knew that this was not for him. 'I'm not sure,' he said. 'I've never done this

275

before. I don't mean I've never . . . you know . . . I've been married, but she died. But I've never been with a . . . a working woman before.'

'It's all right. Lay yourself down here and I'll sort you out.'

He was still trembling. Slowly, he knelt, then stretched out beside her. She didn't even kiss him. With a deftness that amazed him, she sorted him out. It was plain that she knew all the tricks of her trade, yet this fact served only to terrify him. 'Stop,' he groaned. But it was too late. He was spent before he had even started. Anger loomed over the horizon and he tried to keep it there, but she made a mistake. She laughed. 'Eeh, you have been on short rations, haven't you? Never mind, I won't charge you full for that.'

She wouldn't charge him full? 'You should have let me go at my own pace,' he told her.

She laughed again. 'Well, according to what you said before, that was your pace. Not my fault, love. Not my fault if you can't hold your horses.'

The night darkened. He knelt and looked down on her. She struck a match and lit a Woodbine; he could see the make-up clogging a face with enough lines to carry a network of miniature trains. There were open pores on her nose. Her mouth, as she sucked hard on the cigarette, was pursed and the upper lip was positively furrowed.

She held the match and stared at him. 'I've got you now,' she said triumphantly. 'Ramsden's stall, Bolton market. I bought a lemon jumper off you last winter and it shrank when I washed it. You can't win, can you?' She laughed again, was clearly amused.

Derek Ramsden entered a place the edge of which he had seen before – his own particular hell. He almost stood back and watched himself, became a mere spectator to the frenzy which followed. She struggled. For a thin woman, she was unbelievably strong. When she finally passed out, he removed the belt from his trousers and strangled her. The Woodbine continued to burn in the grass beside her and he ground it out angrily, making sure it was as dead as she was.

If he had been shaking earlier, he was now like a man with a neurological disorder. A body. He had a body at his feet and he didn't know what to do with it. Had he really done this thing? Had he allowed rage to overcome him to such a point? 'I could hang,' he whispered. 'Why couldn't I stop myself?'

She was forty-five if a day, he thought as he stared at her. Even in near-darkness, she was ugly. She was ugly inside and out, she was disposable, she was a prostitute. Gradually, the shaking subsided and he found himself in possession of a different feeling, something he might have described as victory. He had excised a weeping sore and the world was all the better for his action. Women such as this one should be jailed so that innocent passers-by would not get themselves into difficulties.

Her children would be better off. The town would take them, would put them somewhere safe with a decent family. A glow began to spread itself across his chest – he had done the town a favour and there was one less diseased creature wandering the streets tonight.

As the sun sank, Yuspeh went into the back garden to make sure her treasures were settled for the night. To other people, the chickens were identical, but Yuspeh knew every feather and every character trait. The birds were Rebecca, Naomi, Esther, Sarah, Charity, Ruth, Patience, Joy, Peace, Jezebel – she was busy already looking for a cockerel – and Hilda. Hilda was noisier than the others, so she had been named after Hilda Barnes, who would not recognize silence if it hit her hard in the face.

Yuspeh placed herself on a backless chair whose function these days was to act as a stool. It was a quiet evening and, as summer was coming to a close, there was a freshness in the air, a threat of autumn. She turned and looked through the window, saw Jakob and Anna in each other's arms. 'I am a lucky woman,' she told Jezebel. 'But you feel not so lucky, huh?' she asked the chicken. 'Already I am in trouble with Mrs Barnes. If I bought a cockerel, she would be running me out of the village.'

Unimpressed, Jezebel got on with the task of eating supper.

Anna came out, Jakob by her side. 'Mamme, we want to ask you something.'

'Asking is what I am for. What is it now?'

Anna wanted to return to work. She had not worked since the birth of her only son, and now that he was about to start his secondary education she thought it was time to help her husband in the business. But first she needed Yuspeh's blessing.

'So. You are to do this English thing, then? You leave your parent alone and off you go without looking over shoulder?'

Jakob said nothing – he knew his mother. Anna, who also knew Yuspeh of old, sighed dramatically. 'Oh, well. If you wish me to stay here and drink tea all day, so it shall be.'

Yuspeh nodded. 'Thank you. Then I shall not want for company when my grandson he goes to Bolton School. There is only so much to keep an old lady entertained, and alone is not entertaining.' She walked past them and into the house.

Jakob looked at his watch. 'Two minutes?' he asked his wife.

'Two minutes,' she agreed.

They stood and watched the lunatic chickens for a while. The birds did a lot of 'talking', were very inquisitive and seemed drawn to human company – and to canine acquaintance, as long as the canine was Monty.

'What's she doing?' asked Jakob.

'She's putting the kettle to boil and searching for sugar lumps. She'll be lucky – there was no sugar at the shop today.'

Yuspeh clattered out of the kitchen. 'Where is sugar?'

'We have none,' her son replied.

'Hmmph.'

'Your mother does the best "hmmph" I ever heard.'

'Yes. It is a wonder, isn't it?'

Yuspeh glared at them. 'You really think I will stop you from the work? I don't want any peoples here under my feet. Yes, you do the English thing and I shall be quite content with my darning and my knitting. This is a mother's place, in the background and not to be seen and never remembered.' On this note of pathos, she re-entered the house.

'How did we do?' Anna asked.

'One minute and forty-five seconds.'

'That's good. She is making up her mind more quickly these days.' Then they both laughed, because they knew Yuspeh's game. Right from the start, the answer had been yes, but she pretended to make them suffer all the same.

Dealing with a corpse was not easy. She hadn't gone stiff, but she was an awkward thing to package – getting her back into her coat was not easy. Rose, whom he had known in the biblical sense not at all, and whose acquaintance he had made just about half an hour earlier, seemed determined to make the task in hand as difficult as possible.

'Slow down,' he ordered himself, 'you've got all night.'

He belted the garment, then dragged her to the van, noting that her shoes had fallen off. They would need to be burnt, he supposed. Alive, she had seemed as thin as a rake; dead, she was leaden and very hard work. He made space in the back of the van by piling boxes of stock on each side, then he manhandled her into the narrow centre aisle. Her feet hung out, so he

280

jumped out, bent her knees and forced her to fit the area he had created.

Shoes. Where was her bag? Had she carried a bag? Yes, he remembered her saying that she had contraceptives. He found the cheap plastic item, stuffed her underwear into it, picked up shoes that had probably seen better days and threw these possessions into his vehicle. When the door was slammed shut, he took what seemed to be his first breath in hours. God, what had he got himself into? And why was he smiling?

He had silenced her, yes. He hadn't wanted her talking to her motley friends about Derek Ramsden who had a stall on the market and no stamina. His name would have been mud within a fortnight. But that wasn't the reason for the smile. In spite of his terror, Derek Ramsden was elated. That one would never laugh at him again, would never laugh at any poor beggar. She had needed shifting. The world wanted clearing of women like that. He was simply getting rid of garbage and there was no harm in that.

For a couple of hours, he sat in the driver's seat. Cars passed by down on the main road, but no-one would notice him back here with his lights off. He hoped no courting couples would come this way, but he had to take a chance on that, as he did not want to be driving around for too long with a corpse in the back of his van. Would she spoil any stock? Did bodies leak after death, did they urinate?

'Oh, shut up,' he told himself. There was no

point in worrying about a few twin sets and blouses, was there? One thing was certain – if Derek wanted to carry on practising on prostitutes, he would need to cast his net further afield – Blackburn, Bury, even Manchester. He ate three squares of chocolate, combed his hair, waited for the traffic to die down.

As he sat with nothing to do, he began to ponder the death of Bernadette Bradshaw, the girl from Rivington Cross. Her murderer had not been discovered, even though her body had floated to the surface of that reservoir. If he disposed of Rose in the same way, even if she did get found, her murder would probably be attributed to the same person who had killed the other one.

That was the answer. He waited until midnight, then began the drive up to the highest moors. Anxious not to attract attention, he kept his speed down and drove with extra care. The idea of being stopped by police while the deceased Rose was on board was not a happy one.

There were still a few lights on in the village. He did a tour of the main street, saw the black-clad Jewish woman in her front room, possibly reading if the tilt of her head was anything to go by. A couple of bedrooms at the vicarage were illuminated and he wondered whether Caroline was there, whether she had finally plucked up the courage to go home.

Parking the car as near to the reservoir as he could manage without detection, he realized that he had quite a difficult walk ahead of him through trees and bushes. But that was better than carrying her through open spaces, he told himself sternly. He needed to be alert, because Caroline had told him a few tales about poachers and baiters of badgers. 'You'll be all right, Derek,' he advised the face in the rear-view mirror. 'Just wait. You've nothing to lose by hanging on a bit.'

It had been a long night and the enforced waiting was getting him down. She would be as stiff as an ironing board by this time, he mused. It would be like handling a manikin out of a dress shop window. But he had to do it, must dispose of her here and now before the problem became insurmountable. It was time.

When he opened the rear doors and tugged at her, she made a sound. Startled beyond measure, he leapt backwards, heart pounding, temples throbbing, hairs on the back of his neck suddenly prickling. Had he not killed her? Cautiously, he stepped forward and touched her; she was as cold as ice. As he had disturbed the corpse, her final inhalation of air had bubbled its way past constricted vocal cords. His hands were sweating and he dried them on a handkerchief.

He pulled her out by the feet, cringing slightly when her skull made a quiet thudding sound as it hit the mossy pathway. Turning her round, he placed one of his hot hands under each armpit and began to drag her towards her final resting place. It was a long haul and she seemed to grow heavier with every yard he covered. Murder was, indeed, a complicated business.

At last, he was at the water's edge. The rim of the reservoir sloped slightly and its contents were contained against flood by large rocks, one of which he chose to use as weight. He tied together lengths of rough twine taken from a few boxes in his van. It was in common use in the sphere of packaging and would afford no clue should Rose decide to resurface at any stage.

Rolling her and the stone to the edge was not easy, but momentum was gained when body and stone moved of their own accord down the incline. Her final audible contribution to the world was a splash as she and the boulder entered a water butt large enough to quench the thirst of Lancashire. And she was gone. Transfixed to the spot, he watched ripples as they disturbed a surface which, only moments earlier, had been smoother than a dark window pane.

Galvanized by fear of discovery, Derek dashed back to his van, jumped in, started the engine and reversed onto the quiet section of road he had chosen. He was home and dry; Rose, on the other hand, was home and wet. Pleased with this contained witticism, he began the drive back to his house where he intended to dispose of her few belongings. It was as if she had never existed.

It was a clear, bright morning with a slight nip in the air. Brian Butlin, who took a constitutional each morning come rain, hail or snow, missed the dog. Stella had been his companion every day until Caroline had disappeared, so Brian

284

was delighted when Monty chose to accompany him from time to time. The rascal belonged to the whole village, it seemed. His nomadic tendencies were becoming legendary; on many occasions, he was in receipt of several dinners each day, because he excelled at appearing hungry and seemed to have an inner mechanism which served to advise him when different households would be dining.

'You ate kosher yesterday, I take it?'

For answer, the sheepdog offered a non-committal woof. So far, he had breakfasted at the Forrester house and at the salon, and after this walk he would probably get another plateful at the vicarage.

'It's a good job you are thin by nature,' said Brian, 'or you'd be the size of a house. If I ate as you eat, I'd never get into the pulpit.' But Monty was riveted to something interesting in a bush, so Brian, who was talking to himself, decided to have a word with God. He advised God that help was needed, because he, Brian Butlin, felt tongue-tied each time he considered negotiating with his absent wife. 'Find me the words,' he pleaded, 'and help me tell her how much I love and miss her.'

The dog dashed off again, leaving Brian to follow whilst deep in thought. His reverie was shattered by barking so loud and high-pitched that it threatened to remove tiles from roofs. 'Monty!' he shouted. 'Stop that at once. You'll have the whole of mankind awake.'

The dog arrived panting, tongue lolling at an angle from his jaw.

'What's the matter, silly dog?' asked the vicar.

Monty emitted a low growl, turned, ran a few steps, came back. He was clearly ordering Brian to follow him. 'All right, all right, I'm coming.'

The anxious canine raised his tail and took Brian to the edge of the reservoir. This time there was no need for Monty to swim, because the body was close enough to touch. But Brian did not touch. It was plain that the woman was dead. She was face down in the water and motionless. Around her middle, twine advertised the fact that she had been tied to some kind of weight. It was Bernadette Bradshaw all over again.

Too shocked to remain upright, Brian allowed himself to collapse into a sitting position. He looked at Monty and Monty looked at him. It was obvious that the dog understood the situation perfectly. 'Monty,' said Brian, his breathing fast and shallow, 'you'll have to manage this, because I seem to be incapacitated. Get help, but don't bring a child. Go on. Find someone.'

Monty ran off towards the vicarage while Brian attempted to find his own feet. He closed his eyes and prayed again. There was a dedicated killer on the loose – that much was plain. For two females to have died in the same way and within a matter of weeks was too hard a coincidence to swallow. These murders had to be the work of one man and nobody would be safe until he was found.

Monty found the death place. It wasn't the graveyard in which his mistress lay among many others; it was where she had been placed until her burial.

John heard the dog scratching at the door and barking furiously. 'Hold your horses, Monty,' he yelled. He laid a coffin lid on the floor and allowed the dog inside. Immediately, he knew there was something greatly amiss. Monty, for all his gypsy ways, was a polite dog, one who knew how to adapt his behaviour to suit most social occasions. This was not the 'indoors' Monty – no, this was the dog who ran wild like a fox in the fields. 'Eeh, what's happened to you, lad?'

But Monty was beyond reach. He acted as he had with Brian, to-ing and fro-ing between John and the door. While John remained still, the dog became more frantic, calming slightly only when the man showed signs of following him. John knew better than to argue; the dog had found something and he needed help. The undertaker called his wife. 'Yvonne? I'm off out for a minute – won't be long.' When the 'All right' had reached his ears, he followed the hysterical dog through the back door.

Monty decided not to run. He had all he needed in the form of John Horrocks and it was best to keep pace with his companion. Occasionally, he allowed a small growl to find its way out of him, almost as if he were giving thanks to the man walking beside him.

They made their way through the woods towards the water. When the clearing came into view, Monty barked just once, then took John to where Brian was still seated.

John Horrocks placed a hand on the man's

287

shoulder, but his eyes were fixed to the horror which bobbed gently on the reservoir's surface. Another one. He swallowed audibly. 'Shall I help you up, Mr Butlin?'

'Give me another moment, John. I think I'm about to lose my early morning tea.' The vicar retched into the long grass. When he regained his stomach, he spoke again. 'Don't lift her out – there's nothing to be done.' He smiled at the dog. 'He swam the last one in and disturbed the evidence – such as it was. Let the police find this poor soul exactly as she is.'

'Shall I go and fetch them?'

'Yes.' The trembling vicar put an arm across the sheepdog. 'Stay with me, Monty,' he begged.

Man and dog sat side by side at the rim of the huge lake. After what seemed like an hour, last month's ghastly scenes began to repeat themselves. Brian was helped home, where he sat all day without a morsel of food. And the dog, who knew too much about humanity, remained by his side throughout. For the first time in weeks, Monty knew real hunger.

But all the same, he sat by one of his masters and waited for the healing to begin.

TEN

The meeting was held in St Faith's school hall. The Reverend Brian Butlin had been elected chairman and he stood at the front while people from Rivington Cross, Rivington itself, Horwich and other surrounding villages packed themselves into the body of the hall. A damped-down hysteria was the component which glued together the many participants. There had been two murders and the police seemed to be getting nowhere.

Brian banged on the edge of a small stage where children had been putting on shows for many years. This had been a happy school in a happy village, but there would be no pantomime or Nativity play tonight. The meeting was about staying safe.

The vicar cleared his throat. 'Quiet, please,' he began. He looked at all the faces in front of him and knew that any one of them could be a double murderer. 'Sergeant Shawcross will be along shortly and he will talk to you about what the police need to know and how to keep your homes secure and yourselves safe. With regard to what the police want, remember that the smallest thing, something you would normally fail to notice, might be the key to finding this man. All summer, since late spring, we have had the moor-walkers here. They drift through, call at the post office and general store, buy something, leave again.'

'We'll never remember that lot – too many of 'em,' shouted a man from the back. 'One thing I do know is they cross farmland and leave gates open. They should be stopped. And now, one of them's a killer.'

Brian waited until a buzz of conversation had died. 'This is hard for me to say and would be difficult for any of us to say, but the murderer could well be a local man.'

A heavy silence was interrupted by just one 'Never!'.

The vicar continued. 'Or it might be a regular visitor, someone who walks the moors frequently, someone who has family here. Yes, that hurts. But the fact must be faced. We may know this man. He could be sitting in here tonight with the rest of us. He probably looks perfectly ordinary and he certainly will not have the word "murderer" tattooed across his forehead. The man is someone's son, husband, father, brother. You may have spoken to him today and, nastiest of all, he could be in the chair next to yours.'

Mildred Cookson piped up. 'Well, it won't be my fellow. He couldn't knock the skin off a rice pudding and anyway, he wouldn't even stir himself to come.'

The whole room seemed to release some tension with a ripple of nervous laughter.

Brian smiled. 'Yes, that's another thing – try to keep up your spirits and to support one another. It's a frightening time for all of us, but we must not allow ourselves to be influenced too greatly, as we have families, jobs and homes to care for. On the other hand, we do need to be aware.'

Alan Shawcross arrived and Brian beckoned him. 'Sergeant Shawcross will now advise you with regard to safety measures. And please, I beg you, be aware that neither of those poor dead women was a resident of this area. I know Bernadette used to live here, but Rose Martindale never did and Bernadette had been in Bolton for many years. If the killer is a resident, he seems to have chosen his targets well away from Rivington Cross. That does not make the dead less important, but it does mean that he seems to be killing away from here and carrying the bodies up to the reservoir.' He stepped away and allowed the policeman to take over.

At the rear of the hall, a fat man sat, hands resting on knees, face arranged into an expression tailored to express concern. The person who had murdered Rose Martindale had done him a great favour; were the man to be arrested, he would probably be charged with both crimes. With his blood screaming for a double whiskey, Father Michael Sheahan offered whispered excuses to his immediate neighbours, then left the hall.

He walked the few hundred yards to the presbytery, saw the old Jewish woman crossing the road – no doubt on her way to the meeting – and opened his door. There was a copycat killer on the loose and his behaviour served the priest well. With any luck, Bernadette Bradshaw would remain no more than a nightmare and would have no power to harm him.

He poured a hefty drink and sat down with the *Bolton Evening News*. Yes, they were looking for one man in connection with both killings. The headline was reassuring, as the whole town seemed to believe that a murder spree was under way. Sometimes, life was almost good.

Yuspeh Feigenbaum looked neither left nor right as she marched through the central aisle of St Faith's school hall. She parked herself on the front row and stared at the speaker. He was delivering a lecture about women's needing to walk in pairs or in groups, especially in the evenings, and about children's staying away from the reservoir and the woods. 'The fellow hasn't hurt a child so far, but we have no way of knowing what he will do next.'

Yuspeh had come for one reason only – to hold the hand of the woman in the next seat. This second murder could bring back the torment that had plagued Celia Bradshaw since the death of her older daughter, and Yuspeh dreaded a relapse. As things were, Celia was going to her work every afternoon and had even begun to think of returning full time.

A man near the door stood up. 'I think the

blokes should get out there every night and watch,' he said.

A few more males chorused their agreement.

Alan Shawcross was not impressed. 'Now, look here,' he said, 'there'll be none of that caper.'

Immediately, the black-clad Jewish lady was on her feet. 'Why?' she asked. 'If the men want to watch to keep us safe, what is problem with that?' She turned and faced the audience. 'It is to your credit that you wish to protect your families.' Having made her pronouncement, she sat down.

The policeman scratched his head. He had a soft spot for the woman who travelled about with a pram filled with groceries and chicken feed. 'Mrs Feigenbaum . . .' he was proud of his mastery over the name – he had fought hard and long to learn it, 'we cannot have vigilantes. The law is the law and civilians can play no part except to keep their eyes open.'

She was on her feet again. This time, she walked a few paces and stood beside the policeman. She addressed the gathering. 'If you want to walk in the woods, this you can do and no-one has power to stop you. Should you happen to meet friends in woods, that is just happening, yes? Like accident.'

Alan was not going to win, because she was on a horse as tall as the room and it was going for the blue rosette. 'Remember when child went missing two years ago? All of you went out to seek. Oh, the police is needing you then, yes? Why not we find this man? We found child, is that right?'

A resounding chorus of 'Yes' travelled back to her.

Yuspeh looked at the sergeant, her eyes challenging him. 'Twice he has killed,' she told him in a voice that travelled well. 'Twice. Once he must be caught – only once. Why should it matter who is doing the catching? You have not been managing, have you?'

Alan Shawcross held up a hand and waited for silence. 'And if he has a gun? And if he is here, now, listening, what about—'

She cut him off. 'If he is here now, we are seeing him and we are telling him we are ready to get him.' To the man by her side, she whispered just four words. 'He is not here.'

Beneath the general hubbub, she addressed him again. 'All in towns around know where is reservoir. Man from here would leave bodies in different place. I tell you something else, Mr Policeman – he will not come here to Rivington Cross no more. Is in all newspapers. Let these men feel they can look after family, give fathers dignity. In the end, we all are just family and no more. He will not come here again,' she repeated.

The sergeant blew his shrill whistle and silence fell immediately. 'This will be handled by the force,' he insisted. 'We have men coming in from Salford and Manchester – this is now a huge search. Keep yourselves safe, no more.'

'We shall be safe,' Yuspeh announced before returning to Celia's side.

Alan carried on about locked windows and doors, about what he named 'voluntary curfew', then he left the rest to the group's chairman.

Brian repeated his request for vigilance, then wound up the meeting. He had a distinct feeling that Yuspeh Feigenbaum had stolen the last word and a small part of him agreed with her. When he had declared the session over, he watched a group of men and women as they gathered round the old woman. Picking up his notes, he made for the door, where he found the sergeant.

'She's a rum one, that old Mrs Feigenbaum,' said Alan.

Brian agreed. Sometimes, a matriarchal figure was no bad thing.

He was suddenly wanted by everyone, or so it seemed. When the little Catholic girl entered his study, Brian Butlin shook her hand and told her how sorry he was about her sister.

Invited to sit, Amy placed herself in a chair at the opposite side of his desk. 'He's killed somebody else now.' Her voice revealed a deep sadness, which fact troubled him greatly. Above all, he wanted the Bradshaw family to survive their terrible tragedy without sinking into the depression reputed to be courting the mother. 'Why do people kill people, Father?' she asked.

Brian shook his head slowly. 'I don't know why. And Rev will do, child. Or Mr Butlin – I'm not asking to be called "Father".'

'Sorry.'

He thought for a fleeting moment about priesthood and was glad that he had been able to marry and produce children. Marry? When would he find the courage to see her? And the children needed no-one but each other and their friends, it seemed. 'I am glad you came to me, Amy.'

She wasn't supposed to be here, was forbidden to mix with those whose predecessors had been responsible for the killing of Catholics. 'I trust you,' she said. 'I think everybody trusts you.'

'Thank you.' She had omitted to mention, of course, that her own pastor, wedded to a bottle, was not a man in whom a person might be eager to confide. 'Was there something in particular you wanted to ask me?'

'Nettie,' she said after a deep breath. 'I listened on the stairs. When they . . .' The child gulped.

'Take your time,' he coaxed.

'When she was found . . . when we found her, when Monty dragged her to us, I knew straight away from her hand. And the nail polish – it was her colour. Even before they told us, I was sure it was our Nettie.'

'Yes. And you listened on the stairs?'

She nodded. It had been Amy's experience thus far in life that little of moment would ever be divulged by her parents in her presence. 'They had to look at her in the hospital – to see how she'd died.'

'I know. That always happens.'

He was a nice man. Suddenly, Amy wasn't afraid any more. He understood people and he wasn't going to fob her off with stupid excuses and lies. 'I can't tell Mam and Dad what I heard. It would make them so sad and Mam has already been very ill. Mrs Feigenbaum and the chickens helped her, you know.'

'Yes, Amy. Mrs Feigenbaum is a wise woman.'

She wriggled slightly in her chair, searching for words.

'Whatever you choose to tell me will go no further unless you advise me otherwise. I may not be a Catholic, but I am a pastor and this is my parish. You do not attend my church, yet your welfare and that of your family remains my concern. It all goes with the job.'

Tears began to prick and Amy blinked wildly in an attempt to clear her vision. She had to tell a dreadful truth and saying it to an adult was going to make it all the more real. 'When they looked at Nettie, they could tell she'd had a baby. I heard Mam saying that he was Adam and he'd been adopted.'

Brian felt some moisture in his own eyes. That an eleven-year-old girl had carried such a secret was abominable. It was clear that she understood fully the implications and that she was deeply distressed. 'Amy, look at me.'

She obeyed, a few droplets of saline escaping down her cheeks.

'Do not sit and weep for her – she is with her Lord and she doesn't want you to be unhappy.'

Amy sniffed and rummaged in a pocket for her handkerchief.

Brian waited until she seemed better composed. 'Dear girl, that is not the worst sin in the world. I take it that Nettie never married?'

For answer, Amy simply shook her head.

'She hurt no-one but herself. Always remember

that. Your sister brought into the world a little boy who is probably giving great joy to a couple who might never have been parents. Nettie made them into mother and father by giving them the child they wanted. You know that some people are unable to have babies?'

'Yes.'

'Then comfort yourself by believing that Adam is with people who love him. For that family, Adam is a gift from God.'

A new confusion entered Amy's mind, thoughts which had never plagued her until this moment. Was she being selfish? She put the new concept into words. 'I wanted to find him. But I don't think anyone would listen to me, and that was why I decided to talk to you. Well, no, really it was Maddy who said I could trust you with anything at all. But after what you just said, Mr Butlin, I wonder if I should leave it all alone.'

Brian understood her very well. She had come to ask him to find her sister's child. 'You wish me to locate him? Or do you want me to tell you how he is rather than where he is? If I can discover the truth, that is.'

'I don't know.'

This girl was a worrier. Amy was naturally cautious and he watched her while she went into battle with herself – her need to meet Nettie's son fighting the new understanding that she might disturb his life. 'What's the right thing to do?' she asked.

To some questions, there were no clear answers. 'I don't know, either,' he replied honestly. 'I suppose you cannot wait until your mother is better?'

'She'll never be well enough for this,' Amy sighed. 'It's something I'm not supposed to know, isn't it? My mother has changed a lot. She's not as . . . strict as she used to be – about church and all that, I mean. But she hurts. And the thing she hurts most about is Nettie. I think she didn't like the way my sister behaved – too many boyfriends – and that's why she sent her to live somewhere else. I don't know enough, you see. I'm not allowed to know.'

Brian stood up and walked to the window, gazed out at the graveyard. 'So you will have no idea about the age of the child?'

'No. And Nettie never even mentioned him.' She watched him as he turned quickly to face her, questions in his eyes. 'Yes, I know everyone thought I never saw her, but she used to visit me. Mam and Dad didn't know, of course. She started coming to look for me when I was about seven or eight and we liked one another – loved one another. Nettie and I didn't want to lose touch ever again, so she used to come up to Rivington Cross and we met in the woods. It was the same day and time every other week and, if she missed, I just used to go again two weeks later – unless it rained. She didn't come if the weather was bad. She couldn't get a message to me, you see.'

'Yes, I certainly do see.' He saw prejudice and a total lack of charity. He saw a mother who had rejected her child and now suffered the guilt that had arisen from such implacability. Celia

Bradshaw's recent brush with insanity had arisen out of the knowledge that the chance to heal the rift with her older daughter had disappeared for ever.

'Now I'll never see her again.'

Sometimes, this job was a heartbreaker, and this was one of those times. Amy was eleven years old, but was going on forty. She owned a wisdom born of cleverness, duplicity and the overwhelming wish to keep her parents and her sister safe. The child had been a bridge for Nettie and a protector of her own parents. 'What do you want me to do, Amy? Would you like more time to think?'

She straightened her shoulders. 'Perhaps I could know where he is when I am older. For now, I'd like to believe that he is safe.'

He returned to the desk, carrying with him the painful knowledge that Amy was old enough to know that she was too young. Such wisdom was a heavy weight for shoulders so narrow. 'I shall do all in my power,' he said. 'Your sister kept her surname?'

'Yes, she was Bernadette Marie Bradshaw.'

'Address?'

'Twenty-five, Bromwich Street. She lived with a girl called Iris Moore. That's all I know, really. Oh, they both worked at Woolworth's.'

'Right.' He smiled at her. 'Thank you for telling me your secret. Would you mind very much if I burdened you with mine?'

Amy stared at him. An adult wanting to share a secret with a child? 'No, I don't mind,' she replied.

'I thought it would be a fair swap and that you should be the first to know.' That was not the truth, because his own children ought to have been his initial port of call, yet he needed to make this child feel safe. 'You won't tell anyone?'

'No, I promise.'

'Because I must speak to Simon and Sarah first. But, as you have given me your confidences, I shall share mine and you may keep them for just a little while.' He leaned forward and lowered his voice. 'I know all about the bell house. The key is under an urn on a nearby grave and my twins have been using the building for several years.' Sarah and Simon had even made their own home, a retreat in which they could grow up at their own pace. Was he a bad parent?

Amy giggled unexpectedly. 'They think no-one knows.'

'Yes. Well, I believe I may just surprise you all. I shall run electricity into both rooms, but I shall not invade. You will still be able to keep all adults out of there. It could be made quite pretty. And there is a reason for my sudden interest, Amy. With a murderer about, I shall need to come and fetch all of you from your homes and return you when your meetings are ended. We must keep safe. We must protect the bell house and all who use it.'

'Yes. Thank you.'

Brian stood up. 'Not at all. It has been a pleasure and a privilege, though I wish happier circumstances had brought us together.'

Amy thanked her mentor yet again and left

301

the vicarage. As she ran across to Maddy's house, her step was lighter than it had been in days. And she would keep Mr Butlin's secret until the cows came home.

The newspapers were spread all over the living room floor. He was famous, as was Rose Martindale. They would never work out who it was, he thought almost gleefully as he peeled off every word and stored it in his brain. Police were fairly certain that they were looking for a man who had murdered twice, who had deposited two bodies in the reservoir at Rivington Cross. Well, they were wrong. Derek and the other fellow were the only two people in the world who knew how mistaken the investigators were.

He glanced at the clock. It was almost nine and his stall was booked from eight, so he had better shift himself. His usual pattern must be maintained no matter what, he advised himself as he fastened a tie and smoothed his hair at the mirror. 'You have rid the world of a piece of evil,' he told the glass. Prostitutes did not deserve to live, and already he itched to— 'Get a grip, Derek,' he mumbled. 'You can't run a war with a one-man army.'

When he was halfway down Deane Road, he saw her. She was wearing a straw hat and it was pulled low over her face, but he would have recognized that walk anywhere. Caroline Butlin moved like a lady. She did not display the gait of someone condemned to stand on her feet behind a counter all day, was not possessed of the curved shoulders that resulted from factory work, all that to-ing and fro-ing between mules or looms. Even from behind, he knew the woman who had driven him over the brink.

In an attempt not to draw attention to himself, Derek Ramsden pulled into a side street, applied the brakes, jumped out and locked the van. To hell with the market – he had more important business on hand. If anyone asked, he would say he had been visiting a new supplier who had looked too promising to be allowed to cool.

Keeping a safe distance and walking at a pace he imagined to be casual, Derek followed her. He noticed how she gave the market a wide berth, knew that she would have expected him to be at his post from eight o'clock. Three days each week he spent on the market – the other two and a half were allocated to his domestic clientele and she had been one of that number. This was one of the days when Caroline Butlin would assume that her ex-lover would be a fixed point on life's map, stall 43, Bolton Market, dresses on a rail, cardigans and jumpers folded on the counter. She was wrong.

He followed her down Great Moor Street, past Timothy White's chemist shop, past Gregory's and onto Deansgate. She crossed to the sports equipment store and he watched the assistant taking a lacrosse stick from the window. She was kitting out her kids for school. Was she living back at the village? No. Had she been travelling down from the moor, she would not have been walking along Deane Road. She liked walking. He remembered her saying that early on, when he had first introduced her to the joys of cut-price clothing. So desperate for love and attention she had been in those days, the days before— No patience, that was her problem. He hadn't really hit her, hadn't been as rough as he had been in youth. Beryl. It was best not to think about Beryl.

He pursued her and the lacrosse stick to Moor Lane Bus Station, hid behind a telephone box while she boarded the Ribble single-decker that would take her to her children. She was not living there. Had she been living there, she would have travelled in her husband's car and would have come from a different direction.

There was one other possible conclusion: the woman he loved, the female whose steps he had just dogged, was now bursar to the school known as St Anne's. Which meant that she continued to live in the Wigan Road area and that he would be able to find out exactly where she had placed herself. It should not be too difficult. Somewhere, probably in his own neighbourhood, Caroline had taken a room or a small flat.

He walked back to his van at a leisurely pace, decided not to take the road to Rivington Cross. No. For the rest of today, he intended to fulfil his duties as a retailer. If anyone wished to know why he had arrived late at his post, he would claim a hangover. In an environment that was predominantly male, hangovers were accepted as a normal hazard. He could watch the school whenever he chose. For now, Caroline could remain in blissful ignorance while he decided how to run the next scene in his own show.

* * *

Yuspeh Feigenbaum was a woman on a mission. With fury beaten into every step, she marched through the village, her ageing frame steadied by George's pram. She knew what she had seen, oh yes. And no-one on this planet could possibly get away with the crime to which she had been a witness on this very day. As she passed the vet's house, she slowed slightly, eyes moving to the door of the surgery, then back to the contents of her pram. He would know. He could get the stuff analysed. If Yuspeh had to sell her jewellery in order to pay fees, she would have Hilda Barnes charged with attempted murder. 'She was trying to commit chickencide,' she decided aloud.

The detached cottage belonging to the vile woman stood in its own grounds and was set back off the pavement. Yuspeh threw open the gate, pushed her pram inside, not caring as she scraped paint from wood. This would never again be used as a baby carriage, while the woman who lived here deserved to have her gate spoilt.

She lifted the brass door knocker and allowed it to clatter home. 'You will open up now, Mrs Barnes,' she screeched in a voice that caused several passers-by to slow down. 'I saw you. George saw you. Mrs Celia Bradshaw saw you. And the poison feed I have here with me. Come out at this moment.'

Mildred Cookson poked her head out of the doorway of a terraced cottage across the way. 'What's the matter, love?' she called.

Yuspeh turned. 'My chickens is matter. Anna is

gone to work with Jakob, so the woman thinks I am alone. I am not being alone. I am having my grandson and Mrs Bradshaw with me. Chickens are now in house, while Celia and George they clean up the poison food.'

Mildred left her house at a speed that amazed Yuspeh. Once again, the old woman clattered the door knocker.

'She's in,' said Mildred. 'I saw her running like the wind not five minutes back. I thought she must have had the devil on her tail.'

'She had me on her tail,' replied Yuspeh smartly, 'and she would be happier with devil chasing, for even devil could not be as angry as I am. She tries to kill my chickens. Across field she is come, then she pokes this strange-smelling chicken food through holes in fence. We rush to pick up chickens – feathers everywhere. Now chickens in kitchen and my poor George Josef and my friend is picking up food.'

Councillor Alec Barnes opened the door an inch or two and was knocked backwards when Yuspeh threw her weight against it. 'Some of it is in pram,' she told him. 'Your wife is chicken killer. This I have seen with mine own two eyes and the eyes of some other people also.'

Mildred was right behind Yuspeh – in more than one way. For years Hilda Barnes had patronized her, and since the debacle in the salon very few villagers had spoken to the wife of Councillor Barnes. 'She objects to the chickens, Alec,' she piped. 'Hilda, I mean. I'm not that keen on them meself, but I wouldn't be trying to kill them. Your Hilda's never been right since she got thrown out of the hairdresser's. She's had fancy ideas and daft airs about her ever since you went on the council. Any road, she's gone too far this time. She'll have to be prosecuted.'

A muffled scream made its way from inside the house.

Yuspeh turned to Mildred. 'See? Hear? This is guilt of woman shouting now. She is in fear.'

Alec Barnes stepped out onto the path. 'Mrs Feigen . . . Mrs Fei—'

'Feigenbaum,' she snapped. 'Feigenbaum is my name. What?'

'I can pay you. I can give you compensation—'

'Can you help my poor chickens and the kitchen where they make mess?'

He scratched his head. 'Erm . . .'

'Can you dry tears of my grandson and calm nerves of Mrs Celia Bradshaw who is already hurt with other things? Money is not everything.'

While Alec Barnes turned and closed the door behind himself, Mildred whispered to Yuspeh, 'Get every penny you can out of him – he's worth a few bob.'

He addressed the angry woman again. Several people had gathered at the gate, and Alec's cheeks were bright with embarrassment. 'Mrs Feig—'

'Enbaum,' Yuspeh finished for him.

'Embalm,' he said lamely.

Yuspeh tutted her impatience. 'Embalm is dead bodies, what my chicks could have been had we not run out and sniffed at this food. Your wife, she is coward and she runs away when we come to garden.'

307

'Yes.' He tugged nervously at a cuff of his shirt. 'I think we can arrive at some satisfactory arrangement, Mrs . . . Yes. And we shall be selling up here and moving to Bolton as soon as possible.'

'Good,' snapped Yuspeh.

'I shall visit you later and sort out details,' he promised. 'I am very sorry for your trouble, but please, I beg you, don't take Hilda to court. You will be well compensated.'

For answer, Yuspeh dragged her pram backwards down the path, Mildred rushing to get out of the way of the advancing vehicle. On the pavement, they stood with a small gathering of people who were discussing this most recent piece of excitement. Ignoring comments and questions, Yuspeh spoke only to Mildred. 'Thank you for coming to help me. But I am thinking I wish it could be as easy to get rid of the man who is killing two women.'

Mildred nodded her agreement. 'I know what you mean.'

The old lady made her way homeward, stopped again outside the vet's house, all the while grumbling under her breath about people who could not leave other people to get on with peaceful lives. Meanwhile, she saw men and women running and laughing as the latest piece of gossip was spread the length and breadth of the village.

She did not go in to see the vet. Instead, Monty joined her, feathery tail giving her a welcome. 'Is just you and me, Monty,' she said gravely. 'When you look at life, the only sense is

308

from you and from me. Come on, boy. You rescue chickens and I rescue Anna's kitchen, or we shall both be in doghouse by evening time.'

Caroline stepped off the bus and almost collided with the old Jewish lady. 'Sorry,' she said. 'I nearly lost my lacrosse stick there.'

Yuspeh glared at her. This was the mother of Sarah and Simon Butlin, a fine pair of twins who had befriended George, Amy and Maddy. 'No problem,' she said. 'You know, sometimes, I am understanding why you go. This Hilda Barnes woman has tried to kill my chickens.' She walked off, leaving Caroline with a jaw that had dropped slightly. Chickens? There was a murderer on the loose and old Mrs Feigenbaum was concerned about her poultry?

The vicar's wife pulled herself up. There was a murderer about and she had abandoned her children, so what right did she have to criticize anyone? Curtains twitched as she walked along, but she held up her head defiantly and ignored the watchers. She had done wrong, but who here could cast the first stone? Goodness, she was beginning to think in Brian-speak – that would never do. This was the home of her children and she would visit them whenever she pleased.

The sour-faced housekeeper opened the door. The look she gave Caroline was not exactly welcoming, but why should that matter? Brian came into the hall. 'Thank goodness,' he exclaimed, his eyes fixed to the lacrosse stick. 'The good sisters passed on my message, then?'

'Of course they did.' She gave him the stick,

which had been wrapped from top to bottom in brown paper.

He laughed. 'I see they tried to disguise it. A lacrosse stick is probably a thing that can never be mistaken for anything else.'

'True.' There followed a moment of awkward silence.

'They will be back soon.' He stopped short of inviting her into the living room. This had been her home for many years and he would not relegate her to the status of visitor. But he led the way. Betty followed them into the room. 'Would you like tea or coffee, Mrs Butlin?' she asked.

'Thank you.' Caroline delivered a smile that was meant to be reassuring. Instinct told her where she stood; the woman feared for her position and Caroline understood that perfectly. 'Coffee, I think,' she replied. 'And a biscuit would be nice, Mrs Thornton. I seem not to have eaten much today. Nerves, probably.' She sat down.

Betty, a born filler of stomachs, was immediately solicitous. 'You have to eat, you know. I can soon throw some bacon and eggs together. Or a sandwich.'

'Perhaps later,' answered Caroline. 'And may I say what a fine job you have made of this house. It sparkles like a brilliant-cut diamond.'

Betty preened. Mr Butlin was a lovely man, but he never noticed much. She had once spent a whole morning sorting out his shirts and socks, but her labours had brought forth no comment. Perhaps that was one of the reasons for Mrs Butlin's behaviour; being taken for granted was not everyone's cup of tea. Or coffee. 'Thank you, Mrs Butlin. I'll get the coffee on. Mr Butlin?'

'The same, thank you.'

When Betty had left, the married couple sat and gazed at the pattern on the carpet. It was a busy enough design, lots of flowers and leaves against a cream background, but it was not enough to hold attention indefinitely.

'How are you?' he managed eventually.

'I am well, thank you. Yourself? The twins?'

'Very well, indeed.'

'Good.'

'Yes.'

She noticed that the wedding photograph remained in its usual place. What had she wanted or expected from this man? And how on earth had she imagined that life might be good with Derek Ramsden? That she should have experienced such an overwhelming physical passion for the creature was beyond her comprehension. 'These murders,' she said. 'Terrible. Are the children safe?'

'I hope so, Caroline. Trust in the Lord is one thing, but this seems to be the devil at work – and *he* even found the temerity to tempt the Son of God. But I have reached a decision. We now have a group of six children – our twins, Maddy Horrocks, Amy Bradshaw, George Forrester and James, Mrs Thornton's son. They use the bell house.'

Caroline grinned. 'The place about which we know nothing at all.'

'Quite. It will be a bell house once again, because I intend to run a cable across for

311

lighting and for an electric bell, which will be installed here on an outside wall. At the flick of a switch, the whole village will know that the children are in need.'

'I should be here,' she said softly.

'I know.'

She stood and walked to the window. There was something afoot. In a village, there was always something afoot. People bustled to and fro, stopping in small groups to discuss developments. 'Someone tried to poison Mrs Feigenbaum's chickens,' she said as she watched folk moving about. They were probably discussing hens – plus the arrival of the vicar's delinquent wife.

'Hilda Barnes, I imagine,' replied Brian. 'Anti-Semitic, anti-vicar, anti-everything except Bolton Corporation. I hope she enjoys a better quality of sermon when she moves to the metropolis. I fear she judged me to be boring. Many people do.'

Caroline swallowed hard. 'What must you think of me?'

He offered no reply, because nothing came readily to him. And what did she think of him?

With her back still turned to him, she whispered, 'I am so sorry. It was a total aberration and I shall never account for it, even to myself.'

'You know where we are,' he replied. 'But I gather that you need some time and perhaps I need time, too. I shan't ask why you are living with Cross and Passion nuns, but feel free to tell me whenever you are ready.'

Caroline returned to her seat. This time, she

did not lower her head as she spoke. 'I have been raped,' she said softly. 'I have been raped repeatedly. A job at the convent came up and I went for it. Mother Olivia recognized my fear and gave me a small flat along with the bursar's position. I hide there.'

The anger which arose in Brian was uncontainable. Raped? This beautiful, fragrant woman whom he loved beyond expression? Word, words, where were the words? He jumped up and left the room, almost colliding with Betty in the doorway.

She swerved, saved the coffee, watched him as he dashed up the stairs three at a time.

'Put the tray here, please,' said Caroline, her voice unsteady.

Betty's mouth hung open. 'Mrs Butlin?'

'Yes?'

'He's . . . he's crying. Oh, I'm sorry – I know it's no business of mine, but seeing him like that – you don't expect it, do you?'

'No.'

Betty could see that the vicar was not the only one in a state. Caroline Butlin was shaking from head to toe. When the tray was set down, Betty hovered. She had not the slightest idea of what to do in this situation. Should she follow Mr Butlin? Should she remain with the wife? Or ought she to go out and find the children, keep them away from all this? In the end, she decided to let nature run its course. 'I'll . . . er . . . I'll get on with my jobs.' Gratefully, the housekeeper returned to her own domain and carried on with her shortcrust pastry.

313

After a few minutes, she heard Mr Butlin coming downstairs at an ordinary pace. It occurred to Betty that she was no longer worrying about her own position in the household; her main concern now was for the well-being of the man who had employed her. She felt sorry for the wife, too. Oh, what could she do? How was a person expected to cope with grief when she knew it was none of her business?

Caroline entered the room. She touched Betty's shoulder. 'Thank you,' she said. 'Thank you for looking after my family and the vicarage. I cannot express my gratitude, it is so . . . boundless. May I ask one more favour?'

Betty's eyes pricked. 'Course you can.'

'Would you tell the children to be here with all their friends at about seven o'clock? That includes your boy, I believe. The Rev is taking me out for a drive and a bite to eat.' She inhaled and the breath shook on a buried sob. 'We have much to discuss.'

Betty smiled. 'The Rev'? What a wonderful title. Those two syllables had contained something approaching affection, pondered Betty as she nodded her encouragement. 'Yes, I'll tell them, Mrs Butlin. And – well – I hope you don't think me too forward, but I'll be praying for both of you.'

'Prayer does no harm, Mrs Thornton. Oh, and your pastry looks wonderful. Apple pie?'

'Yes.'

'Save me some, please. One of my favourites, apple pie and custard.' She turned to leave, caught another thought, turned in the doorway.

'And you may tell all those six ragamuffins that the Rev and I have gone about some secret business.' An impish grin paid a fleeting visit to Caroline's lips. 'Better than that – tell them we are going to deal with the bell house.'

Betty's jaw slackened for a moment. 'They think nobody knows. You've only to look at that daft dog to see where they're all hiding. Private gang, my foot – they're about as private as an old man in a greenhouse with his tomatoes.' Betty stopped. 'You're not taking it off them, are you?'

'No, but don't tell them that.'

'All right.'

When the car had driven away, Betty Thornton carried on with her duties. She added cinnamon to the apples and some fancy fluting round the edge of the crust. This was to be an extra-special apple pie, because the Rev's missus would be partaking of it. And Betty wasn't frightened any more, because God was good, Mr Butlin was good and his wife would come good. It was only a matter of time . . .

ELEVEN

The fury was almost overwhelming. In silence, Brian drove to Bolton and stopped at the Pack Horse Inn for lunch. Recognizing the drastic change in him, Caroline made no attempt to start a conversation; what might she have said, anyway? After hearing 'I have been raped', the man who had been her husband for fourteen years had scarcely opened his mouth.

They played with steak and kidney pie, plus an assortment of vegetables, both plates advertising minimal disturbance when a waitress removed them. 'Is there something wrong?' the woman asked. 'You've hardly touched your meal – do you want something else?'

The vicar's innate kindness and self-control struggled to the surface. 'Everything is fine, thank you. We have had some bad news and it seems to have affected our appetites. There is nothing amiss with the food.'

The woman said how sorry she was for their troubles, offered them a pudding, was sent for two cups of coffee and the bill.

Brian managed to look at his wife. Had he been a decent and attentive husband, she would never have left home. Had she never left home, she would not have been subjected to such a dreadful ordeal. There were dark smudges under her eyes, the sort of bruises that sometimes appeared on peaches left too long in the fruit bowl. She was beautiful. Had he ever told her properly how beautiful she was and how much he loved her?

Made uneasy by the fixed gaze, Caroline shifted in her chair.

'It was my fault,' he said at last.

'Nonsense,' came the swift reply. 'I went of my own accord, abandoned two children and scurried off in the direction of some imagined excitement. You must take no blame at all.'

He swallowed a mixture of emotions that bubbled in his throat. 'I have not told you how much I love you – not for a long time. I treated you as a fixture and I am deeply sorry for that. Now you have paid for my neglect and I cannot forgive myself.' And he had never experienced such anger, either. 'Will you wait for me here, please? There is something I must do today, but I shall be gone no more than half an hour.' He lowered his head. 'I am so, so ashamed of what I am, Caroline.'

A pale smile arrived on her lips. 'You are what you are, Brian.' The smile disappeared. 'I beg you – stay away from the market.'

He rose to his feet. 'Half an hour,' he repeated before marching out of the restaurant. Outside, he straightened his shoulders, turned and walked along Deansgate. 'You made no promise,' he mumbled to himself as he paced past St Patrick's church, strides lengthening as his resolve hardened.

The market bustled, just as it always had. It was a sea of people, some emerging along with a terrible smell from the fish market, others crowding round stalls where colourful characters announced special prices just for today, slight seconds, a job lot for the gorgeous lady at the back. The gorgeous lady at the back might well have been a relative of the stallholder, a plant rooted into position as a draw for gullible shoppers. That was how it worked, mused Brian as he approached his target. Derek Ramsden had advertised his goods to Caroline, but they had proved to be shoddy and dangerous.

At last, he reached his goal. 'Hello, Reverend,' said the salesman of second-hand furniture. 'And what can I do you for this bright, happy day?'

Brian cast an eye over the wares. 'You can do something very special,' he replied. 'Whatever I buy, you must deliver today.'

'Fair enough, but it'll be getting late – where are you?'

'St Faith's Vicarage, Rivington Cross. Now, those six dining chairs at three pounds apiece – what do you say to fifteen for the lot? And the table – shall we say five?'

'For a man of God, you drive a hard bargain,' grinned the stallholder. 'Anything else?'

'The chest of drawers and the small cupboard – ten pounds? Cash on delivery?'

'Done.' The man spat on his hand and held it out. Brian amused himself by doing the same. It was time to let go some of his old ways and this was as good a beginning as any. 'I'll have the money ready for you this evening – I don't carry a great deal of cash.'

'See you later,' called the man as Brian walked away. 'I've never been cheated by a vicar before.'

Brian bought curtain material, two poles and some hooks. Betty could throw together a couple of pairs of curtains and a matching tablecloth for the upper room of the bell house. And in that recently acquired cupboard, the children of Rivington Cross would be able to keep their written thoughts and hopes in old exercise books. Their biggest secret was gone, of course, had been stolen by adults out of necessity. With a murderer about, the village needed to know where its children met to play.

He wandered about for a few minutes, bought some enamel mugs and a pile of second-hand comics and books. All the time, his eyes wandered across the market and along the far wall where stood stall 43, Derek Ramsden's Cut Price Apparel for Ladies. After parking his purchases with the seller of enamel tableware, Brian finally followed where ice-cold fury had been leading him from the start of this expedition. He was no longer heated, no longer near to tears. The knowledge he had gained today had been swallowed right down into the pit of his stomach, leaving no room for steak and kidney pie and certainly no space for the mercy and charity he preached to his flock.

Derek Ramsden looked up. He had been pricing some twin sets and, expecting a customer to be the owner of the newly arrived shadow, he applied the smile he reserved for discerning ladies. His lips froze and he jammed them together determinedly. There was nowhere to run. Because his stall was at the very edge of the market, he always draped a piece of material across the back in order to hide masonry and to make his small emporium more attractive to the clientele. He felt his Adam's apple moving in his throat and, gasping in fear, he stepped back through the makeshift curtain into the small gap between counter and wall.

Brian was there before him. Derek stopped in his tracks – this was a very large man. 'Yes?' The syllable emerged as a squeak, its final consonant deformed by the slight lisp which had cursed this man from infancy.

Brian heard himself in the pulpit preaching about how to turn the other cheek and advising his congregation that all sin was forgivable. His hands, curled into fists, longed to smash Derek Ramsden's face into the middle of next week. He would never forgive this man – God might, but Brian wanted his revenge. Revenge? How quantifiable was that commodity? How justifiable? But he was not just a vicar – he was a man and the man wanted to roar, longed to tell the world about this dreadful creature. Civilization, he decided, was not always an improvement. The primitive in him needed to fight and his education held him back.

'What do you want?' asked Derek.

The vicar's voice was as quiet as he could make it. 'In truth, I want you dead. For what you have done to my wife, I should like to see you jailed, at least. But I cannot and will not sully her name in the way you have dirtied and hurt her body, you despicable piece of dross.'

Derek Ramsden gulped noisily. 'What's she been saying? We didn't get on, so I threw her out, and—'

'Nonsense.' The tone raised itself slightly. 'You raped her. She may be a married woman and a mother, but she is an innocent. She has never come into contact with a being as low as you are and was completely unprepared for your violence. Decent people do not usually encounter the abnormal. You are a thing from the very edge of life, a criminal and a destroyer.'

'Bloody rubbish.' God, if a customer were to arrive and hear all this going on—

'I may be a vicar, but I am also human. You will stay away from my wife, from my family, from my church and from my village. Take this warning and heed it well – I played rugby in my time and I did not always play fairly. If you drive me to it, I shall put you into hospital and both of us in jail. Do I make myself plain?'

Derek shrugged. 'I hear you.'

The nonchalance with which the retort was uttered was the final wisp of straw. Brian seized the trader's shirt and lifted him from the ground. 'I could take you with one hand, Ramsden. What's the matter? Can't you speak? Am I squeezing the oxygen out of your puny little frame?'

'Put . . . me . . . down.'

Brian obliged. The power of his own fury was beginning to alarm him. In this moment, he suddenly knew that there was probably one murder in every man and that he was looking into the terrified eyes of his own potential victim. He hated Derek Ramsden, wanted to watch him suffering, needed to hear his pleas for mercy. 'Breathe the same air as Caroline again and I shall separate you from your need to inhale. Do you understand me?'

Derek nodded.

'Sometimes I am not a preacher. Sometimes, I am a chap with a family to protect, and during those times I shall be watching you. So.' Brian brushed imaginary dust from his clothes, wiped his fingers on a handkerchief. 'Now I go to make my peace with God. You can simply go to hell by any route you choose to take.'

Derek stood back, waited until the damned fellow had walked away, then came out through the makeshift curtain. The stock was down. Someone had taken the opportunity to help herself – or himself – to half a dozen cardigans. He watched the vicar as he picked up his purchases and stalked out of the market. 'I'm not done with you,' he muttered defiantly, noticing how the man of God towered above the rest of the crowd. He was a big bugger and big buggers fell hard. 'No, I'm not bloody finished, not by a long chalk.'

Brian walked back into the Pack Horse. She had moved to a table in line with the door and he saw straight away the lines of worry on her forehead. 'Here I am,' he announced with false cheeriness. 'Curtain material, poles, *Beano*, *Dandy* – all's right with the world. I bought some bits of old furniture and they will arrive tonight.'

She stared blankly at him. 'What?'

'The bell house. Recent developments mean that nowhere is safe, so I shall furnish the place, see them all securely to and fro, install a bell – yes, it will be a bell house again – and all will be well.'

She shook her head. Everyone knew the history of the bell house, how it had been built too small to contain the bell and how a man had been forced to run in and hit it with a hammer just before services. 'A bell in the bell house?' she asked. That would be a novelty, indeed.

'An electric one. Lighting, too. Oh, and a paraffin stove with a good guard around it.'

Caroline shook her head yet again as he dropped and retrieved curtain poles. He had changed immeasurably and with extraordinary suddenness, it seemed. 'Brian? Where have you really been?'

'To buy stuff,' he answered truthfully. 'Shall we go? The man is coming to run the cable across to the—'

'Sit,' she said.

He sat.

'You have been to see Ramsden,' she accused him. 'I can tell. This metamorphosis of yours does not fool me in the slightest, Brian Butlin.' She waited. 'Well?'

'I . . . had a word or two with him, yes.'

'And I told you to stay away from the market.'

'Did you?'

'You know I did. There is nothing wrong with your hearing. What happened? If you angered him—'

'I lifted him off the ground with one hand – heard his shirt tearing, as a matter of fact. And I told him to keep his distance – or else. Where other than at Bolton Market would I go to buy second-hand furniture? And there he was, bold as brass and very puny. I dealt with him.'

This man was not her husband. The man Caroline Butlin had married would not swat a fly, let alone threaten a man and lift him up with one hand. And there was in Brian's eyes an expression of triumph, as if he had just solved the world's problems in a single swoop. He had done this for her and she should be grateful, but she knew Derek Ramsden too well. 'He will do something now,' she said. 'He bears a grudge and I bore the marks to prove it. Brian, he is dangerous. There's . . . there's something wrong with him – with his physical self. He cannot be a man – with a woman, I mean. His failure produces an insanity the like of which I never thought to encounter. Your treatment of him will probably result in the same reaction.'

He shook his head. 'What can he do?'

Caroline leaned forward and lowered her voice. 'He can hurt our children.'

The Town Hall clock struck in the distance. 'Then I shall kill him,' he replied.

'And you will hang, which event will damage Simon and Sarah even further. When I told you to stay away from him, I knew what I was about.

324

The man is a maniac. None of us is safe now.'

Brian placed all his parcels on the floor. 'Then we must go to the police and tell them all we know. He will be charged with rape and will be removed from society, then all—'

'Then everyone will know exactly what happened to the twins' mother. That should be an excellent beginning when they start at Bolton School in a couple of weeks. Brian, you should have listened to me.'

When had he listened? he asked himself. So busy preparing sermons, so actively involved in the lives of his parishioners – but when had he taken the time to notice this precious woman? She was sensible, bright, educated. She was the girl he had chosen to share his life and he had neglected her to a point where she had become restless enough to leave behind a whole way of life. 'I am a fool,' he said.

'You made a mistake.'

'A dangerous one. I had not thought him to be quite so bad.'

'A rapist is always bad,' Caroline whispered. 'The trouble is that the person who has been raped is tainted for life. If the rape gets reported nationwide, she will never heal – neither will her children. I don't want them to grow up afraid, Brian. I don't want them suffering nervous illness later in life.'

He was a ham-fisted fool, he decided. He had rushed in where angels, in their infinite wisdom, would have taken a back seat. How much more damage might he do? 'Oh, God, I didn't think.'

'No. Neither did I when I rode off with him

towards a new dawn that was painted in very thin watercolours. The greater blame is still mine.'

'As is the greater knowledge – and I ought to have bowed to that.' He bent to retrieve his purchases. 'Come along now. Let us make the den for our children and their friends – they need somewhere to play and it is clear that they don't want adults around.' Could he blame them? What a mess that village had become, and no fault could be attributed to the younger members of society. Bodies in a lake, the wife of a councillor trying to kill an old lady's chickens, Amy searching for a nephew, James afraid for his future. And, on top of all that, a vicar's wife who took refuge in a convent.

'I still need time, Brian,' said Caroline as they left the inn.

'I know. Take all the time you need. I shall always be there.'

'It's very nice,' pronounced Sarah. Her twin demonstrated his agreement by nodding his head. They owned chairs, a table, some mugs and a pile of children's books and comics. No-one but Jay read *Beano* or *Dandy*, but politeness meant that nothing could be said.

When all six children had made the required noises, Brian and Caroline left them to their own devices.

'It is nice,' insisted Maddy. 'And very kind of Mr Butlin to think of our comfort.'

'And our safety.' Simon's tone was gloomy. The beloved wife and mother in St Faith's graveyard would no longer guard their key. The key would hang in the vicarage kitchen and Simon intended to make notices saying *NO ADULTS ALLOWED*. These would be fixed to both doors of their no-longer-secret den. 'And we can still use candles,' he added. 'No need to use the electric light if we don't want to.' Candles made the whole thing spooky and exciting. 'But we are still forbidden to go near the reservoir. I like the reservoir.'

They arranged themselves around the table, Maddy at the head, George opposite her. There was no question appended to the matter – Maddy was in charge and George was her deputy. 'How obedient shall we be?' was their leader's first query. 'Obedience is boring, but we have to admit that they are sometimes right.' There was no need to identify the 'they'. The 'they' were usually over five feet in height and ruled the world. In Maddy's opinion, a good job was not being done.

'If we get found out doing something wrong, we could lose the bell house,' offered Amy. 'And it's . . . well . . . it's just good to have somewhere to come without grown-ups.'

'So we don't get caught,' said George. 'You should try living with my grandmother. She knows when you are even thinking about being a breaker of rules. Sometimes, I feel that my skull is made of transparent plastic. She misses absolutely nothing.'

Jay agreed, his expression suitably woeful. 'Mam's the same. Without even going upstairs, she knows I've left clothes on the floor. Even if we did find the murderer, we'd be in trouble.'

A corporate breath was released into the room, each child adding to the sigh of resignation.

'I think Ma will come home soon, too,' announced Sarah. 'And I am glad about that, but it will be one more to watch us. Three adults just yards away.'

Jay shook his shorn head. 'No. I reckon your mam will send my mam away. My mam always says there should be no more than one woman at a time in a kitchen.'

Simon laughed. 'What? You have to be joking, man. My mother can destroy a fried egg – all black and curly on the edge and the yolk still raw. She's hopeless. I love her, but she's still hopeless. She's not a kitchen person.'

'She's not a cleaning-up person at all,' Sarah added. 'Anyway, she's got a job at your school, Amy and Maddy. She's staying at the convent and she looks after all the money. Very good at arithmetic, is Ma.'

Maddy and Amy had already heard snippets about Mrs Butlin and the convent. Neither girl could understand anyone who chose to live among the sisters. In their opinion, it was almost like volunteering to serve time in prison without having first committed a crime. Maddy's dad was always saying 'It takes all kinds to make a world', and he was clearly right.

'Come on,' said Jay after a short silence. 'Best get back to the house. In winter, we'll be fetched and taken back because of the dark. It'll be like being little kids again.'

'You are a little kid,' grinned George.

'I'm nine,' insisted Jay. 'Not far off ten – and you're only eleven.'

'Nearly twelve,' said the older boy.

The ensuing scuffle ended the short meeting. George and Jay left the small building together, the former holding the latter in a wrestler's headlock.

'Be your age,' chided Maddy.

George obeyed, not because he wished to be compliant, but because he needed to impress Maddy. For quite some time, he had needed to impress Maddy. And he could not work out why.

Monty loved Yuspeh's chickens. While the weather was warm, he often spent the night in their midst, soothed to sleep by their little clucky sounds, sometimes surrounded by fussy, feathery creatures who snuggled up to steal his warmth. He slept in their house in another house, one of his own which had been brought in section by section until it made a kennel within the hen house. Chickens invaded his space, but he was quite content in their company.

He lay on his back, all four legs in the air, while Esther and Naomi groomed him. They charged nothing for this service and he was grateful for all the attention to his long, furry coat. Suddenly and for no apparent reason, his left ear clicked to attention. He rolled, making sure that all birds were out of danger, then stood on guard in the kennel's doorway. There was something afoot. Lights were doused, which meant that most people slept, but there was

329

movement somewhere within the dog's sixth-sense radar. The air smelt wrong. An extra ingredient had invaded his territory and he objected to it with every pore along his spine. Hackles rose and he cleared the hen run in a single leap. Esther and Naomi held a short conference about his behaviour, then returned to their nest boxes and settled down.

The thing on the road had been here before. It was connected to badness, but not to the first badness – the one Monty had swum in to the shore of the reservoir. It was the second badness. The dog sat in Yuspeh's gateway and forced himself not to growl. There was evil in the vicinity and he needed to watch it without being discovered.

Derek Ramsden was furious. He hated religious nutcases of any denomination and he detested Brian Butlin most of all. Being trounced by a man of God was not Derek's idea of a good day, so he had stayed awake deliberately in order to come out here and look at the lie of the land.

Was he safe? A blue light further along the road advertised the police station, but he had no intention of staying long. He stared up the path leading to the vicarage and, narrowing his eyes, assessed that there was a letter box. Paraffin, some cotton waste and a bit of luck should suffice. Not tonight, though. Tonight was just a reconnoitre job. He would wait a few days or weeks until today's little episode was buried in the past; after a suitable time, he would do what needed to be done.

Stealthily, he released the handbrake and allowed the van to roll silently down the moor. He had cut his engine when arriving and, thanks to Mother Nature's design in this area, he had been able to come and go without detection. Or had he? A blur of movement sent a stab of fear into his ribs, but it was just a dog. Folk should keep those creatures inside at night, he told himself. His heartbeat slowed and he carried on rolling, but the dog was keeping up with him. Its teeth were bared and the whites of its eyes gleamed whenever a street lamp lit them.

Finally out of reach of all buildings, Derek pressed the ignition button and shot forward. That had been a weird experience. The same dog had been around before – he remembered seeing it on more than one occasion. It was as if the animal had read his mind. 'Bloody rubbish,' he said aloud as he made his way towards Bolton. It was only a dog, after all.

An air of gloom had descended on Maddy's bedroom. She and Amy stood side by side, each taking turns to look at her reflection in a cheval mirror. 'It's horrible,' said Maddy.

Amy agreed. It was the hat that finished it off, a great big brown velour item with a brown-and-yellow band encircling it all the way just above the too-deep brim. Rules dictated that this brim should be upturned at the back and down at the front. 'We look a bit like air-raid wardens,' said the smaller girl. 'And the coats could be rejects from army surplus. Especially mine, which is a sin.'

'Yes, it's bad,' agreed Maddy.

Amy's mother, for ever careful, had purchased a coat large enough to see Amy right through to the sixth form. No more than four inches of leg could be seen below its hemline. Socks were brown, knee-high, and sported two yellow stripes round the top. The gymslip was not a conventional two-buttons-on-each shoulder type, oh, no – the nuns had gone for a cross-over style. 'In brown again,' sighed Maddy as she unbuttoned the heavy coat. The clothes on their own were a terrible weight – she dreaded to think of carrying a satchel filled with books. 'We shall become round-shouldered and old before our time,' she added mournfully. 'You were right, Amy, this is the end of our childhood. No child could wear this lot.'

'They want us to be ugly so that boys won't look at us,' Amy concluded. 'Who in their right mind would want to walk about looking like this? It's not as bad for you – at least your coat's the right length. And I'm still hopeless with the tie. Why should we wear a tie? We're not men and we never will be.'

The tie, in brown-and-yellow diagonal stripes, was a nuisance. There was also a little zipped purse on a cord. Regulations dictated that it must rest on the left hip, with the plaited cord over the head and on the right shoulder. 'I'm fed up,' moaned Amy. 'I look like a refugee orphan in somebody else's clothes.'

In addition, the two girls were the rather-less-than-proud owners of brown gloves – to be worn at all times except inside school – great big lace-up outdoor shoes, sandals for inside, a divided skirt for physical training, a drawstring bag for gym shoes, and a satchel, also brown. The divided skirt had been tested by both mothers, who had been forced to ensure that hems were no more than three inches from the floor when the wearer was in a kneeling position.

'What are you doing?' gasped Amy. Maddy had removed her hat and was trying to make a pleat in the back to render it smaller. 'You'll never get away with it,' she added, deep shock welded into the words.

'Some do,' Maddy replied.

'Yes, but they're in fifth and sixth forms. When they're fifth and sixth, they could be working and earning. You never see a first former with a pleat.'

'Times change,' Maddy insisted. 'The hat is too big and I hate having elastic under my chin – it makes me all goose-bumpy. It'll blow off if I don't make a pleat. It's a necessity.'

Amy grinned. If Maddy Horrocks put her mind to it, she could probably persuade angels that sin was the norm. 'Shall we go down, then? Get the fashion parade over with?' Rivington Cross was inordinately proud of its five grammar school entrants. Yvonne had closed the salon and had invited happy parents to attend the unveiling of their uniformed offspring. George, Sarah and Simon would be downstairs already. 'Come on, Maddy – you'll have the hat ruined.'

'You sound like your mother.'

'She's not as bad as she was,' said Amy.

'I know. But you still sound like her.'

They clattered down the stairs in shoes that might well have been designed for jungle warfare. 'I feel daft,' Maddy groaned.

'You look daft. It's that dent in your hat.'

They stood at the door leading to the salon, both listening to a buzz of conversation. The twins' mother could be heard and Maddy mouthed her pleasure at her companion. Although Sarah and Simon seldom gave voice to their problem, the whole gang knew that they wanted their mother home and wanted to keep Mrs Thornton, too. Maddy opened the door an inch or two. 'We look like wrecks,' she warned. 'No laughing.'

Yvonne dragged the door inward and looked at her daughter. 'She's been fiddling with her hat,' she told the small congregation. 'I knew she would. I've seen St Anne's girls in town – the older ones. They don't wear their hats – they walk in front of them.' She removed the item from her daughter's head, returned it to its original pristine condition, then handed it back. 'No fiddling,' she said.

The two girls stepped into the salon. Maddy, game as ever for a bit of fun, struck a modelling pose and strutted up and down in front of the row of washbasins. Her commentary said it all. 'Here we have Madeleine,' she pronounced in as near to the King's English as she could achieve. 'She is wearing the latest in potato sacks – courtesy of the Farmers' Union and thanks to the inmates of Strangeways Jail. Note the cut of the gymslip . . .' She peeled off her coat.

Yuspeh Feigenbaum clapped her hands together in glee.

Maddy continued. 'The socks, ex-army issue, have been hand-knitted by residents of Prestwich Mental Hospital. The stupid purse is to be worn thus.' She performed a demonstration. 'The Cross and Passion badge on the purse is to be displayed at all times, because Mother Olivia said so.' Maddy turned. 'Come here, Amy.'

Amy, fighting back laughter, obeyed.

Maddy's tone became sombre. 'This is what happens when a girl is forced to wear too big a coat. Turn round, Amy.' When Amy was displaying the back of her coat, the incorrigible commentator continued. 'Here we see a slightly different design which can double up as wedding dress with train as long as a girl doesn't mind being married in a chocolate-coloured garment.' She looked at Celia. 'It's swallowing her, Mrs Bradshaw.'

Jakob Forrester, who had taken an hour off work, jumped to his feet. 'This we can save,' he said. 'No charge, no material lost and we shall fix it for you.'

'Thank you.' Amy smiled. All she wanted was to look as bad as everyone else. Definitely not worse.

Sarah, Simon and George were all immaculate in Bolton School's sensible navy blues and greys. Maddy envied them because they wouldn't get Catholicism crammed down their throats for about an hour each day. And they looked like normal people.

'Very nice,' said Caroline Butlin.

Maddy fixed Mrs Butlin with a look that was meant to be steely. 'We don't agree,' she replied for herself and her companion. 'Brown is the most miserable colour on earth and this yellow makes us look ill. On top of that, we've got nuns.'

'I know,' answered the vicar's wife. 'I have them too, because they employ me as bursar. They are nice women. In fact, I believe the lay teachers are tougher than the nuns.'

Yuspeh, deliberately obtuse, chipped in. 'Tough is no good and requires a good soaking overnight. This I have to do with meat from the kosher butcher in Bolton. Never tender. So I shall remember to cook just nuns and no other teachers.'

The tension was broken and Yvonne served tea and cakes. George whispered to Maddy, 'See? How well trained my family has become? They drink tea and eat cakes in a Gentile household. Isn't civilization a wonderful thing?'

Maddy dug him with her elbow and told him to behave himself. Mr and Mrs Butlin were seated side by side, which was a good thing, and Celia, who seemed almost dependent on Yuspeh, sat with her husband, Yuspeh, Anna and Jakob.

The moment was a defining one, mused John Horrocks as he bit into an eclair. His little girl was no longer a little girl. Soon, she, Amy, Sarah, Simon and George would outstrip their parents when it came to formal education. Proud as a peacock, he watched his daughter as she made small talk with adults and children alike. The job had been a good one, he decided. His Maddy definitely came up to scratch, but she was right – the uniform was a mess and no mistake.

There was a peace about the place, a level of tranquillity that managed to outweigh even the chattering of women. Brian Butlin followed his wife into territory he had never expected to invade, and was immediately struck by the beauty of the convent. A few young postulants smiled and giggled as he passed, but that small event failed completely to break the mood. 'It's wonderful,' he whispered.

'And it has television.' Caroline led her husband into the tiny flat. 'See?' She pointed to the envied item in the corner of her sitting room.

He perched on the edge of a small sofa. 'Are you sure the Reverend Mother won't mind?'

'I asked her if you could come. She became quite flustered and pleased – apart from a very old priest and the occasional bishop, they are completely unused to the company of men. I expect they see fathers of the pupils, but not in here – school is separate.' She went through to her kitchen to make tea.

'Caroline?'

'Yes?'

He took a deep breath. 'Do you think you will ever be able to consider coming home?'

She leaned against the sink. That he should want her back after what she had done was a miracle indeed. 'I am still in thinking time,' she reminded him. 'But yes, I expect I shall be back if you and the children will have me.'

Brian's fists closed and he was reminded of his attack on Derek Ramsden. But this time, he felt only joy. He would not press her, must not press her. Patience was a virtue he had long mastered, and he must employ it yet again.

They drank their tea, then Caroline led her husband through to the chapel. She wanted him to be there for choir practice and longed to see his reaction when the nuns sang. From a back pew, the couple heard the spine-tingling sound of soprano voices raised in praise of God.

> *'Panis angelicus*
> *Fit panis hominum*
> *Dat panis coelicus*
> *Figuris terminum . . .'*

Brian felt every hair on the back of his neck rising to attention. All around, Stations of the Cross showed Christ's suffering as He made his way to crucifixion. Over the altar, a magnificent but small rose window coloured the scene, afternoon light piercing through blues, reds, greens and yellows. The whole thing was brutally exquisite, painful and heart-rending.

'Pauper, pauper, Servus et humilis,' sang the choir.

Then the scene in its entirety was ruined by the choir mistress, a tiny nun with a speaking voice that might have stopped an express train. 'Mary Josephine – are you hearing a different accompaniment? You were up there all by yourself like a crow sitting on the Town Hall clock. I never heard anything like it. Oh, well, it'll have to do, I suppose.'

Brian hid his face behind a hand. The phrase 'sublime to ridiculous' had just been thoroughly illustrated.

The nun fidgeted with some papers and announced that *Tantum Ergo* would be the next piece for Mary Josephine to ruin. But if this were ruination, Brian Butlin felt he could settle for it any day of the week. He dabbed his eyes, blew his nose and hoped that his wife would not imagine that he had been driven to the brink of tears.

'Beautiful, isn't it?' she whispered.

'Yes.' They were doing something together, were sharing precious moments of joy – and that, in Brian's opinion, was where the true magnificence of this occasion lay.

TWELVE

Derek Ramsden had slaked his thirst, had eaten yet another meal of fish and chips and was ready to face yet another afternoon on Bolton Market. Or was he? He looked around the room in which he had just taken lunch, saw half a dozen cups, some glasses, two greasy plates, wrappings from several dinners. In a corner, a pile of clothes threatened to tumble from the chair on which it sat. What was happening to him? He had managed for long enough without Beryl, so why had he suddenly become so incompetent?

He had missed a whole morning, had slept while he ought to have been making a living, was in danger of losing his income. And it was all her fault. Oh, she had been happy enough to leave her husband and kids, but had she shown any patience? They were all the same, bloody women, wanted their own way, instant gratification, good clothes, money, a freedom supplied by some idiot of a man who was willing to ignore his own wants and needs.

Wants, needs? Who was providing for Derek Ramsden's requirements? No bugger cared whether he lived or died – that was the cold, hard truth. Something had to be done, so much was plain. A thick layer of dust coated each surface in this and every other room; he could not remember when his bed sheets had last been changed and washed. Routine. He remembered a routine he had followed for years – washing on Sundays, a bit of cleaning each evening, ironing a job for Monday nights. The house had never sparkled, but it had been acceptable.

It had all slipped away from him and the task was now too big. He needed a woman. It would have to be a competent female and not the sort he occasionally pursued when darkness had fallen. Not that he had picked up anyone since the Rose Martindale episode – he was too afraid to even contemplate using a prostitute again. Women laughed at him. They made him see red and it was all their fault, yet he was the one who would hang should he be caught.

Postcards. He had seen some in a drawer of the sideboard, and he emptied it, found them and rooted round for a pen. Small newsagents placed adverts in windows for a shilling a week, so he would take advantage of that service. He found a piece of paper and composed his notice.

BUSINESSMAN REQUIRES WOMAN TO DO
LAUNDRY AND IRONING, PLUS CLEANING
AND SOME COOKING. MUST BE
EFFICIENT AND TRUSTWORTHY,
REFERENCES ESSENTIAL. APPLY BY
LETTER TO THIS ESTABLISHMENT.

When he had copied the words onto half a dozen postcards, he slipped them into a pocket and prepared to leave for the market. There were plenty of small shops along his route, so he could spread his message far and wide. She would have to be plain, he decided as he climbed into the van. Yes, plain and of a certain age. All he needed was a char. Pretty women were for a different purpose altogether and, for the time being at least, he wanted no truck with them.

Celia Bradshaw was finally back at her work full time. She liked her new boss, found Linda Marshall to be fair and an excellent doctor. It was nice for the women of the village to have a female practitioner for a change – not all ladies could discuss intimate problems with a member of the opposite sex.

She was filing notes when Linda came in from her rounds. 'I must have driven thirty miles this morning,' grumbled the doctor. 'What do you say to a spot of lunch in the pub, Celia? A nice ploughman's with a half of shandy?'

Celia smiled and nodded her agreement. Dr Marshall treated her as an equal rather than as a part of the furniture. Her predecessor had been a decent enough chap, but he had taken for granted that his staff would always be there, that his coffee would be on his desk at nine o'clock each morning and that the establishment would run like a well-oiled machine at all times. Not only did Linda Marshall make her own coffee – she often made one for Celia and for the new district nurse.

In the pub, they ordered lunch and took a table by the window while waiting to be served. Linda studied her companion. 'Are you all right now, Celia?'

'Much better. Nearly back to what you might call normal – whatever that is. I mean, it's still hard, knowing that Nettie and I never got along. But time will heal in the end. I have to be patient with me.'

'Then you might want to halve the dose of those pills. They were only a temporary measure and it's best not to become dependent.'

The receptionist rummaged in her capacious handbag and brought forth a full jar of tablets. 'Untouched,' she said triumphantly.

'Well done.'

Celia placed the container back in the bag. 'It wasn't the pills,' she said. 'It was Yuspeh. And the chickens and that daft dog – and my other daughter, of course. But Yuspeh was the main one.'

The meal arrived and Linda attacked her portion with gusto. A morning spent travelling from farm to farm had left her famished. When the edge had been removed from her hunger, she spoke again. 'Friends are vital when tragedy strikes. Family too, of course.'

Celia smiled. 'All my life as a Catholic, I have been told how bad the Jews were for killing Jesus. They were condemned to wander the earth for all time and I actually feared them, you know.'

'Really?'

'Oh, yes. We were told that Jews were a breed

343

apart, cruel and uncaring. Yet I have never met anyone as wonderfully kind as Yuspeh. Her daughter-in-law is nice, but a very quiet sort of woman – you hardly notice she's there till she comes out with one of her wisecracks and has you rolling on the floor. Their house has turned out to be my second home.'

Linda Marshall had no time for religion, no matter what its form. She didn't believe in any supreme being and was convinced that mankind was merely an ape that had mastered the arts of communication and killing with weaponry. 'It doesn't matter who helps you, Celia,' she said. 'As long as you stay well, take comfort whenever and wherever you can.' She paused, buttered a shive of crusty bread. 'I understand that you have stopped attending church here in the village.'

Celia paused, a glass halfway to her lips. 'Yes.'

'May I ask why?'

The older woman placed her glass on the table. 'I got into trouble with Father Sheahan.'

'Really?'

'Yes. He told me off in confession for consorting with the Forrester family – that's Anna, Jakob and young George. But mainly, it's Yuspeh Feigenbaum. He accused me of exposing myself to bad influences.'

'Did you answer him?'

Celia blushed. 'I did. And I said things I should never have said in a church, so then I had to go to St Patrick's in town and make my confession all over again. The priest there didn't care about me associating with Yuspeh. He said there's good and bad everywhere. So I catch a bus to town every Sunday and go to Mass there. Amy comes with me sometimes, but she usually goes to church here with her friend.'

Linda Marshall stared through the window, her gaze fixed on the presbytery. Although she was not a religious woman, she could sense evil and the damned priest embodied it. 'I don't like him,' she whispered, 'and neither did Phil Bennett.'

'I know. He's a tough priest, is Father Sheahan. Old-fashioned. He sticks to every word of the New Testament and won't tolerate any disagreement.'

Linda wiped her mouth on a napkin. 'There are things I can't say – Hippocratic oath and all that – but Dr Bennett gave me information about the priest that made my blood run cold. He had no absolute proof, but he thought there was something very unsavoury about Sheahan. He told me that several children – girls in particular – have managed to become disturbed and badly behaved and that Sheahan is at the back of it all.'

Celia shrugged. 'Amy never said anything. Maddy Horrocks doesn't like him, but I can't remember her ever saying why. It may be because he shouts a lot and Maddy knows her own mind – old head on young shoulders, that one.'

The doctor finished her lemonade shandy. Michael Sheahan would stay away from the brighter girls, she mused. He would pick on loners, children who had few friends and nowhere to run. If Phil Bennett had been right, that was.

'He's gone diabetic, hasn't he?' Celia asked.

'He has indeed.'

Celia leaned forward. 'He has a problem with drink, you know. Irish whiskey. I hear he has it brought up in boxes of twelve from a place in town. Makes you wonder.'

'Makes you wonder what?'

'Well – when he's preaching, is it him talking or is it the booze? It pushes people over the edge, does strong drink. I swear I could smell it on him that night in confession when he told me off. See, he's only a man at the end of the day, isn't he? You know, sometimes . . .' The words died.

'Sometimes?' the doctor prompted.

'Well, like I said – I wonder. You know how people are – thinking in quiet times. And I start pondering over what's right, who's right. I've been taught that only Catholics go to heaven. Well, I'm not so sure about that any more. There's a few Catholics I know who shouldn't be let in the corner shop, never mind heaven.'

Linda Marshall smiled to herself. The importance people placed on religion was a constant source of bemusement. What did any of it matter when life was so fragile and so quickly over? Roman Catholic, Anglo-Catholic, Methodist, Jew, Buddhist – they were all here for so short a time, why spend it worrying about an afterlife that probably didn't exist?

'I'd best get back to my filing,' said Celia after glancing at the bar clock. 'And you've a very full

346

surgery tonight – looks like there's a stomach bug about.'

Linda sighed. 'Refrigerators should be given free to the entire population. Food goes off so quickly in summer because people can't afford to store it properly. And the cost in terms of medical bills is appalling – all for the want of a bit of ice.'

Celia grinned. Tainted food was one of her new employer's hobby horses. 'We're getting one,' she said proudly. 'The Forresters have one and I've been saving up. You can set a jelly in half the time with a fridge. And you can keep a bit of ice cream in the top bit.'

'Quite,' replied Dr Marshall. 'But the main thing is fresh meat and—' He was walking past the pub, swaying from side to side, the biretta slipping down his sweaty forehead. For how much longer would he survive as an alcoholic diabetic? 'Look at the state of him,' she said, almost to herself.

'He should be ashamed,' agreed Celia. She had ceased to be surprised by herself. The old Celia had been buried alongside Nettie – well, she hoped that the old Celia was gone. 'It's a very bad example for young people.'

But Linda Marshall worried about the young for a very different reason. If this man was a paedophile, the whole weight of Rome would come to the fore should anyone attempt to expose him. He was quite the most detestable man it had ever been the doctor's misfortune to meet.

'Come on,' chided Celia. 'They won't get better without you there, will they?'

The two women walked back to the surgery in comfortable silence. Celia returned to her files and Linda, alone in her consulting room, continued to watch the large, shambling figure as it made its way to the home of a parishioner. Rivington Cross nurtured in its bosom the vilest of creatures, but he walked about wearing a mantle bestowed by some high-ranking cleric many years ago.

He should be stopped. Phil Bennett had been at a loss, as was she. The idea of questioning children – even those who were now adults – was not palatable. And, as she had said earlier to her receptionist, there was that blasted Hippocrates to consider. The Greeks had done a lot of good in this world, but the father of medicine, so long respected and admired, had tied the hands of a woman who itched to know the truth. She smiled to herself. There was something she could do – she could double the loathsome man's dose of tranquillisers.

Beyond tranquillisers, it was hopeless. Linda Marshall sat down, picked up some notes and lost herself in more immediate problems. A child who needed a tonsillectomy could be dealt with; the evil priest must be returned yet again to a back burner.

Betty Thornton was afraid of allowing herself to feel happy. If she became too happy, it would all be taken away from her like a burst balloon.

She was not without her reservations – any woman working in an area where two female bodies had been discovered was going to have a few misgivings – but she loved her job, was a born home-maker, and revelled in her status as housekeeper. James was content – there were trees to climb and a few conkers had begun to appear on the horse chestnuts, and the lad was in his element. He knew where foxes lurked, had seen a badger in twilight, loved his own little room tucked under the eaves.

It was a grand house, the sort she had never expected to see, let alone occupy. But every time she thought about Mrs Butlin, Betty's heart dropped all the way down to her summer sandals. Mr Butlin still loved his wife – that much was plain each time the woman came to the house. It was the way he looked at her – his expression would have pulled at the heartstrings of any onlooker, Betty felt sure.

'I want him to be all right,' she said as she stood at her bedroom window. But she wanted herself to be all right, too; wanted James to continue to be settled. The boy had embraced the move from the very first day and he played properly with Simon, George and the girls. There had been the usual rough-and-tumble, but no nastiness had risen to the surface. James belonged, fitted in, was fast becoming a part of village life.

'Mam?'

She turned. 'Hello, James. Have you tidied your room?'

'Yes.' He continued to hover in the doorway.

'Well?'

'Promise you won't get mad at me.'

Her shoulders drooped. 'What have you done now?'

'Nothing. Well, it's nothing, but it's something.'

She shook her head. What a way to start the day – James with one of his convoluted conundrums. 'How can it be nothing and still be something? You'll not be joining Simon at Bolton School in a couple of years if you can't make a better job of explaining yourself.'

Jay inhaled deeply. 'I don't want you worrying, Mam. I had a talk to Mr Butlin a while back. He said we won't have to leave even if Mrs Butlin does come back. He says we can stay here or he'll find us somewhere else to live round here and a few people want help in their houses, so we won't have to go back to Claughton Street and I won't have to go back to Sunning Hill and—'

'Breathe!' she ordered. 'You're going a funny colour. And you shouldn't be making a pest of yourself, mithering like that.'

Jay breathed. 'I thought you'd be pleased.'

She was pleased. 'Oh, go and put the kettle on, James. I'll be down in a minute.'

Alone once more, Betty wiped her eyes on a handkerchief. Her son had cared enough, had loved her enough to talk to Mr Butlin. Sometimes, James almost made her cry for the right reasons and this was one of those times. He wasn't a bad boy. But he had better wash his hands and face before breakfast . . .

Yvonne was combing out Mildred Cookson. The hair was deteriorating fast and the owner of the salon wanted to be sure that she would not be blamed for it. So, while Mildred was the only customer, the bull's horns needed to be seized. 'Now, love, you'd better listen to me and I'll talk fast in case we get another customer. Whatever you've been using on this head of yours has taken its toll. You're losing your hair, Mildred.'

'Give over,' came the swift response. 'We always thin out in our family when we get a bit older. My gran was as bald as a coot by the time she was eighty.'

'But you're not eighty, are you? Look.' She held a mirror close to the back of her customer's head and reflected the view in the over-sink glass. 'See? You've a spot there nearly the size of a two bob piece. You'll have to let the bleach grow out to give yourself a chance. I'm not saying your hair will definitely all come back, but I'm telling you now, if you carry on, you've no chance.'

Mildred burst into tears. 'I knew it wasn't right,' she sobbed, 'but when I do the roots, the bloody stuff goes all over, so . . .'

'I know, I know. So the whole lot gets a good dousing every time. Now. Look at me. Look at me, Mildred. You've got to let it grow out. It's so porous that it takes ages to dry and it's breaking. It has to go – we have to get rid. And the best way to do that is for me to cut it within an inch of its life—'

'But I'll look like a man. I can't. I can't lose it, Yvonne.'

'You can. I've got a wig and you can borrow it. I'll style it for you and you can keep it nice in between. All we do is tell everybody you decided to go a bit darker – it's like an ash blond. I'm telling you now, nobody will know. These wigs are all the rage in America – everybody's got one. But I want you to come back tonight after I'm closed and I'll cut this lot off. For a kick-off, you'd be too hot in a wig with a load of your own hair underneath. Then take the wig off at night – I'll lend you a stand to put it on – and let the air get to your scalp. Your old man will just have to put up with it. Refer him to me if he misbehaves.'

'But Yvonne—'

'Shut up. There's somebody coming.'

The front door crashed inward. 'I am sent,' announced Yuspeh Feigenbaum.

'Are you?' Yvonne's eyebrows moved upward.

'I am.' Yuspeh plonked herself in a waiting chair and picked up a magazine.

Yvonne's eyes met Mildred's in the mirror. 'I'll just finish setting you, then, Mildred.' She peered over her shoulder. 'Was there something you wanted, Mrs Feigenbaum?'

Yuspeh threw down her magazine. 'This is hairdressing shop, yes?'

'Er . . . yes.'

'And I have hair, so I am come because I am sent. My grandson, George – he does the sending. He tells me be cheerful and look cheerful. He tells me wear colours and get hair done, so I am come for hair done, then I shall buy clothes and become a scarlet woman.'

Mildred choked on a mixture of laughter and grief, but Yvonne was forced to carry on as

352

normal – a customer was a customer, after all. Since her arrival in the village, Mrs Feigenbaum had worn her hair scraped into a bun and her clothes had always been black. 'Right. Well, you read your magazine while I finish Mildred off. Then we'll see what we can do for you.'

Yuspeh pretended to laugh and picked up the magazine again. 'Do for me? What can be done here with this? And I am not frightening anyone. George says I would frighten horses because I always am in black. He says women of England does not wear the black. So, I shall buy red cardigan and be cheerful.' Looking as cheerful as a funeral party, Yuspeh applied herself to a recipe for chocolate mousse. 'A lot of eggs is needed for this mousse,' she said. 'Soon, Celia and I shall have many eggs.'

Mildred did not know where to put herself. After the agony concerning her hair, the comic character in the waiting area was too much to bear, so she excused herself and went to the ladies' washroom.

Yvonne sauntered across to Yuspeh. 'You want it cutting?'

'No. I do not. It is George wants it cutting.'

'Then don't have it done if you don't want it done.'

For the third time, Yuspeh placed her reading matter on the table. 'He is going to the Bolton School. I shall go to school when there is something happening there – plays, exhibitions, parents' evenings. He is ashamed for me.'

'Ashamed *of* you.'

'Yes, that is what I say. All the English bubbahs

wear bright clothes and hair short. Well, those who have not been put away into nursing home by people who do not care. So this I shall do with clothes and hair. For what is a woman made but sacrifice?'

The door to the washroom opened, closed again. It was clear that Mildred's hysteria had not settled.

'You should be yourself,' advised Yvonne.

'I am myself. Who else would I be? I am Yuspeh Feigenbaum and I did not say my name was any other.'

'I didn't mean that.' Yvonne was treading on the thinner end of her own patience by this time. 'I meant wear what you like and have your hair the way you want to wear it. Don't let your grandson tell you what to do.'

Yuspeh grinned broadly. 'Very well, I tell truth. I am wanting this for me, but I am blame George. It is my way. Now, do I have time to go for a newspaper?'

'Yes.'

When the old lady had left, Yvonne opened the washroom door. 'You can come out now, you daft bat. I've had some lunatics in here in my time, but Mrs Feigenbaum takes the full packet of biscuits. Here, let me sort you out.'

While she covered Mildred's bald patches for the final time, Yvonne realized that she was scared. What if she made a mess of the old woman's hair? It looked as if it hadn't seen scissors for a hundred years.

As if reading the hairdresser's mind, Mildred asked, 'What are you going to do with her?'

'No bloody idea,' Yvonne answered. And that was the brutally honest truth.

Maddy was in her element. 'There were people living on the moors long before Bolton was invented,' she told her audience. 'They could keep watch from up there and they made camps.'

Jay, flicking through a copy of *Dandy*, knew when he was out of his depth to the point of total immersion. Desperate Dan he could cope with; the Mesolithic era was rather like school – it was talked about, but it was best not taken too seriously. He licked a grubby finger and turned the page.

'They've been buried,' insisted their leader when she got no response. 'And some of them were buried with ceremony. That means they were sort of civilized and tried to do things properly.'

'Were they dead?' asked Jay.

Maddy sighed loudly. 'I suppose they were dead, but the Tumulus was a strange one – he was practically kneeling and he had a cup and a spear with him – he might have been in the middle of his dinner. Now, all these graves have stuff in them – not just bones, things. They had knives and plates – all sorts of bits and pieces to see them through the afterlife. So there was belief in some sort of god, wasn't there?'

After a heavy silence, she waved a sheaf of papers. 'See – 1825, skeleton with beaker. 1851, bones of young people and animals. Flints, flints and more flints. These were Stone and Bronze

Age folk. Breightmet – cremation urns found by the dozen. There was one skeleton dug up with an arm missing – folk could see where it had been chopped off. They were probably trying to do surgery. Some of this stuff goes back to eight thousand years BC. Am I wasting my time here?' Her father had always been interested in the history of burial rituals, because that was his business, and Maddy had begun to take an avid look at the same subject. 'Am I talking to myself, you lot?'

George was messing about with a boy scout knife. 'This bit for taking stones out of horses' hooves – I wonder if I'll ever find a use for it?'

Maddy glared at him until he put the offending item on the table. Jay snatched it up and started to scrape dirt from his nails. It was clear that the meeting did not share Maddy's enthusiasm for the ancient history of the Pennine Moors.

'Look,' she shouted, 'big tombs. They made caves shored up with slabs and put artefacts with their dead.'

'What's arty-thingies?' asked Jay.

'Read a comic,' came the swift response. 'What I mean is they knew. They knew there was another place, another kingdom. So they accepted that there was a king and that king has to be God. A creator. There are hundreds and hundreds of people buried—'

'Yes,' agreed George amiably. 'They're out there in our graveyard.' He waved at the bell house door, sighed. 'Sorry. I know, I know – you mean dead Ancient Britons.'

'They weren't even Britons,' answered Maddy. 'They were just people who lived on hills so that they could see others coming.'

'It's a history lesson,' complained Sarah, 'and we aren't even in a classroom.'

Maddy was fast approaching boiling point. 'It's more than history – it's our beginnings – it's religion – it's what keeps us all together but separate.' She looked at her sketches of the Pennine Pike Stones. This was a wonderful piece of work and it was leading her . . . somewhere, but no-one was in the slightest way interested. If she closed her eyes, she could see those long-ago people dressed in animal skins, all of them pushing and pulling at heavy stones to make chambers for their dead. It was awesome.

'Maddy,' said Simon. 'We aren't quite up to the mark with this stuff, and—'

'Good heavens!' Maddy jumped to her feet. She would have the last word, no matter what. 'They had God,' she repeated. 'Middle Stone Age – Bronze Age – they recognized an afterlife.'

'And your point is?' Simon was becoming hungry.

'The point is that I don't know what the point is. I shall fix all this stuff to a board – when I find a big enough board – and perhaps some of it will get through your skulls by the time you're fifty. I think what I am saying is that Cave Man was right and we've messed it up.'

George retrieved his knife from Jay. 'They all died in their thirties and they lived in holes. What's clever about that?'

'I'm talking about faith,' she snapped. 'Not

about their living conditions. What they believed in was simple and beautiful. They didn't need churches and temples – they did it properly.' She meant— Oh, what did she mean? It had all gone haywire somewhere along the line and there was a very simple answer staring her in the face, but she hadn't the ability to reach out and touch it.

Sarah stood up and walked to the door. 'Maddy means it was less complicated, I think.'

'Thank you.' The self-appointed teacher of this delinquent class smiled. 'It's something like that, but . . . It's something like that.' She would need to go to the reference library in Bolton. Those long-dead people meant something. They had left messages, standing stones, burial chambers, monuments. There had to be a reason, a plan. 'I'll find out more,' she said. Then, with the air of a lecturer whose students had not come up to scratch, she gathered up her papers and left the arena.

'I think we got about two out of ten between us,' groaned Simon.

George smiled. Maddy had a bee in her bonnet and she would not rest until the buzzing had stopped. 'She was just being Maddy.' He smiled. 'She was just being herself. Come on, gang – time to eat.'

The urge was upon him again, had been re-appearing for days on end, but he had managed to overcome it thus far. The knowledge that he had ended the life of Rose Martindale gave rise to diametrically opposed emotions; he felt elated and, at the same time, frightened to death. Yet he needed . . . He needed not to become a serial murderer.

He stood up, threw down the newspaper and combed his hair. A shave might have been a good idea, but he couldn't be bothered. The Rose Martindales of this world deserved everything they got – including a stubbly chin. Was he going to pick up another Rose? 'A Rose by any other name would smell as putrid,' he mumbled. Perhaps he should walk down to the Lion for a pint instead. He could have a game of darts, or he might play dominoes with some of the older men.

Older men. Derek was no spring chicken and it occurred to him that he would soon be one of that number – a poor old man whose few pleasures included dominoes, cards, joke-telling in the corner of some smoky bar. The chair opposite his in this very room had been un-occupied for years – apart from those few days with Caroline Butlin. Caroline Butlin, the fragrant flower who had turned out to be bindweed whose purpose had been to choke him almost to perdition. Empty chair, empty life, empty future – was he ready for such isolation? Beryl had been gone for years. How many years? And she had left him deliberately, had taken her own life. They were all the same – self-absorbed, greedy and impatient.

The van keys were in his hand. He could not remember picking them up, but he was holding them. The city of Manchester was just a few miles away; there were other places – Bury, Burnley, Blackburn, Bolton – all the B-towns in a row like sitting ducks – where should he go? There were more people in a city, he reasoned inwardly. Liverpool with its dock road had for centuries provided women to service incoming sailors. It was a hello and goodbye place, here today and gone tomorrow – there would be plenty of flesh in Liverpool. But Manchester was nearer.

The door bell sounded and he froze immediately. Had he left any clues, had police traced him? He could not pretend to be out – he had lights blazing all over the place, since dusk was arriving earlier now. Fear almost choked him as the bell was pressed again. Whoever stood outside on the steps was not going to give up easily. After a deep intake of breath, he walked down the hall and opened the door. Relief almost caused his knees to buckle when he opened the door. 'Yes?'

The woman seemed nervous. 'Erm . . . I know it's late, but I saw the card in the shop and I left a letter, but you haven't collected it. So I mithered on until the shopkeeper told me who you are and where you live. Has it gone?'

He was lost for a moment. 'Has what gone?'

'The job – cleaning up, washing, ironing.'

Derek managed a tight smile. 'Oh, that? No, I haven't found anybody.'

'I can cook. I don't mind cooking. And I can start any time, no problem.'

She was small, only about five feet in height. The Liverpool accent caused him to recall his thoughts from a few moments earlier, when he had been contemplating . . . 'Come in.' He pulled the door wider. 'It's a mess. I've been a widower a long time now. The job, you see – it keeps me busy.'

She nodded her head. 'Market. I've seen you there – I've bought stuff off you. You're in a corner near the wall, am I right?'

'You're right enough.' He showed her the front room. 'Just dusty in here,' he said. 'Once a week's enough – I don't use this room much. I live in the back. The back room's a lot worse.'

She grinned. 'Look, lad, don't you be worrying over me. I've done enough cleaning in my life to make it second nature. My Bertie's a messy monkey, God love him. Daughter's gone now, so it's just me and Bertie.'

He took her into the back room, the kitchen, up the stairs. 'Third bedroom's just storage – leave it,' he advised. 'Stock in there and stuff that's been collected over the years. Second bedroom just once in a blue moon, but this is my room and it's a disgrace.'

It was a disaster zone. It stank of sweaty socks and filthy sheets, but the woman remained unimpressed. 'Look, if you've lived down Scotland Road, you've seen it all. Give me a week's trial, eh? If I'm no good, sack me on the spot and don't pay me. All right?'

He led her down the stairs. She was the right age, he decided. She was too old to care whether he could satisfy a woman. She was beyond the stage where everything was expected for nothing in return. Also, she wittered. Beryl had been a witterer until the depression had taken her over. There was something solid and

361

comforting about a woman of a certain age, one who had a lot to say about the small things in life. 'Make us both a cup of tea, then,' he said. 'Oh, and what's your name? I'm Derek Ramsden.'

'I know,' she replied, 'and I'm Ellen Langton. We used to live in Liverpool until after the war, then we followed our daughter to Bolton. Now she's done a disappearing act, so I don't know why we bothered. Bertie's still working in engineering, but I've got to the stage where a nice little job in a quiet house would suit me down to the ground.' She went into the kitchen and started clattering.

While she rattled cups and saucers, she continued with what Derek termed the 'wittering'. She talked about how she missed her grandson, about the price of getting Bertie's shoes soled and heeled, about her neighbours. 'They think we're stupid because we talk different. But we're not stupid.'

She poked her head into the living room. 'Mind, we might be stupid if you think about it. Our Betty – the daughter – came to live here and went Methodist. I ask you – Methodist?' The tongue clicked. 'We're Catholics from way back and she married a Catholic, too, but he got killed in the war. Nice lad, Jimmy Thornton. Anyway, next news – she's gone Methodist. We tried our best, but she wouldn't listen. And now – where is she? Gone, that's where. So perhaps we are stupid for trying to make her buckle down. Could have stayed in Liverpool, couldn't we?'

The gears in Derek's head began to mesh. Had she said Thornton? Because that rang a bell and the bell was attached to the departed Caroline Butlin. He accepted a cup of tea and Ellen deposited herself in the chair opposite his, the seat that had belonged to Beryl. It was nice just to have someone there – anyone – just a person who listened and had something to say for herself. 'I've no religion,' he told her in case she had ideas about converting him to something or other. 'But I've no objection to religious people.'

Ellen smoothed her skirt and placed cup and saucer on a low table. 'I've got past that with our Betty,' she told him. 'All I want is to see my grandson. If you think about it, kids are all we've got that means anything.'

'I've no children,' he told her.

'Oh. I'm sorry.'

He, too, was sorry. This very evening, he had been thinking about dominoes and loneliness, a pint every evening, then back to an empty house, no-one to care for him, no comfort. 'I . . . er . . . I might have an idea about your daughter.' Taking a few sips of tea, he gave himself time to come up with the right words.

'What?' she asked, her body moving forward in the chair.

'It's very awkward,' he said carefully. 'You see, I had a bit of an argument with a bloke – a vicar, as a matter of fact. We don't see eye to eye. His wife was involved – I don't need to give you the details – and the pair of them have been trying to damage my reputation ever since. I can't afford damage, not while I'm in trade.'

Ellen nodded her encouragement.

'I don't know where the wife is now, but she left the vicar, and – well, the top and bottom of it is that I think your daughter is keeping house at the vicarage. I can't be sure, but I did hear the name once. I seem to remember a child being mentioned, so it could be your Betty. You said Betty Thornton, didn't you?'

Ellen Langton's eyes were wet.

'You never mention my name, though,' he said. 'Promise me. No matter what happens, keep me out of it.'

'I will, I will. As God is my witness, I'll say nothing.'

'All right. It's St Faith's, Rivington Cross. It's a live-in job and she's been there all summer.'

Ellen jumped up. 'I don't know how to thank you,' she said, her voice mangled by sobs. 'I was meant to come here, wasn't I?'

He took her to the door. 'Start tomorrow,' he said. 'There's a key under the plant pot to the right of the bottom step. Three hours a day, three days a week. All right?'

'Yes. Thanks.'

Her mind was clearly on other things, so he grabbed her arm. 'Remember, Ellen, not a word.'

'Right. Not a word.' She almost ran down to the pavement, allowing the gate to swing closed in her wake. He listened to her quick footfalls as she made her way home to her Bertie. 'What have I done?' he asked himself as he shut the door. He didn't know the woman, yet he had trusted her with information that could damage himself.

He cleared away the teacups, decided to tidy his room and change the bed linen. It was daft, and he knew it, because he had just employed someone to cover these very tasks. But he didn't want her thinking ill of him; he needed her to be on his side, yet he could not work out why – not completely.

THIRTEEN

One of the sights most pleasing to Betty Thornton was the children, all six of them, playing in the graveyard. At first, she had considered such behaviour disrespectful, especially when Monty became a part of the equation. But, having thought about it, she had decided that she wouldn't mind kiddies and a dog running and playing on top of her bones after her own death. People came, laid flowers, wept and left, but the dead were never alone in St Faith's graveyard, because they had happy young visitors every day.

The gang had developed a sixth sense, too, and they always went into the bell house when folk came to tend graves. On days when there were actual burials, they disappeared into thin air until the grave had been filled in. They were good children. Every time, they gave Betty or Brian the location of the thin air they intended to visit, and they had stayed away from the reservoir since the discovery of Rose Martindale's body.

Betty's gaze slid sideways and rested on the trees behind which lay the huge body of water. A lake of such a size – whether man-made or created by the hand of God – was a menacing presence, so why were children so drawn to it? Natural curiosity, she supposed. Fairy stories were terrifying, yet children of many generations had been kept amused by the wickedness of stepmothers, bad fairies, giants and ogres. She shivered. Terror had not driven her back to Bolton, had it?

She rinsed and dried dishes, found purse and shopping list, decided that the day was warm enough for just a cardigan to top her dress while she went to the village post office and general store. Stopping first to add *tea* to the list, Betty stepped out into a glorious late-summer day. She also stepped into Mrs Butlin, who was making her way up the path. 'Good morning,' said Betty.

Caroline placed a hand on the housekeeper's arm. 'Is he in?'

'I think he's in church.'

There followed a slight pause. 'You don't approve of me, do you, Mrs Thornton?'

Betty felt heat in her cheeks and knew that it showed. 'I'm not here to judge, Mrs Butlin. I'm here to get on with shopping and cleaning.'

'What I did was wrong. I feel wretched about it.'

How else should she feel? Betty Thornton asked herself. Was she expecting bunting and a brass band every time she got off the bus? 'It's nothing to do with me.'

'It has affected you,' said Caroline. 'And you fear me – I can sense that. Look, whatever happens in the future, you and your son will be taken care of.'

'I know that,' replied Betty. 'Your husband told my James that we'd be all right. I've shopping to do.'

Caroline bit her lip. 'If I do come back, you'll stay, won't you? Can we start with a clean sheet? Please?'

Betty looked down at her list. 'As long as there's tea and sugar on it, yes.' She raised her eyes and met the gaze of a woman who had done wrong. 'There's no such thing as clean sheets, Mrs Butlin – especially when our kids have slept between them.' She raised the shopping list. 'There's always something written on my sheets of paper, too. We're all sinners. I was frightened, yes. My sin was that I wanted your twins to be without a mother just so that I could keep my job and live up here.'

Caroline's shoulders relaxed. 'Perfectly understandable. Brian won't let you down and neither will I.'

Betty blinked back the saline. 'You go and find him, then I'll make us a nice cuppa when I get back.' She marched on, her step lightening as she approached the gate. She was going to be fine. Most important, James would be staying up here with his friends.

She crossed the road, looked at potted plants outside the general store side of the post office, and watched a total stranger emerging from the shop.

'Good morning, Mrs Thornton,' said the total stranger.

Betty felt a slackness in her jaw, waited for the light to dawn. When the woman placed her purchases in a coach-built pram, the penny dropped. 'It's you!' she exclaimed before she could stop herself.

'Everyone is a you or an I.'

'Well.' Betty took a pace backward to get a better view. 'I wouldn't have known you except for the voice. You look so . . . so different.'

Yuspeh Feigenbaum held forth for several minutes. She was not different. She was still a poor old Jewish woman who had left Poland and was grateful to England for a home, a son, a factory, a beautiful grandson, an excellent daughter-in-law (God should protect Anna), her good friend Celia and her chickens. She was greatly indebted to Bolton School for recognizing George Josef's genius, to the children who played with him, to Yvonne Horrocks for the new hairstyle. 'I am now looking cheerful,' she finished.

'That's a lovely cardigan,' offered Betty.

'Yes, I agree. I was trying a red one, but this pink is better for my skin. Now, I am able to do the blending in.' She made her farewell and pushed the pram homeward.

Betty shook her head slowly. Yuspeh Feigenbaum would never blend in. She was eccentric, bossy and wonderful.

Yvonne came out of the shop. 'So – what do you think of my latest creation?' She waved a hand in the direction of Yuspeh.

'You've taken ten years off her,' replied Betty. 'It's a beautiful style and it makes her face so much softer.'

Yvonne grinned. 'You should have been there. When I undid her hair, it was down past her waist. Every time the scissors clipped, she closed her eyes and muttered some kind of prayer. I was sweating cobs by the time I was halfway through. She's never had it cut since she came to England.'

'I wouldn't have dared,' said Betty.

'I felt as if I was going where no human had gone before. And can you imagine what she would have said if she hadn't liked it?'

'I don't want to think about it.'

Yvonne moved a little closer. 'Was that Mrs Butlin getting off the bus before? I thought I saw her when I came out of the salon – we were running out of tea.'

'Yes, she's here.'

Yvonne lowered her voice. 'What do you think?'

Betty raised her shoulders. 'It's not my place to think, Yvonne.' She decided on a return to the original subject. 'One thing about that old Jewish lady – she's got this village covered better than the police have. I notice we still have men patrolling after dark. She's good at motivating folk, isn't she? I like her.'

Yvonne accepted the tactic gracefully. 'We all love her, Betty. She's becoming one of our treasures, isn't she?'

'She's a one-off, that's for sure.' Betty went into the shop to make her purchases.

When she emerged, shopping basket in one hand, purse in the other, Betty's heart went into overdrive. She could not believe what she was seeing. The buses from Bolton, which arrived every twenty-five minutes, brought all kinds of people from the town. But the woman she saw was carrying no maps, was not wearing heavy walking boots and protective clothing. Oh, no. This one harboured no interest in ancient standing stones or in researching Rivington Cross's two beautiful churches – this was a person on a far more dangerous mission.

There was nowhere to run. Betty considered the idea of dodging into Hair By Yvonne, but she could not, because she had promised Mrs Butlin a nice cup of tea and she needed to stay in that lady's good books. Dreading a repeat of scenes from years gone by, Betty crossed the road to face the woman who had become the bane of her life. Mother? Ellen Langton didn't know the first thing about being a parent.

Betty plastered across her face what Ellen had always termed her 'bold' look. With lips set in a hard, straight line, shoulders back, head held high, she went to meet her female maker.

'So,' was the first word of the expected diatribe. 'I've managed to track you down at last.'

'I noticed,' Betty replied. 'How did you do it?'

Ellen tapped the side of her nose. 'I have ways,' she replied darkly. 'Call it a mother's radar.'

Betty didn't know what to do, but she wasn't going to allow her uncertainty to show. 'I may live here, but it's not my house.'

'Oh?' Ellen decided not to give too much away. Derek Ramsden had been very generous and she was not about to betray him. 'How's that? I thought everybody paid rent.'

'Housekeepers don't. Now, if you don't mind, I need to get back to my chores. I've people waiting for me.'

'Right. Well, being as I've come all the way from town, the least you can do is let me see my grandson and give me a cup of tea.'

'It's not my house, is it?'

Ellen continued to feign ignorance. 'Then whose is it? Have you got yourself a fancy man? You're certainly looking a lot better – colour in your cheeks and a bit of flesh on your bones. Looks after you, does he?'

'Go away.' The two words were forced between teeth that were almost gritted. Speaking more clearly, Betty continued, 'Get the next bus down to Bolton and don't bother coming back. As for James, I don't want his head filled with Catholic rubbish. Do you think I'm stupid? Did you think he wouldn't tell me you'd had him baptized in your back kitchen? You've no rights over him, none at all. I won't have you anywhere near him.'

Ellen changed up a gear. 'Don't you talk to me like that, lady. The sacrifices I made for you—'

'Rubbish. You wanted another Bertie – not a Betty – and didn't I know it? Stood there outside the shops while you went on about your cystic ovaries and how you'd never be able to give Dad the son he'd always wanted. I was a disappointment from the start and you made sure I was in no two minds about it. Why do you think I did that first disappearing act when I met Jim? And why did you follow me?'

'Because you're my daughter.'

Betty placed her shopping on the pavement. 'James is my son, but I don't own him. Nobody owns anybody. We're born and we need help for a long time, but the helpers don't own us. You can't tell me what to do, and that's what's upsetting you. I'm a Methodist. It suits me. It's wholesome, simple and down to earth.'

Ellen's teeth were suddenly bared. 'You're a baptized Catholic, and so is our James. So what are you doing living with a Church of England vicar?' Her hand shot up and covered her mouth, but she had let the cat out of the bag.

Betty, deliberately composed – outwardly, at least – asked, 'How did you know?'

'A woman on the bus told me. You've got my grandson living in a vicarage. It's not right.'

Betty shook her head slowly. 'It's bigotry like yours that makes for trouble in this world. I've been a bit like you, so I know what I'm talking about. The difference is, my fight has been against Catholicism. It's a cruel and unforgiving faith and I want no truck with it. James will find his own way. He comes to chapel with me now and then, but I'm forcing nothing down his throat except how to behave well. He was wild down there.' She waved a hand in the direction of the town. 'He's different up here.'

'Oh, he'll be different all right. He'll be listening to folk who left the one true faith just because of some king who wanted a divorce or to cut women's heads off—'

'More to it than that,' snapped Betty.

'And which school's he going to in a couple of weeks?'

'St Faith's. He'll be all right.' Betty retrieved her basket and stalked off in the direction of the vicarage. Aware that she was being followed, she allowed the front gate to swing shut, heard it opening again, marched to the door. 'You're not coming in,' she threw over her shoulder.

'No problem to me, Betty. I'll sit on the step and wait for James. He'll turn up sooner or later.'

Betty closed the door and leaned against it for a few seconds. This had started out as another lovely day: bright sunshine, kiddies gone to play, Betty's plans organized – bedrooms, bathroom and stairs to be done. What now? she wondered. Ellen Langton was the determined sort and she would probably sit on the step till the cows came home – or until Mr and Mrs Butlin came home. Whatever were they going to think of their housekeeper? What sort of woman left her own mother to sit on a stone step?

She carried her purchases into the kitchen, put them away, filled the kettle. The best thing was to place her trust in God, because she had not the power to resolve the current situation. She had never been able to communicate with her mother. Ellen was blinkered, prejudiced and stupid. No, that was the root of the difficulty, wasn't it? Because Ellen was not stupid at all. She had allowed herself to be browbeaten and contained within a doctrine and she wanted everyone else to fit into the same mould. 'Yuspeh Feigenbaum should get her teeth into this one,'

374

muttered Betty. 'She'd show her who's who and what's what.'

The back door opened and the Butlins walked in. Caroline was blushing and Betty suddenly realized that these two were going through courtship for a second time. It seemed like a good idea, too. Perhaps more folk should separate, have a break, then come back all new and fresh. 'Mr Butlin,' she began, 'there's a woman sitting on your front step.'

He frowned. 'Really? Why didn't you bring her in?'

'Because I'm the one who locked her out. She's my mother and she's as cracked as an old teapot. There's always a scene when she finds me. I didn't want you to have to put up with it.'

Brian nodded pensively. 'You don't get on, I take it?'

'We get on fine,' replied Betty. 'As long as she gets on the London train and I catch the one for Glasgow. Oh, we're good at getting on. But she isn't good at knowing where to get off. I can't shift her. She baptized my James when he was about four, got the priest in and holy water and all that rubbish.'

Brian did not enjoy hearing any faith being classed as rubbish, but he could see that his housekeeper was not quite herself. This was a calm, good-natured woman and such behaviour was not what he might have expected from her unless circumstances were extreme. It was becoming clear that circumstances had travelled well past the post in this instance. 'What would you like me to do?' he asked.

Betty found no answer that did not involve a shotgun.

'We can't leave her there,' said Caroline. 'I think we must bring her in and talk to her. There's no other realistic solution, is there?'

Betty leaned against the sink. 'I suppose not. But prepare yourselves. Oh – remember that she can be very nice. Until you step on her toes, then get out of her way as fast as you can. She has a few screws loose. In fact, I sometimes think her door's fallen off its hinges altogether.' She rattled a few dishes in the sink, plainly uncomfortable.

Caroline and Brian left the kitchen and closed the door. Betty carried on making tea for two people – her mother could wait until she got home. She lifted the tray and carried it through. Ellen was sitting as nice as pie, legs drawn to one side, hands folded in her lap. 'Here comes my daughter,' she pronounced, irony trimming the words.

Betty said nothing. She placed the tray on the table and marched back to the kitchen, closing the door in her wake.

Caroline came in. 'I'll ... er ... I'll just get another cup.'

Betty made no reply. She picked up a knife and started to peel a potato. Caroline whispered, 'I bet you wish that potato was your mother, eh?'

Betty shook her head. 'Sometimes, being a Christian isn't easy. I could throttle her, Mrs Butlin. All my life, she has made a show of me wherever I've gone – school, friends' houses, church. And mark my words – if she's being polite, watch your backs.'

'We will.' Caroline returned to the living room.

'I've had trouble with her all my life,' Ellen was saying. 'All I've wanted is what's best for her. She married a Catholic – a nice lad – but she wouldn't have my grandson baptized. Then her husband dies and, next news, she ups and joins the Methodists. You could have knocked me over with a feather duster. What's the matter with her?'

'Nothing,' replied Brian. 'She is one of the nicest women I ever met in my life. What do you say, Caroline?'

'A treasure.'

'Well, you don't know her like I do. She's wilful and scheming. All I want is my grandson to make his first Holy Communion in his own church. What's wrong with that?'

Brian placed the cup in its saucer. 'Mrs Thornton wishes her son to make up his own mind. When she first arrived, she was concerned about sending him to our school, as she does not want him indoctrinated. I explained that he would not be pushed or pulled in any direction – that was all she asked.'

Ellen thought about that. 'We're Catholics from way back,' she said.

'As are we all.' Brian stood up and placed himself in front of the fireplace, hands clasped behind his back. 'People change. We have to make room for that. I belong to the Church of England and you belong to the Church of Rome. There are differences, but it's still the one God and the one Saviour. It's just a matter of interpretation.'

377

Ellen wondered for a moment about her soon-to-be-employer's involvement with this couple. Hadn't he said something about the wife? Perhaps she bought clothes from him. But weren't these two separated? She felt sure that Derek Ramsden had mentioned separation and a fight between himself and the vicar? She decided to hang for the full sheep. 'I was talking to this woman on the bus on the way up from town,' she lied. 'She said you weren't living together and that was why Betty was keeping house.'

Caroline ironed out the awkward moment without any difficulty. 'I'm away on retreat,' she said, before taking a sip of tea. Seamlessly, she continued the thread. 'I'm with Catholic nuns, as it happens – those who run St Anne's school. I've been hired as bursar and we decided – Brian and I – that a retreat was a good way for me to learn the ways of the convent.' She paused. 'Also, it's time some gaps were bridged.'

'Some gaps will never be bridged,' answered Ellen.

'Then that is a great pity.' Caroline smoothed her skirt.

It occurred to Brian in those few minutes that he did have a clever wife. She was dealing extremely well with a woman whose nastier edges were beginning to show through the thinning veneer of manners.

'I'd like to see my grandson.' Ellen stood up. 'I've not clapped eyes on him since he got shifted from Sunning Hill Primary. Even then, I could only look at him through the railings at playtimes. She won't let me near him, you see.'

Brian bowed his head as if deep in thought. 'I think you should go home, Mrs . . . er . . .'

'Langton.' She stared hard at him. 'You've no right to keep him away from me.'

'Nor have I the right to go against the wishes of his mother. I'm afraid we have reached stale-mate. Would you like me to drive you back to town?'

'James has gone away with a group of friends for the day,' said Caroline. 'They will not be back until this evening.' Inwardly, she prayed that the children would not come bursting in at any second.

'I'll find my own way home, thanks.' Ellen Langton snatched up her bag and walked to the door. Before opening it, she turned to the vicar. 'Nothing will come between my grandchild and the church,' she said quietly. 'If I have to move to this village and bide my time, I will. But he will be back in the fold, you can be sure of that.' She made her exit, slamming every door as she left.

Caroline jumped up and ran through to the kitchen. 'Are you all right?'

Betty was staring out at the graveyard. 'She'll be back,' she said mournfully. 'And soon.'

'Yes, I had the same thought,' said Caroline. 'What can be done?'

Betty raised her shoulders. 'There's fire, flood and famine. Then there's my mother. She's been a part of my life for so long that she's just another natural disaster. No matter what I do, no matter where I go, she happens.'

'I'm sorry.' Caroline sat at the kitchen table.

'It's not your fault.'

'I know, but I'm still sorry. Will she do anything silly or nasty?'

Betty turned from the window. 'Nothing would surprise me. Her sister – my Auntie Doris – married out – a Baptist, he was. Mam never left them alone for a minute. She had priests and all sorts knocking at the door. In the end, Auntie Doris and Uncle Ed upped and left Liverpool. God knows where they are, but that's what she does to people. She drives them to distraction.'

'And she followed you to Bolton?'

'Yes. She put an advert in the *Evening News* and offered a five pound reward for information leading to me. I never saw the ad, of course, but my next door neighbour came into enough money to buy new winter clothes. Then Mam dragged my dad away from his job and his friends and forced him to come over here. She's a nightmare.'

Caroline didn't know what to say. She had heard of fanatics from many denominations, but she had not had so close a view before. 'So, do you move on yet again?' she asked after a pause. 'You're settled, as is your son, and it would be a great pity if you were forced out by this nuisance. Why give her the power?'

Betty sighed heavily. 'You don't give my mam power – she takes it. Hours I spent on my knees as a child, doing novenas. I wasn't even old enough to know what a novena was, so I just counted the beads till the prayers were over. She watched for my sins, wrote them down so that I wouldn't forget them in confession. The sad thing is that her every move is a sin and she doesn't recognize it. She thinks she's perfect.'

'I am so sorry, Betty. Is it all right if I call you Betty?'

'It's my name.'

'I'm Caroline.'

Brian came in. He stood by the door and watched the two women as they sat together at the table. Betty had become one of the family and he didn't want her to leave. James, too, was enjoying life in the country, but what on earth could be done to stop that terrible woman from coming to the vicarage or from buying a house in the village? 'We should not let her spoil your life,' he said.

Betty smiled wanly. 'She can't be stopped. She's like a racing car without brakes. And she doesn't even know she's wrong, you see. With my mother, there is the Catholic way and the wrong way. No argument, no negotiation. I'll have to get my thinking cap on.'

When the Butlins had gone off to find their children, Betty allowed everything to pour out of her eyes. Tears of misery wet her cheeks and huge sobs racked her body until she was exhausted. Did she have to move on again? Why should she disturb James? Why should she disturb herself? She dried her eyes.

The village would mind her. If Mam moved into Rivington Cross, Betty would make sure that everyone knew the score. 'Time to stand up for yourself, girl,' she said as she walked up the stairs. The cleaning could wait for another day, because Betty was going to have a bath, get changed and buck up her ideas. She would not leave this house until she was ready, and that was that.

The day began in innocence, everything predictable and calm. Trade on the market was lively enough to put a smile on Derek Ramsden's face and several untraceable pounds in his wallet. The problem at home had been addressed and Mrs Ellen Langton would be starting her job today. He would be returning to a feast – Lancashire hotpot, perhaps, or meat-and-potato pie – and all was well within the narrow world he knew and understood.

Until she came along. He had watched her tottering about between stalls, the high-heeled plastic sandals causing her to stumble from time to time, her face over-defined with panstick and rouge, lips made ruddy by generous applications of lipstick. She was a bottle blonde, which fact was advertised by darker growth at the roots of her hair, but she was pretty enough, he supposed.

She wasn't buying anything. She toyed with table linens, stood for a while and listened while Potty Tommy went through his comedy routine, the fast talk, the jokes and the juggling with crocks. Derek watched covertly while she fiddled with a cheap handbag on the luggage stall, noticed when she picked up several pairs of stockings and dropped them casually into a capacious shopping basket of woven straw.

When she had left the market after threading

her way past exterior stalls, she met another woman, a dark-haired piece who received the basket of shoplifted goods and made off with it. This second thief was wise to stay away from the actual crimes, as she had an unforgettable silver streak that ran right through hair that was mainly brown. He had never before seen this particular pair of females, though he had witnessed many such operators in his time as a market trader. But he had not been a victim on this occasion, so he kept his counsel. If folk wanted to stand by while their goods were stolen, that was their problem.

He ate his lunch of bread and cheese, chewed on an apple, drank tea from a Thermos. Business picked up again after two o'clock and Derek enjoyed a productive afternoon. With his wallet full to bursting, he wrapped surplus notes in an envelope which he stashed in a back pocket, then began the task of dismantling his stall and packing stock into the van.

His new housekeeper was still there when he arrived home, and the wittering began as soon as he entered the house. He demolished a chop, vegetables and gravy followed by a delicious apple crumble. The sound of her voice did not irritate; it served only to make him feel secure, because it was normal, an echo from the past, reflecting a proper home, a mother, a father, a family. But what was she talking about? 'Come again?' he said.

'That's why I waited for you. Now, I don't know what happened between you and that vicar – and I don't need to know – but she sat there bold as brass and said she's on retreat at the convent. A vicar's wife? Have you ever heard anything like that in all your life?'

He had not heard anything like it and he told her so.

'She says she's the bursar or some such thing. As if Catholic nuns would employ a Church of England vicar's wife. And why should she go on retreat? You can't even talk on retreat. Nuns become like a silent order when they go on retreat – they can talk for about half an hour every day, I think. It's all very fishy.'

He nodded while she carried on about her grandson, the evil ways of her daughter, the wickedness of the Church of England. So, it was confirmed. Caroline had definitely taken the job and she was living just a couple of hundred yards from where he sat. His hands itched and curled as if he held her throat between the fingers. Deliberately, he forced himself to relax. Ellen Langton must notice nothing.

'I thought about moving up there with my Bertie, but after them two murders – well, you can't be too careful, can you? And that's another thing – what's our Betty doing settling near the reservoir? Is she not worried about that lad of hers? They've already found two bodies in the water, but does she care?'

'Terrible,' he muttered vaguely.

Ellen picked up her raincoat. 'I'd best get my bus,' she told him. 'I've given your bedroom and this room a good bottoming, but the rest's had just a lick and a promise, because I'd your dinner to do. I'll be back tomorrow, only I might not see you – I waited specially to tell you what happened at that vicarage.'

He stood up. 'I'll drive you,' he said. 'You shouldn't be out on your own at this time, not with a murderer about. I don't mind you using buses during the day, but I'll see you home tonight.'

Feeling very pleased with her new employer, Ellen climbed into the passenger seat and thanked him. 'It's nice to know I work for somebody who cares,' she said. 'She's very good-looking, isn't she?'

'Who?' He started the engine.

'The vicar's wife.'

He shrugged. 'Can't remember. I do know he didn't like me going up there to sell her a few clothes. I suppose he wants her wearing stuff out of fashion magazines, but a vicar's wages won't run to that sort of thing. I was doing them a favour, but some people don't appreciate help.'

'That's what I say. I mean, I could help her, couldn't I?'

'What?'

'My daughter. I could help her to bring James up. But no. She's got herself fixated on Methodism. Turn left here, Mr Ramsden. People who don't want help never give help, do they?'

'No, they don't.' He paused for a moment. 'Do they seem to be getting on all right – the vicar and his wife?'

She pondered before answering. 'I'd say so, yes. I mean, I wasn't there very long, but he looks at her like she's some sort of film star. So they must have got over whatever it was. Me and

385

my Bertie have had our ups and downs, but we always get over the rows. You do, don't you?'

'Eh? Oh, yes, I suppose so. My wife died quite young, so I'm no expert.'

'I'm sorry. I saw your wedding photos. Very sad.'

'Yes.'

He dropped her outside a two-up-two-down in Goldsmith Street, turned the van round and set off for home. On a sudden whim, he made for town. The house would be back to its usual silent self and he needed the clatter and chatter of people while he thought about Caroline. The bitch would be back with her other half soon and he could scarcely bear the thought of that.

In the Wheatsheaf, he ordered a pint of bitter and sat on a bar stool, downing the beer quickly. He asked for a second, then looked to his left. The woman with the silver streak sat next to him. Knowing how she earned her living, he guessed that she would be open to offers. 'Would you like a drink?' he asked.

'Thanks,' she replied, revealing unexpectedly good teeth. 'I'm Lily. Lily Holdsworth. I'll have a rum and black, please.'

He ordered her a double. 'Haven't seen you around these parts before,' he said.

'I'm from Blackburn,' she said. 'Just staying with my sister for a while – she lives up Breightmet.'

He nodded. Breightmet was fast becoming a sprawl of hastily erected post-war council houses. Her sister was doubtless the bleached blonde who had harvested goods from Bolton

Market earlier in the day. 'Nice to meet you,' he told her. 'I'm ... John.' Unsure of the reason, he chose to give her his middle name. 'Breightmet's quite nice, isn't it?'

She grinned. 'If you like pebble-dash and problem families. The woman next door to our Eva's got seven kids. It's like listening to the Battle of Britain every day – banging, slamming and screaming. That's why I came out tonight. And the bloody buses run when they feel like it. It's the back of beyond up yon – and a lot of it's just a building site – bricks and cement mixers everywhere. I'll not be sorry to get back to my own house.' She picked up her drink. 'Cheers,' she said.

Derek made his second pint last the whole evening, but he got three more doubles into his companion before offering her a lift home. As they walked to the van, Lily stumbled several times, and for the final part of the journey she placed a hand round his lower back in order to steady herself. 'Eeh, I'm ashamed,' she said more than once before they reached the vehicle.

He helped her into the passenger seat, managed to get the address out of her, then, after leaving town behind, began the tedious business of threading his way through a labyrinth of ill-lit and poorly finished roads. Lily was snoring. With her jaw slackened by sleep, she was no longer attractive. The silver streak, which had so recently lent her an exotic appeal, was just a patch of grey above a forehead into whose lines had been pressed too much face powder. She was a mess and he could not find the address she had mumbled.

He turned a corner and she slipped sideways, her bag falling from her lap and onto his feet. After stopping under a street lamp and applying the handbrake, he retrieved the bag and some loose contents that had slipped out of its open top. As he stuffed these items back into the container, his hand made contact with a thick envelope and, almost immediately, he knew what she had done. Lily had been drunk and continued so, but she had been sufficiently alert to relieve her victim of his afternoon's takings.

Derek shook his head. He had watched this woman's sister going about her business, had smiled to himself because he had escaped, but now he realized that he had been the most severely bitten of Lily and Eva's targets. She had not clung to him – she had robbed him. He inhaled deeply, noticing that the night had suddenly darkened. Bitch. She was just another of them, a taker, never a giver. She had taken his time and his drinks, had accepted a lift, had robbed him blind.

The van leapt forward, its kangaroo behaviour the result of Derek's anger. He was shaking and control of his legs was a near impossibility. 'Easy, Derek,' he whispered. 'Don't wake up Sleeping Beauty.' Out in open countryside, he stopped and sprang from the driver's seat. Dragging her out was easy. He removed her lower garments and was pleased beyond measure when she woke. While he raped her, he told her why she was being punished. 'Thieving, lying, stupid, ugly tart.' He was quickly spent, but the experience had been one of the most satisfying and exciting of his whole life.

Bleary-eyed, she stared up at him. 'Why?' was all she managed.

'The money. You stole my money.'

Lily raised herself on an elbow. 'It was hanging out of the pocket – I was looking after it for you.'

'Liar!' His fist made sharp contact with her face and she passed out again.

Derek made himself tidy, walked back to the van and opened the rear doors. From within, he took the small hammer whose function was to pin up the curtain at the rear of his stall. Twice he smashed the head into her skull, noting a pleasing crunch when bone shattered into grey matter.

'Oi!'

Derek froze.

'What do you think you're doing?' Two men walked quickly towards him across the field. 'Stop!' one yelled as he jumped into the van.

He drove off at a furious pace, no lights switched on, no chance of them getting his number. 'Vans like this are ten a penny,' he told himself once he was out of immediate danger. Slowing down, he turned on the lights and headed homeward. He should not have gone out. Lonely silence was one thing, murder another matter altogether.

Only when he entered the house and switched on the hall light did he notice the state he was in. The knuckles of his right hand were torn and bloodied, while his clothing was spattered as a result of the hammer attack. He was grass-stained, too, and one knee of his trousers was torn.

He filled the bath, stepped in and scrubbed himself until he felt almost flayed of skin. The mirror told him that his face was unmarked, but he needed to get rid of the clothes. A thought struck him – there was the hammer, too. Anyone peering into the van tomorrow morning was sure to notice it on the passenger seat. Wrapping himself in a dressing gown, he walked downstairs, picked up the evening paper and let himself out via the front door.

After unlocking the van, he folded the hammer into the paper and lifted it out. The road was deserted, thank goodness. He locked the van and ran up the terraced path, flung himself inside, leaned against the closed door. When his knees gave way, he sank to the floor and sobbed until he had no tears left. He wept not for her, not for the one whose brown and silver hairs clung to the weapon on the floor. Derek Ramsden grieved for himself and for what he had been forced to become. There was no justice in this world and he was living proof of that fact.

FOURTEEN

'What have I done? What have I done?' He rocked back and forth in the chair just to the right of the empty grate. The elation had evaporated and he could scarcely recall the excitement he had experienced while hurting her. He swallowed and changed the words in his head. While killing her, he reminded himself. The greatest joy had arrived not with the rape, but with the contact between hammer and skull.

He had ended the lives of two women, a Rose and a Lily. Both had been named for flowers and neither had resembled in the slightest way the blooms in question. A rose was a fragrant item until the thorns dug in – harsh laughter and coarse remarks about his manhood. Rose Martindale had ended up in the reservoir where the other girl had been found. He could not remember the name of the first victim, because he had played no part in her demise.

Now, a Lily. There had been a spray of lilies on top of Beryl's coffin, long-stemmed white trumpets with tapering, orange-yellow tongues. Beryl – why hadn't she loved him enough to help him? Why had no-one ever cared sufficiently to lift him out of the pit into which he had fallen?

Derek Ramsden had trusted only one woman, and that woman had been his beloved mother. Edna Ramsden had worked herself into the grave to build up the business that now belonged to her son. There had been no lilies on Mother's coffin, because lilies had been beyond reach of the family purse back then.

Elegant flowers, they were. Simple, beautiful and pure. Lily Holdsworth had owned none of those virtues; she had been cunning, ugly and soiled. He stared at the envelope in his hands, noticed that it was marked and stained by what might have been lipstick or rouge from that disgusting handbag. Pulling out notes, he screwed up their container and threw it into the blackened maw of the empty grate.

There had been very little light. Those two men would not recognize him again – of that he felt sure. He remembered seeing no-one of his acquaintance in the Wheatsheaf, but Lily had been noticeable because of the streak in her hair. Panic paid a visit to his chest, causing his heart to race along like a Grand National favourite. Everyone knew him. 'Think, think,' he ordered himself. 'You gave her a lift up Bury Road, then left her. She said she would walk across the field. You offered to take her all the way to the house, only she said she wanted to walk – needed to clear her head.'

Anyone might have done it, he mused. But there was the van. It was a common enough breed and there were hundreds of them out and about each day, but would two and two make four? Would the barman remember serving him and Lily, would the men in the field mention the Morris? Round and round his brain the problem played, like a film on a continuous loop.

Old Ernie Entwistle entered the recipe. Ernie would help. Derek would offload the van first thing tomorrow and get Ernie to falsify the paperwork on another one. A larger vehicle had been needed for some time and the iron was hot – time to strike. Ernie Entwistle's garage was just a mile down Deane Road and its owner was not averse to bending the rules slightly when one of his customers needed to terminate a relationship with a vehicle because of some minor infringement. So, he would get rid of the Morris, acquire a better van and swear blind that he had owned it since early this evening.

He suddenly realized how exhausted he had become. In spite of tensions, he drifted into sleep, but there was no rest for him. Time after time, he drove the head of the hammer into a temple until her skull was reduced to pulp, but she continued to walk. The other one followed him, too, as did the two men in the field. They ran faster than the van; he could hear their laboured breathing as they chased him. Fists hammered on the rear doors of the vehicle and there was no escape, no chance for him—

He woke with a start when the front door

slammed. God, who was that? Had they come for him, had the police traced him, would he finish up at the end of the hangman's noose?

'You still here?' Ellen Langton poked her head into the room. 'It's gone nine, you know. Oh, it's not a market day, is it? Have you had your breakfast? Shall I do you bacon and eggs? Tell you what, it was a bit nippy this morning. It smells of autumn out there.' She bustled off into the kitchen and carried on chirruping. It was like having Mother back. Mother had always provided a running commentary while preparing a meal or washing clothes. He dozed again until she touched his shoulder.

'Well,' she cried when he jumped to life, 'your nerves are like stretched wires – have you been working too hard?'

He stumbled to the table and eyed the feast of bacon, two eggs, sausage and black pudding. She had seen the Morris van outside. If people were questioned, his goose would be cooked good and proper – and he couldn't face bacon, let alone goose. 'I'm not hungry today,' he told her.

'You've got to eat, Mr Ramsden. Where would the world be if our working men didn't have a cooked breakfast? Up the Mersey without a lifeboat, that's where. If my Bertie couldn't eat his breakfast, he stopped at home, no messing. I stand for no nonsense, me.'

He should have married an Ellen Langton, a woman who made sure that her man ate properly and wore woollens in the winter. All he had wanted from Beryl was the chattering and a bit of comfort in the bedroom department, but

394

she had been as cold as a Frigidaire. She hadn't cared. Tears brimmed.

'You don't look well to me.'

'I've a cold starting.'

She sat down, put a hand on his forehead. It was a cool, comforting hand and he wished he could feel it for ever. 'You're not right, son,' she told him.

Not right? Of course he wasn't – he'd killed two women, hadn't he? 'It's the loneliness, you see.' Shocked by what he had just admitted, Derek burst into tears, the saline accompanied by racking sobs.

She stood and placed her arms around him, drawing his head into a bosom that managed to be matronly in spite of its flatness. 'You'll find somebody, lad. A fine man like you with a nice house and sense enough to make a good living – loads of women would give their eye teeth to marry you.'

'My mother would have loved this house,' he wept. She would. A garden on four levels, wrought iron gates, leaded lights in the windows, proper bathroom with running hot water. 'She never even saw it. I would have brought her here, you know. From the front bedroom, you can see right across town. She would have been as happy as a queen. She was a queen, my mother.'

Ellen chased away a few tears of her own. Everyone – including Betty – got just one mother and every mother was a queen. 'What have you done to your hand?' she asked.

Immediately, he was on his guard. 'Oh, I had

a bit of an accident on the market, not looking where I was going.' Lily's face must have been a mess before it saw the hammer, because his knuckles were certainly bruised. 'I'll be all right – I'm a quick healer.' But there was a part of him that would never heal. It was the part that missed his mother, a wife, a day-to-day companion. It could not be filled by dead women, could it?

'You need a rest,' she ordered. 'Stop there while I make you a nice cup of tea and a slice of toast. I'll eat some of this – I'm not letting it all go to waste. It's a sin, is waste.'

Yet again, Ellen was Mother, though she scarcely resembled the dead Edna Ramsden. Mother had been weighty, arms huge, belly huge, heart enormous. 'Where you live,' began Derek carefully, 'there's no garden. If you ever get fed up, you and your husband, you could stay here rent free. I've two living rooms and plenty of space upstairs. It gets quiet, living alone in a three-bedroomed house. Think about it.'

He was more than lonely, thought Ellen Langton as she washed dishes. Derek Ramsden was desperate for human contact at a level that went beyond selling clothes and handling small change. The man wanted a family and he dreaded isolation in old age. She understood that, but wasn't sure she wanted to give up her own home. Bertie wouldn't move in here – of that she felt certain. It was a damned shame, though. No man should be left to struggle alone in this cold, heartless world.

Derek, still in dressing gown and slippers, fell asleep again in the armchair. Ellen peeped through the kitchen door, an egg-and-bacon sandwich clutched in one hand. Poor bloke. He looked so isolated and vulnerable sitting there with his head leaning against the chair's wing. He needed the love of a good woman, that was all.

He slept all morning. Inside his head, he knew that Ellen was around, that she would protect him from all harm, so he slumbered peacefully, because his mother was with him and nothing further could go wrong.

Brian Butlin had searched records going back ten years and had come up with absolutely nothing. No Bernadette Marie Bradshaw had registered a birth in Bolton, so there was no evidence that an Adam had ever existed. Because of the dog collar, Brian was able to persuade people to talk and, of course, he was given access to baptismal records in churches of all denominations.

He sat in his car on Bromwich Street, conjured up a picture of Amy's disappointed face. This was his last chance, he supposed. He climbed out, locked the door and walked up the path of number 25. In this house, Nettie Bradshaw had lived, and he prayed with all his heart that she had discussed the baby with someone – anyone would do. All he needed was to give Amy some hope, yet he felt none himself as he allowed the door knocker to clatter home.

The door opened a fraction and an eye

peeped out. 'I'm not interested,' announced the female voice attached to the eye.

'I'm not here from a church,' he answered hastily. 'Please don't shut me out – you are my last chance.'

The door opened an inch at a time. 'Well?'

The owner of the scratchy voice, a woman who carried a cigarette as evidence of the cause of damaged vocal cords, was almost as broad as she was tall. 'I'm busy,' she snapped. She wore a dirty wraparound pinafore, lisle stockings whose state of near-collapse imitated a pair of concertinas and an expression that might have soured milk in ten minutes flat.

'It's about Bernadette – I mean Nettie Bradshaw. She lived here, I believe.'

'She's dead.'

'I know she's dead. May I come in, please?'

She allowed him into a brown hallway that might have been any colour at all before becoming stained by nicotine and neglect. 'I live in the back,' she said. 'Rest of the house is for lodgers – I'm a widow.'

The chaos defied description. A line of tobacco-coloured washing hung low in front of the fireplace and there was nowhere to sit. The almost square female placed herself in a chair with a week's newspapers on its seat. This enabled her to seem taller sitting down than she had while standing up.

Brian inhaled, coughed, inhaled again. Oxygen seemed rationed in this establishment. 'It's about Nettie,' he repeated.

'Aye, you said.' Deftly, she pulled another

Woodbine from a packet and lit it from the cremated remains of the previous one. 'Police have been time and time again – I got fed up with brewing endless pots of tea. It was terrible. Nice girl, Nettie, liked a laugh and a joke – she's missed.'

'This is a delicate question and I shall come straight to the point. Did she ever speak about a child?'

'Oh, aye.' The woman nodded her head with a vigour that was at odds with her general condition. 'I think it were an Amy – little sister – lived up in one of the villages – where she died – Nettie, I mean.'

'But no other child?'

'No. Who do you mean?'

He decided to proceed no further with this particular line of questioning. 'Didn't Nettie share her room?'

'Aye, they were in the big downstairs front. But when she died and after all the fuss had settled, the other girl upped, left and emigrated to Australia with her mam and dad. Never heard from her since, not so much as a postcard. And I look after me lodgers, you know. Do you want a cuppa?'

Nothing on God's earth could have induced Brian to eat or drink in a room as filthy as this. 'No, thank you. I have other calls to make. But could you show me the room in which Nettie lived?'

She heaved herself up out of the chair. 'I'm Mary Browne, by the way.' She huffed and puffed her route to the door.

'Brian Butlin, vicar of St Faith's, Rivington Cross.' He followed her down the hall and was completely unprepared for the sight of Nettie's room. It was pristine, newly painted and papered, decently furnished. The woman clearly did look after her guests, but seemed to be propelling herself towards a very premature grave. 'It's beautiful,' he said. 'A credit to you.'

'I charge extra for cleaning,' she replied, pride colouring the tone. 'But I do a good job – takes me all week, like. No time for myself.'

'Make time,' he advised.

Mary Browne clapped a hand to her mouth. 'You know, I'd forget my head if it weren't screwed to the rest of me. See – come back with me – there's something she left and I weren't going to give it to the police. They open things, do police. They don't care, you know. Hounded my Gordon to death, blaming him for stuff he'd never done. That's how come I'm a widow – my husband took a heart attack when they charged him with receiving stolen goods. Hmmph. Give a dog a bad name, eh?'

How she remembered the location of things in such turmoil was a cause for wonderment, pondered Brian as she opened one of many tins. 'I keep all policies and suchlike in these,' she explained. 'They'd have a better chance in a fire, you see.'

The woman was right to fear fire – there were cigarette burns on the rug, brown stains in a long row on the window sill where she had rested Woodbines; even the eiderdown covering the crumpled bed was full of burn holes.

'Here it is.' Triumph gleamed in tiny, fat-encased eyes as she waved her prize. 'This is what she left. Out of respect, I took good notice of what it says on the envelope. Police would have had it ripped open straight away, but I weren't going to let them have it. See.' She passed it to Brian. 'I were going to give it to somebody – a lawyer or a doctor – but you'll do nicely because you live up yon, don't you?'

He nodded. 'Thank you, Mrs Browne. I appreciate your trust in me.'

'Well, if you can't trust a vicar, you can't trust anybody. Read the envelope.'

It had been written in capitals and the ink was black.

TO BE OPENED BY AMY BRADSHAW WHEN SHE IS 21 YEARS OF AGE. NOT TO BE OPENED BY ANYONE ELSE. B.M. BRADSHAW.

'See, wishes like that have to be stood by, that's what I say every time. She might be dead, but what she wanted still counts. Otherwise, her life was a waste.'

Brian's opinion of the slovenly woman had changed completely. She had moral fibre and a code to which she had adhered in spite of temptation. Anyone would have wished to open the letter – his own inclination might well have been to throw caution to the winds in the hope of identifying a murderer. 'The answer's in here, isn't it?'

'I'd say so.' She lit yet another cigarette. 'I worked that out for myself. Some days, it's plagued me halfway to death, but I managed to stop and think. Nettie Bradshaw likely mithered long and hard before writing that lot. It's thick – oh, yes, I've run my hands over it a fair few times. She loved one person in this world and that were her little sister.'

'Yes.'

Mary ploughed on. 'And I thought, right, this is going to be what the coppers want, but it's not what the dead girl wanted. Nettie won the argument every time. I'm glad to be shut of it, to be honest. It's up to you now, isn't it?'

'It is.'

She smiled at him. 'You'll be the plagued one now, son. Put it somewhere out of easy reach – with a lawyer or one of them accountant men, or stick it in the bank. How old's the kiddy now?'

'Eleven, I think.'

Mary blew out her cheeks. 'Ten years is a long time. But to me, what's in that envelope is Nettie's dying wish. She'd not rest in her grave if we went against her. Good luck with it. I shall think about you.'

Brian surprised himself by walking across the room and planting a kiss on the lady's forehead. Because she was a lady, a person with standards, a woman who had worked out her own agenda and stuck to it. 'You're a remarkable soul,' he told her. 'May I visit you from time to time?'

'Aye, lad. I'll try to be a bit tidier when you come again.'

'I'll take you just as you are, and gladly, Mrs Browne.' He left the house with a lighter step, but, as he sat in his car and thought of Amy, the

402

sadness returned. He had nothing to tell her. She must not be informed about the existence of Nettie's letter, or she might well spend the next ten years in a state of worry and mixed expectations. No, he would not confine Amy to one of life's waiting rooms.

He started the engine, waved at the figure in the doorway of number 25, and set off for home. Amy, a diligent child, would do well. Nettie had done well, too, because she had chosen the age at which Amy would have reached her majority and completed her education.

Love did survive beyond the grave. The proof of that rested in a brown envelope in a black car which would stop soon at the bank. No-one would be tempted to interfere with Nettie's plan. Brian would make sure of that.

Maddy and Sarah were alone in the bell house. Jay was messing about with the dog in the graveyard, George and Simon were searching for conkers, while Amy had gone to town to buy instruments for geometry. 'It's algebra I dread,' sighed Sarah. 'No way can X and Y mean anything to me. Pa was showing me something called an equation and it made about as much sense as a page of Greek. It's all brackets and squiggles.'

Maddy agreed. She owned little enthusiasm for mathematics and would have preferred to immerse herself in history and English. 'We have to do Latin,' she grumbled.

'So do we. You need an ancient and a modern to get into university. I mean, I can understand the need for French – France is a neighbour and we might go there one day. But who speaks Latin?' Sarah plonked herself on a dining chair. 'Not long now until we start.'

'I know. The day we left primary school, Amy was sad – she was talking about the end of childhood and all that kind of stuff. I thought she was being a misery, but now I think I know what she meant. We'll need to be tough. Especially those of us who have to go to nuns. As for Latin, it's supposed to help with what they call word-roots. We'll get used to it in time.'

The two girls sat for a while in the gloom, thoughts as dark as the shuttered upper room of the bell house. Although they were now the proud owners of two electric lamps, they chose darkness because it suited their mood. The prospect of seven years at grammar school did not appeal, while the idea of adding on three for university was utterly appalling. Ten years was a long time – almost as long as their lives thus far. 'We'll be old,' muttered Maddy.

'I know.'

'And others will be working at the age of fifteen. We'll be old, but we'll be babies, because we'll still be at school. What are you going to be?' Maddy asked.

'Fed up,' answered Sarah obtusely.

'I know – but a fed up what?'

Sarah shrugged. 'I might want to be a vicar, but I can't. Stupid, isn't it?'

It was stupid. The more she thought about it, the further away Maddy got from working out Christianity. 'It's a maze,' she said to herself.

'I don't really want to be a vicar,' mused Sarah. 'I think it's more that I feel I should have the choice and I won't, because I'm a girl.'

'It's all stopped making sense to me,' Maddy complained. 'Either we have free will or we don't.'

Sarah, who thought Maddy was continuing to talk about limited choices for women, agreed. 'We're only women.'

But Maddy hadn't meant that. She had recently indulged in one of her lengthy thinking sessions and was hitting a brick wall every time. 'What if Pontius Pilate and Herod had both said no? One was a Roman governor and the other was in charge of all Judaea, so if those men of power had decided to refuse, there would have been no Christianity.'

Sarah blinked. She was still struggling with the unfairness of gender and was not keeping up with her friend. She opened a box on the table. 'We're nearly all in here now.' She had holy water for Amy and Maddy, a Book of Common Prayer for herself and her brother, and a frayed tract about the evils of alcohol to represent Jay. 'I only need something Jewish.'

'What?'

Sarah closed the box. 'I'm listening now.'

Maddy threaded her way through the Garden of Eden and into the Land of Nod, to which Cain had been banished after the first recorded murder. She stumbled through brothers and sisters who must have mated with one another, then paused. 'God gave free will to Adam and Eve. But when they took it – all that stuff about apples and snakes – He threw them out into the world.'

'Yes.'

Maddy concentrated. 'Jesus was sent to die. He had to die. It was his duty to die. That way, He could open the gates of heaven and all believers could pass through. But there was no choice. He was forced to die.'

'Yes,' repeated Sarah.

'Well.' Maddy inhaled deeply. 'If He was born to die, they were born to kill Him. Stands to reason – there had to be a victim, so there had to be killers. It wasn't their fault. On the cross, He said, "Father, forgive them, for they know not what they do."'

Sarah scratched her head. 'So what's it all about, then?'

'That's my question. It doesn't make sense. Free will can't come into it. It's like that algebra with a few squiggles missing – doesn't mean anything. Those who crucified Him were . . . well . . . like robots. They were God's robots. Free will had to be switched off, because it was all planned for them. So we can't believe in free will if we accept that those people were created by God to kill Jesus.'

'Because if they'd had free will they could have said no.'

Maddy nodded. 'Well, the ones who put the nails in and all that couldn't. They were just doing what the boss said. The boss was the robot. Pontius Pilate had to let Jesus die, so he was . . . predestined – that's the word – to murder Jesus. The same goes for Herod. I'm having a bit of trouble with all of it. I certainly don't belong with nuns.' She grinned.

Sarah stared down at the table. 'God planned the whole thing, then?'

'It looks that way, yes.'

'God killed his own son? That is scary.'

Maddy grinned. 'I know. Sometimes I get a bit tired of being a genius. Come on, let's go and find conkers.'

They ran off to the edge of woods whose deeper parts were now forbidden territory. With George and Simon, they plucked the fruits of horse chestnuts and made furtive plans involving vinegar, varnish and baking. The final summer of true childhood was drawing to a close, and they embraced it to be treasured for all time in their minds and hearts.

He woke from time to time, heard the vacuum's drone, dishes and pans being rattled in the kitchen, running water, her footfalls as she made her way around the house. Safe in the knowledge that a matriarch was on the premises, Derek slept like a child. Nothing could hurt him while his mother was nearby; no-one on God's earth had ever dared to touch the son of Mrs Ramsden.

He ate soup with bread, snoozed again, dreaded the moment when the front door would close behind her. She crept about with his lunch tray, was clearly doing all she could to avoid waking him. He smiled when she hummed the tune to 'Rock of Ages', remembered Sundays at church with the family, shiny shoes, sailor suit, white socks.

Something propelled him to sudden wakefulness and he sat bolt upright in his chair, ears straining to catch the slightest sound. Had she gone? Had she left him here to face those nightmares all over again? She would have said goodbye, wouldn't she? He stood up, stretched cramped muscles, tried not to think of a broken body in a field up Breightmet way.

She was on the stairs. He could sense her presence, could almost reach out and touch her . . . her fear. Swallowing painfully, he allowed the excruciating truth to enter his mind. Ellen Langton knew. That damned hammer – where had he left it? His clothes, the splashes of blood – how could he have been so stupid? She knew that he was awake. And he knew that she knew that he was a killer.

Slowly, he made his way to the door. Simultaneously, she clattered down the rest of the stairs and into the hall. She had to be stopped. He grabbed her just as she reached the front door. 'Please,' he gasped. 'Let me explain. It was a fox. I think a car must have hit it, so I put it out of its misery.'

Ellen opened her mouth and screamed. Fascinated by the size of this sound, he froze for a moment. How could a woman so tiny produce a noise so massive? He clapped a hand over her mouth and she bit him hard, sharp little teeth cutting like razors. The air darkened and he hit her hard across the jaw, almost bursting into tears when he heard bone splinter. She folded into a heap at his feet and he joined her on the floor, his body rocking as he took in the magnitude of his problem. He had killed two women and a third one knew about the second. There were no choices. 'I can't help it,' he moaned. 'It's not me, it's something in me.'

From a brown paper bag, the bloodstained clothes spilled. She had collected her evidence and had clearly intended to remove it from the house. 'You shouldn't have gone quiet,' he told her. 'I was all right while there were sounds.' Underneath the clothing, the hammer was loosely wrapped in newspaper. A fox? What kind of fox owned dark brown hair with silver streaks? Congealed blood held strands of Lily Holdsworth's crowning glory, stuck them to the weapon. And now? And now, he had to dispose of Ellen Langton.

She was as light as a child. He carried her into the bathroom, removed her clothing, tried not to look at fluttering eyelids, worked hard to blot out those soft moans. As he beat her to death with the hammer, tears streamed down his face. 'Mother,' he wept. 'I'm sorry, I'm sorry.' No lilies for her coffin, no expensive cars, no wake. She was in the bath, yet blood covered two tiled walls. 'It's finished now,' he told her. 'No more hurting, Mam, no more cancer, no more crying.' He stroked the battered head. 'You'll be all right now. God is good, Mam. God is good.'

Chickens grew at an alarming rate of knots, doubling and trebling their original size within a matter of weeks. They began to nest, were producing the occasional egg, and Yuspeh was becoming uncomfortable with the whole thing.

But she knew the rules. The kosher code was clear and plain – no sick or injured animal could be slaughtered for food.

Anna, George and Jakob began to torment her as soon as the hens had reached a decent weight. The family had eaten their evening meal and Jakob leaned back expansively, hands resting on a replete stomach. 'That was very good, Anna. But I have a sudden yearning for chicken. Soon we shall be able to bring the butcher and he can prepare one of Mamme's birds. We shall have roasted chicken and, perhaps, some soup from the remainder. I noticed that Hilda has a good, firm breast on her, so she should be first.'

Yuspeh clicked her tongue. 'I am happy that Hilda Barnes, for whom I have named my noisy bird, is gone from this village. But Hilda Hen is not well. I am thinking she was eating some of the poison food from the other Hilda.'

'Pity,' sighed Jakob. 'What about Esther? She is promising.'

The senior citizen of the family eyed her son. 'You don't know from any of their names, so there is no need to pretend.'

Anna spoke up. 'He does. He knows each and every one of them. Esther came into the kitchen and was in one of his shoes last week, so he knows her very well. He had her feathers sticking to his socks for one whole day.'

George fought a giggle that threatened to erupt from his throat at any minute and he drowned it with a mouthful of water. After swallowing noisily, he fixed his face in angelic mode. 'Esther would make a good dinner,' he said.

'She has the limp,' announced Yuspeh. 'We cannot eat a bird who is having the limp.'

Anna nodded. 'She got the limp because Jakob's shoe was the wrong size for her. Jakob, you must make sure that you put away your shoes, or we shall go hungry.'

Yuspeh eyed the three criminals who surrounded her table. How could they contemplate eating those sweet, innocent chickens? 'You are having no heart,' she informed them. 'These chickens are too young for eating and this you know well. They must live a longer time than this.'

Jakob fiddled with his knife. 'So, will you wait, Mamme, until they are so old that they must be boiled?'

The old woman stood up. 'I am not eating any. You are not eating any. They are for eggs. Celia is coming with me into the business of selling eggs. My chickens is not for meat.'

Anna sighed. 'But you said that the English chickens were no good.'

'They will have to do for us,' snapped Yuspeh. 'My chickens you will not eat. This is my final word.'

The three of them burst into gales of laughter while Yuspeh picked up the *Bolton Evening News*, rolled it up, and slapped each of them in turn. Unable to read some of it, she had found a use for the local publication at last. She muttered about people who tormented old women and hens, then she cleared the table in a furious rush. Women were built for suffering and she suffered very well.

*   *   *

Making her smaller had not been an easy task. It had involved an axe and some carving knives, but the results rendered her inhuman and, therefore, easier to look at. He parcelled up the remains, placed them in his van, then scrubbed the bathroom until it shone.

Making sure that he had collected all stained clothing, hammer, axe and knives, he drove off into early dusk with no idea of his eventual destination. The evening was cool, and for that he felt grateful. Ellen Langton had been dead for several hours and he had no wish to be reminded of that each time he breathed. But there was no smell, at least.

He spread her about all over the place, dropping some parts into the Irwell, placing others in thick hedges, a couple of parcels on the outskirts of Rivington. Let them believe that the killer was the one who had killed that first girl, some person from one of the villages.

He disposed of all tools and knives in the river, then took the clothing and, after weighting it down with stones, placed hers in a disused well, his own in a rubbish dump at the back of the Bolton ring road. It was done. But he had to act quickly and carefully now, or all would be lost. 'Stay calm,' he said repeatedly as he began the most frightening leg of the journey. This was the weakest link in a hastily constructed chain and he needed to be on an even keel, sensible, concerned, yet casual.

A light burned in the house on Goldsmith Street. Mr Langton was in, then. 'God, I am

412

scared,' Derek breathed. He closed the van door quietly and approached his goal. This had to be done – there was no other chance for him. He knocked, waited, knocked again.

The door opened. 'Mr Langton?'

'Yes, that's me.' The man yawned. 'I'd dropped off in the chair, lost all track of time.'

'I just wondered what had happened to your wife. I brought her home once, so I knew your address. Is she ill?'

'What?'

'Oh – sorry. My name's Derek Ramsden and your wife started to work for me recently – house cleaning and so on. But she didn't arrive today, so I wondered whether she was ill.'

'Oh, I see. Are you him from Wigan Road? The chap with a stall on Bolton Market?'

'Yes, that's me.'

'Well, I've not seen Ellen all day. As far as I knew, she'd gone to work. I thought you'd kept her on for a few extra hours. She never arrived, you say?'

'No. I've been in most of the time – I had paper-work to do – and the hours slipped by, because I was up to my neck in tax forms. Then I nipped out for a bite to eat and a pint, read the paper, went home. Before I knew it, it had got to half past eight and I thought I'd come round and see how she was. I wonder where she's got to?'

Bert Langton frowned. This wasn't like Ellen. Ellen was a woman you could set your watch by, a creature of habit, predictable, a believer in routine. 'I'd best tell the bobbies,' he said. 'She's not one for stopping out, you see. Hang on while

I get my coat. Will you run me down to the central station? It'd be best to go there instead of the local one.'

On the way to town, Derek stopped at a red light. He glanced sideways at a small shop, saw that the board advertising the local newspaper had been left out. His jaw dropped when he read the headline. Surely not. He shivered and turned to his taciturn companion. 'I'll drop you and carry on if you don't mind. Bit of a headache after all that paperwork. Good luck. I hope you find her soon.' When he had deposited Bert Langton outside the police station, he drove home as quickly as he could.

The paper was lying on the floor just inside the door, had probably been there since five o'clock, but he had been too busy to look at it. The headline glared up at him, thick and bold, the message burning its way into his consciousness until the headache he had pleaded threatened to become a reality. WOMAN SURVIVES HAMMER ATTACK IN BREIGHTMET. His stomach rose, but it was too empty to prove productive.

She was conscious. She had defied all odds and had lived through surgery performed to remove splinters of skull from her brain. She had a metal plate in her head. She was beginning to talk to police. She was a miracle. She was his ticket to the gallows.

Derek listened to his heart as it drummed heavily in his ears. They would come for him. Because of Ellen, he had not changed his van. Lily would remember him. People in the Wheatsheaf would remember both of them.

The men in the field would remember the van. He was doomed.

What should he do? How much money did he have in the house? Angry and terrified, he lurched into the living room and sat down. 'Think, damn you,' he ordered himself. He didn't need to worry about Rose; Rose was a different kettle of putrid fish and someone else could be blamed for her murder. But the real mess was Lily the thief and Mam. No, that hadn't been Mam, it had been the Liverpool woman. Ellen. Ellen Langton.

But before Rose, Lily and Ellen, there used to be a Caroline. She lived . . . where was she? Oh, yes, she was living in St Anne's convent – who had told him that? And hadn't he suspected as much after seeing her on Deane Road that day? No, he had believed that she must have taken a room in the Willows Lane area. Switch out the lights – yes – that was a good idea. Switch out her lights. As he stumbled from the darkened hall and back into the blacked-out room, he knew that he was on borrowed time.

He heard one of Mam's sayings – 'Might as well hang for the full sheep instead of for a lamb.' One hand flew to his throat – already, he could feel the rope tightening. The takings – he still had today's takings. No more markets, no more customers, no more freedom. 'Run, run.' There was a song, wasn't there? 'Run, Rabbit, Run', was the title. Women had always liked him until the bedroom business. *Run, rabbit, run.*

Thinking straight was an impossibility. Petrol can. Rags. Shed. Convent. Caroline. The vicar . . .

Kill, kill. *White cliffs of Dover* – where had that come from? Vera Lynn. Songs from the war, running across a foreign field, into a boat and back to England – *white cliffs of Dover*. Shed. Petrol can. War – this was war. There was only one soldier for the next incursion. *Learn to fight your own battles, Derek* – Mam again. In the bath, pieces, red everywhere. No, that had not been Mam, it had been the other one, the thin one.

'Get away,' he muttered. 'Far away. Sell the van and get a car.' Everything he owned was here – a house with no mortgage, his bits of furniture, photographs, memories. He reached out and grabbed a picture of Mam, one he had taken just months before her death. How well she had looked – a little thinner, bright smile, pretty hair. Weight loss had been a harbinger of terrible times, months of agony, watching, waiting, sometimes even praying for her to go. But he hadn't killed her. The one woman he should have killed had been allowed to live and to suffer unspeakable agonies.

Rock of ages. She had been his anchor, his stability, his rock of ages. How had he managed to arrive at such a mess? It was not his fault. 'You shouldn't have left me,' he told her. Mam had been the love of his life and a part of him had died with her. Money, bankbook, keys, clothes, the photograph of his mother – these he would collect and the rest he would probably never see again.

Midnight found him in West Yorkshire. He settled down in the back of the van, his bed constructed from clothes he would never sell.

416

Tomorrow, he would empty them out, throw them away, because his life had already been lost beyond retrieval. New car, bed and breakfast, shave off his moustache, dye the hair. After that, he had something to do, but he could not remember the details.

Caroline was the core and her husband was woven into the fabric. There was nothing more to be lost – he would hang for the full sheep and not just for the lamb. Mam had been right. She had always been right.

FIFTEEN

The Caveman Covenant was completed. It was pinned to a board in the upstairs-downstairs chamber of the bell house and all had signed it.

'Should have been done in blood,' said Jay, not for the first time.

'He's been reading Richmal Crompton again,' sighed Amy. 'We're not William and Ginger,' she told the younger boy. Amy wasn't completely sure what the Cavemen were, but they were nothing like the determinedly dishevelled William Brown and his cronies.

'We've got a dog,' Jay insisted. 'We could be the Famous Five like Enid Blyton writes about. They get loads of adventures.'

'Six plus dog,' George said. 'We're Cavemen.'

Jay picked up his catapult and tested its elasticity. If the murderer returned, Jay was armed with a dozen varnished conkers and the weapon with which to propel them. The Caveman thing was all daft, anyway. A girl was in charge and that was the problem. She was clever and he didn't understand half of what she said, but there should have been a boy in the leader's position – it stood to reason. The weapon was satisfactory, so he laid it on the table and prepared to be bored.

Maddy switched on the light installed by a local electrician. She nodded at Amy, who opened a hardbacked exercise book in order to take the minutes of their first truly official meeting as Cavemen.

The chairman and inventor of the club read out the covenant. 'We believe in God,' she began, 'just as Stone Age people believed in God. We do what we think is right and we use our common sense, not the rules of adults. We agree that we would have been better off without prophets—'

Jay chipped in. 'What's a prophet?'

'We've done that already.' Maddy glared at him. 'Read a comic.'

'I've read them all.'

'Well, shut up, then.'

He shut up. She rambled on about prophets thinking they were closer to God than anyone, about them daring to interpret God's will for the world, about Christians and Jews disagreeing, about Christians arguing with Christians. She moved on to Dead Sea Scrolls – whatever they were – the Gospel of Thomas, the Gospel of Truth, churches taking money from folk and grown-ups talking a load of rubbish. Well, he agreed with that bit, at least.

When she had finished the list, Maddy declared, 'Someone is wrong. The Jews, the

Christians and the Muslims can't all be right. We believe only in God.'

Amy laid down her pen. She couldn't keep up with Maddy. The problem was that Maddy Horrocks took some giant leaps of faith and no-one could find the stepping stones in order to follow her. 'Do we not believe in Jesus any more?' Amy asked. 'He was a good man.'

'So is my dad,' Maddy replied smartly, 'and your dad, and the twins' dad and George's dad.'

'Mine's dead.' Jay's tone was mournful.

'And we're sorry,' said Maddy. 'He died because of religion.'

Jay glanced at the faces of the gang. All wore expressions of uncertainty and he was glad not to be the only slowcoach. 'He died because somebody shot him,' he said.

'Why did they shoot him?' She was in patient mode now.

'Because of the war,' he yelled.

'And why was there a war? Because a so-called Christian nation decided to spread out and get rid of Jews. It was religion. We don't need it and we don't want it. So we are going back to caveman times and believing in God without all the rest. If you don't want to be a member, fair enough. We have free choice. The point is, you believe what you want to believe and not what you are told to believe.' She listened to herself. In telling them to believe what they chose, she was ordering them to believe what she believed to be right. She was tumbling over words in her head, was seeing no light. The labyrinth was getting more intricate by

420

the minute, but Maddy didn't know how to stop.

Sarah and Simon nodded, Amy kept her thoughts to herself, but George spoke up. 'Everything we know has been taught. You are saying that there's no point in anything. Why stop at religion? Why not say there's no truth in science and that the earth is flat?'

Maddy shrugged. 'That's up to you.' She hadn't reached wherever she was going and had no true concept of her own destination. 'Believe what you like. But why should there be so much separation when we all have the same God?'

George nodded thoughtfully. 'Oh, I agree about all the arguments.' He was with Maddy in theory, but he had family to consider. He could imagine Bobbee's face if he started to propound the caveman theory while seated at the Shabbat table. She would probably have a heart attack, so he had to tread carefully. 'I have to honour the traditions of my own people,' he said.

Maddy laughed. 'So must we – Amy and I. But we can go through the motions for the sake of the ones we love, can't we?'

Sarah spoke up. 'I know what she means about all the different Christian churches, but I don't know anything about the Jewish faith. Maddy is coming to Evensong one Sunday and we shall go to Mass.'

George clapped a hand against his forehead. 'Then the whole village will have a heart attack.'

Sarah smiled. 'We'll be hidden. Maddy will put us in confessional boxes and we shall smuggle her into the vestry. It's the principle, you see. We'll do it because we can.'

421

Simon concurred. 'Makes sense to me.'

Jay was still trying to work out the bit about prophets. 'Who do Jews follow?' he asked.

'Moses and we've already done him,' replied Sarah. 'And some others.' She could not remember the names.

'And that religion, the one I'd never heard of . . .' He looked at Maddy. 'You said it before.'

'Islam,' she replied. 'They're Muslims and their prophet was Muhammad, but they believe in Jesus, too. He's one of their prophets.'

Jay decided to place his faith in catapulting and tree-climbing. But even in his innocence, he managed to deliver a parting shot to Maddy Horrocks, female chairman of the Caveman Club. 'So this means that you are our prophet?'

Maddy went very still. 'I don't know,' she admitted finally. 'But at least I say I don't know. I'm not waving a New Testament and a pile of holy pictures under your nose – which needs wiping, by the way.'

Jay sniffed and walked out of the room.

'Lift up a stone and you will find me there.' Maddy was trying to quote from the gospel of St Thomas, a work unrecognized thus far by any church, so it suited her. 'We don't need buildings,' she said. 'All that money in Rome and London – it's wrong. We can pray in a field. Shall we go?'

'To pray?' Simon asked.

'Oh, for goodness' sake.' She laughed. 'To play. We have only a few days left, so let's use them.'

* * *

The hair colour had turned out rather badly, but it would have to do. It was described as auburn lights, or some such nonsense, and it had made his hair slightly red, but it also rendered him different. The biggest change was to his face, which seemed rather blank without the punctuating moustache. His upper lip was pale, too, so he acquired some make-up to fill in the gap.

Derek was staying in a bed and breakfast on the outskirts of Huddersfield and wasn't doing very well at being alone in an alien place. As he dared not talk to anyone, he spent much of his time in the car, a dark green Austin that had seen better days and many, many miles of road. In the evenings, he sat in a sparsely furnished room and talked to his mother. Evenings were the worst, as he saw no movement beyond the odd passer-by beneath his window. When tired, he had a tendency to become confused – and confusion allowed in the anger again.

The photograph rested on a bedside locker. For an hour at a time, he stared at it until he imagined that she had moved within the frame. If only she would; if only she could come back and take care of him now. 'Rose laughed at me,' he told her, 'and Lily stole my money. I know how hard you worked to set us on our feet, so why should she take what you and I have earned? Then Ellen.' He paused. 'She reminded me of you, but she wasn't you. No-one can ever be you.'

He would have enjoyed Ellen. If she hadn't gone and done everything wrong, if she hadn't snooped about among things that were none of her business, life might have been all right. She had chatted and cooked, had cleaned his house, and now . . . and now she was all over the place in parcels. He swallowed, turned his head, allowed his gaze to fall on a cheap straw shopping bag he had bought in an arcade. He would look in a minute; he would have to look soon, needed to know the truth.

The newspaper lay right at the bottom of the basket. He had folded it so that the front page was not visible, but he must get it out, needed to see. Slowly, he bent and retrieved his purchases – two bottles of pale ale, some cigarettes, a quarter-pound of Mam's favourite Mint Imperials. And, of course, the paper.

The shock was a hammer blow. He had been named and described in the national press as a person who might help with inquiries. His disappearance was mentioned, along with a full description of his person. The mirror was a comfort, as it reflected a man who bore no resemblance to the newspaper's depiction. 'I am not Derek Ramsden,' he repeated several times. He was now Matthew Roper.

Returning to the front page article, he learned that he had been recognized drinking with Lily Holdsworth in the Wheatsheaf, that she had continued to improve in hospital and had recovered sufficiently to give a full account of the attack. A lower paragraph informed the world that Derek Ramsden was also being sought in connection with the disappearance of Ellen Langton and the murders of two further women. Two? He remembered Rose, but who was the other one?

'Two in the reservoir,' he recalled aloud. 'And the first wasn't mine.' He wanted to tell them that they were wrong, but he couldn't. Indignant now, he shook the paper. 'I never did the first one,' he snapped angrily.

A pale ale calmed him a little, though its flavour was not improved by a slight taste of mint toothpaste which clung to the glass. But the toothbrush holder was the only container in the room, so he drank the second pint straight from the bottle.

'Car-o-line.' He separated and savoured the syllables. Apart from Mam, Caroline Butlin remained the only woman he had ever loved. Beryl? No, he hadn't loved her. Caroline owned class, elegance and dignity. 'She left me,' he told his mother. 'She left me because I've never been right, you see. Did you know I wasn't right, Mam? Did you?'

Fully clothed, he drifted into sleep that was filled by images of women. They paraded before him, Mam, Beryl, Caroline, Rose, Lily and Ellen. They chased him, hit him, screamed obscenities at him. Except for one. Edna Ramsden simply stood and smiled at him. She was his mother, she loved him, but there was nothing she could do.

Brian was taking no nonsense. The man on the run, the very person who had hurt Caroline, owned a house right on top of the convent. His place had been searched and was under watch, but who knew what a madman might do?

A little postulant opened the door, cheeks

425

brightening beneath the white veil as she noticed his collar. 'Come in, Father.'

He entered. 'I'm not a priest, I am a vicar. But one thing I can be glad of – any man wearing a dog collar is well received in a Catholic establishment.'

She bobbed her head and dashed off to find Mother.

Mother Olivia smiled when she saw him. 'Ah, there you are, now. I believe you visited our chapel during choir practice.' She laughed. 'The choir mistress's bark is worse than her bite – it surely is, for she cannot sing a solitary note and I'd rather she bit me any day. Away in. We'll go to your wife's little flat.'

They walked through mosaic-floored corridors, saints on plinths punctuating the monotony, windows overlooking the school. They turned a corner and almost collided with Caroline and Stella, who wagged happily at the sight of Brian.

'Brian? Is everything all right?'

'No, it is not,' he replied, 'though the children are fine, so no need to worry about them. You are the worry.'

Mother Olivia hung back. 'Would you like me to go, Mr Butlin?'

'No, Mother. Come in with us, because this involves the convent, too.'

They entered the flat and Brian waited until the two women were seated together on a sofa. He settled in the armchair, breathed deeply and began. 'You must come home. I take it you have read the newspapers?'

Caroline nodded.

'And his house is a couple of hundred yards away from here. If he comes back and if he has the slightest idea of where you are – well. Need I go into detail? This convent could be threatened by your very presence – the man is a lunatic. His home help is missing, a woman is in hospital and two more are dead. He probably killed Amy Bradshaw's sister as well as the other one. As for the poor soul in hospital, her face is marked for life. And she is the luckiest of them. Must I say more?'

Caroline had never before heard such power in his tone. That had been quite a speech for Brian, who usually seemed to save his voice for Sundays. 'I work here,' she said lamely.

'I'll get you a car. You can bring Amy and Maddy safely to school. Listen.' He glanced at the nun, then carried on regardless. 'If you don't wish to share a room with me, we can work something out.'

Caroline blushed, but said nothing.

'You are coming home. If necessary, I shall bring Yvonne Horrocks, Mrs Thornton, Celia Bradshaw and Yuspeh Feigenbaum to fetch you. Stella will come home, too.'

Caroline failed to smile, though she made a valiant effort. 'Yuspeh? I have heard all about how she has come out into society at last.' The twins had regaled her with tales of the pram, the chickens that could not be eaten, the hairstyle, the cardigans and skirts. 'Please, not Yuspeh. Anything but George's grandmother. I concede.'

Brian had not expected so inexpensive a victory. But he could sense her worry, had noticed a slope in her shoulders and the restlessness in her hands. Had he been asked to make a list of adjectives that might have been applied to his wife, 'calm' would have come high on the agenda. She was not calm at the moment.

'We'll miss her, so we will,' sighed Mother Olivia. 'But she's been doing a grand job of preparing the books, and, well, she is a married woman and her place is elsewhere. She can drive to her work here. But it will be a wrench to say goodbye to Stella.'

'I'll miss all of you,' said Caroline.

A gleam arrived in the nun's eyes. 'Before you go, give me the keys, then I shall be the holder of both sets.' She giggled. 'I'll be able to watch the television in splendid isolation, so I shall. I can't be doing with a lot of hot and bothered nuns all over the place while I'm concentrating.'

Brian shook his head. 'And the greatest of these is charity, Mother Olivia?'

'Sometimes, charity begins at home.' The head of the convent smiled. 'And I shall be nicely at home in here, thank you very much, with my tea and a bun and the television to watch. Ah, don't be worrying, they'll be let in for *Watch With Mother*, God love them.'

Brian rose to his feet. 'I shall be back within the hour – give you time to pack.' He studied his wife for a moment and wondered whether he would be able to let her out of his sight, but she had to work. He was a lucky man, anyway, because Caroline was coming home.

On Wigan Road, he parked his car and stood at the gates of a small park, his eyes fixed to the

428

house in which his wife had been subjected to the torment of a homicidal monster. His hands curled into fists and he pressed them together, one set of knuckles fitting into the other.

A woman stopped and studied him for a few seconds. 'It'll be wanting a blessing, that place.'

'I beg your pardon?'

She pointed towards the home of Derek Ramsden. 'I live next door and I heard the scream. Told the bobbies and they think it was his cleaning woman – she's never been clapped eyes on since. He put parcels in the van and drove off. I never thought. I mean, you don't, do you? Somebody screams and you look outside, but you don't go thinking it's your neighbour doing murder.'

Brian nodded encouragingly. 'Quite.'

She lowered her tone. 'You being a man of God, I can tell you.' She looked up the road and down. 'I've heard as how he cut her up in the bath.'

Brian swallowed nervously. 'The cleaner?'

'Aye. He'd scrubbed it out, but they still found some blood. They found her hat and coat, too – and her handbag.' She shook her head. 'Take it from me, no woman leaves her bag or her purse. She's dead, I'm telling you. I reckon she was in them parcels.'

Caroline was not safe. He had done the right thing today, he told himself.

'He had a lovely girl living with him for a while. I'm saying girl – she looked to be in her mid-thirties – smart, nice-looking. She disappeared and all. But . . .' Again, the tone was lowered and she glanced around before continuing. 'The bobby who told me says she's accounted for. He said she'd talked to the police in town and that it was a matter for discretion – they're thinking she must have been married.' The final words were spoken in a whisper.

So, Caroline, too, had done the right thing. She had admitted her acquaintance with Ramsden and had stopped another possible search. 'What sort of a man is he?' he asked.

The woman pursed her lips tightly before answering. 'Well, there's a woman lives up the brew – Willows Lane end – and she's known him all his life. She knew his mother and all – a big, fat woman – worked the market. She doted on him. She bathed him every night till he was turned twelve – treated him like a baby. He married Beryl Worthington-as-was – fish and chip shop up Halliwell, her family had. She did away with herself.'

Brian's blood ran cold. 'Are they sure of that?'

She clapped a hand to her mouth. 'Eeh, Lizzie Mellor – what a fool you are.' She stopped and thought for a moment. 'Well, I don't know. He's supposed to have found her when he came home from work – they said she'd been dead a few hours. Oh – that's my name, by the way – Lizzie Mellor. Lovely funeral. More lilies than I'd ever seen in all my life.'

Brian stepped away. 'Thank you for talking to me, Mrs Mellor.'

'Do you want to come in for a cuppa?'

He thanked her and refused politely. He had a wife and a dog to get home and some thinking to do. Derek Ramsden had to be somewhere and Caroline must be kept safe.

The salon was buzzing with it. Two perms had been in residence all morning and, between them, they had cited every instance of every male stranger noticed in Rivington Cross for the past six months. What if the missing man had a partner, was he the only killer, how could they possibly sleep with all this going on? Shampoos and sets had entered and exited, had contributed, argued, changed their minds about hairstyles – Yvonne would have been enjoying herself had the subject been anything but murder.

Yuspeh Feigenbaum dropped the biggest bomb just before lunchtime. Wearing her famous pink cardigan, a grey skirt and – most surprising of all – a pair of slip-on shoes, she made her entrance at a quarter past twelve. Unable to simply walk into a room, the woman always announced herself before plugging straight into any ongoing conversations. In the privacy of her own living quarters, Yvonne had been heard to declare that Mrs Feigenbaum – given younger and fitter days – might have managed tennis doubles without the benefit of a partner. Many people did not realize the true facts about Yuspeh – she was eccentric, yes, but she owned, as Celia Bradshaw and Yvonne Horrocks recognized, a brain more finely honed and brighter than the sharpest, shiniest knife in the drawer.

She stood now with her back to the door, a

hand raised as she waited for silence. 'Ladies,' she began, 'you will thank your husbands for patrols, which must be extended to be longer, because the missing person who was cleaning for the disappearing man is the mother of poor Betty Thornton.'

The ensuing stunned silence did not last for long. Mildred, who had dropped in for a chat while wearing her gorgeous new wig, sat down abruptly in one of the waiting chairs. 'Hell's bells,' she declared, 'and it's him that Mrs Butlin ran off with. Talk about close to home.'

'The bells of hell ring indeed,' sighed Yuspeh, 'and our Monty dog is hearing them all the time. He is in and out of hen house so often that my chickens do not lay eggs. In him there is fear. Hair all along back standing on end, little growlings in his throat. I was with him in the night, because sleep for an old woman can be rare. And he was on pathway making small noises. He would not go back to chickens and would not come in house.'

'That dog knows things,' said Yvonne. 'When the kiddies go to Horwich, he always knows which bus to meet, even though they get off a different one every time. Like that radar thing where they track planes.'

General chatter broke out – they should have a curfew, Ramsden was a bad man and charged too much for skirts, no woman was safe these days and what had Caroline Butlin been thinking of?

Yvonne butted in. 'Hey, hang on,' she shouted. 'Leave Caroline Butlin alone. This place is like the confessional box and don't you forget that. And I've signed no promises about keeping my gob shut, have I? I'm not a doctor and not a priest – a flaming unpaid psychiatrist is what I am, so think on. There's not one of you who hasn't opened up to me about problems. Caroline Butlin had a problem. She's dealt with it and she's back home with her kith and kin. So shut up and move on, or I'll shut up and move on to Bolton. I could charge more down there.'

Yuspeh smiled to herself and sat next to Mildred, told her how she preferred Mildred's hair in the new shade. 'You look younger,' she opined.

Mildred met Yvonne's gaze in the mirror. Not one single person in this village knew about the wig. Only Yvonne, Mildred and her husband were in possession of the precious secret. To earn and deserve the respect of a woman of Yvonne's calibre, a woman had to pull up her socks.

'Poor Betty,' said Yvonne. 'She'll be in a terrible state, because they don't even know where her mam is. Remember that, you lot. Remember that Mrs Butlin is living in a house of pain.'

The buzzing continued, but Caroline ceased to be a feature, which was just as well, because she entered the shop without her children for the first time. She had always used a hairdresser in Bolton for herself, though Simon, Sarah and the vicar came to Yvonne. She made an appointment, tried to ignore the sudden silence.

Yuspeh stood up. 'It is nice to see you back home, Mrs Butlin.'

A chorus of yeses followed the statement.

'Thank you,' said Caroline. 'It is good to be home.' There, it was done. She had faced the village and, hopefully, would soon become yesterday's news.

Betty was still sitting at the kitchen table when Caroline returned from Hair By Yvonne. Neither Brian nor Caroline could work out what needed to be done, as the good woman had spoken scarcely a word since the police had visited.

Caroline made tea and poured a cup for Betty. 'Try,' she said.

Betty looked like a crumpled version of a graveyard ornament, still as stone, grey and eroded by the passage of time.

'I wish you'd talk to me.'

Betty had nothing to say. The woman who had birthed her was missing, was probably dead. The man who had removed her was the very one with whom Mrs Butlin had cohabited and Betty felt numb. How many times had she wished her fanatical mother gone? But not like this, oh, no. Ellen had been cruel in her way, but she hadn't deserved to be murdered – no-one merited that.

'She may turn up,' said Caroline, though she knew she would not. Brian had spoken to a neighbour, who had conveyed messages from a loose-tongued policeman. Ellen's outer clothes, purse and handbag had been found at Derek Ramsden's house. 'Please drink the tea, Betty. I am not asking you to eat, but you must take fluids.'

434

Betty fixed dull eyes on her employer's wife. 'What were you doing with a man like that?' she asked.

Well, that was a response, at least, yet scarcely one Caroline might have welcomed. 'He seemed charming, funny, lovable. I was silly. He hurt me, Betty. He tried to destroy me, body and soul.'

'You were lucky.'

'I was indeed. I found a job and the nuns – they restored my faith in human nature.'

'And destroyed mine.' Betty employed both shaking hands to convey the cup to her lips. She remembered canes and even a whip, recalled the cruel glint in the head teacher's eyes when a child had been judged in need of chastisement. The cup rattled in its saucer when she replaced it. 'Where's James?'

'Out and about with the others, probably near or inside the bell house. He's a beautiful child.'

'She had him baptized, you know.'

'Yes.'

'Against my wishes.'

'I know.'

A long, shuddering sigh made its way out of Betty's lungs. 'She wanted him, wanted the Bertie I ought to have been. From the day he was born, she tried to stake a claim – as if he was a piece of land in the gold rush. All planned out for him, it was – Catholic school, Catholic priests, Catholic nuns. I ran, but she followed me. She wouldn't have been here but for me and James. They'd have stopped in Liverpool.'

'There are bad men in Liverpool, too, Betty.'

'I know, but that one was here.' She took

another sip of tea. 'I feel as if I wished it on her. When I came up to this village, the best bit was that she'd never find me – or so I hoped. Well, she won't follow me now, will she?'

Caroline offered no answer. She reached across and grasped a hand that was far too chilled to reflect the temperature in the room. 'Why don't you have a nice bath? I've some bath salts – very relaxing – you're welcome to use them.'

Betty shook her head. 'I'm waiting.'

'Oh?'

'He'll come, you see. I want to be here when he arrives. James and I are all he has now. Tried to keep the peace over the years, my dad, but he's a quiet man and she ran roughshod all over him. He'll need me now.'

'Yes, I expect he will.'

'I'd best get the food on.'

Caroline gripped the icy hand. 'No, you shall not. I am going for fish and chips – the children will be delighted. They can eat theirs in the bell house and I shall buy them dandelion and burdock. You rest.'

Betty refused lunch, continued her vigil at the table, drank more tea, waited for her father. The children, under the guidance of Caroline, stayed away. James seemed to need them more than he needed his mother, so Betty was left in peace to continue waiting. The boy had accepted almost without question the disappearance of his grandmother and was carrying on as if nothing of moment had happened. 'That was my fault, too,' Betty mumbled into the empty kitchen. Yet how might she have stayed her mother's hand? Ellen would have engineered his First Communion and Confirmation, and she would take account of no-one's wishes when it came to Catholicism. No, James would have needed to be kept away from Ellen until he reached the age at which he could make up his own mind.

Betty went to the bathroom and performed rudimentary ablutions, her ears alert for the front doorbell. She went into her bedroom, looked out at the beautiful village, at houses built from heavy stone, at the cross, the stocks and the cobbled roadway. 'I am so very fortunate,' she said. 'And my mother is dead.' Why could she not mourn?

Bert Langton arrived at three o'clock and was ushered into the kitchen by Caroline, who had kept an eye on his daughter all day.

At last, Betty shifted herself. 'Dad, oh, Dad.' They clung to each other and the weeping began.

'Thank God for that,' muttered Caroline as she left them together. It was clear that Betty adored her father and Caroline was happier now that he had finally arrived.

Bert placed himself in a chair opposite his daughter's and their hands, locked together in the middle of the table, became their lifelines.

'Betty, be brave,' he told her. 'I'd have come earlier, but I had to . . .' He stopped, took a breath. 'I had to identify her wedding ring. It had our names engraved inside. Never once since the day of our marriage did she take that ring off. I knew it straight away, before I

437

looked inside for the names. It was hers, love.'

Betty lowered her head. 'So they've found her body?'

He gulped noisily. 'They've found parts of her.'

'Parts?'

He nodded. 'He's a bloody lunatic – and that's swearing. Came to our house, said she'd never turned up for work – he even drove me to the police station. The coppers found her bag and coat in his hallway – I identified them, too. And her rosary beads and her picture of St Anthony.'

'So she's . . .'

'Yes. They call it dismemberment. They might not even find all of her. When I'd done it – the wedding ring thing – I went for a couple of pints because I needed mull it all over in my mind before coming up here. I can't bear thinking of what he did to her. I don't know how to live my life without her. Yes, she was bossy and yes, she was a raving Catholic – but I loved her, you know. She was my Ellen.'

'I know, Dad.'

'She didn't mean any harm – it was just the way she got brought up. It was all church and praying at their house – she never knew any different.'

'I know that, too.'

Tears the size of two-carat diamonds coursed down Bert Langton's cheeks. 'I'm worth thousands,' he wept. 'She always kept the policies up, did Ellen. I'm worth thousands and I'm worth nothing at all.'

Caroline opened the door an inch or two just

as Bert was saying that he didn't want to go home. 'Stay here,' she ordered. 'It'll be a squash and a muddle, but you must remain with Betty and James. At times like this, you don't want to be alone.'

In that moment, Betty's heart opened and allowed Caroline Butlin a tenant's rights. These were the best of people and Dad would be safe.

Matthew Roper signed his name in yet another register, this time on the outskirts of Manchester. In a city of such a size, he had a good chance of disappearing into the crowds, though he was gaining confidence with every day, because he looked nothing like his old self. Money had not yet become a problem, but it would be difficult in a week or so, because he dared draw nothing from the account of Derek Ramsden. Or perhaps he could – that decision must wait, he told himself.

In the public phone box, he dialled the number he had found in the library directory. Dropping in a few coins, he cleared his throat while he waited to be connected. 'Hello? Convent of St Anne, Mother Olivia speaking.' The Irish accent was almost musical.

'Can I speak to Caroline Butlin, please?'

After a pause, the reply came. 'She isn't available just now.'

Damn. 'I need to locate her. My name's Burrows and I am her insurance agent from the Prudential. I was told that this was her new address.'

'Not any more. She'll be here during

school hours from the beginning of next week.'

'Thank you.' He replaced the receiver. So, she had moved out. Twice, he had driven all the way to Rivington Cross during hours of darkness; twice, he had failed to catch a glimpse of her or her husband. That was the trouble with night times – everyone was in bed. Except that bloody dog, of course. It watched him. When he came through the woods, it was there, waiting in the graveyard. When he drove through the deserted village, it was there, on a pathway across the road from the vicarage. It was a bloody nuisance.

With hands plunged deep into pockets and his head bowed, he made his way back to the small hotel. He read the newspaper, was relieved to find that he had been relegated to an inner page. The police, if they knew anything at all, were keeping quiet. Derek Ramsden was reported as being still on the loose and still unapproachable. Members of the public were advised to keep their distance. 'Bloody fools,' he told his mother. 'I'm no threat except to those who do damage to me. I fight my own battles, don't I, Mam?'

She smiled at him. Mam always smiled at him. But he wished she would speak. No matter what had happened, Edna Ramsden had remained firmly in her son's camp. He had never broken a window, had never sworn at a neighbour, had never put a foot wrong. 'You believed in me. You're the only one who ever believed in me.'

Someone knocked at the door and he jumped up from the chair, every nerve in his body alive with fear. They had ways, didn't they? Fingerprints. No-one had ever taken his

440

fingerprints, but . . . . He had left that woman's stuff in the house and they had found it and they were here now, looking for him.

The knock was repeated.

There was no way out. He tried the window, but it was stuck. The fire escape would be no use if windows didn't open.

'Mr Roper?'

It was a woman's voice. 'Hello?' The word emerged shaky and high-pitched.

'Clean towels,' she shouted.

He opened the door, took the towels, closed the door quickly. This was no way to live. His heart was banging about like a loose wheel, his stomach felt sour, while his mouth was as dry as sand. Every time someone knocked to deliver clean towels or to change the bed, his body jumped into overdrive. There was no chance for him, anyway. Eventually, he would be found and placed on trial, so what was the point in remaining alive?

Something to do. Yes, he still had a mission to perform and, in a moment, he would remember what it was. 'I'll be with you soon, Mam,' he told the photograph. Exhausted, he fell onto the bed and dropped into sleep. He would be all right, because Mam was waiting for him on the other side.

SIXTEEN

The first day of the rest of their lives found Maddy and Amy overladen with goods and chattels. They had satchels and gym bags, indoor shoes, a whole term's lunch money, and the uniform they wore seemed to weigh a ton. They thanked God that Mrs Butlin had come home, because she would ferry them to St Anne's and, on days when her hours of work matched their school day, would also bring them back.

Simon, Sarah and George had already left for Bolton School with Mr Butlin when the two girls stuffed all their belongings into the boot of Caroline Butlin's recently acquired little Austin.

'So grateful,' puffed Maddy.

'So nervous,' added Amy.

'Same here,' admitted Caroline. 'I've worked with the nuns and I have started on the accounts, but it's many years since I was in a building containing six hundred girls. It's rather daunting.' More terrifying, though, was the sense that she was being watched, even followed.

She was constantly tense, permanently on alert, and she managed to relax only when indoors. It was enough to give a person agoraphobia, she thought as she glanced left and right, half expecting to see his face in a doorway, on the upper deck of a bus, in a passing car.

Maddy grinned impishly. 'And you've never been in a school with six hundred Catholics, have you, Mrs Butlin?'

Caroline agreed that she had not.

'We shall all be terrified,' Maddy said. 'I met a fifth former in town when we went for my horrible, clodhopping shoes. My mother was talking to her mother, and the girl told me about her first day. She said the worst thing is the silence.'

Caroline found it difficult to imagine Maddy Horrocks being frightened. She also had trouble envisaging such a large number of girls keeping quiet. Suddenly and almost without thinking, she slammed on the brakes with a ferocity that came close to propelling her two rear-seat passengers into the front of the car. 'Sorry,' she said, 'it was a cat.' It hadn't been a cat at all, but a man with a moustache had been standing on a corner and she had thought . . . 'Sorry,' she repeated.

Maddy had some idea of Caroline's situation, as she had heard her parents talking. In the opinion of Yvonne Horrocks, Caroline should have been in receipt of full police protection, plus a battalion of soldiers. 'It's all right,' she assured their nervous driver. 'Cats are so quick, aren't they? They seem to come out of nowhere.'

So would he, thought Caroline. He had nothing further to lose and she felt sure that he would be looking for her. But she needed to concentrate, because she was carrying precious cargo, so she made the rest of the trip without studying other people on the roads and pavements too closely. She did not notice the man with rust-red hair at the bottom of Deane Road. He was just one person in a long bus queue and she did not even glance in his direction.

They arrived. Caroline parked the car and offered to help her passengers carry their burdens into the school. Maddy refused politely for both of them. It was important to look like everyone else, to blend in without looking like special cases who lacked the ability to work out the simplest of problems.

For years to come, Madeleine Horrocks would describe this day as an introduction to hell. She likened it to how new recruits might be treated on their first day in barracks, with barked orders, no right to reply and no dignity.

Ushered by a determinedly bored sixth former into a cloakroom, they were allocated pegs on which to hang outdoor clothing, cubbyholes for outdoor shoes, small lockers for gym uniform. The older girl, curvaceous and blond, had the belt of her gymslip nipped in tightly in order to advertise her shapeliness. 'You will leave indoor shoes in the holes overnight and you will not remove them from the premises until half-term. First year assembly is in the main hall in five minutes. Leave your satchels here for now; they will be watched. I advise you to keep

444

money in your peggy purses and gloves in your satchel, or they may be stolen. Change your shoes now. No outdoor shoes are allowed beyond the main corridor.'

'What about our shoes?' asked Maddy innocently. 'Won't they get stolen?'

The blonde wandered over. 'Did you speak, brat?'

'Yes, I asked a question.'

'Well, don't. You'll learn by your mistakes, just as we did. Any more of your lip and you'll be on a list. All right?'

Maddy, though sorely tempted to enquire as to the nature of such list, decided that to keep quiet might be best on this occasion. After just two minutes in the dreadful school, she hated it with a passion that was almost overwhelming. She would not stay here. Nothing on God's good earth would induce her to remain in such a place.

They were arranged into lines in the corridor, their marshals consisting of the bored blonde and three others of about the same age. These all wore sashes of varying colours and badges with the word *PREFECT* embossed on the surface. Maddy, who was a player with words, mentally transposed the second and third letters of this title and smiled to herself. Perfect? Hardly.

In the hall, Mother Olivia had placed herself on a podium, the item being a necessity due to her lack of height. A girl at a badly tuned piano murdered a military march so efficiently that it would have defied identification even on the part of its composer. Ninety-odd new girls were

445

lined up and waiting. The room, which plainly doubled as a gymnasium, boasted tied-back ropes, beams and wall bars.

'Good morning, girls.'

'Good morning,' answered a few.

The nun tutted. 'You will reply, "Good morning, Mother Olivia". Shall we try again?'

Maddy was perplexed. They were at grammar school, yet they were being treated like babies. Prayers followed, then all were ordered to sit on the floor with gymslips covering legs.

'Now,' began the headmistress. 'It is my duty and my pleasure to welcome you to St Anne's. You will be divided into classes and houses. All houses will be represented in each class and you will read up on the saint who is patron of your house.'

There followed a list of rules too long and too complicated to make any real sense. There would be no lateness, no running in corridors, no shouting during exterior recreation periods. Girls would flatten themselves against walls to allow teachers to pass and would be polite at all times. Peggy purses would be worn in accordance with the printed information already in circulation, socks should be knee-high during the autumn and winter terms, but white ankle-socks must be worn with summer dresses. No blazers or panama hats could be accepted except in spring and summer, and all girls must wear hats and gloves when outside.

Maddy glanced sideways at Amy, who was clearly working hard to remember the regulations. Why did they have to sit on a hard floor during this rubbish? They could all read, so what was wrong with another printed list of rules? Uniform rules had arrived in the post, so why hadn't this load of tripe come with them? Perhaps it would have put folk off. Perhaps they might be needing permission to breathe.

No girl should ever miss Mass on Sunday or on a Holy Day of Obligation. As the fourteenth of September was to be the feast of the Exaltation of the Holy Cross, an extra assembly would take place when that blessed day arrived. 'We are the sisters of the Cross and Passion,' droned Mother Olivia, 'and we observe that day as one of our special feasts.'

Maddy switched off. She counted ropes, beams and the number of rungs on each section of wall bars. She counted windows and doors, stared at the stage with its blue velvet drapes, supposed that all plays would be Shakespearean or similar. When the others stood up, she did the same, then waited, as ordered, to be allocated to a class.

Another nun arrived with a clipboard and some interesting facial hair. She barked out names – Maddy's among them – and Class One A was formed. Amy was in Class One O and both girls were heartbroken. Never since the age of five had they been separated and that fact placed another black mark on the page Maddy was creating in her head. This was a prison, not a school, and she would run away from it. No, she wouldn't – she would leave with the dignity of which she had been deprived this morning.

Three new classes trooped off to various

destinations, each girl collecting her guarded satchel en route. In class, Maddy was placed in a double seat with a girl named Cynthia. Cynthia owned a nose of remarkable proportions, greasy hair and about a million freckles.

The first lesson was – of course – religious education. A sister whose letter Ts brought forth gushes of saliva told them to 'turn to page thirty-tree' and Maddy thought the first three rows of girls ought to have been furnished with umbrellas. The nun checked her pupils' knowledge of catechism, delivered a lecture on the gifts of the Holy Ghost, then meandered through a homily on duty to parents and to teachers.

A Miss Holmes took over after the first bell. She introduced the class to the joys of mathematics, which would consist of arithmetic, algebra and geometry. She checked that all girls had the correct equipment for geometry, then the bell rang for morning break.

There was an eerie silence in the corridors and a slight buzz in cloakrooms where indoor shoes were removed and outdoor ones were reinstated. Outside in an unevenly paved yard, Maddy searched for Amy. 'God, I hate this,' she snapped.

Amy was surprised. 'Do you? We had a religious lesson, then French. It was all right. I sit next to a girl called Eileen and she's very nice. The French teacher was funny and really French – from France. She told us a daft story in French all about *saucissons*. They're sausages. Mademoiselle Hédouin is good fun. Cheer up, Maddy, you'll get used to it.'

'I won't. I won't let myself get used to it. I feel like starting a revolution, but look at them – they're nothing but a flock of sheep. If the nuns told them to jump in a fire, they'd do it. It's all wrong, Amy. It's worse than infant school.'

'Maddy, don't do anything silly.'

'Like what? Ripping all my clothes off and running into chapel?'

'You know what I mean. Answering back and all the Caveman stuff. You'd get expelled.'

'That may be the ideal answer.' Impatient with Amy, who appeared to be just another lamb for slaughter, Maddy wandered about among other first formers in order to listen to conversations, in the vain hope of finding a few more malcontents. But, apart from the odd complaint about ill-fitting shoes and getting lost when looking for the toilets, she heard nothing of interest. It was plain that everyone else accepted what was happening, but surely she was not the only rebel? There had to be at least one other person here with the guts to think for herself.

The day ground on, lunch at noon, recreation after that, which activity involved the changing of shoes all over again. Maddy was introduced to the joys of geography and French but she paid little heed, as she had no intention of becoming a taxi driver in Paris. How was she going to escape from this place? What would her parents say and do? Could she live with their disappointment? And would she have to attend a secondary modern, the schools for the leftovers who would work in factories and shops?

449

'What is your name, girl?' asked the geography nun.

Cynthia dug an elbow into Maddy's ribs.

'Name?' the teacher repeated.

'Maddy. Maddy Horrocks . . . Sister.'

'Your name is Madeleine, I take it?'

'Yes.'

'Then you shall be Madeleine. Are you intending to daydream your way through this school?'

'No, Sister.' She wasn't intending to be here, so that was the truth.

'Then find the capital of Russia on this map.'

Maddy walked to the front, picked up the cane and pointed it at Moscow.

'Sit down and pay attention.'

Maddy learned a few tricks on that eventful day. She perfected the art of appearing to listen while daydreaming, discovered, during Latin, that she could wiggle her ears if she concentrated and found that she could outstare most of her teachers. These were small triumphs, but they would have to suffice until she could find her way out of this institution for the tame and the acquiescent. It was a pity about the uniform, but perhaps someone would buy it. Because one day was enough and she would not be returning for more punishment.

She did not wait for anyone after school – she was alone and she would do this alone. There was no point in discussing it with Amy or with Mrs Butlin. After collecting all her belongings, including the indoor shoes, Maddy ran down the hill and caught the number 39 to town. Now all she had to do was convince her parents that their dream for her had been the wrong dream. And that was the only aspect that caused Maddy the slightest pain.

Yvonne was astonished. The one thing on which she had always been able to depend was her daughter's temperament. John, too, described himself as 'flummoxed' by Maddy's behaviour. She had begun with reasoned argument and had ended with a tantrum involving screaming, weeping and the slamming of doors. Her parents faced each other across the living room. 'She'll get used to it,' said Yvonne.

John shook his head. 'If there's one thing I know about Maddy, it's this – she makes up her mind and she sticks to it. She's sensible, Yvonne.'

'Sensible? What's sensible about turning down the chance of a lifetime, eh? After one day, too. We all have to get used to things. You've had to get used to laying out the dead and I've needed to cope with everything from baldness to head lice.'

'She's only eleven.'

'Exactly – too young to know what's good for her.'

'You're using the argument from both ends, love. We took stuff on board when we were old enough – she's expected to cope at eleven with things we have never seen. Yes, she's only eleven, so why should we allow her to be so upset? I don't like this, Yvonne. It's not what I expected from her and I don't know where to start. She has to go to school – it's the law—'

'Yes, and she'll go back there tomorrow.'

'How?'

'Mrs Butlin will take her.'

'In chains? Sedated? Tied to the roof of the car? She'll go nowhere in that mood. And, since this is the first time she's been in a mood, we don't know how long it will last, do we?' John leaned back in his chair. What would he have given for a chance at Thornford College, the boys' equivalent of St Anne's? But there had been few options back then, so he had educated himself as best he could, as had Yvonne. Maddy? Maddy was brilliant.

Yvonne leapt to her feet and began pacing back and forth. She stopped abruptly after about ninety seconds. 'John?'

'What?'

'Nip over to the vicarage and grab hold of Caroline Butlin, will you? We need to travel along a different road.'

'What can she do that we can't?'

'She can be *not* one of Maddy's parents. Sometimes, the ones closest to us are the very people who can't help.'

John left the house and returned ten minutes later with Caroline.

'She came home without waiting for me and Amy,' Caroline explained. 'I knew she was safe, because I saw her through the salon window. Is there a problem?'

John gave a brief commentary on all that had happened in the past hour.

Caroline went upstairs and knocked on Maddy's door, entering the room before being issued a verbal invitation. 'Now, Maddy—'

Maddy, face down on the bed, turned her head to the wall. 'Please go away.'

Caroline placed herself in a yellow-painted kitchen chair. 'You have to give this a proper chance,' she began. 'I know how you feel.'

'Do you?'

'Yes, of course I do. We have all been through it to a greater or lesser degree – some when older than you, some when younger. But every one of us hits a brick wall from time to time. Maddy, look at me. Look at me now.'

The child obeyed.

'Brian was talking to your teacher a few months ago. Do you remember being taken into the head's office in your junior school? You did a test – just you – none of the other children? It would have lasted quite a while – over half an hour.'

Maddy recalled the occasion and how greatly she had enjoyed working on a set of very challenging problems. 'He was a funny-looking man,' she said. 'Bald, but with a red, bushy beard. Twinkly eyes.'

'He was a psychologist, Maddy. Do you know what an intelligence quotient is? Have you heard of that?'

Maddy sat up and dried her face on the edge of a sheet. 'It's to do with your brain and how well it works.'

'An average person has a quotient of one hundred to one hundred and twenty. Yours measures one hundred and sixty-four. This means that you are in the top two per cent. Only

453

two people in every hundred – twenty in each thousand – are endowed with such ability. You are cleverer than I am, cleverer than my husband is, certainly a great deal brighter than any of your friends.'

Maddy stared at Caroline. 'But I can't work things out,' she said. 'It's mixed up in my head, and—'

'Because you are still a child, your emotional development is possibly lagging behind. Academically, you are a grown-up. Socially, you remain a child. Do you remember learning to read?'

Maddy pursed her lips and thought hard. 'No. I remember being able to read very suddenly and the book was *Robinson Crusoe*. When I started school, I could read.'

'And all the others were babies.'

'Yes. Except for Amy. She's clever.'

'But not as talented as you are. So, you have a gift. A person endowed with a gift has to repay. You work on your talents, then you pass them on. Work is painful. Obedience for someone of your calibre is difficult, because rules seem silly and, frankly, the people making the rules are not as bright as you are. Maddy, you are cleverer than your teachers. But there is a mould into which you must squeeze yourself and that mould is entitled society. Rise above, but play your part.'

'I have to pretend to be stupid? It's mad up there. I hate it.'

Caroline began the tale of her husband's youth and the years he had spent in boarding school. She spoke of cruelty, slavery to the whim of sixth formers, despair and loneliness. 'He was beaten – literally – with canes. Older boys used new boys as fags – that meant servants. When Brian's mother sent him a tuck box filled with food, bigger boys commandeered it. But he got through and went on to university, became a vicar. You have to pretend to walk to the same beat of the same drum that is heard and obeyed by others. Inside, you can be as free as you like.'

'It's still pretending.'

'Yes, it is. Society is pretence, as you will learn for yourself.'

Maddy stood up and walked to the window. 'I'm not a genius, am I?' She didn't want to be a genius, felt that she could not cope with such a burden.

'No, you are borderline. True genius occurs in less than one per cent of the population. Give the school until Christmas, then think again. St Anne's is not out of step – you are. And St Anne's cannot be blamed for the superiority of your brain. Rules are for the majority and the majority must rule in a democracy.'

'It's a dictatorship by nuns,' said Maddy, 'who want to see us as sausages coming out of a machine, all the same length and all with the same amount of meat in them.' Amy had done sausages today – French sausages. 'I hate the place.'

'Then do well and show all of them that you are on a level of your own.'

Maddy turned and wiggled her ears. 'I learned that during Latin. Amo, amas, amat, amamus amatis amant.' She recited the words with ease, but was prouder of her ear-wiggling.

'You also learned a verb. Without even listening, you took it in. Others will be struggling for days to achieve that. Maddy, you must persevere. Walk with other ranks and appear to keep pace. Inside, where it matters, follow your own star. I am imploring you to stay. For three months. Well?'

Maddy shrugged. 'I expect there is no alternative.'

Caroline knew there was, but she kept quiet. This girl could sail through the entrance exam for Bolton School, but such ideas must be kept on a low light for the present. 'There is no sensible alternative, no,' she agreed.

'Thank you, Mrs Butlin. I shall change my clothes now.'

The bursar of St Anne's RC Grammar School for Girls walked downstairs. Exhausted by a day of lunch money and other accounts, she sank into a chair. 'She'll try till Christmas,' she said. 'I may have a word with Mother Olivia – as long as you don't mind. They have to realize what they have in Maddy.'

'You mean the hundred and sixty-four business,' said John.

'Yes. And all that goes with it – including a tendency to see through solid steel when it comes to academic subjects. She'll go far.'

'As long as she gets to St Anne's tomorrow, that's far enough for us,' replied Yvonne. 'Thank you so much.'

* * *

456

The bell house was humming. Amy struggled with the school song while Sarah, in mischievous mood, was 'helping' her by inventing her own very unsuitable lyrics to the doleful tune. Jay, covered in glue and confusion, was being detached by Simon from pieces of balsa that were supposed to make a model Spitfire, though the result so far resembled the fruits of a bad accident on a very busy road.

George, testing his theory that the upstairs-downstairs floor of the building was out of true, had plainly proved his point, as all the marbles he had placed near the door had moved themselves into a corner. 'Told you it was crooked,' he explained to Simon.

Simon, now almost glued to Jay, answered, 'No, it's the ghosts. They shift everything.' He retrieved his hand. 'Look,' he complained loudly, 'I'm stuck to a wing.'

'Don't try flying,' advised Maddy from the doorway. 'Remember what happened to Icarus?'

'Was he a prophet?' Jay asked.

All chorused Maddy's famous line, 'Read a comic.' Jay explained that he could not possibly read a comic without becoming very attached to it.

'Where did you get to?' Amy asked her best friend. 'We waited for you.'

Maddy made an airy excuse about travelling with girls from her class, then gave poor Jay the once-over. His mother would kill him, she stated baldly. Glue should be attached to pieces of wood and not to boys. She asked whether he liked his new school and he replied in the affirmative, though with some reservations about multiplication and division. 'Will water get this glue off me?' he asked.

He was advised by his friends that he would need to be boiled, sandpapered, flayed of skin and hospitalized, though not necessarily in that order. Fortunately, the lad was becoming inured to the insults and threats of his slightly-elders and he simply carried on ruining aeroplane and clothes. The days when he had been taken in by these five were long past. He tried to scrape some glue off the table, realized that the tail of the Spitfire was now embedded in said piece of furniture, and left the room with an air that was casual, though studied.

'That bit's stuck,' said Maddy when Jay had made his escape. George worked with a screwdriver until the tail shot across the room and broke into pieces. Simon, imitating a bugle, sounded the last post for yet another downed pilot, then they all settled to talk about school.

Maddy volunteered little information. She listened while Amy outlined her French sausages and the twins described the hallowed halls of the best school in the county.

'How did you go on?' George asked Maddy.

'I'll survive it,' was her reply. 'And I learned to wiggle my ears.'

All stood back in stunned admiration while she demonstrated the newly acquired skill. 'And I pointed to Moscow.' Thus she summed up her first day at the school, then she watched while the other four tried to move their ears. No-one managed it. 'Concentrate,' she ordered. 'Think ears and only ears. Keep everything else still.'

George looked at his watch. 'Feeding time at all zoos,' he announced. They locked up their den. Sarah and Simon disappeared into the vicarage, from which building the voice of Betty Thornton rang as she chided her son. 'Why can't you do these things properly? Look at you. How much glue do they put in the kits? Get upstairs now and in that bath.'

While Amy giggled, George whispered to Maddy, 'Did you hate it?'

'Yes.'

'What will you do?'

'I'll win,' she said. And, from that moment, she knew that she could.

The binoculars had been an expense he would have preferred to avoid, but he realized that they had been absolutely essential. He found a clearing in the woods, worked on the focus mechanism and trained the binoculars on the vicarage. She was there. What was more, she was standing near a window with her husband and they were kissing.

Anger rushed into Derek Ramsden's veins, but he managed to hold back a howl of fury. So, he had been a mere diversion that had pepped up the failing Butlin marriage. Replacing the binoculars in his basket, he picked out the photo of his mother. She travelled everywhere with him these days and he was beginning to believe that she was guiding him from the other side. 'See, Mam,' he said. 'Look how they treat me.

It's always been the same. They find me good-looking and funny, then they drop me like a hot brick. It's not fair.'

Edna smiled up at her son, seemed to be urging him on. 'It'll be sorted soon,' he told her. 'Don't you worry, Mam, I'm fighting my own battles, just like you told me to.'

He watched the children as they wandered out of the graveyard, two making for the vicarage – her two – and three moving towards the road. They all had homes to go to, mothers who would have a meal prepared, a comfortable bed of their own and all modern conveniences. Whereas he was condemned to live the life of an itinerant, for ever on the watch, alert and fear-filled.

Home. He wondered whether the police would be inside the house, doubted that the place would be monitored permanently. It would be nice if he could go back for a few hours, better still if the police hadn't found his little stash of money under the boards in the spare bedroom. Could he? Should he? Perhaps the force had given up the search – the days of Derek's front page stardom were waning.

He made his way out of the woods and across fields towards Horwich. Three nights he had come here and this was the first time he had clapped eyes on Caroline. He had also started to mingle with crowds in Bolton town centre, confident because his image was so altered that he had trouble recognizing himself in a shop window. He was Matthew Roper; he was no longer Derek Ramsden. Emboldened by anonymity, he thought he might just about get away with a quick visit to the house – ten minutes – take up the floorboard, get the cash and run. But first he had to wait for darkness.

Assuming an accent he assumed to be posh, he bought fish, chips and a bottle of pop to eat and drink in the car. Then he parked in a little alley-way behind an empty factory and slept for a few hours, Mam's picture balanced on the dash-board. She had to be with him to keep watch. From time to time, he opened one eye to make sure that she was still there, and she was, every time. Mam would never leave him.

When midnight arrived, the bottle-green car rolled down in the direction of Bolton. It stopped in a quiet street off Wigan Road, its occupant leaving quietly after locking the door. He ducked down behind the wall of Haslam Park, eyes fixed on the house that was his, bought with his own hard labour and the money left by Mam and Beryl. It seemed deserted, but, just to make perfectly sure, he went via the back, over the wall and into a flower bed. Silence.

Behind a loose brick in the coal shed, he felt the spare back door key, a monstrous object about four inches in length. Dared he? After a minute's thought, he chose as weapon the shears with which he had once trimmed privets, and carried them to the house. The police had not changed the lock and he let himself into his own home, removing shoes in case footfalls might be heard next door. Even the aroma of the place belonged to him and he breathed it in greedily, relieved beyond measure to be on ground that was familiar to him.

He was back. It took a while for his eyes to adjust, but he began to make out shapes of familiar objects, many of which had been moved. How dared they touch his stuff? Some of the furnishings had been Mam's and he hated the thought of alien hands in contact with her chair, her sideboard, her life.

Upstairs, he entered the bedroom he had always used for storage, crawled about and found the loose board. The tin was still there, a biscuit container manufactured to commemorate the wedding of Prince George, later King George V, to Princess Mary of Teck. Good. He had money, at least. But it might not be enough, so he picked up Mam's jewellery box. Once he had explained his intentions, she would surely understand, because she had always insisted that he should stick up for himself. The sale of his mother's treasures would not be for trivial purchases – it would be to keep him safe and that was what she had always wanted for him.

When he was downstairs and almost at the back door, he heard the noise. It came from the hallway and was clearly the sound of a key being turned in the lock. So, they were watching all the time. Quickly, he was out and through the back gate in a matter of seconds. He climbed into the car, turned it round and headed away from Wigan Road. 'You're too fast for them, Derek,' he said. 'I mean Matthew.' Forty minutes later, he was in his little room at the Manchester bed and breakfast. Oh, yes, he was too quick for them. He kissed his mother's photograph and slept the sleep of the just.

She was suddenly an adult who had temporary ownership of teacup and saucer. Madeleine Horrocks, aged eleven and a bit, was seated in the headmistress's office with a hot drink and biscuits. 'We're not ogres, you see,' Mother Olivia was saying. 'And yes, we are very much aware that you were picked out to do one of those new-fangled tests. I can also tell you that you gained top marks in the entrance examination and that the one point you lost was because of a hastily spelt word of several syllables. That was in your composition. Free Will was the title, if my memory is correct.'

Was this a challenge? Maddy wondered.

'Your faith will be hard fought for. You have a brain of tremendous elasticity and that makes you fortunate, but, at the same time, unfortunate. It will be a burden and a blessing both.'

Maddy could have listened all day to this woman. Her voice was soft, much quieter than it was in assemblies. Irishness displaced some of the words and the whole thing could have fitted very well to music. 'I am not a genius,' she said. 'They come off worst.'

'Do they now? And what do you know of genius?'

'A genius often sticks to just the one thing. Beethoven did. The cruelty was that he lost his hearing – that's almost like a painter losing hands and eyes. I want to do everything.'

The little woman knew – as she had always known – that St Anne's occasionally received a child who was a cut above, and that such children were troublesome. They were also troubled, sensitive and inclined to indulge in too much thinking altogether. 'Is there not one thing that you want to do over and above all else?'

Maddy pondered. 'Not really. I want to teach, explore, dig up sites where there are bones and all kinds of things used thousands of years ago. I want to write books and travel all over the world. I'd like to do piano and guitar, act in plays, learn tennis and swimming properly – I can swim only a bit. Get married, have children, fly an aeroplane—' She stopped. Sister Olivia was laughing.

The nun dried her eyes. 'You are going to be needing more than one lifetime, I can see that.'

'I expect I won't get to do all of those things.'

Mother Olivia didn't know about that. Madeleine Horrocks was going to be a worker and the sky was her limit, with or without the aeroplane. 'Look, child, I know this is difficult for you and I am not going to pretend otherwise. You are one among six hundred. Yet you are one alone. To some extent, that is true of all girls out there.' She waved a hand towards the corridor. 'Mrs Butlin told me what I already knew – she also told me of your unhappiness. Madeleine, we are here to help and I shall be your personal mentor. But that is to be our secret, because favouritism is not encouraged.'

464

Maddy smiled. 'I'm not your favourite, anyway – I'm too much of a nuisance.'

'That is true. But I shall always be here and you may send me notes when you are troubled or in any kind of difficulty. I will not lose you, Madeleine Horrocks. And I have vanity enough to know that I shall bask in your success one day. Now, be off with you, for I have a school to run.'

Maddy rose to her feet. 'Mother?'

'Yes, child?'

'The word I got wrong – what was it?'

'Transubstantiation. You missed the second S.'

'I shan't do it again.'

'That I can believe.'

When the girl had gone, Mother Olivia sat and grinned to herself. Madeleine was a trouble and a treasure, and it was an honour to have her in the school.

Caroline poked her head in from the attached bursar's office. 'All right, Mother?'

The grin broadened. 'I met my Waterloo, Caroline. She has brains enough for two and the ability to change the way this world works and thinks. But it will be a hard road for her, because she also owns a beautiful soul. She'll break and mend my heart time and time again, but I would not give her up for all the leprechauns in Ireland.'

Caroline blinked. 'But there are no leprechauns in Ireland.'

The headmistress shook her head. 'Another of little faith. Away with you and get me the education offices in that town. I've girls here too poor to be paying dinner money and the town will pay. Tell them I am on the warpath again.'

Caroline went off to warn the Town Hall that Mother Olivia was disgruntled. She had known that the nun would love Madeleine. Everyone loved Madeleine – especially that young Jewish boy . . .

SEVENTEEN

Emboldened by success as a master of disguise, strengthened by his small victory over the police, Derek spent more and more time on the fringes of Rivington Cross. He had entered his house under the nose of guards and had got away with money and jewellery. The national press had found other matters on which to concentrate, leaving Derek Ramsden to feel as free as the proverbial bird. The lisp he had worked on; if he controlled the positioning of his tongue and spoke slowly, his speech improved no end.

Holly Brook Farm, about two miles north of the village, had been deserted for some time. The barns were in reasonable shape, though the house itself required a great deal of work. Roof tiles had slipped and shunted into gutters, rainwater goods had fallen away from walls and the land, clearly fallow, had not been rented out to other farmers. And it cost nothing. At Holly Brook, there was no landlady to ask questions and, best of all, there were no other tenants.

In one of the barns, he found an old table and a chair of moderate stability. These he placed in the kitchen. An aged paraffin stove boiled his kettle and kept him warm during September evenings and nights. From a camping shop, he had acquired two sleeping bags, an inflatable mattress and a pillow; with one sleeping bag doubled over on the mattress and the other worn for warmth, Derek was as snug as a bug in a rug.

His only ornaments were Mam's photograph and her jewellery box. These he displayed on the table and he often talked to Mam while he ate and just before going to bed on the kitchen floor. Food was bought from a variety of shops and he managed to cook bacon and eggs on his little stove, so life was bearable. Just about.

Until he thought about *her*. But for her, he would have been all right. None of the other stuff would have happened had Caroline Butlin not given him the glad eye. He chose to forget his pursuit of her, recalling only her expressed pleasure whenever he had called at the vicarage to deliver clothes. She was a temptress. She had pushed him so far that he had . . . What had he done?

Oh, yes. Rose and Lily. Ellen he could not remember properly, because she had been sent by Mam to try to help him and it had all gone wrong. 'Where was I?' he asked the photograph.

They pushed you too far.

He smiled. Mam was here again. She had made the journey from the other side and she was guiding him. 'What shall I do?' he asked her.

468

You have to fight your own battles, Derek. You know where she is, and she must be punished for what she did to you.

Yes. But that wasn't going to be easy, was it? She had a husband and two children and . . . and she had someone else, someone who had been connected to Ellen Langton. Betty. There was a Betty and, he thought, a son of Betty. 'She's never on her own.'

But she works at that school, son. Where the nuns are. Follow her or wait for her, stop her. You have to sort her out before she does more damage. She is not fit to be allowed to wander. She hurt you, Derek. She hurt you most of all.

This was true. He had thought of burning down the vicarage so that everything would disappear in one fell swoop, but there were the watching men. They walked about at the oddest times after dark and Derek knew why – they were searching for a murderer. 'I never killed the first one.'

We know that. You and I know the truth and that's all that matters. I'm here. I'm always here.

He remembered cream teas, strawberry jam, Mam in front of the fire with her stockings rolled down. The brown mottles on her legs had been baked in by the heat, but she would not alter her ways. Lisle stockings covered the damage and Mam wasn't the sort to worry about appearances. Her gravy had been wonderful. Nobody on earth could match her gravy. She used to say that the secret lay in elbow grease.

Have a rest. Take it easy, because this is your biggest job of all.

469

There was no point in trying to argue with Mam. She always knew her mind and was not averse to giving away pieces of it. No shopkeeper had dared overcharge her, because Mam's wrath was legendary. 'Right-oh,' he told the photograph.

Then he lay down on his makeshift bed and wished he could go home to his own bedroom, but both he and Mam knew that he never could and never would. There would come an end to all this, he told himself as he looked up at a flaky ceiling. He was far from sure of the shape of the end, but he realized that he could not continue indefinitely in this way of life.

I'll sing you to sleep.

He drifted away on 'Rock of Ages', a slight smile on his lips. She would be here when he woke. It had taken her long enough to come back to him, but he was sure that he would never lose her again. Wherever he went from now on, his beloved mother would accompany him.

The room was cramped and Yuspeh, as was her wont, had provided – with help from other women – sandwiches and cakes sufficient to feed a small African nation for two days. If these meetings had to happen for a reason that was less than good, Yuspeh would make sure that people got some pleasure out of them. She checked that everyone had food and drink, then stood at the front of the school hall to make an announcement.

Anna eyed her mother-in-law. Yuspeh Feigenbaum had taken over Rivington Cross in a swoop so effortless that no-one had even noticed. Jakob smiled at his wife. 'They will all be at Shabbat with us soon. We shall be squashed out of our own home.'

Anna laughed. 'They love her, though.'

'My mother is a lot of things, Anna. She is wise and old, she is inquisitive and she is everywhere – as are her chickens. But yes, she is loved.'

Yuspeh eyed her audience. Yvonne would not be here as she was currently minding the children – all six of them. But John would come, as would the vicar . . . as would his wife. She noticed Betty Thornton with her father – poor man, may God protect him and his from further harm.

The old lady held up her hand. 'Tonight will come a very brave young woman to talk to you.' The Catholic priest had slipped in at the back and Yuspeh eyed him for a moment. He was too fat to slide in without being noticed – and she did not like him. She could not fathom the reason for this deep antipathy, but it had interfered with her train of thought, ah, yes. 'She is concerned for the village, so she comes so that you will understand better the man who has been killing people. Because of that man, Derek Ramsden, we are going to continue watching our village and taking extra care of our children. He has killed three times and has put one woman into the hospital.'

Caroline Butlin walked in with her husband. He planted a kiss on her forehead, then steered her through to the front of the hall. 'Here we are, Mrs Feigenbaum. Caroline?'

471

She turned to face her public and her own crime. Brian nodded at her reassuringly. 'We are all friends here,' he told her.

After clearing her throat, Caroline began. 'I worried about myself for a long time and went to stay elsewhere while I came to terms with what I had done to my husband, to my children and to me. It was not an easy time. I had to account for myself to myself and it was a case of facing my own grossly bad behaviour. But I have decided to tell you what I and the police already know.

'I went to the police after the attack on Lily Holdsworth. There was no alternative, but they were very kind and they kept my name out of it, because I am a married woman.' She glanced at her husband. 'I am a very fortunate married woman,' she added.

'It is my duty to tell you that the man is a rapist. I shall not go into details, but I ask you to believe that he hurt me more than once and that I know him to be capable of damaging and killing almost any woman. Obviously, I have given a great deal of thought to this matter before coming forward, because I am now exposing my family to ridicule caused by my own stupidity.'

People moved in their seats and a few mouthed sympathy and encouragement.

'Thank you,' she said. 'Your support is appreciated. Now, Derek Ramsden.' She took a deep breath. 'There is a cleverness in him. He is, I believe, mentally ill, but I feel sure that he will have changed his appearance. Self-preservation

472

is his primary goal. Many know him from the market and I think he will have shaved off his moustache, will possibly be wearing spectacles and may have changed the colour of his hair. He is . . .' She looked to Brian for support and he came to stand beside her.

'I'll do the rest,' he said. 'The man is clearly fixated on my wife. He is not too fond of me, either, since I confronted him in the market. I am not proud of my behaviour, yet a part of me wishes now that I had followed my baser instinct and incapacitated him, because the world would be safer without him.

'Police believe he killed Bernadette Bradshaw as well as the other poor soul who was found in the reservoir.' He stopped for a moment, thought about Nettie's letter, the one he had retrieved from Mary Browne. Did it contain the very truth that was needed now? Should he open it? No, no, he could not, must not. 'I beg you all to be vigilant.'

Caroline joined him, placed a hand on his arm. 'There is one more thing,' she said. 'Derek Ramsden has a problem sounding an S. When he talks quickly, the lisp is quite pronounced. Those of you who have not shopped at his stall will have been unaware of that. Thank you.'

There followed a pause, then a cheer went up, its leader the irrepressible Yuspeh. 'Well done,' called several people as Caroline gratefully accepted a cup of tea. She had done all in her power to stop Ramsden and, now that she had faced the village en masse, she felt cleaner.

Yuspeh gave her a big hug. 'Of you I am

proud,' she said, 'and of your husband, you must be very proud.'

'I am.'

From the back of the hall, a fat man in black watched the proceedings. They had a Jewess in charge and the promiscuous wife of a vicar as the main speaker. How tasteful. As for Bernadette Bradshaw, Michael Sheahan knew perfectly well that the man on the run had not killed her. But the real murderer of Bernadette Bradshaw answered to God and only to God. He refused tea and a sandwich, had no intention of indulging in kosher food. There was a half-bottle of good Irish waiting at home and a sermon to write.

'Father Sheahan?'

It was the vicar. 'Yes, Mr Butlin?'

'Will you not stay for something to eat?'

'No, thank you, I have a parish to run.' He swept out of the room, black cape ballooning around him.

Brian stared at the floor and shook his head. There was something so unpalatable about the Catholic priest. Oh well, perhaps a sandwich and a cup of tea would cover the bad taste in Brian's mouth.

'I'm doing it, Betty, and let that be an end to it.' Bert Langton's Liverpool accent was stronger when he was arguing. 'Look, girl, he killed my wife – your mother. They've started finding her in bits and pieces all over the place, so I'm off with John Horrocks to do my stint. Don't try to stop me, missy, because my mind is made up.

474

And if I find him, I'll bloody kill him – and that's swearing.'

Betty had never before heard such a long speech from her father. Buried under the weight of his garrulous wife's constant torrent of words, Bert's voice had seldom managed to reach the surface. 'Dad, be careful.'

'What do you take me for? I didn't sail up the Mersey on the last banana boat, you know. And I'll be investing in this village, won't I? Once the insurance is through, I shall have that cottage that used to belong to – what was her name? Husband on the bins?'

Betty almost smiled. This was her real dad, the one she had never met until lately. He was funny, determined and full of love. 'Hilda Barnes. And he wasn't on the bins, he was on the Town Council.'

'Same thing, then, because they're all a load of rubbish. Anyway, Mr Butlin's lent me the deposit and the solicitor says the Barnes people'll wait because of my tragic circumstances.' He leaned back in his chair. 'Rivington Cross will be my home, so I will be part of it. I'm glad I've got you and our James. If it wasn't for you two, I don't know what—'

'Stop it, Dad. We'll look after each other.'

He would look after his daughter and grandson, all right. They'd be owners of a decent house when he died, and that was all thanks to Ellen and her insurance policies. 'She'd go without food before she'd miss a payment to the Prudential.'

'I know.'

'And she loved you in her way.'

'I know that, too.' The problem had been that Ellen's love for the church had always stood at the front of the queue, well ahead of affection for friends, for neighbours, even for family. But Dad didn't need reminding about any of that. Remarks he had made since coming to lodge with the Butlins proved that he was well aware of his deceased wife's shortcomings.

'Stay with John while you're out there,' his daughter commanded. 'Don't be going off on your own if you think you see something.'

'I won't.'

'And don't get too tired.'

He sighed. 'All right, Mother. Can I go now?'

'Wrap up. It gets cold later on.'

Bert kissed his daughter and left by the front door, crossing over to the shops belonging to Yvonne and John Horrocks. This was a bad carry-on and no mistake. Ellen had been looking for a little cleaning job and had landed not on her feet, but in a bath and— He didn't want to think about it. She would have been dead, anyway, before that creature began to . . . began to do what he did to her remains.

They bought a pint at the pub, stood outside while they drank it, then went on patrol. John had promised Bert's dead wife a good funeral once she had been retrieved, had even offered to drive her coffin over to Liverpool, all for no money, but Bert had put his foot down. Ellen had another little policy just for funerals, and she would pay for herself to be buried with all her family in the city of her birth.

'I was talking to Caroline Butlin before,' said John, 'and she reckons he's not far from here. Intuition, she calls it.'

'My Ellen had that, but it did her no good in the end, did it? Mind you, she'd only seen him a couple of times when he . . . you know. But female radar's a mighty force, John. Women sense things. I don't know whether they're nearer to animals than we are, or whether they've developed past us, but they do know stuff.'

'Yes. And so does that blinking dog.' John pointed at Monty, who was seated at Yuspeh Feigenbaum's gate, every hair on his back rigid. 'We've been having a bit of trouble with him lately.'

'Whose is he?' Bert asked.

'He's his own,' replied John. 'Belonged to an old lady who was found dead – he still goes to her grave every day. First time I met him, I was laying her out and this here dog was asking me questions with his eyes. So I took him into the back and showed him where she was. After that, he adopted everybody. Nobody owns Monty – he owns us. Oh, and he gets two or three dinners a day and sleeps with chickens. He's leading the vicar's dog astray, too.'

Bert was studying the dog. 'I wonder if he knows him?'

'Who?'

'Ramsden. I wonder if Monty's seen him and can smell him. I mean, you can shave off your 'tache and dye your hair, you can wear specs and put weight on – anything you like – but a dog still knows you.'

477

'Yes.'

Bert patted the dog's head, but got no response. 'I thought I'd have known him again. He came round our house that night – the day he killed my Ellen – asking where she was. Pretended she'd never turned up for work, you see. Bold as brass, drove me down to the cop shop, never blinked an eye. I wonder . . . no, it doesn't bear thinking about.' But John had been forced for some time to live with the idea that Ellen might have been in the back of the van that night. 'He's got to be stopped. There's a young woman still in hospital.'

'And two dragged out of the reservoir,' John added.

Suddenly, the dog relaxed, yawned, wagged his tail politely and went off in search of his feathered bedfellows. 'Whatever it was has gone. Come on, Bert. Let's do the rounds.'

There were several stretches of deserted road between Bolton and Rivington Cross. Some were more deserted than others. From most, a farmhouse or a shed could be seen in the distance and Derek was taking no chances. He hid the car on a dirt track, took up an elevated position and used his binoculars. Caroline now owned a car – he had seen it the previous night. It had been parked on the vicarage driveway and that bloody dog had been parked across the road. Two vigilantes had completed the picture, and Derek had scooted off at speed via graveyard and woods, back to his vehicle and to Holly Brook Farm. But now, at last, he owned the upper hand.

What was he going to do with her? Damn, he had left Mam's picture behind. He would need to take Caroline back to the farm and, when he had done with her, she must be dropped else-where. Another of his mother's sayings raised itself from beyond the grave – *never on your own doorstep, Derek*. He could still hear her, but she was louder in the presence of the photograph. The farm was his own, and Caroline Butlin must not remain there. There were hills and vales a-plenty, so that goal would not be too difficult.

The road below him wound its crazy way through pleats of land, its tortuous route partly the result of nature's positioning of moors and further dictated by arguments on the part of long-dead farmers who had fought for every inch of ground. He saw the car, watched as it dis-appeared into a bend, waited for it to reappear. What if it was the wrong car? What if she stopped in time? What if she killed him and her-self in the crash? He found himself smiling, because the single answer was that he didn't care. Wherever he went, Mam would be there and that was all he wanted.

He jumped into his vehicle, started up the engine and waited for a few seconds before pulling out into the road. At the last moment, he realized that he did not need to die, so he leapt out and hid in a ditch. She was very near. His heart raced, bounced about and tried to break out of his ribcage. Oh, God, he could hear the screech of brakes. The collision was not loud. Derek peered through long grasses, saw her getting out of the car, watched her as she bent down. She was shouting names – she was not alone. He ducked down when a girl climbed out of the rear seat. A second girl followed.

'Are you hurt?' Caroline was asking.

Both answered in the negative.

'I can't leave the cars,' she told them. 'Someone else may get hurt – I shall have to walk down the road and stop traffic.' She felt too shaken for driving. 'I know there won't be much traffic, but I mustn't take the chance. You two go home as quickly as you can. Leave your satchels here – they're heavy. Get help and make sure the doctor sees you.' Her mind was all over the place. She was in shock – that much was plain – but she managed to worry about Maddy and Amy. There was a killer about . . . Yet she could not leave them here to be hit by another car. No, they must go and she must stay. They would be together, would be moving targets, would not be run over.

'Shouldn't one of us stay with you?' asked the taller of the two girls.

'No, no. If either of you becomes ill as a result of the bump, she will have the other to look after her.'

The girls left. When he had assessed that they should be out of earshot, he climbed out of his ditch, grabbed Caroline from behind and bounced her head on the bonnet of her car. The resulting limpness disappointed and angered him – he had wanted her awake and aware. After dragging her into the back seat of his dented car, he drove off towards the farm. She would wake, he told himself. And when she did,

480

Caroline Butlin would regret the day of her birth.

Sergeant Alan Shawcross scratched his head. 'Are you sure the girls said she was going to walk down the road to stop traffic?'

Brian nodded. 'Traffic comes up the moor at this time of day – it seldom goes down.'

'Well, she's nowhere to be seen. Look, get back to the village and tell my lads to send somebody to shift this car. If we leave it any longer, we could have a pile-up.' He stared hard at the vicar. 'What? Mr Butlin?'

'He has her.'

'Eh?'

'Derek Ramsden has her.' As he spoke the name, Brian's blood seemed to turn to ice in his veins. He shivered. 'She has been his main goal, you see. That man is an insane demon.'

Alan thought about it. 'Look, I bet she'll be at home when you get there.'

Brian looked into his wife's car, remembered the conversation with Lizzie, whose surname he failed to remember. She was Ramsden's next door neighbour. Ellen Langton had left her bag and purse in his house, and no woman went anywhere without her bag and purse. 'We're lucky that he doesn't have Maddy Horrocks and Amy Bradshaw, too.' He pointed at the satchels.

'Don't touch anything,' ordered Alan. 'There's a chance that his prints may be on your wife's car. If you're right. Perhaps she just forgot all the stuff and walked home? It's not that far.'

481

'No.' Brian's voice was soft. 'She would not leave an obstacle in this position when she knew full well that others might be hurt. And she would have taken her own and the children's bags with her as well. I tell you, he arranged this accident. It has been choreographed down to the last detail. The car hit by Caroline was empty. Both girls said that. He was in the ditch. He drove his car down that lane over there, left it slewed across the road and hid in the long grass.'

Alan Shawcross decided to err on the side of caution. 'Shift yourself, Mr Butlin. Get up yon and tell my men to phone Bolton Central.' This was fast becoming a crime scene. The vicar was correct – no woman in her right mind would walk away and leave all her things in an unlocked car. She was in her right mind now, but she mustn't have been when she'd left her husband for this character. 'We need some back-up. Go on, hurry up.'

Brian did as he was told, praying all the way back to Rivington Cross. He dashed into the vicarage, was told by Betty that his wife had not returned, then ran across to the police station. Every second counted now. A constable phoned through to Bolton, was promised immediate help, asked Brian where he was going.

'To collect men,' he answered. Everyone who was not at work must join the search. 'I can't just sit and wait.'

'But—'

'But nothing, constable. I am going to look for my wife.'

* * *

She lay on the floor like an oversized rag doll and he wondered what he had ever seen in her. Her legs, splayed at strange angles, were covered in laddered, torn stockings whose tops were visible. The face, bloodied, swollen and bruised, bore no resemblance to the one he remembered, so beautiful and calm. 'She's a mess,' he told his mother.

Mam made no reply.

Derek picked up the photograph. 'Mam? Why aren't you talking to me?' The smile on Edna Ramsden's face seemed to have slipped slightly. She was clearly displeased and he wondered why. 'Oh. I suppose you won't talk to me until she's gone, eh? You want it to be just you and me again. Well, I can understand that, because I owe you everything. But I can't get rid of her for a while yet, because I want her awake. Anyway, I might leave her here when I've done, and find somewhere else for you and me. Never mind. She'll wake up in a minute, just you wait and see.'

He ate a sandwich, drank tea, sat with his mother and bided his time. He was in no hurry. Caroline Butlin was going to suffer and he was looking forward to that.

There were eight of them and they split up into four pairs, Brian attached to the man who was now his temporary lodger, father of Betty Thornton, husband of one of Ramsden's victims. They were the ones chosen by Monty, who ran ahead repeatedly, turned, barked, ran on again.

Brian stopped while Bert Langton regained

483

his breath. 'Do you want to go back?' asked the younger man.

'No. If you are going to find the bugger – sorry, Vicar – I want to be there.'

The dog was going frantic. He seemed unable to be still for a second and Brian wished, not for the first time, that the animal could speak. It was plain that Monty knew what he was about and that there was, according to him, no time to waste. 'We must shift,' the vicar told his companion. 'Monty knows what he's doing, but there's no point in you making yourself ill, Bert. Let me go on and you follow as best you can.'

Bert was forced to admit that age was holding him back and that Caroline Butlin might well lose her life as a result. 'Right, you go on. I won't be far behind you.'

Brian ran ahead, the dog leaping and yapping until at least a mile of ground had been covered.

Then, suddenly, Monty stopped, a low growl curdling its quiet way out of his throat. He had learned these hills until he knew them like the back of his own paw. As he and Brian had not been confined to roads and pathways, their journey to the edge of Holly Brook Farm had been as straight as the flight of a crow. Again, the dog growled a low rumble of warning.

Brian, who had come to know Monty well, understood. 'We go softly from here, is that it? Stay by me, boy.' He followed Monty, who remained barely two feet in front of him, across land that was lying fallow. The house hove into view and Monty flattened himself in the weeds. 'Is she in there?' Brian asked.

Brown eyes stared up at one of the many people who were loved by this precious canine. A sound emerged from his chest as he tried to communicate what he knew. The bad one was in there. The bad one had been coming and going for some time. It was up to Brian now.

'God bless and keep you, Monty.' There was no time for any further prayer. He had to reach the farmhouse ahead without being seen, and that would take some concentration.

Brian strode ahead. He was on his own and he felt it.

She groaned.

Derek stood up, opened his penknife until the sharpest blade was on show. No man would ever look at Caroline Butlin again. 'Hello, lover,' he said, menace etched into each quiet syllable.

She opened one eye – the other seemed to be glued in the closed position. Where was she and where were the girls? Then she focused on him, saw the knife, knew that she was staring death in the face. Perhaps this was what she deserved as payment for her terrible behaviour. Her face burned and her neck felt as if it might be broken. She moved fingers and toes, knew that her nervous system remained in one piece. Not for long, she thought as he brought his chair and sat beside her. The knife glistened.

'Thought you'd got away from me, did you?'

She offered no reply.

'Your two little friends will have raised the alarm by now. Mam and I have decided to leave you here when I am finished. She always told me not to dirty my own doorstep, so you can have my house and we'll move out.'

He had finally gone completely crazy, she decided. There could be no point in reasoning with a madman, and anyway her mouth was filling with blood. She swallowed the nasty substance, shuddered as it went down her throat.

Derek noted the shiver. 'Ah, so you've finally got enough sense to be scared of me. I killed Rose and I killed Ellen Langton – I think her daughter's staying at your husband's house. Lily lived, though. And I never killed the first one. I'll write and tell them that when I have time. After I've done you.'

He was delivering a strange mix of sanity and total lunacy, thought Caroline. And his voice was so calm that he might have been reading from a storybook. Not that any of it mattered – she would be dead in a minute or two. She found herself thinking of her children and Brian; she hoped that death would be quick and that her murder would not prevent the children from doing well in life. Her head ached and throbbed.

He jumped up. 'I am going to cut your face first.' The tone was almost conversational. 'Then I'll kill you off slowly, because you were the one who made me like this. I was doing all right till you came along, managing without a woman. My mother was the only real woman in my life – the rest have been rubbish.' He knelt down and placed the knife an inch from the open eye. She closed it automatically. 'This'll cut through skin,' he said. 'And—' A sound from outside reached

486

his ears. He paused, waited, reminded himself that foxes were becoming cheeky these days.

Stroking Caroline's cheek with the edge of the knife, he carried on speaking. 'Beryl left me, you left me and the others used me for money. But you? You did the most harm. You are filthy, not decent, not fit to be a mother. No-one will recognize you when I am finished – not even the bloody vicar I saw you kissing the other day. Remember? The boring man you left behind to come and live with me? My mother never left me. Proper mothers stay with their children.'

'Ramsden?'

Derek froze for a second, then turned to the door. It was her husband. Derek glared. 'Move one inch and I'll put this knife straight through her eye and into her brain.'

Brian strode on.

'Stop!' He drew back the blade as if preparing to stab with all his weight behind the thrust.

Brian stopped. 'Do that and I swear by Almighty God that I shall kill you. For my wife, I am prepared to do just about anything. Put down that knife.'

'Make me.' Derek blinked. In the last few seconds, life had become very complicated. He should have taken the two girls as well. Could he have managed all three? 'Don't budge an inch,' he told Brian.

Brian remained perfectly still, but a whirlwind entered the farmhouse. In a blur of black and white fur, Monty leapt onto the kitchen table, picked up the photograph and dashed outside with it.

Derek dropped the knife. 'Mam!' he yelled at the top of his voice. 'Mam, don't leave me.' He moved towards the door, seemed oblivious of Brian's presence. When Brian hit him on the chin, he buckled like a broken ornament. The vicar rubbed his sore fist, thanked God and school for rugby and the strength it had given him.

Caroline had passed out again. Brian rushed to her side, knelt and felt for a pulse. She was alive.

Bert, breathless from running, entered the arena, a framed photograph clutched in a hand. 'The dog came flying at me with this,' he said. Monty was behind Bert. He passed the man and, with his teeth bared, sat next to the inert form of Derek Ramsden. 'Who the hell's that?' Bert asked, pointing at the unconscious man.

'It's our favourite monster,' Brian answered.

'Get away – that's red hair, and— He's dyed it and shaved off the moustache. Clever, these lunatics, aren't they?' Bert found that he was talking to himself, because Brian was concentrating on his injured wife. 'Can I do anything?' He looked at the woman on the floor. 'She's been battered, God love her.' He thought about Ellen and his eyes threatened to spill. 'I'll go, lad. You stop here and watch him and her.' He picked up the knife. 'What's the name of this place? For the police and the ambulance.'

'Holly Brook. Tell the ambulance to hurry – and the police. Because I am afraid of myself, Bert. If he moves so much as an inch—'

488

'I know, son, I know.' Bert dashed off to fetch help.

On a beautiful day towards the end of September, Brian prepared to bring home his wife. She had suffered severe concussion, a broken cheekbone, and the loss of a pre-molar. For two weeks, she had been in hospital, because brain damage had been a possibility and her emotional state had been dreadful. But she was on the mend and had been given permission to come home as long as she did not work.

Remembering the day of the big visit, Brian smiled to himself. Half the convent had arrived – much to the consternation of the ward sister – and had given a recital of Gregorian chant. Patients had gathered from all surrounding wards to listen to the purity of soprano and mezzo voices, painfully perfect and totally dedicated. Even the dragon-like staff nurse had brushed away a tear after the *Credo*. There was an undeniable beauty in Catholicism, so reverently was the music delivered, so carefully was the Latin guarded and kept ancient – none of the modern School Certificate stuff in the *Gloria*. Caroline loved that music and Brian was looking for records of Gregorian chant so that she might listen to the beautiful sound while convalescing.

Betty bustled in. 'You're early. And I see you're taking my dad.'

'Yes. We have something to do first. I think you know what it is, but suffice it to say that it is vital for both of us.'

'Yes, I know. Still,' she grinned in an effort to cheer him, 'you won't get Yuspeh along with you this time.'

'Thank the Lord for that, Betty.' They had moved on to Christian names and he was glad about that. 'The food she brought! She completely reorganized the ward, you know. There was an old lady at the end nearest the office, and Yuspeh demanded all new pillows and a cot side for the bed. She commandeered clean sheets for my wife and ordered a total remake of another woman's bed. The staff were terrified when she offered to work there on a voluntary basis – I think there would have been an all-out strike.'

Bert arrived in his best suit, navy pinstripe with waistcoat and blue tie. In his wake, an excited James bounced. He had a real granddad, a granddad all his own who liked kicking a ball about. 'I'm going to have two homes in Rivington Cross,' he told Brian. 'I can choose where I sleep.'

Bert laughed. 'Yes, you can choose where you sleep as long as your mam says so – and don't you forget it.'

Bert kissed his daughter, rubbed a fond hand through James's curls, then followed Brian to the car. This was going to be a hard day, but it had to be faced. They drove in near-silence towards Prestwich on the outskirts of Manchester, each man deep in thought as he drew nearer to his goal. It was a goal they wanted not to need, yet they did need it.

Not a word was spoken for several minutes after they had pulled into the grounds. 'Silly, isn't it?' asked Brian, needing to break the sombre mood. 'We know he's in there and that he'll be sent to a prison hospital, yet here we are like a pair of doubting Thomases.' He had pulled many strings to achieve this visit. Only his status as a man of God had enabled him, husband of a victim, to enter this place with Bert, husband of a woman murdered by Ramsden.

Bert offered the opinion that Thomas had probably been the most intelligent of the disciples. 'He needed to see for himself. Like we do. He was sensible.'

'Maddy Horrocks would agree with you,' said Brian. 'She's been digging about in the Dead Sea Scrolls trying to find something about Jesus saying there should be no churches. They don't believe in churches.'

'They hardly believe in Jesus,' said Bert, 'so I don't know why they're bothering. Cavemen – I ask you. Is it a phase?'

'Of course it is. Come on, Bert.'

They followed a man in green cotton overalls through a maze of corridors. Each door had to be unlocked before they went through it, locked again so that they could move on. They stopped by a cell with an internal window. 'There you are,' they were told. 'That's your man.'

It was. He sat cross-legged on the floor, his lips moving constantly. 'Is he speaking?' Brian asked.

The orderly pointed to a photograph on the wall. 'We took the frame away, because he might have done himself a mischief. He talks to her all day. The alarming thing is that she answers –

491

though only he hears her, of course. Other than that, he says just the words he used to the police when he was arrested. "I am not Derek Ramsden, I am Matthew Roper." '

Bert sobbed. This was the devil who had killed his Ellen. She was buried now – well, all the recovered bits had been interred – in Anfield in her beloved Liverpool. 'What makes monsters like that?' he wept.

Brian put an arm round his friend's shoulder. 'Buck up, now. We needed to see him. I couldn't have brought Caroline home without coming here first. For you, this is a part of bereavement. You've faced it – we both have. We can walk on now.'

They walked away, then drove to Bolton Royal Infirmary.

Caroline, still faintly bruised in body and spirit, came home with them. Brian sat with her for hours and answered her questions – yes, Maddy had settled, so had the twins at their school. Yuspeh's chickens were fine, Amy Bradshaw was doing well, Bert's insurance money would be through any day and Betty would come and go between the two houses.

The twins visited her, brought her flowers and the biggest conker ever found in the woods. Betty carried in tea and told them all about the mad beggar who was the new minister at the chapel in Horwich, all doom, gloom and damnation. 'I think I might settle for St Faith's,' she said, 'if you'll have me and seeing as you're not really high church.'

When they were alone again, Caroline

reached out for her husband's hand. He wasn't just a husband – the man was a hero who had featured in just about every national newspaper. He had saved her. 'I am a fortunate woman,' she whispered.

'And a tired one. Go to sleep. I shall be here. I'll always be here. Everything will turn out well, please believe me.'

She closed her eyes and slept.

EIGHTEEN

The beginning

On the day before Amy Bradshaw's twenty-first birthday, a man of the cloth sat on the steps of Bolton Town Hall. Behind him, twin lions couchant lay in wait for whatever might befall this city-sized town; opposite the vicar, in the square, a mother figure held in her arms a dying son. He had been dying for some years, and he represented all who had given their lives in two world wars. Columns around the sculpture bore names of the fallen; in a few months, people would bring poppies, while the Mayor, wearing an appropriate expression and a chain of gold, would stand and pay tribute to the sons of Bolton.

It didn't mean anything, Brian said inwardly. It was just words – and ceremony brought back no-one, did it? He should not feel like that. He was a preacher and words did mean something, but . . . Each mother, wife, son, daughter, would

494

walk away towards another tomorrow and none of their men would come home. Was he depressed? No. But he carried in a pocket the weight of Amy Bradshaw's future and it was a heavy, sad burden for one man. Ten years ago, he had placed it in a rented vault in the bank. Half of him wanted to tear it up and throw it to the winds, but Nettie Bradshaw had made her wishes plain and Brian was a man of honour.

The letter was not going to be an ordinary one; it had been written by an older sister for a younger sister and, had Nettie not died, would probably never have reached Amy. Oh, God, what was he doing? And what had he achieved for Amy? Over the years, he had made attempts through welfare departments to locate Amy's missing nephew, but his efforts had yielded nothing. He had been hailed as a national hero for a couple of days after the capture of the lunatic, but all he had wanted was success in his pursuit of Adam, the son Nettie had given away. A hero? Never.

He thought back to the day of his victory over Derek Ramsden, about how the event had altered him as a pastor. Gone was the era of pallid, monotonous sermons. Since the time of his wife's near-death, Brian Butlin had been alive. From near-loss had come salvation and he had embraced it gratefully. Yet during recent days the envelope had sat at the front of his mind and had troubled him greatly; he was about to alter the shape of a young woman's life and he did not feel much like sermonizing at present.

They were all home. George Forrester from Oriel, Maddy Horrocks from St Hilda's, Amy from a Liverpool training college, the twins, James Thornton – yes, the Cavemen were back. Amy had already changed. During her training at a Catholic institution, she had quietly left her faith and no longer attended any church. Typically of Amy, she had attracted no attention to herself, but that was her way. Amy needed no bells and flags to accompany her decisions. Rumour had it that Amy had met a nice young man in Liverpool, but no-one had yet seen him. Tomorrow, she would open this envelope and, perhaps, would find two items of information – the location of her illegitimate nephew and the identity of Nettie's killer.

Right up to the day of his suicide, Derek Ramsden had screamed his innocence in this respect. Not once had he denied the murders of two other women, but, during increasingly rare clear-minded periods, he had maintained that Nettie's death was not on his conscience.

Brian had been the only outsider at Derek Ramsden's funeral. Insiders were nurses and doctors, because no member of Derek's family had ever put in an appearance. His mother's photograph had gone into the coffin with him, and the insane man, dead these five years, had finally disappeared for ever.

He stood up, stretched his legs and walked towards his car. The summer of '61 was proving pleasant – warm, but with a gentle breeze that prevented the sun from wreaking too much havoc on the north of England. Brian sat in the driver's seat and pulled the envelope from his pocket. 'It has to be done,' he said aloud. Then, for a reason he would never bother to analyse, he went to visit a woman who, over the past ten years, had become a firm friend. The friend he sought had known Nettie, had never met Amy, had no knowledge of the existence of a baby born to Nettie, but she had been the original keeper of the letter.

Mary Browne opened her door, cigarette in its usual place of residence between nicotine-stained lips, the wraparound pinafore pulled tight against her bulky body, concertina-ed stockings spilling down towards grey slippers.

She removed the Woodbine and smiled at him. 'Hello, Brian. What brings you today? I thought you would have been walking the hills looking for inspiration for your Whit sermon. And look at the state of me – get in here before the neighbours see me, I'm all of a doodah.'

Brian grinned and obeyed orders. Mary put him in mind of old Yuspeh Feigenbaum, since both acted the matriarch and expected instant compliance.

Her room had been tidied over the passage of time. It remained utilitarian, but Brian, who had proved himself capable of being just as in-transigent as she was, had wielded a paintbrush, put up shelves and introduced large ashtrays to the establishment.

Mary filled the kettle, lit the hob, reached for cups, then paused. 'It's time, isn't it, son? I were thinking about you earlier on, and I thought to

497

myself that she had to be well turned twenty. Is it soon?'

He nodded. 'Tomorrow.'

'Have you got it?'

'I have.'

Mary lowered her bulk into a chair. 'That's gone over fast, hasn't it? Ten years, eh? How is she doing, young Amy?'

Brian sighed. 'She's left the Catholic church, is a qualified infant teacher and intends to teach in a state school. Oh, and she is very beautiful – rather thin, but quite spectacular.'

'Nettie were good-looking and all. But she wouldn't let you say so.' Mary paused. 'You won't be able to tell me what Nettie wrote, will you?'

'I may not know myself. I'm just the postman, Mary. If she chooses to tell me, fair enough. But I shall not be able to pass anything on.'

'No.' She rose to deal with the whistling kettle. 'Sometimes, I wish I'd opened it. But that's just me being nosy.'

Brian disagreed. He had come here to keep company with the one other person who knew how he had been tormented over the past decade. Convinced of Derek Ramsden's innocence regarding Nettie's death, he had wanted very badly to tear into the letter, because it might well contain the name of the real murderer – as well as some details about Nettie's child. But he had held fast and now, wondering whether Amy would agree with his behaviour, he had come to share his concerns with Mary.

'Whatever happens, Brian, it's never going to be your fault.'

'She might berate me for not telling her earlier. That's in my mind all the time – that she might have wanted to be told sooner whatever it is.'

Mary poured tea. 'Well, I know one thing for sure. You honoured Amy's dead sister. Come rain or shine, your conscience is clear.'

'Is it?'

'Yes, so drink your tea, grab a shortbread and shut up – I've dusting to be getting on with. I can't sit here supping, lad. Come on, shape yourself.'

He obeyed the woman who had become a sort of mother to him, the one to whose squalid room he had bolted after the attack on Caroline. Instinct had always told him that this fat, slovenly woman, who kept her lodgers' accommodation in perfect condition, was a good person. 'My faith's been tested a few times,' he informed her now.

'Aye, so has my patience.' She glanced at the walls. 'We should have had that ice blue. I told you at the time we should have had ice blue. But no, you had to have the green, didn't you? You were wrong.'

He was wrong, but he sat in this place where he was allowed to be wrong, where he was not minister, husband, father. Here, he was just a man and he drank his tea gratefully.

Yuspeh Feigenbaum, who did not specialize in silence, was as quiet as a mouse. For years, she had watched her grandson and his beautiful *shikse*, had suspected that love was on the agenda, had spoken to George on several occasions. He had not listened. Perhaps his ears had taken in the sounds, but Yuspeh had failed to persuade him. Had she tried hard enough?

The quiet Anna was the one who erupted now. 'He went to Oxford and she went to Oxford – three years they have had together.'

Jakob sighed. 'What did you want me to do? Set up a business in Oxford? We could not afford the rents. Or would you have me attending college with him and following him every evening? Anna, this has happened.'

Anna walked to the window and looked at the church of St Faith. In that bell house, invisible from here, the seeds had been sown. 'For years, Maddy said this, Maddy said that, Maddy thinks, Maddy believes – what did we do to deserve this?'

Yuspeh placed a sugar lump between her teeth before taking sips of dark, hot tea. She didn't know what to say or how to feel. This was disconcerting, since Yuspeh advertised her opinions at every bend in life's road.

'Mamme?' There was a terrible sadness in Anna's voice. 'Mamme, what are we to do?'

Yuspeh rattled the cup into its saucer. Although she appeared younger in the face than she had ten years earlier, her frailty showed in poor walking and limited control over all four limbs. As she was often heard to bemoan, she was a slave to arthritis and this was what happened to women who had worked hard to raise a family single-handed after the death of a husband. 'I don't know,' she replied.

Jakob sighed loudly. 'Well, there is, as they say, a first time for everything.'

The old woman glared at him. 'You may have reached your half of a century, but you are still my son. I like her. I have always liked her. Sometimes, an old woman who has done her best all her life is confused. Confusion I am allowed. It is all a mixed-up thing in my head and a weight in my heart. Do not ask me any more.'

'But, Mamme—'

'Mamme is not here,' declared Yuspeh. 'She is outside with her chickens.' On this note, she left the room with all the dignity afforded by sore bones.

She sat on her stool in the garden and watched Monty with his chickens. This was not the original Monty, but the young one had developed most of the characteristics owned by his sire. 'Hello, my brave little friend,' she said. 'Your daddy was a wonderful dog.' Yes, Monty had been spectacular, yet he had not mated with his own kind. This crossbreed, half sheepdog and half English retriever, was the beautiful result of an unscheduled coupling. 'Sometimes there comes a corner we must turn,' she said to herself.

All Monty's good traits had come out in his son and the five other siblings born to a retriever bitch. The owner of the bitch had been angry, because her pedigree animal had been 'spoilt', but if this was a spoiling, it was a good one. There had been a queue a mile long to foster Monty's offspring. The other five, all female, were dotted around the village like a pack of scattered cards. 'They are loved,' she told him, 'as you are loved.' And love was everything.

But Judaism counted, too. 'You see, Monty, a Jew is born from an old and wandering nation, a proud nation from which has come many clever people in the sciences and in the arts. Now, we have our homeland and we may go there, but this is my grandson's home. England is his place and he fits into it like a hand in a glove.'

The faith, too, mattered. The Forrester/ Feigenbaum household was not Orthodox, but it followed the day-to-day laws of the oldest religion on earth. Cavemen? She could not prevent the smile. 'From where came the thoughts of these children?' Looking up, she cast her eyes along the ridges of moors that covered the remains of many ancient tribes. 'The ideas come from earlier even than Moses.' Who was right? And who was qualified to judge who was right? God alone held that power.

She looked over her shoulder. 'Jakob? Have you been listening to the ramblings of an old woman?'

He nodded. 'To sit Shiva for my son would grieve me a great deal.'

'Yes. I cannot think of him as dead just because he marries the girl he loves. The day of his wedding, do we stop taking baths and wearing leather on our feet? Do we cover and drape the house because we cannot enter with him the happiness?'

'Anna is the most grieved,' he said. 'She feels that she has failed her son, because the strength of faith depends on the mother. I cannot look at her eyes, Mamme, because they are empty.'

Yuspeh glanced at chickens and dog. 'They have it right, Jakob. The animals seek not for pedigree or breed, they simply continue. My head is in a turmoil. I am too old for this.'

'So am I,' breathed Jakob. 'Yes, Mamme, so am I.'

Only once in Maddy's life had her temper been lost. She had not settled immediately at school and, after one day, had declared her intention to leave. The tantrum had been an eye-opener for her parents and they knew now – just as they had known back then – that she would make her own decision and adhere to it. Caroline Butlin's brand of sense had sent Maddy back to St Anne's and brains had got her through school and St Hilda's. But love, the strongest and fiercest of all emotions, was taking her away from everything.

Yvonne rattled her way through the days, concentrating on the hair of 'her' ladies, looking after the new, carefully coloured regrowth sported by Mildred Cookson, cutting, perming, setting and drying the locks of Rivington Cross. John, in his lonely, silent world, worked with the dead, offered condolences to relatives, cleaned the hearse, worried about his only child. She was marrying out. Not only was she marrying out, she would be making her promises in front of a civil servant in a registry.

They closed both shops for the evening, played with a meal for which neither had an appetite, lit a small fire when evening cooled the air.

'There'll be no stopping her,' John said.

'I know, love. He thinks the sun shines out of her and she knows she's found the right man. I'm just glad he's not from America or Africa – we'd have lost her good and proper.'

'London's not that far,' mused John.

'But there's a lot of land between Jew and Christian. I asked her what religion she belongs to and she said she's a Deist. Just one God, she says. No prophets. I thought she would have grown out of that at Oxford. Well, I'm going to no register office do, John. I can't bring myself to face it.'

The doorbell sounded. John went to answer it while Yvonne began to tidy the table. Hearing a voice whose owner she neither liked nor respected, she abandoned the task and sank back into her chair. This was all she needed, Father Flaming Sheahan and his sweaty, bloated body – it was enough to put anyone off religion and food for life.

'I'm here to see Madeleine,' he announced without preamble. Entering the sitting room, he cast baleful eyes around the area. 'Out, is she?'

'Yes.' She pointed to a chair and hoped he wouldn't perspire into it. He stank of drink, too, and she wondered how he had managed the short distance from the presbytery. He should have been dead ages ago, but only the good died young, it seemed.

He settled his bulk and waded straight in. 'I hear she is to marry that Jewish boy. You realize that she will be lost if she does?'

Yvonne did not answer; she knew the score

504

well enough and didn't need Sheahan to bang his drum all over the subject. He was a mess. Not for the first time, Yvonne thanked God for the advent of Father Bernard Shaw, a young priest who had arrived recently to help the ailing incumbent.

John looked at the priest, then at Yvonne. 'We know all about that, Father. We also know that neither of them will budge. They're twenty-one and their minds are made up.'

The priest's lip curled. 'You should have put your foot down years ago when she started all the bell house nonsense. What do you expect when you allow her to associate with all and sundry?'

Yvonne sniffed meaningfully. 'She's an intelligent girl and she mixes well. Maddy found her own friends. Now, she's an adult and we can't do a thing about this. You'll have to talk to her.'

The priest, who had already crossed swords with Maddy, had no real wish to repeat the episode. He had seen her leaving the house earlier with *that* boy and was here to work on the parents. In his opinion, Madeleine Horrocks was too bright for her own good. 'She won't listen to me,' he told them, 'but she may honour her father and her mother. Have you tried?'

'Of course we have,' shouted John. 'Do you think we've stood here like two shop window dummies? We've done all we could.'

'And it wasn't enough.' Sheahan settled himself in the chair. But he did not rest for long, because the door opened and in stepped Maddy.

'Ah,' he blustered, 'there you are.' He struggled with his displaced centre of gravity, attempted to shuffle forward to the edge of his seat in order to stand.

'What do you want?' Maddy asked. 'Don't you think you've said enough – all that rubbish about eternal hell and damnation?'

'Remember who I am.' The visitor's face was purple.

Maddy tapped the toe of a shoe on the carpet. 'Yes, I know who you are. You're an old drunk who imagines himself important—'

'Maddy!' cried Yvonne.

'It's all right,' the girl told her mother. 'This is your house, and if you want him in it, that's up to you. But either he goes or I go. I shall stay with Sarah Butlin until he's gone.' On the word 'he', she pointed to the priest.

'Ah, the vicar,' he spat. 'You'll go to a vicar and you'll marry a Jew, but you aren't at home in your own parents' house.'

John stepped into the arena. 'She is at home. I think you'd better go, Father, before any more damage is done.'

Sheahan finally managed to stand, his bulk impeding him and rendering him breathless. 'You'll burn,' he told Maddy.

'Then you'll have company, Father Sheahan.' Her chin raised itself, both hands rested on hips and her pretty mouth set itself into a narrow line. 'Because any man who drinks his congregation's money is a thief. Mortal sin in your book, is theft. I'll see you when you get there.'

He left the house, slamming all doors in his wake.

Maddy looked at her parents and grieved for them. She was spoiling their dream, was going against everything they believed. 'I'm sorry,' she said, 'but I have loved George since we were fourteen. And I've had less trouble from him than from any so-called Christian. I have escaped the hungry clutches of a few Catholic boys, I can tell you. George respects me. He's my future. I am choosing my own future.' On this note of high melodrama, she swept out of the room.

While Yvonne wept quietly, John cleared the table. There was nothing else to be said. Their daughter had outstripped them in all areas of life and now, as an educated young woman, she was in possession of arguments they had not the ability to counter.

'Stop crying,' said John. 'She could be marrying a wild Irish Catholic with a fondness for drink and for wife-beating. Look at that Eugene McCrimmon. Six kids, he's given her and she'd a lovely black eye last week. She spends her time traipsing kids round building sites trying to get money from him when he's already drunk it.'

Yvonne dried her eyes. 'I know.'

'And we're still not happy.'

'I know.'

John, determined to look on the better side, patted his wife's hand. 'Buck up, flower. In the end, she'll inherit a tailoring business and all the bobbins of cotton she's ever wanted.'

Yvonne tried to smile. 'She can't sew a button

on and you know it. Did you see her last week with the hem of her skirt held up with sticky tape? She's not what you might call domesticated, is she?'

'Well,' sighed John. 'You never know – he might get used to having his boiled eggs raw or as hard as bullets. Just a minute – it was seven kids, wasn't it?'

'You what?'

'That Eugene McCrimmon – didn't she have twins? I wish you'd try to keep up with the conversation, Yvonne.'

She thumped him with a cushion. He was trying to tell her that this wasn't the end of the world – and she knew it wasn't. It just felt like that.

The village was buzzing. Brian knew that he could not pass on Nettie's letter today, even though Amy had turned twenty-one. In truth, the letter might have ruined her party, so he would be forced to wait until she was one day older.

Caroline, who had been listening to the music emerging from the church hall, came back into the house. 'Shall we pop over to the hall for a while, dear? I got her a little pair of pearl studs – she had her ears pierced while she was at college.'

'Yes, we'll go over for a while. Everyone else is there and there's no danger of any sleep with all that noise.'

'What's the matter?' she asked.

The matter was a letter he was unable to

deliver. 'Ah, it's just that here we are, our children at the party, the party in my church hall and I didn't know about it. So much for vicardom.'

'The caretaker takes care of all that – hence the title "caretaker". Are you sure you're all right?'

He nodded, took her arm and led her out into the garden. It was a lovely night in late June, navy blue sky sprinkled with stars, a new moon hovering above the houses, Monty Junior sitting on the path, his face wearing an inscrutable expression. Brian bent to pat him, thought of Monty Senior, the dog who had died while pushing a small child away from the wheels of a car. The very next day, Monty Junior and all his sisters had been born and Yuspeh had claimed the one male. Like his father before him, he belonged to this section of the village, travelled from vicarage to Yuspeh, from Yuspeh to Celia, from Celia to Yvonne. Stella was long-dead and Monty Junior was much appreciated in the Butlin household.

Caroline laughed. 'Perhaps young Monty here doesn't like Floyd Cramer?'

Brian straightened. 'Who?'

'The music. I think the pianist plays for Elvis, but that one's called "On the Rebound" – it's a Floyd Cramer solo.'

'Ah.' He was no clearer, though he had certainly heard of and suffered Elvis Presley. Sarah played him on her Dansette, volume right up, her poor father below trying to write about the Holy Ghost visiting the apostles. Life was becoming too noisy altogether – and he was growing older. 'Come along, dear.' They walked across to the church hall, but Monty stayed where he was, sensible dog. Brian wished he had cotton wool for his ears, but it was too late for that.

Amy was seated with a good-looking young man. Her parents, with the Forresters and Yuspeh, sat at the other side of the hall, the body of which was packed with gyrating young people. He saw James, Maddy, George, the twins and many others from their schooldays.

Amy came over and introduced them to her partner – he seemed to be Bill, though the information had to be lip-read. She accepted the pearls, kissed Caroline, kissed Brian and spoke some words of thanks that were cruelly drowned at birth. When the younger couple had drifted off, the vicar and his wife endured 'Hello Mary Lou', 'Halfway to Paradise' and something particularly dreadful named 'Runaway'.

After that, they did the running away, giving Monty an unscheduled supper and repairing to the relative peace of their bedroom. Betty was away for the night at her father's cottage, a building much further away from the church hall. 'Lucky Betty,' remarked Brian as he lay beside his wife. 'This is a sign that they are all grown up and all rebellious.'

'It's only music.' She laughed.

He wasn't so sure. 'They've grabbed their own place, their identity. It's all tied up with this music and no, I don't know what I'm talking about.'

'Stick to the Holy Ghost,' she advised with mock solemnity.

'Yes,' he replied. 'Even when people speak in tongues, it probably makes more sense than that cacophony. How are we supposed to sleep?'

Caroline read a few pages of a novel, smiled to herself when he started to snore. How was he supposed to sleep? 'With a conscience as clear as yours, you will always sleep,' she whispered.

'Where is Bill?' Brian asked. He had half expected Amy to have company, but she was taking her morning constitutional by herself.

'He's driven back to Liverpool,' she said. 'His mother's sick.'

'I'm sorry to hear that.' He looked out over the reservoir, noticed that Amy was standing near the spot to which Nettie's body had been dragged by Monty Senior. Should it be done here? he asked himself. She had to be alone – he knew that much. And, in his sleep, among many tormented dreams, he had approached a place where a part of the mystery was threatening to unravel. Ten years, it had taken him – and he could still be wrong. 'Amy?'

'Yes?'

She looked like a subject for a painting, features perfectly balanced, long, slender neck, a sheen on the dark hair, eyes shining with health. God, what was he doing here? 'Bill seems pleasant. Not that we could talk to him, of course.' He was playing for time, assessing her mood. What did mood matter? If she was happy, that might be changed; if sad, she could well become sadder.

'Yes, it was noisy. I had some lovely presents – look.' She held out her left arm and displayed a splendid watch. 'That's from Mam and Dad. Thank you for these.' She was wearing the pearl studs.

Brian didn't know much about fashion, but this child – young woman, he reminded himself – had the sort of skin against which pearls gained an extra sheen. 'You look beautiful,' he told her.

Amy laughed. 'The image of my sister, or so I am told.' She looked out over the water. 'I think of her as here, not in the cemetery. Sugar pink nail polish, lipstick to match, one and eleven-pence each from Woolworth's.'

He couldn't do it where Nettie had been found.

'I still miss her. She made me laugh, you know, always saw the funny side of life.' Home had been a dreary place and Nettie had been a bright light to which Amy had been able to run. It was better now. Mam and Dad had relaxed some-what, and Amy thanked Yuspeh Feigenbaum for that. Celia was no longer dyed-in-the-wool Catholic; she had become more rounded in mind, if not in body. 'I'll always miss Nettie.'

Brian swallowed a massive lump of pain. It sat in his chest like a knife that twisted and threatened to make its cruel way through his entire system. 'Of course you will always miss her. She was important.'

Amy shrugged. 'It's still in my mother's mind, you know. All the time, she suffers, because she was the one who sent Nettie away. It wasn't Dad. Dad just lets things happen. I see Mam staring into space and I know what's on her mind. There's nothing I can say or do to make her feel better.'

The knife turned again. 'Amy?'

'What, Mr Butlin?'

He dragged in some extra oxygen. 'There's something I have to do. I wonder if you would come back to the vicarage with me?' He suddenly knew the very place. 'The bell house,' he said. 'No-one goes in there any more. You are going to need to be alone.'

She frowned. 'Why? What's wrong?'

'Nothing is wrong – well – nothing . . . er . . .' Words failed him. He stared at the ground. 'Your sister left a letter. I took it from her land-lady ten years ago. Instructions written by Nettie on the outside of the envelope were very clear. It was to be given to you and only to you when you reached your majority.'

'A letter?'

'Yes.'

'Ten years?'

'I'm afraid so. Mrs Browne – she's the lady who owns the house where Nettie lived – ought to have given it to the police, but, like myself, she decided to follow the wishes of your sister.' He raised his head. 'We withheld evidence. We both honoured Nettie's request.'

'She wrote to me?'

'Yes.'

'Why?'

Brian felt as if he were wading through

quicksand. 'Well, there must have been things she wanted – needed – to say to you when you reached twenty-one. I suppose she wrote everything down in case . . .'

'In case anything happened to her?'

He nodded.

'Do you have it with you?'

'Yes. But because we don't know what to expect, I think you should go into the bell house, switch on the light, close the door and . . . and read it. It's something that should be done in solitude.'

They walked together in silence away from the reservoir, through the trees and right up to the bell house door. 'It isn't locked,' he told her. 'Go in. Here you are.' He dragged from a pocket the full weight of his conscience. Should this have gone to the police, should he have burnt it, ought he to have given it to Amy a few years ago? Had he needed to give it to her at all?

She took it, mouthed her quiet thanks and shut herself away from him.

Brian stood for a while, his eyes wandering over a graveyard that contained the remnants of hundreds of souls. There were marble headstones here and there, but most of the older ones were made from the very same sandstone out of which church and bell house had been fashioned.

Was she all right? Should he stay, should he go?

Monty Junior arrived. He sat, feathery tail waving slowly, head cocked to one side, tongue lolling. Nothing of moment happened in the

514

village without the presence of this ubiquitous dog.

'You're Senior all over again, aren't you?'

The dog whined softly, looked at the bell house door, touched Brian's leg with a paw.

'What?' asked the vicar. 'Do I go away?'

The dog turned, looked over his shoulder and began to walk towards the vicarage.

Perhaps he was hungry, thought Brian. Or perhaps angels did come down to guide humanity at its most senseless. The dog saw a magpie, barked and gave frantic chase. Brian smiled wanly. Monty was a lot of things, but the term 'angel' was a bridge too far.

My darling Amy,

It is hard to know where to begin, but, if you are reading this letter on your 21st birthday, that means I have gone somewhere. I have sat up night after night wondering what I could put down on paper and all I know is that it's not going to be easy for me to write or for you to read.

I was a quiet kid with no confidence. Mam was strict, Dad was always asleep or delivering the mail, so I was a bit lonely at home. School was all right, but I am not as clever, nowhere near as successful as you are going to be and I didn't do very well. I suppose I couldn't be bothered, since I had other stuff on my mind most of the time.

This is all about Father Sheahan and what he did to some of us girls. He always picked people like me with not much to say for themselves and he took us into the presbytery or the vestry one at a time. He raped us. I was eight years old, I think, when he first

515

raped me properly. I saw him through the windows with other little girls and knew that it wasn't just me.

He said I was helping him with God's special work and told me never to speak about it. Mam would not have believed me anyway, so I just kept away from him as best I could and I sometimes played truant from school.

For my last two years at the school, he never got me. I thought I was safe, because he liked little girls best and I was growing tall. But he found me one day when I was fourteen and told me off for not helping him with God's work. I tried to fight him off, but he did it again. It happened in the woods.

I went a bit wild after that – boyfriends and staying out late – but no-one else ever did sex with me. It was something I never wanted to do again. Mam was very angry with me, but I wouldn't listen and I just got worse. One night I stayed out altogether, but I slept at a girl's house and Mam wouldn't believe me when I said I wasn't doing what she called dirty things.

I started to put weight on and old Dr Jameson told Mam I was pregnant. She went mad. She was screaming all over the house at me and hitting me and it was awful. She asked me over and over again to say the name of the baby's father, but I knew she would never have believed me. So she got it into her head that I had been with a lot of boys and she found me a room in Bolton. She told everybody I was working in town and staying with her friends. By that time, I had left school, because I was fifteen. Mam and Dad paid rent on the room in Bank Street over a shop. They brought food and told me never to go out. It was hard, because the war was on and I felt very alone.

516

Mam and Dr Jameson had a plan. Mam probably didn't leave the house much and she wore padding so that all of Rivington Cross would think she was expecting, then she came to stay with me at the end and everyone thought she was in a nursing home somewhere because of severe anaemia and she could have no visitors except Dad.

When you were born, I called you Amy. That was all I was allowed to do, choose your name. A boy would have been Adam. Mam took off her padding and went back to Rivington Cross with you. I never saw you again until that day when I stood outside the playground and talked to you through the railings. I knew straight away which one you were, because it was like looking at a picture of me from years ago. That was when we started to make our plans to meet in secret. Amy, you were meeting your mother, not your sister.

Dr Jameson died. He was the only one apart from Mam and Dad who knew the truth, that I was your real mother. You were born in Bank Street and delivered by a midwife who didn't know me. Mam gave her some money and pretended I was somebody called Bertha. I was very sad after you were born and Mam and Dad had to keep me in food and rent because I could not work. I was crying all the time and it took me a long while to stop crying and get a job. From the moment you were born, I loved you with all my heart. You were mine and you have always been mine – nothing to do with bloody Sheahan – may he burn in hell for all eternity.

I have started to be angry instead of scared, Amy. Every time I see you I want to tell you, but you are too young. There was a gun in a barn at Eccles

517

Farm and I took it with some bullets in a box. I found it while I was waiting for you. I always hid till the last minute before going to the woods, because I was scared of being seen. That Maddy girl talked to me once and she is so nice. She will never tell Mam that you are meeting me. That girl is the best sort of friend you could have, so make sure you never lose her. She watched out for us many a time and I know she thinks the world of you.

Amy, I took that gun and threatened him with it. He knows I want to kill him and I may well do that unless he gets to me first. If you are reading this and if I have been killed and not by accident, the killer is Michael Sheahan.

I am sorry that you have that man for a father, but you are a good girl with enough sense in you to know that you can walk away and be just yourself. I wish I had lived to see you grow and become a woman. I wish you were not reading this and that we were in my room and I could tell you face to face. There is a small parcel enclosed – use the contents as you see fit. The present is for your birthday, sweetheart. I am crying and I don't know why. This letter will probably be thrown away when you are 21 and I shall come for you and take you out for something nice to eat. We can go to the Pack Horse and sit in the best room like two ladies and you will never read this.

More than anything I am writing to tell you how much I love you. You are a beautiful child and a wonderful intelligent girl. I am so proud of you, my daughter, my shining little girl, my princess, my angel, my Amy.

Your mother for all time, Nettie.

* * *

He came out of the vicarage and waited. Amy might well need somebody and he was the only one who understood the significance of this day. The dog waited, too, ears cocked, tail stilled, tongue tucked away in his mouth.

She ran out of the bell house, a whirlwind in a yellow dress, feet scarcely touching the ground as she fled across the graves.

'Amy!'

She ignored him, so he ran into her path, his body tensed against inevitable collision. Wrapping her tightly in his arms, he felt her heartbeat through two sets of clothing. 'Amy, calm down.' He had been right. In that moment, he knew that last night's dream had skirted the rim of reality. She had just discovered exactly who she was. 'Come inside with me.'

Her teeth chattered in spite of the day's warmth. 'I have to go. I have to talk to my—' To her grandmother. She continued to shiver.

He marked the pause and hung on to her firmly. 'Unburden yourself, child – it will go no further.'

'She . . . she . . . Oh, my God.'

'Come on,' he urged. 'Let's stick you together in one piece, shall we? We can go into my study and simply sit while you work your way through.'

She stilled slightly and looked into his eyes. 'You know, don't you?'

Brian nodded. 'But I didn't work it out until I was asleep last night.' Ten years, and he had never cottoned on to something that ought to have been staring him in the face. 'Was Nettie your mother?'

Amy nodded. But she could not say the rest of it. The whole thing was too raw, too nasty and painful. 'She stole me. Celia Bradshaw stole me.'

'Celia is still your blood. She probably did what she thought best at the time. People make decisions every day and those decisions alter the course of others' lives. Please don't do anything rash. Shall I send for Maddy?'

'No, no. I'm not ready.' There was the parcel, the bits of paper, the rest of it. 'I'm twenty-one and I feel like a five-year-old.'

'You're hurt.'

'Yes, I am.' She opened clenched fingers. 'See what she left me. I remember her taking the photo of me.' The locket snapped open and Brian saw two sisters who were not sisters, one a child, the other a woman in her twenties. Nettie's face was almost obscured by a lock of Amy's hair. 'She cut that bit of hair on the same day – when she brought the camera. I was . . .' She bit down on her lower lip. 'I was so important to her that she blanked out her own face with my hair.'

Brian was going to weep and he must not. He sniffed back tears and emotion. 'It's a lovely locket, Amy. It's your mother's twenty-first birthday gift to you. She must have loved you a great deal.'

Amy's chin raised itself in a gesture that advertised something not far short of defiance. If Nettie had been allowed to keep her baby, she would have been happy. Perhaps she would not have wandered about looking for revenge if she had hung on to Amy. They could have had fun. 'We were both robbed,' she told the vicar now.

520

'Please come in,' he begged.

'No, thank you. You did the right thing, Mr Butlin. You did what Nettie wanted and I am grateful to you for that. Let me go. I have things to do.'

'There is a danger here, Amy, a chance that you will do something many people will live to regret – including yourself. An hour or half an hour with your thoughts could make all the difference.'

The beautiful dark eyes clouded over. 'I can make no difference to my sis— to my mother, can I?'

He remembered sitting opposite the war memorial. Amy Bradshaw had just put his own thoughts into words. No matter what anyone did or said, Nettie Bradshaw would remain dead. She would not get so much as a poppy by way of remembrance. 'What will you achieve today, though?'

'The truth,' she replied. 'I shall get my grand-mother to admit the truth, then—' Then what? She opened her mouth and drank in oxygen in an effort to immobilize her stomach. Then him. She had to deal with him.

'Is there anything I can do?' he asked.

She studied him. He had grown leaner and more handsome with the passage of time. 'Mr Butlin, you are the best man I know. You would lay down your life for any of us, and we all know that. But today, you can do nothing.' She pulled away from him and walked homeward, envelope in one hand, locket in the other, sheepdog at her heels.

Brian walked quickly to the bell house, entered the dank, dark interior, did not bother to switch on the light. On a chair he had bought a decade ago, he sat and sobbed until he felt dry and drained. Some days, belief in a benign deity was sorely tested.

She didn't go home. She had no home yet. In a few months, when Bill's mother had improved, Amy would make a home with him. The locket owned a long chain, and she had placed it round her neck without needing to fiddle with a fastener, which was just as well, she mused as she sat by the edge of the reservoir. There were things she needed to do, but she could not compose a list, an order of service. As batsman, she had too many runs to make and there were several bowlers to be faced.

The letter, now tear-stained and slightly crumpled, she knew off by heart. On this very spot, the first Monty had swum in Nettie's body and . . . and the priest had put her there. She glanced to her left, saw, in the distance, smoke rising from a chimney at the presbytery. No, she would not go there. For the first time in her life, Amy needed an audience.

The dog licked her hand.

'Where do I start, Monty?' He didn't seem to have an answer.

She picked up herself, Nettie's letter and a few pieces of paper that had been tucked away with her locket. It was time. The dog followed her towards the main road, but stayed out of the battle zone. He settled to wait in the front garden, supervising traffic as it passed. She would be out again soon.

In the end, there was little need for words. As soon as Amy entered the house, Celia's gaze glued itself to the huge silver locket that hung down a now stained yellow dress. 'That was your grandmother's,' she said, her heart slightly out of rhythm.

'Great-grandmother's.' Amy folded her arms. 'It needs cleaning. Silver doesn't thrive unless it is worn. It hasn't been worn for a long time, has it?'

'We looked for it after . . . after it had happened. I thought perhaps it had been pawned.' She remembered receiving all her daughter's goods and chattels, remembered asking the police about the locket.

'It was left to me. It has been in a bank vault since Nettie— since my mother was murdered. Good thing she wasn't wearing it the day my father killed her, isn't it?'

Celia dropped like a stone into an armchair. How many times had she tried to beat the truth out of Nettie? 'Your father? You know who he is?'

'Yes. And you will all know by tomorrow.' She had nothing more to lose. The greatest treasure – her own mother – had already been removed.

Amy turned on her heel, left the room and went upstairs to pack. Furiously, she threw her things into cases, not caring about creases. Celia would not stop her – neither would Arthur. They had lived a lie for over twenty-one years and

Amy was content to leave them guessing for the moment. Why should they be given a truth they did not deserve? They could learn the full story tomorrow, just like everybody else. The other plan festered as she threw shoes, dresses, cardigans and coats into bags. If her grandparents wanted the details, they could stand in line with the rest.

Where would she go? Not back to Liverpool, not yet. Not to Maddy, either, because Maddy had her own preparations to make. She would go to Mr and Mrs Butlin. He was the only other person in this village who might have the slightest chance of understanding her fury. She was glad he had stopped her in the graveyard, glad he had forced her to steal some thinking time. There would be questions from Sarah and Simon, but they would not last for long. 'Tomorrow,' she said to herself. 'It will be done tomorrow.'

She placed the cases and bags on the stairs, allowing them to slide and crash their way into the hall.

Celia arrived from the living room. 'Where are you going?'

'Away from you. If you had left me with my mother, she would probably be alive today. This is the end of your biggest sin. You can go to confession now and relieve yourself of guilt.' She opened the front door and threw all her possessions outside. Before she left, she spoke a few more words. 'Be at Mass tomorrow. Here. In the village. Not in town.' She slammed the door, paused for a moment, took the key from her bag and posted it through the letter box. Smoke continued to rise from a chimney on the presbytery roof. Tomorrow morning, there would be the fire to go with it.

Weekday Masses were not well attended. Father Bernard Shaw welcomed the small congregation and began the service. '*In nomine Patris et Filii et Spiritus Sancti,*' he intoned. On a large chair to one side of the altar, Michael Sheahan supervised the proceedings. To him had fallen the task of easing the young priest's passage into parish life. So far, the arrangement was a satisfactory one, since Father Bernard was a good cook and passed no comments about the evils of alcohol.

Sheahan narrowed failing eyes and peered towards the back of the church. Surely he was imagining things? What would that dreadful Jewish woman want from a Catholic Mass? She was sitting with Celia Bradshaw, who was no longer a regular communicant in this church – didn't she usually go to town? For a few moments, the senior priest toyed with the idea of stopping the Mass – there was no place for a Jew in his church.

Yuspeh, to whom Celia had fled in the wake of yesterday's disaster, held her friend's hand tightly, but her gaze was fixed to the occupant of the chair. The man was evil, she was sure of it, and that such evil should thrive under the guise of a priest was more than abhorrent – it was criminal.

She squeezed her friend's hand again, knew that she was this woman's sole support. Celia's husband had gone to work as usual after making very few comments about the situation, though he had grumbled on about inevitability and the truth always emerging in the end. Yuspeh, fearing yet again for Celia's sanity, had decided to accompany her this morning. Young Amy had issued not an invitation, but a command.

The Mass thus far had been interesting, though Celia's tension precluded any concentration on the part of the visitor. When, after fifteen minutes had passed, nothing of moment had happened, Yuspeh tried hard to relax. But Celia remained as stiff as a board, her whole body rigid with anticipation.

At last, the door of the church crashed inward. Amy Bradshaw, smart in a grey-blue suit and with her hair pulled away from the lovely face, did not bless herself with holy water. She marched up the centre aisle, stopping about halfway. From her handbag, she took some slips of paper.

Father Shaw, just about to lead the *Sanctus*, paused. 'Would you care to sit down?'

'No, thank you.' Amy angled herself so that she faced the older, seated cleric. 'Hello, Father.' She paused on the word, then began to read from the papers in her hand, dropping each one to the floor when she had done with it. 'Bernadette Marie Bradshaw,' she began, 'murdered 1951.' She dropped the first piece. 'Gone,' she said. 'Gone, Father.'

He squirmed.

'Alice Mallinson, three weeks in a mental hospital 1949, suicide 1958. Shall we pray for her, Father? Shall we?'

He tried to stand up, failed, sagged into the chair.

'Julie Barnes, Margaret Foley, Annette Charleson, Daphne Melia.' Papers fluttered to the ground. 'You raped each and every one of them when they were children. You raped Bernadette Marie Bradshaw for the last time when she was fourteen years old. She found some of your other victims and left their names and addresses to me. In raping Bernadette at such an age, you made a big mistake, Father Sheahan. Before you stands your sacrilege. I am its embodiment.' She took a deep breath. 'I am your daughter and I am forced to live with that knowledge for the rest of my life.'

The congregation, riveted and beyond embarrassment, remained seated. There was something new about the young woman they all remembered – she might have been a top barrister at the Old Bailey. And what was she saying?

The door opened quietly and Brian Butlin walked in, closely followed by three policemen. 'Amy,' he said softly, though the whisper carried. 'Come along now. Let's phone Bill, shall we?'

A figure leapt up and ran along a side aisle all the way to the front of the church. Before anyone could stop her, Celia Bradshaw was near the altar and had drawn blood. The priest, his cheeks torn by her nails, pushed her away. But she kicked him and began to scream words Amy would never have expected her to have known.

The policemen dragged her off and placed her in the custody of Brian Butlin. While he held on to her, the sergeant and two constables led Father Michael Sheahan into his vestry.

Amy cast her eyes over her audience. 'Carry on,' she said. 'Just pretend this never happened. You're good at that, aren't you? I wonder how many of your daughters were affected by this demon? Or will you hide the truth amongst the *Kyries* and the *Glorias*? You sicken me.' She swivelled on her heel and left the scene, pushing past the woman who had acted as mother to her.

Outside, she cast off her shoes and ran like the wind until she reached the reservoir. 'I did it, Nettie,' she said. 'He'll be charged.' Derek Ramsden had not been lying. He had not murdered Nettie. Amy sat there for hours, moving only when pains of hunger and thirst drove her back to the vicarage. She limped along, high-heeled shoes sticking out of her handbag.

Betty Thornton welcomed her. Sarah, Simon and Jay took her into the parlour and sat with her. The news had spread like wildfire, and although this trio had watched Amy at the edge of the water, they had decided to leave her exactly where she was. Sometimes, a person needed to be alone.

They ate sandwiches, drank tea, waited for Maddy and George. The silence, broken only by the clatter of crockery, was heavy. No-one knew where to begin, but Maddy would cope, or so they hoped.

Amy finished her meal and realized just how hungry she had been. 'So, have you all been struck dumb?' she asked.

Jay shrugged. 'We don't know what to say. Your mother's got the doctor out to see her.'

'That isn't my mother.'

'You know who I mean.'

'Yes, I know who you mean.'

George and Maddy came in, the latter throwing herself down by the side of her best friend's chair. 'Good God, Amy, why didn't you tell me?'

'There was nothing to say and a lot to be done. And before any of you asks, no, I am not ashamed of Nettie and no, I don't care who my father was. He doesn't count.' She turned to Sarah. 'Remember the box you filled?'

Sarah nodded.

'Let's bury it today. It has to be today. Once Maddy and George are gone, the bell house probably won't be used by any of us. I think Mr Butlin has his eye on it for storage. And I want to put my real mother's name in the box and a little piece I have written about her. I've a photograph of Monty Senior, too. He should have a place with us. What's in the box already?'

Sarah listed everything. 'Book of Common Prayer for Simon and me, holy water for you and Maddy, something about abstinence – that's from when Jay was supposed to be a Methodist – and a Star of David for George.'

Amy nodded. 'We'll put Nettie and Monty in it and we'll bury it with the rest of them.'

They knew who the 'them' were. Amy referred to ancient times when men and women had inhabited the hills that surrounded Bolton. The group could also see that Maddy was suddenly not the leader any more and that Amy had taken the reins. It would not be for long, as the bell house Cavemen had not met in years.

They trudged up the moor and George used a trowel from the vicarage shed to dig a hole. As they lowered the box into its final place of rest, a sadness spread among them. They were piling earth on top of six dead childhoods and on a sister who had really been a mother. They were saying goodbye to those heady days of balsa wood and glue, of picnics on hillsides, of innocence, Desperate Dan, treacle toffee and secret code words. They were saying goodbye again to Monty. Son of Monty whined, then scampered off in search of rabbits.

Amy stood up. 'There, it's done.'

Maddy and Sarah wiped away tears. 'I wonder who'll find it?' Sarah asked, a little sob in the words.

Amy answered. 'It just goes on. We live and we die and someone else comes along in hundreds of years and finds our box.'

'I feel a bit dead,' Maddy said.

Amy smiled bravely. 'Well, don't. You've got so much ahead of you. Then, when you have children, it starts all over again.' She lowered her head. 'I have to make things right with the people who brought me up. Celia and Arthur did their best, you see. I can't punish them for much longer. We aren't kids any more, are we? No point in sulking and putting a good woman into hospital.' She walked away and left them all behind.

'We're grown up,' said Maddy quietly. 'And she is older than all of us.' There was a reason why Amy had been born so quiet and level-headed. Any other person might have gone insane, but this precious girl walked on. She would always walk on.

Even the boys felt lumps in their throats as they watched Amy getting smaller in the distance. 'That was horrible,' Jay said finally. 'She must be cut to pieces inside.'

'No,' replied Maddy with certainty. 'Amy knows exactly who she is and exactly where she's going. Burying the box was her first step into the future. She will be all right. Won't she, George?'

He cleared the emotion from his throat before answering. 'She'll be great. We'll all be great. Sarah the pharmacologist, Simon the art historian, Jay the physics boffin, you, Amy and I the teachers of the next lot.'

'I wonder if they'll bury boxes? The next lot, I mean,' said Simon.

George hugged his fiancée. 'Ours will,' he said. 'We'll make sure they're cavemen.'

Amy was returning from the post office when she met Mrs Feigenbaum. The old woman no longer used George's pram, but depended on a stick to help her along, and on this occasion she appeared flustered and far from steady. 'Amy,' she cried, 'thank God I find you. And so glad you came home to Celia, because she loves you and home is where you should be. Come now, for we must go inside. Something is happening.'

'What?' asked Amy, taking hold of Yuspeh's arm. 'Is someone hurt?'

'They will tell you now and you must not

worry. Celia was with me collecting eggs when they came to fetch her.' She pushed Amy gently towards the front door, then followed her inside.

Father Shaw stood up as soon as Amy and Yuspeh entered the living room. He wore an expression that put Amy in mind of the day when she had walked into his church and pulled it down stone by stone. 'Did you want me?' she asked. He seemed a decent enough chap, rather embarrassed and nothing at all like his predecessor.

Celia rose and put an arm about the girl's shoulder. 'Sit down, love,' she begged.

But Amy preferred to stand. 'What's going on?'

The young cleric cleared his throat. 'I had a visit from the police,' he said. 'Father Sheahan has been murdered in prison.'

The mantel clock ticked loudly. Amy looked round at all the people in the room, then walked through to the kitchen. 'Tea or coffee?' she shouted. Her heart maintained its usual steady rhythm while she made the drinks; she carried a tray through and invited everyone to help him or herself. 'Chocolate biscuits.' She picked up a wholemeal and prepared to bite into it. 'Who killed him?'

'They think he was set upon by several,' answered Father Shaw.

Amy nodded, chewed a mouthful of biscuit, swallowed. 'Decent criminals have no time for his sort. We shall not be attending the funeral – I think I can speak for my parents.' They were her parents. For twenty-one years, Arthur and

Celia Bradshaw had cared for her. Perhaps they had done wrong, but they had not deliberately hurt her or Nettie. Amy had settled her mind on the subject and was determined to get on with life, no matter what life brought to her door. This was a minor irritation, no more. She was not interested in Father Sheahan, alive or dead.

'Are you all right?' Celia asked.

'Of course,' came the reply. 'Do you expect me to mourn? I shan't even bother to dance on his grave. Oh, I got some of that new shampoo, Mam. I'll just go and try it.'

Father Shaw stood up again. 'Please do not think ill of all priests—'

'I don't. I left the church because I don't believe in the pope.' She excused herself and went upstairs.

Yuspeh sighed dramatically. 'From this generation, we get the straight answer, Father. My grandson, he marries soon a Christian.' She shook her head. 'They know better than we do and that is the problem. Education is the curse.'

Upstairs, Amy stripped off her clothes and went into the bathroom. Her hair would be good for Maddy's wedding and that was her only concern. Her father, Arthur James Bradshaw, was the local postman. One mother was dead and the other was getting better. And this new *Silvikrin Shampoo for Shining Hair* had better work.

The Pack Horse had followed Amy's instructions to the last detail. In the smaller private dining room, staff had laid a table for six, had placed a sign above it that read *THE LAST SUPPER* and had even pinned up Simon's clever cartoon of cavemen.

Five of the bell house Cavemen were seated at the table, and a sixth was on her way. This was to be George's and Maddy's last night as single people and the whole party was to spend the night at the inn. Neither bride nor groom had wanted to endure the wedding morning in the company of a disappointed mother, so this had been the best solution.

Maddy and George had engaged in spirited arguments about disappointment and its measurability. Maddy insisted that a Catholic mother could win a medal in the subject, while George had been heard to declare that a Jewish mother could take Olympic gold and a PhD in the sport. The whole match had been declared a draw and this party had become the happy compromise. The last supper was Amy's idea, of course.

'She has changed,' said George.

They all knew whom he meant.

'She's beautiful,' groaned Jay, 'but she treats me like a kid. What's two years, huh? She's twenty-one and I'm nineteen – yet she won't even go out for a drink with me.'

'Read a comic,' suggested Maddy, flinching when Jay clouted her with his napkin.

Sarah laughed. 'Remember the glue and the planes? Remember when we stuck poor Jay to the chair and he had to get out of his trousers before he could leave the bell house?'

The laughter stopped when Amy entered.

The spitting image of her mother and of Audrey Hepburn, the woman was a showstopper. Sleeked-back hair allowed emphasis on a perfect face, dark, liquid eyes being the most arresting feature.

'I could kill Bill,' whispered Jay.

Maddy smiled and her own eyes were wet. Little, skinny Amy Bradshaw, who had never said boo to a goose, was probably the most amazing-looking female in the north-west – if not in the whole of England. What was more, the once-shy girl had begun to realize that she was special, and the way she moved was graceful, almost regal.

But there was little of royalty in the 'film star' who collapsed in a chair and declared that her stomach believed that her throat had been cut. 'I've had nothing since breakfast,' she wailed. 'For God's sake, somebody get me some food before I die of starvation.'

They dined on melon, smoked salmon, chicken, ice cream served with hot chocolate sauce, then pints of coffee. 'Is the reception in here?' asked Amy.

Maddy nodded. 'There'll probably be just a few of us, so we can take food parcels home.'

'We'll need to.' George's voice was gloomy. 'As a cook, my wife-to-be is a disaster. I shall be poisoned.' It was his turn to be swatted with a napkin.

Maddy stood up at the end of the meal while George poured champagne. She reached across to the next table and picked up four packages. When the bride and groom had been toasted,

Sarah, Simon, Jay and Amy were each presented with a gift. 'That's from both of us,' Maddy told them, 'and we have one to take with us to London. A local artist did them – they're signed.'

Amy opened hers and put a handkerchief to her face. 'It's our childhood,' she said, her voice muffled.

The prints were of the bell house, its history penned beneath. Sarah read it out, the story of a bell purchased in Wigan hundreds of years ago, the inability of workmen to accommodate it in the church tower. 'The bell house was constructed to take it,' she read, 'but it was made too small to allow for movement and the bell had to be sounded by striking with a hammer.'

'Where's the bell now?' asked Jay.

'In the tower,' chorused the other five.

'Much dented by said hammer,' added Simon.

'How did they get it up there?' asked Jay, and then, before the others chipped in, he ordered himself to read a comic.

They talked well into the night, unearthing memories, interrupting each other, putting the past to bed.

'I think,' said Jay just before the party dispersed, 'I think that we had a marvellous childhood.' He glanced at Amy, whose mother was dead. 'Most of the time, anyway.'

Amy caught the glance. 'I wouldn't change a minute of it,' she declared. 'Except for what happened to Nettie.'

They squeezed the final dregs of champagne into their glasses, and George spoke the final toast. 'To Nettie,' he said, 'and to her beautiful daughter.'

A bedecked and joyful party of six arrived at the register office ten minutes before the appointed time. Maddy, in her wonderful ivory suit, wore a pillbox hat and carried a spray of cream flowers. Woven into the bouquet was her dead grand-mother's pearl rosary, while her husband-to-be, resplendent in a suit made at his own father's factory, paid homage to his ancestors by wearing a yarmulke. While striding towards a future they were determined to forge for themselves, they were deliberately expressing the respect due to those who had raised them.

At the appointed hour, the four guests took off to sit and wait for the bride and groom.

George smiled at Maddy. 'It's now or never. If you want to change your mind, do it out here, please.'

She dug him in the ribs. 'You're not getting out of it as easily as that, lad. Remember, I knew you when all you had was a wall – oh, and some scuffed shoes.'

'I think I loved you then,' he told her.

'Don't be silly – we were eleven.'

'We'd better go.'

'Yes.'

They walked towards the register office and entered it together, stopping in the doorway for a few seconds before approaching the front. Maddy gasped and gripped George's arm. 'They came,' she breathed.

'Of course they did.'

Yuspeh, resplendent in a mauve coat with matching hat, waved her gloves at them. With Jakob and Anna, she sat at the groom's side of the aisle. Mary Browne, whose stockings were not wrinkled today, had her eyes fixed on Amy. 'I can't get over the likeness,' she kept whispering to Caroline and Brian.

Arthur and Celia Bradshaw were there, along with a handful of other Rivington Crossers and, right at the front on the bride's side, Yvonne and John Horrocks had taken pride of place.

'It's going to be all right,' Maddy told her fiancé.

'Look,' he said. 'There's my very best man.'

Placed between the registrar and his clerk, clearly in the position of overseer, was an extraordinarily clean Monty. He wore a black bow around his neck and a distinct air of authority. Betty Thornton, who had scrubbed the dog this very morning, kept a steely eye on him. If he so much as whimpered, he'd be for the doghouse in more ways than one.

Monty scratched an ear, wondered what all the fuss was about, worried about the stupid bow, thought there might be food involved at some stage. With food in mind, he decided to hurry matters along somewhat. He walked down the centre of the room, stopped in front of the young couple and barked a gentle order. Then, at a pace that might have been described as stately, he led bride and groom to their places.

Anna cried, Yvonne cried, Mary Browne cried.

But Monty, who knew his own importance,

538

made no further noise. He supervised the vows, wagged his tail when the registrar announced that George and Maddy were man and wife. Soon there would be food, and that made the world an excellent place for a dog to be.

THE END